KILLERS FIVE

"Who're you?"

"My name is George C. Babel," was the quiet reply. "And now, John, if you will place that order here on this little table—"

"Orson!"

Just that one word came in a booming roar of command from the outlaw leader. Then a man-made hell exploded in the close confines of the restaurant.

Orson flung himself half sideways and his hand streaked to his right hip. It slapped leather and started up, and then double crashes of smoke and flames spurted from Babel's black-clad hips. Triple streams of fire ripped into Orson's hulking chest. They drove him backward like the heavy blows of an axe against an ox's head. The streaks smashed him through and through and sent him down against the wall against which he had been leaning, and which was now blood-splattered.

GUNFIRE AT SALT FORK

"You know why we're here," Evans said. "Poke Kendall wants you. You can walk, or be carried out feet first."

"Evans, get out of here before it's too late," Jonathan Carr said. "Get back home and stay there while you still got time!"

"Hell I will!" Evans bawled, and clawed wildly for his gun.

From his left hand Carr's .44 spat fire, the crashes of the weapon deafening in the new courtroom. Under the shocking impact of two bullets Evans went down.

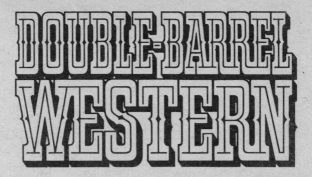

DOUBLE-BARREL WESTERN

KILLERS FIVE
and
GUNFIGHT AT SALT FORK

—————WILLIAM HOPSON—————

LEISURE BOOKS NEW YORK CITY

A LEISURE BOOK

April 1989

Published by

Dorchester Publishing Co., Inc.
276 Fifth Avenue
New York, NY 10001

Printed in the United States of America.

KILLERS FIVE

ONE

The thing had its inception that day in a certain Rocky Mountain territory when two young brothers and a phlegmatic Swede named Aven Larson stood at the mouth of a mine tunnel hidden in the wilderness. The older of the brothers, twenty-one, carried a buckskin bag containing approximately sixty thousand dollars in gold, which would be added to some ten thousand dollars more that Judge Calhoun was holding for them in town.

They had run into the pocket two days before while driving stubbornly along the two-foot wide vein holding its position beneath a low ledge in the tunnel. Larson—a rather religious Swedish friend of their late father, who now worked for the boys—had put in the shots just before coming out for dinner. When, after eating, they went in again, the fumes and smoke of the dynamite had cleared, revealing a mine tunnel splattered with chunks of gold-studded rock.

They had shot out a rich pocket, a very rich pocket. There might be an even bigger one, as Aven thought likely, or the vein might continue on. But they wanted to get that dust out of there.

"All right, Jim," eighteen-year-old Tom Kent said to his older brother. "You go out the back country way, as usual, on foot over the mountains. I hate to see yuh have to make these long trips, but Jennifer and his crowd might stumble onto us. They've got these mountains staked out, watching for us. They've finally figgered this mine is too rich to be recorded, and they'll even try torture if they get yuh. So be keerful. Tell Ellen all I told yuh, because I cain't write, and Aven's thumb is too sore fer him to do it for me this time. You just go ahead and give sixty thousand in gold to Jedge Calhoun to add to

5

the ten thousand more he's holdin' fer us. But git enough cash fer grub and some for Ellen and the baby."

Although less than nineteen, this ignorant young mountain boy who could neither read nor write had married a year back and had a two-months-old baby girl. He had married a woman three years older than himself—a town woman who was easy to look at, vain, and who had raged at him when she found out that there was to be a third one in their lives. So worried young Tom Kent took her to town and went back to his wild life with his brother, in search of the quartz vein their prospector father had been certain was somewhere in that particular section of the rugged hills.

And now those two had found it, and had hired loyal and honest Aven Larson to help work it. Meanwhile, whispers were going around that the gambler Jennifer was becoming increasingly interested in the lovely but vain Ellen Kent.

"Yuh needn't worry about Jennifer ketchin' me," Jim Kent said to his younger brother and to Larson. "That steamboat river card shark might be handy with a deck, but he never had much time left to learn how to foller a mountain man's tracks."

And in this Jim Kent was partially right. Jennifer knew nothing about a country where in certain wild sections various Indians of the warlike tribes were still making occasional raiding forays; but he was clever enough to know that a man with money can hire skill—including an Apache tracker. Thus it came about that Jim Kent left the hidden ledge deep in the wilderness country carrying a long-handled brush cut from a limb. With it he took time to blot out every visible track. He did it for twelve miles, keeping to rocky ground whenever possible, until he came out into open country. Here Jennifer's hawk-eyed Apache, circling like a blood-hound, finally picked up his trail.

Kent camped that night, unaware that a lurking form

lay in the brush less than sixty feet away. He wrapped himself in his blankets, still in his moccasins, and went to sleep. When he awoke he saw dim forms closing in like ghouls and, seeing the Indian, Kent sprang with his knife out and got the Apache in the throat before something—a gun butt in Jennifer's hands—exploded on top of his head. The blow cracked his skull, and it wasn't until daylight that, half out of his mind and babbling, he regained consciousness.

The fire was burning brightly and four men were cooking breakfast. One of the men was the gambler Jennifer, sitting on a rock ten feet away and still looking immaculate in his neatly cut clothes—black-mustached, black-eyed and handsomely intelligent. The other two were Carl Bonner and Ed Alden, the gambler's satellites.

The fourth man was Sheriff Ben Johnston.

Johnston was the oldest of the four, and he was only thirty. The others were in their middle twenties. Jim Kent tried to call out to the sheriff; then his mind cleared enough for the truth to dawn, and he sank back again with lips clamped tight.

He kept them tight during the next two hours while they pressed their thumbs against his cracked skull, hung him by his thumbs, and finally resorted to hot faggots against the soles of his bare feet. But the blow of the gun butt had, in reality, been a blow of mercy, for by now he was too far gone to feel anything. He was unconscious, and a cursing and frustrated Martin Jennifer recognized the inevitable truth, directing a final blow of his boot to the limp form on the ground.

"Hang him up, damn him!" he snarled. "Swing him and leave him for the buzzards! We'll stay staked right out here until that kid brother of his comes to see what happened." For he knew that they would never be able to back-track the trail now.

Bonner and Alden got a rope from the sheriff's saddle horn and slipped the noose over Jim Kent's head. They dragged him by the neck to a tree fifty yards distant—a tree that clung precariously to a ledge with half its roots exposed—and it was there that they swung him and left him hanging, his limp body turning slowly as the rope unwound.

Back in the mine, eighteen-year-old Tom Kent went on working with Larson. They had built a crude but effective Spanish *arastra*—a rock-bedded pit around which a blindfolded mule plodded, dragging rocks over the ore to crush it—and they kept on working with the ore taken out.

A week passed, and Jim Kent was due back. . . . Ten days passed, and Jim Kent had not yet returned. . . . On the fourteenth day his younger brother, rising at daylight, packed food for a trip.

"Yuh stay right here, Aven," he said to the Swede, who sat across from their crude rock stove, puffing his pipe. "I'm going out the same way Jim went. You wait till exactly a week from today. Effen I ain't back by then, yuh'll know we're in trouble, so yuh go out the opposite direction and circle around to town. Nobody knows yuh work for us. Nobody'll suspect yuh know where this mine is effen we're in trouble."

Larson nodded and went on puffing his pipe. He was about forty years old and brown-bearded from a touch of German blood in his veins. He watched the pack on young Tom's back bob around a turn and the gully become deserted; after which he knocked the dottle from his pipe, got up, stretched, and went back to work in the tunnel. Had he been a greedy or a dishonest man, he, who had himself hunted for the ledge with the boys' father, might have made himself a rich man. What he did was to wait; and then he set out on a long trip afoot, circling far and wide before he got to the county seat. He arrived on the day that young Tom Kent, heavily manacled between two of the sheriff's deputies, was sentenced by Judge Calhoun to not less than fifty nor more than seventy-five years in the Territorial Penitentiary for the murder of his brother, Sheriff Ben Johnston witness. Larson sat in the back of the crowded little courtroom, unseen and unheard; but his shrewd Scandinavian eyes above the beard saw something in Judge Calhoun's face that the judge thought was hidden. Larson knew then that Calhoun too was in on the frame-up. The unholy five had schemed and schemed well. They had got the gold, all right—which the crowd believed to be a fable—but they had not learned the secret of the mine.

And honest, cunning old Aven, sitting there watching a screaming, fighting, incoherent young mountain boy led out of the courtroom by the sheriff's deputies, knew they would never learn it.

So out of the lives of the people of that Rocky Mountain town went young Tom Kent, a tragic figure as he disappeared from the room. At least Aven thought him tragic. He had lost a brother by murder and been framed into a living hell of prison for it. And now he was to lose the wife whom Martin Jennifer wanted, as well as the gold that the five intended to use to build up their own little cattle and land empire in Texas. And because the lovely but vain Ellen Kent was not worthy, the gambler got her. Hardly had the prison doors closed behind her husband when Judge Calhoun granted her a quick divorce. Jennifer married her, and went away with her and Kent's girl child.

Jennifer and his new wife went straight to Texas, to a section where land and cattle could be had for a song. Two weeks after their arrival, he wrote his cronies that he had found the place all were looking for. This sent Bonner and Alden south in a wagon with all their belongings. A month later Sheriff Ben Johnston resigned his office and quietly disappeared.

Calhoun, however, stayed on for all of six months, for he was a cautious man by training. He remained superficially the same kindly, church-going young judge whom people respected for the manner in which he had dealt with such a cold-blooded Cain as young Tom Kent.

Six months later, though, the judge too left, having developed a bad case of "lung trouble." He said he was going north. But, with the heartfelt best wishes of all for a speedy recovery from his "illness" still ringing in his ears, he went south to a mere village named Partridge. Here the others had taken over a sizable ranch.

Bonner and Alden were looking after the cattle. Ben Johnston was getting ready to run for sheriff. Martin Jennifer was poring over newly bought books on banking practices. And the five decided that the judge, instead of practicing law and looking after their legal interests, would be of far more value to the expanding cattle combine in his former judicial capacity. So they began laying the foundation for their five man empire.

And in the Territorial Penitentiary far to the north, the young mountain boy Tom Kent began his first year in prison.

TWO

On a day nearly twenty-one years later the rain beat down in the mountain country several miles above the thriving town of Partridge, and up there under a sharp cut bank a man squatted over a tiny fire. For three days now he had been sitting up there waiting for the rain to subside. He had come back, this man whom the world—and the prison officials too—thought dead. He had come back to take a terrible revenge upon five rich and highly respected men who comprised the Sunset Land and Cattle Company and who were the cream of Partridge's horse and buggy set:

Martin Jennifer, the banker and the president of the

company, who had married his faithless wife and taken their daughter.

Carl Bonner and Ed Alden, vice-president and general manager respectively of the bank and cattle company.

Rugged, fifty-one year old Sheriff Ben Johnston, who was rich from much stock in the company.

And benevolent, kindly, church-going Judge Calhoun.

The man sitting up there under the cut bank knew all about them. He had it all down in a thick volume in his saddle bags. They had done well with the sixty thousand dollar pocket and a few thousand more the "kindly" judge had been keeping for the two mountain boys of twenty-one years ago. One's bones were dust in a crude grave far north in another state, but for three days and nights the other—he now called himself George C. Babel—had holed up there while the rain continued its steady downpour. Luckily the time was the full of spring and the wetness not too cold.

Another man might have been impatient and cursed the weather while he turned and twisted to ease the pressure upon his thigh muscles. Babel did neither. A single glance at his finely chiseled features and ascetic eyes back of his glasses would have shown two things: that Babel was above such things as cursing; and as for becoming impatient—what were three or four days to one who had learned patience during twenty-one years in a cell?

He had been eighteen then. He was thirty-nine now. He looked little more than thirty.

So Babel sat there over his tiny fire beneath the cut bank high above the drenched plain, the water dripping from the lower edge of the yellow slicker spread overhead on sticks like a tent top. It was tied hard with piggin string. Most of the time he let his gaze sweep the sodden terrain below. Now and then, when the moisture clouded up his thin, gold-rimmed glasses, Babel carefully removed them, wiped the lenses dry with a white pocket handkerchief, and put them back on again. Prison lights had done that to Babel's eyes; prison lights while he read and absorbed the knowledge contained between the covers of more than five thousand volumes.

And somehow neither the glasses nor his slender, sensitive fingers seemed to go with the heavy black guns he wore beneath his dark coat; surely they didn't go with the fine features and ascetic eyes. Twenty-one years and five thousand volumes. He had learned much.

Babel thought about it that day a few miles above his destination, seeing again the wild youth of the mountain country as he sat in the little courtroom, manacled between two of Ben Johnston's deputies, and heard Calhoun brand him as Cain and pronounce sentence. Then a trip by train—his first—to the Territorial Prison; the clang of the gate behind him; formalities and a cold warning from a cold warden; and then, in tow of a big ex-cowpuncher guard with a carbine across his arm, he was led along a rocky passageway past a row of rocky cells to one in the corner.

The yellow-toothed guard seemed to be hugging a huge joke to himself, for he kept chuckling as he opened the cell door.

"We're puttin' yuh in with ol' Crazy Coot," he grinned. "He's a nice ol' man, but so batty that not a convict will stay long without goin' crazy hisself." And he chuckled as he shoved Youth inside to where Age sat on the edge of a comfortable bunk: a fat and jolly looking old gentleman in a sort of cassock and wearing sandals on his bare feet.

That would have been all right, save that the guard had been reading the newspaper stories of young Tom Kent's trial. And because he was that kind of a man, who hated prisoners, he made a coarse remark about the wife of the prisoner.

The mountain youth still loved this woman who had been unworthy of him, and naturally knew nothing of her impending divorce action. A work-hardened young fist exploded through the perpendicular bars. It smashed the guard in the mouth, and when he got up two of his yellow teeth were pushed in at a queer angle, loose and spewing blood. He bawled a curse, and two others came running, one with a doubled rope nearly an inch in diameter. They barged into the cell and dragged out the shaven-headed youngster and beat him down until he lay bruised and bleeding. Then they tore off his shirt and went to work with the heavy, water-wetted rope, working on that particular area over the kidneys. Five minutes later, panting and cursing, they picked up the unconscious form by his arms and legs, carried him to a pitch black dungeon and threw him in on a cold rock floor.

And all the time it went on the fat and jolly looking old man in the cassock sat on the edge of his comfortable bunk and watched, smiling.

At sundown of the fifth day the prisoner came back. His lips and cheeks were a mass of bluish, puffed flesh and the blood on his scalp was dried and caked hard. He came bent over like an old man, each step a step through a hell of agony, and they kicked him through the door of the old man's cell again. From the floor he looked up into the eyes of the man in the cassock.

"That was the first lesson," the jolly looking prisoner said, making no move to help him. "Fortunately it is also the most painful. The others won't be so hard."

"Yuh at least—could help a man— Oh, God, I can't stand it!" he burst out in a moan, and lay there on the floor, like a dog that has been run over by a wagon and lies panting, its haunches smashed, in the road.

"You just imagine you can't stand it, my son," the cassocked one said in his kindly way. "You'll learn in time that pain is a matter of mind and can be controlled. And the correct pronunciation is 'you,' not yuh. Yes, I could help you up on the bunk, but the second lesson you must learn is never to depend upon any person but yourself. Therefore, though my heart goes out to you, I dare not, for your own sake, assist you. But if you can summon up enough strength to get up on the bunk unaided, I shall be glad to look at your injuries. My name, by the way, is Zarkov. My crime? Well, what does it matter? I am a Greek."

That was the beginning of "George Babel's" life in prison and his meeting with the scholar who was to become his teacher. Zarkov stripped him and examined his injuries, aware of the terrible pain in his back and bladder and groin. He took salve from a medicine cabinet and smeared him from head to foot. He took more medicine and fed it to the other. The pain lessened, and Babel, a wild youth of the mountain country who could neither read nor write, watched him.

He paid no attention to the couple of thousand books that covered the walls all the way to the ceiling, the writing desk covered with papers in a corner; his eyes blazed and he kept mumbling from between his smashed and swollen lips: "I got to git outa here, you hear me? I got to git out in a week and kill ever' dam' rotten coyote of 'em for what they done to me."

"Out?" Zarkov queried. "Why, you can get out any time you wish."

The shaven-headed youth looked at him, and a snarl broke from his puffed lips. "They said yuh were crazy! No wonder nobody'll stay in here. I'd go crazy too."

"Would you like to go to England?" Zarkov asked. "Here." He picked up a thick volume he had been reading. "Dickens, my son. He'll take you to England. And here in this cell are a thousand other journeys you may take through these books I've paid handsomely to have brought to me. Here you may have as friend and companion all the world's greatest men. You may talk to them. Look up there on the ceiling: a map I drew of all the planets and their course of travel. Yes, my son, perhaps you are more fortunate than, at the moment, you imagine. For here you will learn that the body is but an open cage from which the mind may take flight."

That wild-eyed, furiously raging youth did learn much in the twenty-one years that went by. He amazed his teacher by an ever growing appetite for knowledge until, to the scholar Zarkov's vast delight, it became a gnawing hunger. Latin absorbed his attention most at first, for he discovered in it a key to a world he had never known: that of pen and ink; the written word. Within two years he sat on his bunk in the darkness of the cell and talked to Zarkov in cultured Greek, while the ignorant guards, at first disappointed that he had not asked to be removed, began to shake their heads as they strolled their stations outside.

Almost from the first the young prisoner began to get letters that were never signed, written in a surprisingly good masculine hand. They contained a few dollars, of which the guards promptly took half. With the money more books were ordered. The books came, and at each shipment the student took a tiny hidden penknife and slit under the back flaps and brought forth yellowback notes. With that money Babel bought good food from the outside and many other things. He paid the warden one thousand dollars to knock a hole in the wall so that the cell next to his could be converted into a bigger study for his teacher and himself. Yet the one thing he wanted most—escape—was denied to him, even money not being sufficient to get that.

There was one aspect of Babel's new life, however, that at first surprised and then saddened the gentle Zarkov. Each day he took hold of the bars of his cell and twisted for ten minutes until the cords of his wrists and forearms stood out like steel bands and there came a time when he could take an ordinary book, strip the covers from it, grip it with both hands and tear it in two. He did five hundred fast squats every morning, equivalent to a three mile run up and down a rocky ravine. Five days each month he fasted as a means of developing self-control, and there came a time when, already a legend among the ex-cow-

puncher guards, he became more of a legend by paying
five hundred dollars for gunbelts and two Colts that had
been rendered useless.

It was this last that so saddened the now aging Zarkov,
for the Greek scholar knew now that the man who one
day expected to leave his cell lived only to kill.

So the years passed, and Zarkov died a feeble old man.
Babel lived on, leading a cloistered life in a world beyond
the bars, working, always working. He played the violin
now; his library was filled with the scores of all the
world's great music. There came a time when some well
meaning matron donated a bellows operated organ to the
chapel, and the new warden—there had been many
wardens since Babel first came—asked him if he could
play it.

"I can learn," the prisoner said quietly and paying a
burly axe murderer by the hour to pump the organ bellows, he became master of that big instrument. More
years. . . .

Winters and summers. . . .

Old guards went, new guards came . . . new faces walking by his cell, new faces in lockstep. Babel lived on, ate
in his cell, and worked over his volumes until the night
when the great prison revolt broke out and one hundred
men died in the roaring flames that swept through a block
of old-fashioned cells and licked at the others made of
stone. May years before Babel had made, by visual study
of the original, a key that opened the simple lock on his
cell. On this night he unlocked it as the flames swept
toward him and yelling, cursing guards ran here and there
trying to rescue the very mutineers they wanted to put
down. Directly in front of him Babel saw a man shot
dead, and this man he dragged into his cell before the
flames licked through at his books and turned it into an
inferno. Then, with a rope ladder, he went unseen under
the long porch and up over the walls.

He disappeared into the night through the graveyard,

while his five thousand books burned fiercely behind to char a man's body until it never would be recognized. He stopped at a low concrete marker and bent to touch it almost reverently.

"You were right, Zarkov," Babel said softly. "Through those books of ours I'm taking a journey—*to kill five men!*"

Thus, as Babel sat there under his stretched out slicker, did his mind go back over the long years, step by step over the road of time. Presently he stirred, his eyes going to the sky. By now it was mid-afternoon and the sky looked somewhat lighter. Babel got up and broke "camp."

Carrying saddle and frugal blanket roll, he went down the wet slope to where a great black horse stood under the cedars on the edge of a grassy clearing. Its ears went up at the sound of his footsteps, and Babel went to him: to Black Boy. He ran his hand up the white blaze on the black's forehead, and only a close examination of the clear eyes could have detected something strange about them.

For that great black horse, carefully trained by a man who knew his business, had been born stone blind.

Babel saddled him and set off on his interrupted journey, wearing the slicker.

THREE

The going was slow not because the big black was guided by every touch of the rein and his master's voice but because its hoofs sank deep into the gumbo mud in places where the grass had been washed away. Everywhere about them brown rivulets cascaded crazily down from the mountains above in a mad rush toward distant Willow Creek, now swollen at the middle like a woman heavy with child.

"Martin Jennifer, Bank President," Babel said, his ascetic eyes looking strange beneath the flat brim of the hat. He said it aloud, again: "Martin Jennifer, Bank President—gambler and robber and murderer. They must have been sure of themselves not to have changed their names."

He took off his glasses, wiped them with the handkerchief, then put them back on again.

For the rest of the afternoon the blind black horse with its uncanny sense of hearing and feeling picked its careful way downward, sometimes leaping across narrow washouts and sometimes fighting through rushing muddy waters that slashed at its wet belly; yet always in trustful obedience to Babel's guiding hand. It's surefootedness was an astounding thing to behold.

Babel heard the roar of the rushing creek long before he caught sight of its boiling waters; by now dusk was closing in on him and the black from all sides. He turned eastward along the stream, keeping to the higher ground; and when a mile or more had passed he discovered that the roar of the waters had subsided into quiet. That probably meant the presence of a dam up ahead.

It was then that he caught sight of the two riders on the opposite side of the creek—two dim figures making their way in the same direction as himself and probably toward the same destination: Partridge. One of the men rode what Babel was certain was a part steeldust horse with a white spot on its rump.

Presently, instinct making him keep under cover of the willows, he reached the dam where the waters were running over an outlet to one side, lapping dangerously near the broad, flat dirt top. He saw then that the two horsemen, yellow looking figures in their slickers, were now riding out on top of the solid dirt structure.

"If I get my facts straight," Babel mused thoughtfully, "Partridge and five certain gentlemen of affluence are about three miles below here somewhere. I wonder if by chance those precious five are so afraid of their corpulent and respected selves that they've sent those two riders out to see how the dam is holding?"

Whatever they had been sent for, it was dangerous for George C. Babel. He heard a startled yell from one of them, followed almost immediately by the crash of a Winchester. The slug drummed past Babel's flat hat brim, so close it might have shattered his glasses; or so it felt. It was followed by two more levered ones, whipped out fast, but by now the black was in full motion. Babel swung him about and spurred him head on into a group of cedars. Black Boy went crashing through in blind flight, unhesitatingly, for in the two short weeks the new rider had been astride him the intelligent animal, depending upon a brain to offset the black world into which it had been foaled, had come to trust him. Babel jumped him through into a clearing, cut forty feet to one side as more shots crashed into the thicket, then bent swiftly in the saddle.

He came up with a new model .45-.90 repeater rigged with special sights for bright and dull view shooting; Babel had practiced much of late wth the gun while he rode southward. He said, "Hold it, Black Boy," and swung up the big Winchester. The tiny line of ivory that made hazy shooting a pleasure brought the slickered figure squarely into focus.

Babel didn't pull the trigger; he squeezed it gently. The .45-.90 gave off a spiteful roar and recoiled against his shoulder. With the recoil the man out there went over his horse's head and pitched from sight below the dam, rolling down and down into the gully. The horse broke and fled with reins flying. It did so just as the other man cursed and fought his plunging horse while he struck a match under his raincoat. Then the dark bundle with the long string of hissing sparks dropped to the ground and this man too fled into the darkness, Babel's second shot slashing a long furrow in his dripping hat brim.

"So?" Babel said, and levered out the smoking shell. "Easy, boy—I believe we're going to have a lot of noise now."

He stood there watching calmly; and because he had never considered himself a brave man, he surely didn't feel heroic. Somebody had reason for wanting Willow Creek Dam to go out and send a wall of brown water rushing down below to overflow the trickling bed of the creek, which carried off the superfluous water from the mountains, and flood the town. Babel knew all about the town, because in the book in his saddle bags was a carefully drawn map of it and all the fine big mansions of The Five on a rise above the business section.

But George C. Babel had been in prison for twenty-one years. He had come back to take vengeance upon The Five for murder and perjury. He had come to find out what had become of his daughter, who now would be twenty-one years old.

Why risk himself when he was so near to his goal? Why chance being blown up and crippled for life over something that was of little personal interest to him?

The answer was "Don't do it," and Babel didn't. He sat there talking to his great black horse, which had been trained to be guided by the words of a human being. He sat there, this strange man with the gold-rimmed glasses and the ascetic looking face who wore two heavy guns belted beneath his fine black coat, and waited, the acrid smell of the burning fuse getting stronger in his nostrils. Then the darkness above the dam was split by a lurid flash and a roar of exploding dynamite. Almost immediately water gurgled into the gap, tore it wider, and the gurgle became a louder roar as the released waters went through and poured down the gully in a brown wall that spread out as it hit the lower country.

Willow Creek Dam was gone, and Babel turned the black horse and rode hard through the night.

Partridge never forgot that night of rain when the del-

uge came: a wall of brown water, less than three feet high
because it had spread out after a three mile run, that hit
the town some time after dark. It swept through the lower
business section and another section where a lot of common people lived. It picked up false-fronted buildings of
the smaller kind and carried them as much as two
hundred yards before they smashed into shanty homes
and shacks and other houses.

It missed the big mansions on the higher ground just
west of town.

All night long, wet, mud-covered men waded here and
there, some with lanterns and some without, in answer to
cries of the injured, the pinned, the marooned. And just
when the strange rider on the black horse put in an appearance nobody ever knew. But he arrived shortly after
the deluge, and the big black horse was seen to be wading
unerringly through the hip-deep water to take off some
who had managed to climb up on sheds and the roofs of
porches. Babel quickly learned that there was a rich
young doctor who had a home up there two hundred
yards above the stream, and to it he began to take the injured, the half drowned, the cold. The dead—and they
were numerous—he helped the other men to lie in Martin
Jennifer's front yard near the great white columns of the
Southern plantation style mansions. A man came hobbling
along, trying to use a broken tree limb for a crutch.

"Let me help you, friend," Babel said.

"Thanks," grunted the other, and there was a touch of
forced back pain in his voice. "I work at the livery stable.
Didn't know a thing was happening until I stepped outside into the corral just in time to see that water bring two
houses down against the fence. They broke through and I
was caught in the timbers. I think my left ankle's
smashed."

"Sure, it looks like it, though I know little of medicine.
We'll see if the doctor can get a look at you."

"Emmons is a good man," replied the other, his wet

arm holding onto Babel's neck. "A little stuck up and all that sort of thing, some people say. But I never found him so. I hear tell he's goin' to marry Jennifer's daughter. If I was him, don't know if I'd relish havin' that slick gent for a father-in-law, but that girl is all right. Emmons is a good man."

A smile half crossed Babel's face in the darkness. He was smiling at the thought that a daughter he had not seen in over twenty years was going to marry a man Babel had never seen. For despite numerous trips to the improvised first aid station, he had not yet met the physician who rumor had it would one day be Babel's son-in-law.

He helped the limping livery stable man on, and as they neared a group by a big fire built in a heavy cast-iron kettle some three feet in diameter—a pot of the kind used on ranches to render up lard—Babel heard a cry of pain. He saw a broad shouldered young man of about thirty working over a supine form on the ground, medicine kit and bandage rolls beside him. The light from the fire and several lanterns reflected from brightly polished surgical tools.

"Easy now," came the doctor's calm voice. "I've given him all the ether he can stand. You men will have to hold him. Here—give me a hand!"

FOUR

A big, craggy-faced cattleman who had been kneeling there with the doctor suddenly rose, his face wan with a queer pallor. "Not me, Doc," he gasped out. "I—I—" He whirled away from the fire, went into the darkness and vomited.

"What's the matter with you fellows?" rapped out Emmons sharply. "This man is dying, unless I get some help."

Babel lifted the livery stable man's arm from across his neck. "Sit down," he said.

He pushed through the crowd, and Emmons looked up as the black-coated man said, "What do you want done, Doctor?"

Babel saw a strong, sun-tanned face and keen eyes that appraised him with a quick glance. Then Emmons jerked his head sharply toward the man on the ground, through whose thigh a jagged two-by-four timber, ripped from a building, had thrust its needle point. He rapped out orders as Babel knelt, and Babel obeyed him. His own fingers soon became wet and slippery as he helped to ligature the torn flesh after the timber had been forcibly withdrawn. A glint of admiration came into his bespectacled eyes as he watched Emmons' hands.

This man from back East was a *surgeon!*

"You," Emmons grunted out a few minutes later, as they were finishing, "seem to know the rudiments of surgery."

"A little," Babel said, for among his books in prison had been several manuals on medicine and surgery, and for a time he had worked in the crude prison hospital as assistant to the rather ignorant and low-paid country doctor who looked after the inmates between nerve-shattering drinking bouts. "My name is Babel."

"I'm Frank Emmons. Glad to meet you. Stranger here?"

"A stranger," Babel said. "And now, if you're through with me, I'd better be getting back to town. There might be something else I can do."

Emmons seemed to be inquisitive regarding him, and Babel did not care to answer or parry any questions concerning himself, even from a man now engaged to marry the daughter Babel hadn't seen since babyhood. He went into the darkness again.

He made two more trips into the yard with injured. An hour later, as he started through the wide gateway where a gravel driveway led into Emmons' yard, he saw a burly-shouldered figure loom out of the darkness, carrying a slickered form in its arms. Then the man known as George Babel came face to face with Sheriff Ben Johnston.

Johnston had been thirty when Babel last had seen him. He was fifty-one now, but there was little to indicate it in his rugged figure, for he was still solid as a rock. Babel heard him roaring something to another man about a murder.

"You mean that gent you're carryin' has been shot?" asked the voice of the other.

"Plugged plumb center by a large caliber Winchester," Johnston almost bellowed back. "I found him in the water down on the lower edge of town. Found his hoss too. It's bad enough that a flood had to hit this town of ourn, but now it's murder."

Babel was close enough so that, even in the darkness, he recognized the dead man. Babel had shot him up there at the dam in the defense of his own life. He had blasted the dynamiter out of the saddle without compunction and felt no regrets about the matter now. That slickered figure in the sheriff's arms had, with his companion, spread death and destruction upon people on the lower side of town.

"Too bad I didn't get the other," he half muttered as he stepped aside to let Johnston by.

The sheriff half swung around to face him. "What's that?" he demanded of Babel.

"I said," came the gentle reply, "that it's a pity he had to lose his life that way."

"Well, it's not a pity. It's damned good riddance—even if it's still murder. But don't stand there like a fool, man! Jennifer's daughter has disappeared and can't be found. Martin's frantic. Get out and try to find her—both of you!"

Babel judged from that that Johnston knew the would-be dynamiter's identity quite well. "Damned good riddance" meant that the man probably belonged to some outfit the sheriff didn't like. It was something to bear in mind, Babel thought as he went down the slope again into the wetness of the night.

All over town word had spread that Jennifer's daughter had disappeared. Men took up the search with renewed vigor, and Babel found time to analyze his emotions as he waded here and there in aid, hunting for a young woman he would not recognize should he meet her face to face. Was he to lose his daughter just when he had hoped to find her?

Somebody spread word Jennifer had offered one thousand cash reward for the finding of the girl, and Babel found it ironical to think that the banker was offering Babel's own money to the man who would find Babel's own daughter.

He mounted the black that he had been leading and began anew a hunt among the buildings.

At four o'clock in the morning Black Boy finally played out on him. The work of carrying many double burdens most of the night had proved too much. Babel had a woman in his arms, a young and comely woman of around twenty or so, whom he'd taken from a shed on the lower edge of town. They reached the higher ground out of the water, and there Babel pulled up.

"I'll have to let you down now," he said, bending to lower her to the ground and then swinging down himself to relieve the tired black horse. "My black is about done in. I'd offer you my coat, but it's wet and muddy. I might suggest, however, that you go up on the hill to the house of the man they call Jennifer. They've a tub of hot coffee on the fire, and a cup would prove welcome in this cold."

She laughed at him, something amazingly frank and open in her eyes. He had to admit that she was rather attractive. She also appeared to be self-reliant and worldly. They started walking up the slope.

"Good heavens," she said. "Is it possible that a real gentleman has come to our fair little city—or is it that you, a stranger, don't know who I am?"

Babel smiled and confessed his ignorance.

"My name is Kitty Derril," she said, "otherwise euphemistically known as the bold, bad woman of the town."

He looked down at her amazingly open eyes that told of a woman who, though perhaps ostracized by certain petty, hypocritical standards, could never be low and common. This much her face told him in the darkness.

"You don't look bad to me—I mean," he hastily amended, "you don't appear to be—"

"Oh, no you don't!" Kitty Derril cut in, laughing. "You can't back out of a compliment. I love compliments from any man in Partridge, preferably where they can be overheard by members of our horse and buggy set."

"Why, may I ask?"

"Because I'm the town bad woman," she explained in her frank way. "You see, most small town women of the kind we have upon the hill there have in them a streak of a certain female species, if you get what I mean."

"Meaning that you do not particularly care for the female friends of Jennifer's crowd, I presume."

"Presume is a mild word."

"You dislike them for their opinion of you?"

"Good heavens, no!" she exclaimed, her eyes flashing. "I, care what that mob of snobs thinks of little Kitty? No, it goes further than that; much deeper. It's because of the little people. Over there," and she pointed to the west, "lies Ben Ferguson's outlaw domain. Some say he's a rustler who steals Sunset cattle from Jennifer and his pardners. Others say he's in with Jennifer and his crowd. I have my own opinion. But down in that country are the little people who were driven out by Martin Jennifer and his pals. Uprooted from their homes and herded out like cattle, under the guns of Sunset riders, because Jennifer and his gang wanted more land and still more land. There were men like Ike Slauson and Tommy Corson who tried to fight back—and died helplessly. And there was Jed Berber, whom they haven't been able to kill—yet.

"No, I dislike them because they're rotten and hypocritical. And the only decent one among them is Mary Jennifer, who they say is lost."

"Ah," Babel said softly. They had reached the top of the hill now, and the figures around the distant fire appeared to be little automatons that moved jerkily as though on strings. "Ah. So you know Jennifer's daughter?"

Kitty Derril nodded. "I came here as her music teacher three years ago, until the biddies of the horse and buggy set got jealous of the way men tried to be friends with me. So just to spite them, little Kitty became a little 'wild.' And it was more than the girls could stand. They tried to drive me out of town."

Babel liked her and the frank way she talked. Her warm handshake lingered when he led the tired Black Boy around the back of Jennifer's great mansion to the neatly kept stables. He went inside a long low building where row after row of sleek riding and buggy horses stood dry and blanketed in private stalls. He finally found an empty one. There he unsaddled, threw a warm, dry horse blanket over the animal's wet back, rubbed down his fore and hind legs, fed him and returned to the lower part of town. By now most of the people were gone from the front yard where Emmons had worked most of the night.

Babel saw then that faint dawn was beginning to light up the dark pool of the eastern horizon and that the sun soon would be up to start drying the water-soaked land. He worked his way down among the willows and cottonwoods about three hundred yards below Partridge. Here the water had overflowed onto a flat expanse of sand and still swirled sluggishly around his boot tops.

It was then, in the full light of a new dawn, that he saw the girl's body.

She lay on her back, pinned against a thick screen of willows, her face seeming to rise and fall with the ebb of the creek waters. Only the upper part of the face was visible, white and bloodless; the rest of her form was submerged and resting on the ground. One arm, her right, had so entwined itself in the tangled willows that it had not only kept her face above surface but had prevented her from floating on downstream.

She was about twenty-one or so, and it took no second glance at her wide, intellectual forehead to know that here was no ordinary dance hall girl or waitress or rancher's daughter. There was character and breeding and culture in that lovely countenance with its closed eyes and wet lids.

Babel slogged over to where she lay, braced himself against the gentle tug of the current and bent down. Holding her carefully, he released the entwined arm and then scooped her up. Her body came up dripping, clothed in an evening dress of white silk, and now the torn bodice fell away, leaving her white bosom exposed. There seemed to be no movement of the lungs beneath, and Babel guessed that she was dead.

He carried her toward the higher ground, slogging along through the water for nearly a hundred yards before the water fell away and released its clutch upon his boots. Her right arm dangled at a queer angle, badly broken above the elbow.

He took her over to a grassy spot and laid her down, straightening out the twisted arm. That done, he removed his black coat and carefully wrapped her in its folds. As he lifted her head with its wet coils of hair, he saw that a tiny chain around her neck held a gold locket that had slid around behind and now was entangled in his fingers. As he brought it around into its proper place at her soft throat, a name engraved on it leaped up at him.

Mary Jennifer!

And then a startled sound broke from the throat of the man known as George Babel. It was a strange choked cry, and in it was a sudden, terrible fear and agony.

"My God!" he cried. "It's my own daughter!"

From somewhere he heard men running. He didn't look up. He sat there beside her, gazing down into her face, too stunned even to remember some of the things his books of medicine had taught him while in prison. The running footsteps came closer, men cried out to each other and waved; and then there was Martin Jennifer himself, gray-shot at the temples but the same sleek Martin Jennifer of old, kneeling and taking the girl's wet form in his arms.

"You've found her!" he was almost weeping. *"You've found her!"*

"Yes," Babel heard himself saying slowly as he got up.

He turned and walked away, aloof, alone, like a man in a trance; and men looked at the tall, white-shirted figure with a question in their eyes.

FIVE

Mr. John Metekas opened his restaurant at four that morning and waded in through ankle-deep mud the water had deposited on the front and kitchen floors. He set to work with a will, luckily having a big supply of dry wood piled high in the shed back of his big kitchen. He built a roaring fire in the kitchen stove, and the dry cedar, hauled from the brush-choked brakes a few miles west, threw out heat that soon had the room halfway habitable. Keeping the front door locked, the industrious Mr. Metekas worked steadily, until shortly after sunup the Greek looked up to see a stranger standing in the back door.

"Ah, gooda morning, my friend," the short and hospitable restaurant owner greeted him. "Pretty soon I getta her cleaned out again, eh? You wanta some breakfast?"

"If it isn't too much trouble, yes. And, if possible, a place to clean up."

Metekas stared. His mouth fell open.

"Why, you speak Greek!" he cried out. *"You speak my language!"*

"Some," George Babel said. "Do I get a chance to clean up?"

"My friend," John Metekas cried, running forward and impulsively grabbing him by the biceps—and he noted they were as solid as fence posts—"you get anything in this restaurant. Take off those clothes. I've a tub in back and hot water in the stove tank. I got a razor, clean dry socks. I got anything you want. If you only know how this lonesome Athenian welcomes the sound of his own tongue."

Babel pulled off his wet boots, which the Greek promptly washed out with more water and then laid down almost in the oven of the stove, before getting the neetsfoot oil. He said nothing, though, when the stony-faced man asked for other oil and clean cloths and began to take care of the heavy black guns he wore. Perhaps the man was one of Ben Ferguson's outlaw riders—though he scarcely looked the part, with his gentle, ascetic face and cultured voice.

The Greek shrugged. What did it matter? The man spoke his language and spoke it with the tongue of a scholar. While Babel bathed the Greek cleaned his wet trousers and neatly pressed them with a big flatiron. He brought out a snow-white shirt and dry socks. He wanted to work the neetsfoot oil into the customer's boots, but this Babel did himself. After which he retired into the back room and started putting them on. Metekas found a suitable black coat—his Sunday best—and laid it on the back of a chair.

"Stranger in Partridge, eh?" the Greek said, slicing bacon into the smoking skillet on the stove. It set up a protesting sizzling sound.

"Yes," came the voice from the other room, through the open door. "I arrived last night. My name is Babel. George C. Babel."

"Hmm," John said thoughtfully. "I must tell my friend Aven Larson about this."

"Larson?"

"A strange man, Aven is. He runs a little store down the street and preaches to a small flock on Sundays. I must tell him about George Babel who came to our town amid the deluge. Tell me, why not stay here and build a tower? You speak many languages, do you not?"

"Many," came the reply from the other room.

"But you forget, my friend, that after the deluge and the building of the Tower of Babel, where many languages were spoken, it was wrecked in violence."

Metekas laughed and said jokingly: "If you build one, George Babel, and don't do business according to the interests of the Sunset outfit, I assure you it will be wrecked. They own us, almost. But Ben Ferguson and his two main henchmen, Blade Duval and Buck Orson, and the rest of their outlaw crew, drew a line on the lower side of town and warned Sunset's monied crowd to keep off. That tough dive up the street that was owned by a man named Jose Alveraz was the line where Ferguson told Jennifer's crowd not to pass. And they didn't pass, either. That dive is, or was, Ferguson's hangout when he had the effrontery to come boldly into town flanked by his wild riders out of the brakes, nor has Johnston ever dared go inside and arrest him."

"There have been reports," Babel said in his gentle way, "that Freguson might not be as much of an enemy of the Sunset company as some think. At least, so I was told during the night. But, then, I am merely a stranger who happened to get caught here when the flood hit."

The restaurateur shook his head, and then grimly jerked it toward a .44-.40 Winchester racked over the door entering into the front of his place. He was busy over the stove.

"So I have heard," he said in his native tongue. "I personally take no sides. But I have a premonition that this is but the beginning of more death and violence. It's been in the wind for a long time. And now the dam has burst and wiped out Ben Ferguson's side of town, one of his outlaws has been found shot dead, and less than a minute before you arrived a man came running to say that a stranger wearing two pistols who rode a black horse and called himself Babel had found Jennifer's daughter. Babel, if the finding of the girl makes you a friend of Martin Jennifer, it will make you an enemy of many others—including, perhaps, the outlaw Ben Ferguson. If you remain a friend of some of us smaller people, Johnston and his two tough pistol-carrying deputies may take it that you're their enemy and force you either to fight or leave. In this accursed town you can not remain neutral."

There came a sound from out front, the queer sound made by mud when it clings to horses' hoofs and then flies spattering against the side of a building. The Greek stepped to the doorway for a look out front, and then Babel saw his face turn slightly pale.

"Ferguson! And I can tell from the way he handles himself that he's half drunk. They'll smash up the place again. They always do, and I don't dare open my mouth. Orson is the worst, he and Duval. They toss plates into the air for targets and then jeer at me."

"Trouble?" Babel's voice asked from the back room.

Before the Greek could reply there came a loud hammering on the front door and voices roaring for the owner to open up. Metekas hurried forward and unbarred the door, and several heavily armed men pushed past him into the room.

"We want some breakfast an' we want it damned fast, Greek," Ben Ferguson ordered. "Hurry up."

"It will take time for so many—"

"It will if you stand there gassin' all day," roared the outlaw leader abruptly. "Get busy on it, mister. We've got a little private business to settle this mornin', an' when it's over there's liable to be fewer but better citizens in town, sabe?"

He followed the apprehensive restaurant proprietor back, then gave him a push that sent him reeling into the kitchen. He was a very tall, brown-mustached man, powerful in frame and shoulder width. Strangely enough, he hardly looked the part of an outlaw. His mustache was carefully trimmed, his clothes of good quality, and there was intelligence written on his now liquor-flushed face. Only the liquor seemed to have brought out the base element in him.

His red-rimmed eyes spotted the skillet with its crisply frying bacon.

"Who's that for?" he wanted to know. "You?"

"Why, Meester Ferguson, you see there is another—"

The burly Orson broke in. "Put in some more an' hurry it up. I can do business better with them dam' dirty yellow coyotes up on the hill if my stomach—"

"Cut it, Buck," Ferguson cut in. "You talk too much."

Metekas' hands were trembling a bit as he lifted out the now crisply done bacon strips and held them to drain off the grease. The folk tines shook so that the drops arced off to fall in little splatters on the stove, shooting up long curls of pungent smoke where each drop fell. Some of the other riders, unable to crowd into the kitchen, had returned to the front, to wait. The burly Orson and Duval leaned against the wall back of Ferguson, who stood waiting for the Greek to break two eggs into the frying pan.

The eggs fell into the grease and set up a blubbering splutter.

"Throw some of them boiled spuds into the pan, too."
Ben Ferguson grunted, taking off his hat. "Slice 'em
thin—"

And then he said no more. He stiffened and the hat
dropped back into place on his head while he stared at
the immaculate man who had appeared in the doorway
leading into the back storeroom.

The man was dressed in a snow-white shirt which he
now was buttoning at the sleeve with a final twist of his
slender fingers. He wore dark trousers, freshly oiled boots,
and a brace of lead-studded cartridge belts that encircled
his slab-muscled waist. Protruding from the open-topped
sheaths at his thighs were the handles of two worn Colts.

Babel had been specific in asking for used guns. New
ones were stiff, too hard to break in.

Ferguson, however, paid little heed to the guns—not
when flanked by Orson and Duval. His eyes were upon
the freshly shaven face and gold-rimmed glasses of the
man who stood there, his hair sleeked down. Ferguson
had never seen in any man's face the baffling quality that
lay in that before him, and, half drunk or not, he was no
fool. He asked one question, and he asked it very quietly:

"You working for Martin Jennifer and his crowd?"

Babel appeared not to have heard him; his eyes were
on the breakfast plate in Metekas' hands. The eggs and
bacon strips were on a platter now.

"A cup of coffee, too, if you please, John," he said to
the Greek.

Ferguson's long, stringy-muscled frame stiffened a bit
more. Orson and Duval seemed to take the situation at its
face value, for they spread out on either side like cat-
footed shadows. They didn't straighten. They seemed to
hunch down a little against the walls.

"Them eggs an' that bacon are mine, mister," Ferguson
said slowly. "If you know what's good for you, get out.
You're bucking a stacked deck."

"Two spoonfuls of sugar in the coffee, John," Babel said, in Greek. "And then I think after breakfast I'll go up and see Martin Jennifer."

Poor John Metekas!

He was a courageous man, but not a seeker of trouble. He had faced death and revolution in the Balkans, because it was fight or die. But these cold-nerved Westerners he could not understand! And why must this strange man Babel, who spoke Greek with the tongue of a native—

"What was that you said to him, mister?" Ferguson grunted out coldly. "Spill it. In my lingo."

"I merely stated that I'd like two spoonfuls of sugar in that cup of coffee," Babel said. "That's right, John. Now some cream."

"You said something about Martin Jennifer. Who are you?" Ferguson shot out, the liquor inflaming him. He had been drinking during most of the early morning hours on his way out of the brakes for a showdown with Jennifer and his partners, partly to keep warm in the wetness and partly to give flexibility to his tongue. He had spent hours working himself up into the necessary rage, and now this seemed made to order.

"Who're you?" he spat again.

"My name is George C. Babel," was the quiet reply. "The C is for Crespigny, a name from the English nobility. And now, John, if you will place that order here on this little table in such a manner that I can face these gentlemen while I eat—"

"Orson!"

Just that one word came in a booming roar of command from the outlaw leader. Then a man-made hell exploded in the close confines of John Metekas' restaurant kitchen.

Orson's body moved like that of a huge mastiff sicced by its master. He flung himself half sideways and his hand

streaked to his right hip. It slapped leather and started
up, and then double crashes of smoke and flames spurted
from Babel's black-clad hips. Triple streams of fire ripped
into Orson's hulking chest. They drove him backward like
the heavy blows of an axe against an ox's head. The
streaks smashed him through and through and sent him
down against the wall against which he had been leaning,
and which now was blood-spattered.

He lay with his left arm half pillowing his shaggy head,
something repulsive about his loosely sagging lips. Once
his quivering body moved and he lashed out with a
booted foot, his spur rowel raking a thin line across the
wallpaper, but the action was a reflex. For Orson had
been shot three times squarely through the heart, the area
where the bullet holes entered so small it could have been
covered by the palm of a man's hand.

The first two bullets had been fired simultaneously as
Babel drew, the third thumbed a second time from his
left-hand Colt. But he had fired only the one shot with his
right hand. In the split second when he drew and drove
those first two slugs into the outlaw henchman, he swung
the muzzle of the big six-shooter in line with Ferguson
and Duval, ready to begin two-handed shooting.

Thus he stood with the two smoking Colts held low at
his hips, covering the doorway and all in it, his ascetic
eyes through the glasses looking expectantly at the
stunned outlaw leader and at the tawny-haired Blade
Duval. Then into the gun-shocked silence of the kitchen
came his soft, cultured voice:

"I still say, Mr. Ferguson, that I had a prior right to
breakfast."

Ben Ferguson's face flamed, grew red with a terrible
fury; and for just a moment during which frightened John
Metekas looked as though life had ceased within him, it
appeared as though he would bellow the order that would
mean his own death—for he knew that he could never

buck those drawn guns. Yet there was something not about the guns but in Babel's ascetic face that stayed his attempt.

Ferguson had killed men and seen many others die in his long career of cattle rustling, but never had he met such a man as this gun fighter, Babel.

"Out the front way, all of you!" he suddenly bawled to the men trying to crowd in from the other room. "Out, all of you!"

He whirled, lunging with a hard shoulder at his packed men. Their ranks split, and then chairs and tables went tumbling as booted feet shook the building when they ran for the front and their horses outside. Metekas, looking terribly sick and frightened at the huddled outlaw on the floor, watched them thunder out of town and disappear into the willows.

When he came back Babel was drinking coffee.

"If you value your life, Babel, get out of town," Metekas said. "Mount your horse and leave Partridge this morning, or you won't be alive in seventy-two hours."

SIX

It was about then that Ben Johnston put in an appearance. The front door slammed, and he must have caught sight of two booted feet lying in the curtained doorway that separated the kitchen from the front, for he came hurrying back. He stepped over Orson's lax body and looked at both Babel and Metekas.

"I just saw Ferguson burning the breeze down the street outa here," he snapped. "You plug Orson?" he demanded of Babel.

"I did," was the cool reply.

"Then I wouldn't want to be in your shoes, mister. You've just plugged Ben Ferguson's right-hand man."

He hadn't, Babel noted, changed much from the thirty-year-old sheriff who had been in that courtroom twenty-one years before. He had grown just a trifle heavy about the midriff, but he was still a tough and hard-riding and cruel, dangerous man. Just how cruel and dangerous Babel knew only too well. Burned into his memory was the way a younger Ben Johnston had mounted the witness stand and sworn before Judge Calhoun that he had seen young Tom Kent knife his brother in a quarrel while they were on the way to town, then bash in his head. Of course it had been too hot to pack a dead body all the way to town. So church-going Judge Calhoun had taken the sheriff's word for it, commended him for doing his public duty, and then done *his* public duty by sentencing this Cain to life in the penitentiary.

And who would believe the wild, incoherent ravings of an ignorant young murderer, who had been foolish enough to think he could get free by concocting a hairraising story of a fabulous mine of gold that the sheriff and his friends wanted! Sixty thousand dollar pocket indeed!

Babel could still remember the veiled sneers on the faces of the jurymen and the spectators at such a fabrication.

No, Ben Johnston hadn't changed much. He was still the big-shouldered gun-packing sheriff who handled all cases himself and asked neither horse nor gun favor of any man.

The excited Metekas began to shout explanations, but lost his tongue and switched into Greek. Johnston brushed past him and picked up a coffee cup from a wooden tray filled with clean dishes, neatly stacked. He crossed to the stove and picked up the coffee pot.

"So you plugged one of Ferguson's outlaws right in front of him and got away with it, eh?" he said thoughtfully, as though he still couldn't believe what his eyes told him. "Hmmm."

"As a matter of record, Sheriff, the score is now two," Babel replied. "If I'm to be hanged for this, I can't be hanged twice."

"Two?" grunted Ben Johnston, turning with the steaming mug in hand. "Where's the other one?"

"I believe you had him last night. The man in the slicker. I ran into him and another man dynamiting the dam just at dusk. He didn't seem to like the idea of strangers around and threw a shot at me that missed. I didn't like the idea of his shooting at me, and threw one back that didn't miss. He went over his horse's head below the dam, and when it blew out he was carried into town by the water, where you stumbled across him."

Johnston didn't seem to be very much upset about this. He leaned his broad buttocks against a meat table and looked at the man across the room.

"For a gent who just got in town, you ain't doing so bad for a starter," he said slowly over the cup held to his thick lips. "Where did you come from, mister? What are you doing in Partridge?"

Babel pushed back his partly eaten breakfast and wiped his lips with a handkerchief. "I'm from up north, Sheriff. I've business down in this country. When it's finished I'll be returning where I came from. Are you expecting to hold me for this little fracas?"

"Hold you? Hell, don't be a damned fool, mister. Even if I did hold you, Ferguson or one of his men would plug you through the bars before you'd spent twenty-four hours in jail. And if he didn't, Martin Jennifer would have you out of there in thirty minutes after the way you found his daughter. He worships the ground that girl walks on."

The dead something that had been within Babel since he had left the crowd by the girl seemed to lift. "Ah," he breathed out softly, "then she is not—"

"Dead? No, thanks to you. But she would have been within a few minutes more if you hadn't found her. Emmons got there in a hurry and administered first aid, then took her home and set her broken arm. She's going to be all right. Matter of fact," he said gruffly, "I was on my way to tell you Martin wants you up to the house for breakfast. You better go on up anyhow while I stay here and take care of that"—indicating with his boot the lax body on the floor—"thing there. Martin wants to express his gratitude along with a reward check."

Babel rose and slipped the black coat off the back of the chair, putting it on. It fitted well, for Metekas had been a much slenderer man when he had bought it a year before. While Babel fitted his flat-brimmed hat into place and then punched the empty shells from his guns, he told the sheriff of Ferguson's remarks concerning fewer citizens and Orson's threats anent some "dam" dirty yellow coyotes up on the hill.

Again Johnston surprised him by his imperturbability. The sheriff merely shrugged his heavy shoulders. "Ferguson ain't as bad as he lets on," he said. "Him and his men backed down in the face of one pair of guns this mornin', didn't they? He's allus talkin' too much."

"Perhaps you're right, Sheriff," Babel murmured, and went out, with a puzzling thought running through his mind.

Then it came to him.

If Johnston thought the outlaw leader a four-flusher, why was it that he had never dared to arrest him in Alveraz's dive up the street?

SEVEN

The sun had come out bright and warm now, and the water had disappeared. There was still slick mud everywhere, but most of the boardwalks anchored to posts sunk deep in the ground, had managed to survive the rush of the torrent; and thus Babel made his way up the street.

Here and there a few people huddled around buildings. But there was little activity; they were the only curiosity-seekers. It was strange to stand on what had been a familiar corner and see buildings in different positions from those they had been in the night before. Some were gone altogether, smaller ones that floated easily.

Ahead of Babel a man stood alone on the corner—gray-bearded and vigorous despite his more than sixty years. Except for the whiteness of beard, he was the same Aven Larson as of old.

"Good morning," Babel said. "The town's been hard hit, hasn't it?"

Aven turned his clear, keen eyes upon Babel's ascetic face back of the gold-rimmed spectacles.

"Hard hit, yes, my friend," he replied. "But out of catastrophe always comes some good. It's an immutable law of nature. Wars bring death and privation and pestilence, but once they're done with man can look forward to rebuilding his destiny in a land that, at least, has been cleansed. A criminal commits a crime, yes, but when he's imprisoned or hanged his presence is removed from the world of common people and thus, though somebody among them has suffered, they are free of him. Last night's flood brought death to almost a dozen people and many others suffered injuries, but look at the town this morning. A lot of dirt washed away, and over there on the opposite corner, where a dozen men have died in violent gun fights, a stink hole wiped out. You see?"

Babel had already been looking at the unusual sight while old Aven talked. Before the coming of the flood waters from the dynamited dam's torn spine, the building at which Aven now pointed had been the Cedar Bar, the most notorious dive in Partridge. Run by a swarthy, surly man named Jose Alveraz, the place was Ben Ferguson's hangout when he came in to get drunk, flanked by a dozen heavily armed riders. In it they drank and whooped and fired off their pistols, and even Ben Johnston had not dared to arrest a man inside its bullet-pierced doors. So said rumor.

In it the outlaw out of the cedar-choked brakes to the west had laid down his decree to Jennifer and his crowd to stay on the upper side of the line.

Yet in the church just one hundred yards up the street that elderly, quiet-spoken, educated man who now stood beside Babel had told his humble hearers, the poor from down in the shanties along the creek, that one day God would wipe out that stink hole.

God finally had kept that promise of Aven Larson's too, for the three-foot wall of brown water had hit the small house of worship and picked it right off its flimsy foundation. It had floated Aven's church one hundred yards across open ground and crashed it into the side of the half-breed's boxlike saloon. Church and house of sin now lay there together, both smashed, the saloon certainly beyond all repair.

"We were giving a special box supper for some of the younger children from the lower side of town," Aven went on to explain to Babel, "when I had a strange premonition that something might happen. Mary Jennifer had brought her violin down to play for us, as she or Kitty Derril always plays for us at meetings. We got the children out to higher ground, and Mary made a final trip back for her instrument when the flood hit. By then it was dark and nobody saw her again until a man named Babel, who came to Partridge in the midst of a deluge, found her in the water this morning. Tell her, when you get up to the house, Mr. Babel, that Aven Larson's prayers are being answered. I myself am barred from Jennifer's house."

"This is a strange town filled with strange people," Babel said. "Angry people, too, I judge. Look!"

"Alveraz doesn't look very well pleased, does he?" bearded old Larson said in his slow way, his eyes on the cursing, raging half-breed clambering with mud-clogged shoes among the twisted, broken timbers, trying to find an entrance inside the wreckage.

Alveraz seemed to catch sight of Larson for the first time. His swarthy face contorted anew. He jumped off the end of a broken six-by-six beam and came at a half lumbering run across the street, his feet weighted with mud.

"Look at it!" he yelled out savagely, a slight accent in his voice. "Look what that building of yours has done."

"I am looking at it," Aven Larson said mildly. "A good job."

"You'll pay for it, damn you! You hear?"

"I'll buy the wreckage from you to prevent your rebuilding another."

Rage got the best of the excitable Alveraz then. He forgot everything as he came closer, half crouched, seemingly unaware of Babel's presence.

"You're the one who won't rebuild," he snarled.

And then he came with a roar. He leaped straight at the older man, a long knife flashing in the sun as it was snatched from the back of his collar, its thin scabbard between his shoulder blades. But when he leaped the man known as George Babel moved too.

Just how it happened Alveraz never learned; but his half spring was halted almost in mid-air as two hands with slender fingers of steel caught him. An iron thumb sank into a nerve center back of Aleraz's right elbow, and his roar of rage turned to a scream of excruciating pain as the knife fell from his agonized fingers. There was a grunt, a heave and Jose Alveraz landed flat on his back in the mud of the street.

He fell beside his knife and, despite the mud, there was something pantherish in the quickness with which he snapped off the ground, his eyes blazing with hate and deadly ferocity. But the heavy Colt held low at Babel's right hip stopped him short.

"Drop it," the stranger said gently, his eyes cold back

of the spectacles, his ascetic face expressionless. "There's been enough death in Partridge for one night and day."

"You didn't let me finish," Aven Larson said to the man as the knife fell a second time. "I'll do more than pay for the wreckage. I'll try to scrape up enough money to buy both building and *lot* from you."

Alveraz, however, had forgotten about the man with the beard. He fastened his hate-filled eyes upon Babel's face and half whispered:

"You shouldn't have done that, mister. You shouldn't have done it because Ben Ferguson is a friend of mine. We'll meet again, whoever you are."

And then he was gone, leaving Aven Larson standing there staring after him, a worried frown on the bearded man's face.

"You've made a bad enemy, I'm afraid. You've not only made a bad enemy, but he'll never sell now, and a new Cedar Bar will rise upon the foundation of the old."

Babel left him then, deeming it neither the time nor the place to reveal himself to this faithful friend. He wanted a chance to talk over the past with Larson, to check with him on the facts he had written—now in that volume in Babel's saddlebags.

He wanted most of all to know as much as possible about his daughter.

So the man known as George Babel went up the grassy slope toward the row of great mansions overlooking the town; mansions built with profits from his own money. There were six in all, up the street's length, with trees over the boardwalk and well kept lawns beneath more trees in the great front yards. Curving driveways of gravel arced through the green of the lawns from gates to verandas. Out back were stables and paddocks and pasture beyond.

As he circled toward the stables out back, Babel noticed that several Negro servants were cleaning the last vestiges of last night's debacle from the lawn, carrying away the cast iron kettle in which the big fire had been built.

Babel went directly to the stable and to the stall where he had put the great black horse, past rows of other stalls, each with a name over the chain. The blanket had been removed from Black Boy's back and his dark coat had been groomed until it shone. He had been watered, fed, and rubbed down without being taken from his stall.

"You black rascal," Babel said as the animal twisted its head, its nostrils quivering inquisitively. He ran an affectionate hand down on the inner side of its hind legs to pat it. "You certainly are having an easy time of it."

"You talkin' to me, boss?" queried a strange voice from somewhere nearby, and then Babel saw the speaker's head pop out of the next stall.

EIGHT

The stable hand was a Negro of about forty-five, wearing a red coat and cap. He saw Babel's bespectacled eyes and respectfully touched his hand to his cap.

"How are you?" he inquired. "That your black hoss?"

"I put him in last night—or rather early this morning when he played out on me in the water," Babel explained. "Take good care of him for me, will you?"

"You bet I will. Mistuh Jennifer saw that hoss this mornin', an' he sure went wild. He's the craziest man about hosses I ever seen, he is. I reckon that man love hosses almost next to Miss Mary herself. Every mornin' he gets up early an' comes down here to see about his mounts. He calls 'em his boys. He done took one good look an' says that black of yours is the greatest hoss he ever saw."

"I agree with him," Babel smiled. He unfastened the

snap on the chain across the stall, came out, and snapped it into place again.

"How much you want for him?" the stable hand wanted to know.

"He's not for sale at any price. Not even to your boss."

"Then you sure don't know Mistuh Jennifer. He'll get that hoss somehow." His face fell. He grinned wryly and scratched his head. "I kinda hope so too. Me an' that horse get along swell."

"Then be sure and see that he doesn't remain stiff after bucking the flood waters last night."

"Yes, sir. I took him out an' led him around in the paddock this mornin'. He seems a little awkward. Kind of stumbled when I brought him back inside."

"He's stiff, that's all," Babel lied, "from bucking the flood."

Why let anybody know Black Boy had been born stone blind?

"Yes sir, sure was some flood. They done took away all them poor dead folks in the yard. But I 'spect you better get on up to the house. Boss man's been expecting you. Everybody in this here town talkin' about you this morning, Mistuh Babel."

"Indeed?" Babel said softly, thinking of what had happened in the kitchen of the restaurant. "And just what part of the South do you come from, Ed?"

"My name's Booger, sir. And all us colored boys come from Mississippi. Boss brought us all out here because he done say he used to live along the river and he want this place to be like the South."

It was, Babel reflected, as he went toward the side of the house; and there was bitter irony in the thought. Those Unholy Five had done well with their ill-gotten proceeds from murder and perjury and robbery. With blood money that had built a cattle and land empire they had erected mansions in the Southern style, brought in Southern Negroes as servants, and Babel only hoped that

Martin Jennifer wouldn't carry the farce so far as to address him with a "suh" and offer him a mint julep.

Yes, they had built their great homes up there above town where the grass once had grown thick and wild, and as George Babel went slowly around the side of the house to the front he knew that he would never again sleep a full night's sleep until those mansions were gone and the grass again growing on the spot.

It was not a fleeting wish or a mere thought. It was a vow. He had come back after twenty-one years in prison to wipe out five murderous rogues now living in splendor on the proceeds of their crimes, and he would not stop at merely wiping them out. Those big white eyesores glaring above the weatherbeaten shacks of the flood-swept town below must go too.

There was a line of well tended poplars forming the north side of the great front yard of the ex-gambler's home, and out there Babel caught sight of a tethered horse. It was a rugged cow pony with a Western saddle and there was a Winchester stock peeping from the boot. Wondering whose it could be, Babel passed under the window of the great library, and then he pulled up short as he heard Ben Ferguson's cursing voice inside. The rider of the wild brakes was pacing the floor back and forth in long, angry strides, for Babel could hear his big spur rowels clanking on the luxurious softness of the Persian rugs.

Babel took off his hat and risked his life to peer through a corner window of the room. Luckily for him, the four seated men all had their backs to him. Alden and Bonner were the same, but Judge Calhoun had grown much older. He wore a flowing white Van Dyke beard and had lost weight until he was in reality a skinny old man.

Martin Jennifer sat in a big chair back of a huge desk of polished mahogany amid the splendor of thick rugs and varnished bookcases lining the walls. His sleek black hair was streaked with just enough gray at the temples to give him, at forty-five, a dashing look—the smiling, handsome devil who always had a witty word for the ladies. Babel felt his thin lips curl into a sneer at those four precious rogues. For just a moment there came over him such rage and burning hatred that he felt more respect for that wild figure pacing the floor with clanking spur rowels and cursing than for the four.

Ferguson's hat was off his head and lying on the desk near Jennifer. He was waving his hands and biting out words with hissing fury.

"Confuse the people," he was saying snarlingly. "I was to play the wild outlaw an' do yore dirty work, yuh four yaller coyotes! Not that I minded, mind yuh!" he went on, wheeling to point a finger at the banker and president of the Sunset Company. "It was the kind of job me an' my wild bunch liked: burnin' out nesters, drivin' out the small ranchers when they wouldn't borrow money on mortgages to buy more cattle for me to steal and brand with yore Sunset iron. Oh, I did the dirty work for yuh, all right, but I'm not kicking about *that*."

He reached the other side of the room and wheeled, half leaning against the glassed-in bookcases, and for just a moment Babel thought the outlaw leader was going to start shooting.

Martin Jennifer's voice cut in, sharp and cold and deadly:

"I don't give a sun-beaten damn *what* you're kicking about! None of us do. But you think that because you've been working with us for years you're indispensable. That's where you're wrong, Ben, and don't you ever forget it for one damned moment. Sure—for seven years you've been an outlaw yet not an outlaw, because we protected you. We kept the Texas Rangers out of here. We covered up your crimes. When we couldn't cover them any other way, Johnston pinned them on somebody else, like Ike Slauson and others. He'll get Jed Berber too.

When that wild kid Corson went gunning and might have shot you or some of us from ambush, it was Johnston who put him out of the way. And now you have the undiluted crust to dare set foot in *this house!* If you wanted to see me, why didn't you send word for me to come to your hideout, as usual?"

"I'll tell you why," Ben Ferguson shot back savagely. "Because I wanted to come straight into yore home with its damned highfalutin' finery and tell yuh straight to yore face that we're through, that's why! We're all finished, do you hear? From now on I'm on my own. From now on the very damned cows that I stole from other outfits and branded with Sunset's iron I'll turn around and steal again—from you five rotten coyotes. Some of yore own men are *my* men. Yuh don't know who, and yuh don't dare try finding out. They'll rustle yuh clean and make yuh like it, because yuh can't find any one man or group of men to stop us. Yuh tried it, damn yuh, but I got wise in a hurry."

Jennifer came up out of the chair then, and he came up with something pantherish in his lithe movements. He had a gun in his right hand, taken from the drawer of the desk, and it might have spouted flame had not Judge Calhoun got up too. He pushed into the line of possible fire.

"Now, boys," he said in his church deacon manner, clearing his throat judicially and beaming upon them in benevolent tolerance—the big brother settling a dispute between two hot-headed inferiors. "Now, boys, let's forget all this violent talk and settle this thing like gentlemen."

"Like gentlemen, eh?" Ferguson jeered. "Oh, my gawd-lemighty! Oh, my Lord! Like *gentlemen,* he says! Why, yuh choir-singin' old—"

"Now, now, Ben, cool down and control yourself," admonished the judge, wagging a finger at him. "We must all be sensible. Frankly, I don't see how you expect us to have any patience with you when you come in here shouting incoherent accusations—"

"Accusations, eh? Save my black soul! He's trying to tell me yuh all don't know what I'm talking about! Yesterday afternoon you four and the sheriff, too, hired two of my men to go up there and blast out that dam. You wanted to flood out the lower side of town and clean out all those shacks down there. Maybe yuh hoped to flood out Alveraz's place too, because it was allus salt in yore hides for me and my riders to hang out there in the open right under Johnston's nose. It must have pained hell out of you precious cutthroats when people complained that yore sheriff never arrested me. Anyhow, yuh hired Etheridge an' Gorman to blow out the dam and make it look like an overload of water had done it. So yuh sent them up there, and then you sent that fish-eyed gent named Babel right along behind them, with a Winchester. He was to plug them cold so they couldn't talk afterward."

Carl Bonner half shot up out of his chair. "What's this about us hiring a gunman named Babel?"

Ferguson sneered openly, his scornful eyes flaming at the four.

"Go ahead, act innocent," he jeered again. "But after Babel shot Etheridge dead with a .45-.90 an' put a slug through Gorman's hat, he came on to Partridge, *after levering out the shell from his repeater!* Rod had sense enough to circle back and pick up that shell. He rode hard all night back to the hideout to confess the whole thing, then hit the breeze to town ahead of us on a fresh hoss. He finally located this Babel gent's black hoss in yore own stable, Jennifer. He took a .45-.90 shell from Babel's saddlebags, extracted the bullet, and fired the cap. When he compared the marks of the firing pin they were the same."

And then Babel, listening outside the window, heard him begin an account of the gun fight in the Greek's—

again accusing the four and the absent Johnston of hiring Babel for the job.

"I don't know who this Babel gent is. I don't know where he came from. I don't know how much yuh're payin' him to try wipin' me out, now that yuh've decided yuh no longer need the 'outlaw' who helped boost yuh to wealth. But, by God, I take off my hat to yuh rotten coyotes for picking a good man. Orson was hell on wheels with a Colt, but when he drew on this fish-eyed school teacher looking Babel gent, his gun never cleared leather. Babel shot him three or four times so fast you couldn't see him draw. But we'll get him. Make no mistake about that. We'll get him—and for two cents I'd go back down to the willows below town where my men are waiting and wipe out—"

Babel ducked below the level of the window, having heard enough. He put on his hat and went around to the big double doors. On the front of one of them, chest high, was a brass knocker cast in the shape of a thoroughbred horse's head. He lifted the knocker, and presently, in answer to its call, a perfectly trained Negro servant opened one of the doors and looked inquiringly at the tall man.

"What could I do for you, suh?"

"You may inform Mr. Jennifer that George Babel is here to inquire about the condition of his daughter," Babel said.

The Negro's immobile features broke in a smile of welcome. He stepped back, opening the door wider.

"We done heard all about you, Mistuh Babel, and we certainly is glad about what you done for Miss Mary. You come right in, suh. My name's Edson and I'll go right now to tell Mistuh Jennifer you done come."

Babel went into the splendor of a front hall such as even his books in prison had never visualized for him. Edson took his still damp hat and disappeared.

Then, presently, he heard a voice say, "What's that, Edson? Babel here? Quick, where is he?"

And then Martin Jennifer was coming through the portieres, and once again the man with the gold-rimmed spectacles who called himself George C. Babel found himself face to face with the man who had helped murder his brother, framed him into prison, stolen an unfaithful wife who was now dead, and taken away his daughter.

Twenty-one years.

It had been a long time.

NINE

"Mr. Babel, you don't know how much I'm indebted to you," the suave Jennifer said warmly, shaking hands.

"You'll never know how I feel about it either, Mr. Jennifer," the tall visitor said.

"Come on in," the cattle magnate invited, leading the way.

"Three of my associates are taking care of some— ah—business matters in the library and will be out shortly for breakfast. Meantime, if my daughter's still awake I want you to see her."

"I shall be most delighted," Babel murmured to his host. And then, as Jennifer went toward a large Negro mammy heading toward the parlor stairs with a covered breakfast tray, Babel heard angry shouts that the walls almost muffled, curses from the library, and then the slam of an outside door as Ben Ferguson left.

Jennifer turned and beckoned to Babel. "It's all right, Mr. Babel—I'm going to call you George—my daughter's still awake."

They went up the broad curving stairway that Babel instinctively knew would burn like tinder and up into a sunny bedroom. The Negro woman closed the door behind them as Jennifer went to the huge white bed, bent down and kissed the forehead of the lovely girl who lay there with her right arm in splints. And over Babel there came a terrible surging emotion—a raging heat that made him want to cry out, "Get back from her, you foul animal, you're not fit to touch her with your bloodstained lips! She belongs to me, not to you, do you hear?"

What he did was to stand silent and motionless, his stony face with its gold-rimmed glasses a mask that hid the raging fire burning within his soul. The girl turned her wide, clear eyes upon him, and the smile that had been for her father and Negro mammy left her face. Her lips half parted as a certain kind of wonder came over her oval-shaped countenance.

"Why—why—" she began.

"What is it, darling?" Martin Jennifer said, seating himself on the edge of the bed and bending down. "This is Mr. Babel, who found you this morning in the water."

She was looking at Babel and not even hearing Jennifer's words. "It's—it's something in your eyes," she said slowly. "It's something you can almost grasp, and yet it's terribly elusive. Take off those glasses, please."

Babel obediently took them off, instinctively reaching for the white handkerchief. In doing so he brushed back the front of his coat, and the gesture brought the heavy, brass-studded cartridge belts into view above the shiny handles of the black-butted Colts.

"No," she said slowly, that same strange note in her voice, "it's not the glasses. There's something in your eyes that I've never seen in any man's eyes before. I—I feel as if I'd known you somewhere far, far back in the dim ages."

Jennifer laughed, and Babel, putting his spectacles back on, thought he detected a touch of uneasiness in it. "I'm afraid you mustn't mind her, Mr. Babel. That opiate her fiancé, Dr. Emmons, gave to alleviate the pain in her arm is a little too much. Well, darling," he went on, rising from the bed, "we'll let Mammy feed you and get you off to sleep. Come, George, let's go downstairs and have you meet my associates at breakfast. I've an idea you'll like

Partridge. In fact, after what happened last night, I think
you're going to find our little western community a worth
while place to stay."

"I'm not so sure," Babel murmured in his reticent way,
and he told Martin Jennifer, as they descended to the parlor below, about the killing of Orson in the Greek's place.

Something, of course, that Jennifer wasn't supposed to
have heard about—yet.

Jennifer's reaction was what he had expected. The
banker grabbed him by the arm and almost hauled him
toward the three other men emerging from the library on
the north end of the house. "Boys," he cried out, "here's
the man we've been looking for for two years! Here's the
man to rid the country of Ferguson and his whole gang."

The door had not closed upon the three alone. Ben
Johnston had come out too, and now as the white Van
Dyked Judge Calhoun stuck out a clammy hand, he
nodded his sage old head wisely and his benign eyes took
in Babel approvingly. "Yes, Martin, I believe you're right.
I think, Mr. Babel, that you will like it here in Partridge."

"I have no reason to think so," Babel smiled.

Inwardly he was raging. They, these precious five, were
so bloated with their own sense of power that the thought
he might refuse to turn hired killer apparently never occurred to them. It was plain to see that this powerful
combine of murderers and robber barons was used to getting what it wanted.

Babel made a pretense of eating, slow and fastidious,
handling the silver as his books in prison had taught him.
He studied the five and mentally marked each man. They
hadn't made further mention of his impending job, and
the quiet man with the gold-rimmed glasses wondered
whether they would offer him a town marshal's job, perhaps a deputy sheriff's star, or whether they would revert
to their natural murderous selves and offer him cash for
cold-blooded killings of the kind they themselves once
had done.

Babel though about it, yes, but in an instinctive sort of way. What really occupied his mind was the girl upstairs. She was his daughter, the daughter of an escaped convict now supposed to be dead. How could he wipe out the ex-gambler who posed as her father and yet keep the girl from hating him? And even if he did, what would she say when he told her, "I'm your real father. I went to prison for murder when you were two months old and I served nearly twenty-one years. It's I who have smashed up your way of life and torn down the very home you lived in."

"By the way," he said to Jennifer, "I don't believe I've had the pleasure of meeting the mistress of the household, Mrs. Jennifer."

Martin Jennifer's face changed and for a split second there was an embarrassed silence at the table. Then benevolent Judge Calhoun spoke in his flower voice:

"There has been no Mrs. Jennifer for many years, Mr. Babel. But then, you never can tell—you never can tell!" And the way he wagged a silly finger at the banker aroused in Babel the desire to crush in the old fool's skull with a heavy cut-glass bowl.

Dr. Emmons came in, tall, sun-browned. In daylight he appeared to be in his late twenties, or older. The fact that he owned the end house of the six big mansions pronounced him a man with money. And Babel was glad he owned the end home. Babel had no debt to settle with Mary Jennifer's young fiancé, and he would leave that one standing—alone.

He finished breakfast and left, walking down the grassy slope to town again. The sun had come out hot, as only a Texas sun can come out hot after a hard rain. The ground was already beginning to dry, the mud gone except in the lower spots. Babel went down the street that curved along the bottom of the slope. Here the buildings, with their backs almost against the bank, all belonged to the Sunset company. There was a bank on one corner, with Martin Jennifer, President, emblazoned in gold letters on the front window, a real estate office, a big store, and various other buildings. Across the street had been the shacks on ground desired by the company. The water had caught them and made a mess of things. One of them, a tiny little building, had housed the stock of merchandise of the Sunset Mercantile Company's only competitor. Aven Larson was busy, with the aid of several hired men, prying up a corner of the building and getting it back upon the blocks. Babel walked on. Then he turned as a cheery voice called out:

"Hold on there, my handsome rescuer. Don't pass up the bold, bad woman of the town."

Kitty Derril came toward him, smiling a greeting. In the light of the morning sun she was exceptionally pretty, and she hardly looked the part she had elected to play.

Babel removed his hat, nodding in a slight bow.

"My, you really *are* a gentleman," she laughed. "I see you came from up on the hill. Tell me, did they make you remove your boots before entering?"

"I gather," Babel said gently, "that you don't like the town banker."

The mockery that had been in the girl's eyes turned into open hostility. "I hate every one of them!" she said furiously. "They, with their fine manners and their servants and their society airs. There's only one among them who's got a decent drop of blood in her veins, and that's Jennifer's daughter. How that poor kid ever remained untainted is more than I can understand. And now they're selling her to Dr. Emmons because he belongs to a New York society family."

They had turned as though by common consent and were walking toward the restaurant run by John Metekas, for into Babel's mind had leaped a plan. It was so perfect that he wondered why he hadn't thought about it before. He could use this girl. They sat down at a table and talked over cups of steaming coffee.

"I gather," Babel said, picking up the conversation

where she had left off, "that you don't like Emmons too much either. I was rather impressed by him. He seems like a gentleman."

Kitty laughed bitterly. "He *seems* like one. He didn't act like one the night two years ago when I foolishly accepted an invitation to supper at his home. I found out something that night before I had to escape almost forcibly—something nobody would believe if I told it. Emmons is more than a mere drunkard. He's a smoker of *marijuana* as well. And now, Geroge Babel, you know one of the reasons why I lost my job as music teacher to Mary, whom I still see quite often. Now you know one of the reasons why I'm the so-called bad woman of the town. Emmons got frightened the next day and came to me, offering me money if I'd leave town. He was afraid I'd tarnish his reputation. When I refused, he probably figured that if the story had to spread, he'd better do the spreading himself. So he let it get out that I had stayed with him at his house that night. That's Dr. Emmons, the so-called 'brilliant' young surgeon, who wastes his genius out here in a stinking, hypocritical hole like Partridge, mostly hunting wild game."

Her lips had thinned out, her eyes were flashing fire, and Babel knew that in this girl he had found one of his own kind: one who could and would help in the terrible job of vengeance he had set out to do.

"Tell me, Kitty," he said in his gentle way, "do you know many of the ranchers who have been driven out by the Sunset Company?"

"All of them. Some moved across the state line into a new country. Others are down in the brakes. I take books down and try to teach the kids when I can, also give them lessons in choral singing. Then there are a few like Jed Berber. He's my—fellow. He's down in the brakes with some others, determined to fight it out to a finish."

"I believe I heard his name mentioned. I'd like to meet him some time soon, Kitty—him and the others."

"Jed is true blue. He'd make a great cattleman if Ben Ferguson didn't rustle what few head they managed to get together down there. Say"—and she was eyeing him narrowly across the table—"who are you who can come in her in the middle of a flood, kill one of Ferguson's outlaws in front of his eyes, and then enter the sacred halls of 'Pearly Gates Manor'?"

"You know, Kitty," Babel said, absently taking the pencil from his pocket and beginning to draw doodles on the tablecloth, "I was just thinking how a new co-operative cattle company could be formed over there among those poor outcasts with their own stolen stock. Take the Sunset brand: it's an S Bar like this."

Babel drew the S—on the tablecloth while the girl's eyes watched in brittle fascination. Then he filled in the S into a figure 8 and added lines to make a Lazy B. The new brand was 8B.

An 8 Lazy B.

In the dead silence that followed as Babel carefully erased the brand, the girl's voice came low: "Would you like to meet some of the old-timers who are leaders in that crowd?"

"Very much," was the toneless reply. "If they can be trusted."

"I'll bring them to you whenever you say the word," Kitty Derril answered.

They rose, after making detailed plans, and then as Kitty started toward the door she turned and let her blue eyes play upon Babel's stony face.

"Just one thing you completely overlooked, George Babel. You'll have to make your drives right through the heart of Ben Ferguson's country."

As she opened the door to go out, the sudden rattle of gunfire swept up the street, punctuated with one shrill yell after another. A Winchester slug drummed through the door jamb beside the girl and buried itself in the wall. Gunfire rolled and swelled and the running beat of hoofs sounded as a stream of masked men thundered up to the bank that had just opened its doors. As Babel jerked Kitty back inside and slammed the door, John Metekas reached up over the door leading into the kitchen and took down the .44-.40 repeating Winchester.

"Here—Ferguson has sworn to get me anyhow," Babel said, taking the gun. "Get Kitty under cover back of the kitchen stove. These walls won't stop lead."

He slipped out the back way, levering open the breech of the repeater long enough to expose an expanse of bright shell in the firing chamber. He melted around the corner just as a half dozen outlaws from the willows poured into the bank.

Ben Ferguson, after leaving Jennifer's house and returning to his men, had wasted little time in coming out into open warfare against the cattle barons his rustling had helped boost to power.

TEN

In Jennifer's home, shortly after Babel had taken leave after letting them extract a promise to return and meet their friends, the five men comprising the Sunset cattle outfit went into the library again and closed the door. Martin Jennifer, as speaker, stood with his back to the cold fireplace and surveyed his four partners.

"Well, boys," he said, flicking the ashes from his after breakfast cigar, "things are really breaking our way. You know, people think that an outfit like ours that's worth a million dollars and more runs itself, that we have no worries. They don't know that we have worries aplenty. Nobody ever knew that all these years we've been living under the shadow of a man who, though forgotten by the world, might escape from prison and hunt us down."

A look of horror crossed Judge Calhoun's bony face.

The eyes lost their benign look and became beady, half in anger, half in fear.

"Martin!" he half squealed in shocked dignity. "Good heavens, man, how can you even *mention* such a thing! That's all buried deep in the past and forgotten. We're gentlemen now, and gentlemen don't speak of such things."

"No, Judge, it's not forgotten and you know it," the ex-gambler who had pressed his thumbs against Jim Kent's bashed skull to try making him talk replied. "I've woke up in the night a thousand times seeing Jim Kent swinging from that limb—and we are speaking of it because we're *not* gentlemen."

"I guess you're right," the judge murmured. "I'll never forget the stricken, trapped animal look in the eyes of that wild mountain boy when I passed sentence on him and they dragged him away. But come, Martin, why have you brought up this distasteful subject?"

"Just a prelude to the fact that we're coming into our own bigger than ever. Two weeks ago in that big prison fire up in our old stomping grounds, the Kent man burned up. They found his charred body in the locked cell. That fire lifted the shadow that's been over me all these years. It was more like a cloud that has passed away. But there has been one other shadow, Ferguson, that we've got to erase. For two years now he's wanted to come out in the open. You know—turn respectable and all that sort of thing. We're supposed to use our influence with the Governor and get him a full pardon, after which he'll take over a slice of our huge holdings, erect himself a ranch house, rebrand a couple of thousand head of Sunset cattle. . . ."

"And then get him a haircut, a new suit of clothes, and bring him into our set, eh?" Bonner finished with a sneer. "After a bath of course."

"That was the idea, I guess," Jennifer went on. "And when he came roaring in here this morning and broke clean with us, I knew we were in for it. I still think, Judge, that I should have shot him right here on the spot."

"It'd never have done," Ben Johnston put in. "Duval is a mean, dangerous man with brains of his own. That tawny devil would have split this country wide open. Nope, we've got to wipe them out some other way—and we've got to get them all if it means dynamite under their place down in the brakes."

"Not any more," Jennifer smiled. "For this morning that man Babel is the answer to all our prayers. He's a strange, cold-blooded devil, that man. There's something in his eyes that's as deep and unfathomable as the Orient itself. But if ever a man was sent at the right moment to pull five other men out of a bad hole that easily could suck us all down into ruin and disgrace, that man is George Babel."

They waited. Alden shifted his big body in the chair and rolled the cigar thoughtfully around and around his protruding, purplish lips. He was a heavy drinker but still active on the ranch. His town home was more for show than anything else.

He also was a man of direct action, for he said bluntly: "How much money you think it'll cost us to hire him to wipe out Ferguson and his gang? I ain't puttin' out more'n two thousand for my share, an' that's final. I'll do the job myself an' save that much, if necessary."

The look of scorn the others, even the sheriff, focused upon him told without words their opinion of a man with such crude ideas.

"Don't be a damned fool, Alden," Martin Jennifer said coldly. "That man has got to be handled with kid gloves. He's already had to kill two of the gang, and a good job it was. He'll have to kill that Red Gorman—the whining fool!—because that Etherdige fellow was his bunk mate. That makes three. What we'll do is go to him in the guise of honest cattle operators who are desperate and helpless in the face of rustlers. We'll beseech him to aid us. He's a Western man clean through, Babel is, and he's got that rare combination of brains and a deadly pair of Colts one so seldom sees. Naturally he hates a rustler worse than he does a snake. So, in desperation, we'll offer him two hundred a month and a certain number of shares in the Sunset company, not to kill rustlers—oh, no! That would be too crude—just to ride the range and let his new reputation scare them away. Well, Ferguson isn't a man who scares. He's a vindictive man. He'll go after Babel—and when the showdown comes my money is on that cold-eyed gentleman. Well, boys, I've got to get on to the bank. Coming?"

Sheriff Ben Johnston rose and yawned. "Not me. I'm goin' over and sleep all day. I'm wore out from last night."

The other four got hats and went out. It was less than three hundred yards to the town and the courthouse of red stone sitting up there on a rise a hundred yards back of the bank. They started down the gentle slope, and then there was a movement at the far end of town and a body of masked horsemen suddenly spurred into view from the fringe of the willows down where Babel had found Jennifer's daughter.

"My God, it's Ferguson and his men raiding the bank!" Martin Jennifer cried out, and the four of them halted, too stunned to move as the line of riders swept on.

Guns began to blast. Men working along the street dropped shovels and dived out of sight. Shrill yells and whoops rent the air. As the outlaws swept up the street, firing more shots to clear it of spectators, a half dozen of them broke away in a wave and spurred at the bank porch, the door of which the teller had just opened and propped back. Five men jumped down and ran inside, the sixth holding the horses. He himself rode a part steeldust horse with a white spot on its rump.

"It's that Red Gorman we hired to help Etheridge dynamite the dam!" Bonner cried out in a rage. "I'd know that hoss anywhere. Good God, can't we do something?"

"And get shot down because we're all unarmed?" snapped Martin Jennifer coolly. "Stand still and do nothing and hope they don't see us. This is open war, and Ferguson is drawing first blood."

So the four stood there, watching in queer fascination as a small but important part of their ill-gotten gains was being taken from the bank.

It was then that a man stepped into view around a corner of the Greek's restaurant. He wore a long black coat and a flat-brimmed hat and carried a repeating Winchester in his hands. He stepped out boldly into sight just as four riders who had swept on up to the end of the street whirled around by the smashed church and saloon and came tearing back. They sighted him and bore down with shrill yells, their reloaded guns making short circular motions as they brought them up over their heads and then down again. The snapping reports rolled out across the drying country. Then Jennifer saw the Winchester whip up. He had never believed it possible for a man to lever shots so fast or with such deadly accuracy. Spurts of smoke enveloped the man in the black coat, and the brass shells described glittering circles as they jumped, empty, from the firing chamber one on the heels of the other, the sharp crashing roars slashing savagely into the duller booming of the .45's.

With cool, deadly accuracy Babel shot the four of them to death and swung the gun around toward a guard at the other end of the street. It crashed again, and the guard's horse sank down on stiffened forelegs, then fell kicking. In front of the bank Red Gorman had whirled with a horrible outlaw yell and dropped the reins, yanking out his six-shooter. The outlaw mounts bolted and thundered down the street just as the raiders in masks came running out. And there in that still wet street Partridge witnessed a sight it never forgot: a tall, black-coated man wearing a pair of thin, gold-rimmed spectacles walking deliberately toward five others on the back porch. He held a pair of spouting Colt .45's in his hands and his whole body seemed to be a wisp of bluish smoke that rose and swirled about his hips. Three of the masked men had broken for the protection of the bank and ducked around the corner, grabbing wildly at the reins of frightened horses. One was down on the porch, and Red Gorman was staggering in circles, blood running from his mouth and nose. He went down, got half up again, then fell flat on his face in the mud, his mask off.

And one man on that porch stood alone. It was the tawny Blade Duval, mask torn off and his greenish eyes blazing. A yelling scream of rage was in his throat when he forgot everything in a mad, insane desire to down that black-coated phantom who came on in that slow, even walk while he shot from the hips as though the very devil himself had been his teacher.

He ran off the porch with a rush like the rush of a mad bull, and Babel used up his last two cartridges to bring him down. He lay there kicking and wallowing convulsively in a smear of red, and there was animal ferocity and the wild cruelty of a panther in his greenish eyes as he looked up at the man who had shot him to death, at a face that was merciless.

"Ferguson an' the—rest of the gang'll git yuh," he panted. He coughed and spat red and managed somehow to wipe his sleeve across his lips. "He'll make Jennifer—an' the rest of them yaller coyotes pay, too. . . . Ahh, God!"

He wallowed out his life in a pool of his own blood, and the man known as George Babel stood over him with a blank, unrelenting face and watched him die—a man with no emotion in his heart that boded good for any of them, except for the girl up there in bed.

For in that moment as Babel stood there he knew that

he had become a machine, a killer of men, a man who lived only to destroy, a man without mercy.

He became aware of men yelling all about him. He saw Kitty Derril and Jennifer and the others. He heard her cry out, "Babel—George, are you hurt?"

"No," the man known as George Babel said. "I am not hurt." And he remembered what the old scholar Zarkov had said to him that day twenty-one years ago about pain being only a matter of mind and being controllable. He felt no pain now.

"No," he said again. "I am not hurt."

He turned to walk away, took two steps forward, and then as a tree falls he fell. He lay with arms outspread, the spot of red widening on the back of his dark coat.

ELEVEN

When Babel came out of it again he opened his eyes into splendor such as he had never been able to conceive. He lay in a huge four-poster bed in a room more than forty-foot square. He saw upper tree limbs outside the big windows, and that too told him all he needed to know:

He had been carried to an upstairs room of Martin Jennifer's great Southern style mansion.

The thought brought the faint touch of a sardonical smile to his lips. He was lying in splendor that had been bought with his own gold, in the house of the man he was going to kill.

He twisted around in bed and discovered, with a grunt of pain, that his chest was swathed in bandages and that the pain came from along his side and back near the right armpit. Memory flooded back again and he recalled the fight.

Babel reached over with one hand and got his glasses lying on a table beside the great bed. He put them on and settled back, noticing for the first time that his saddlebags and slicker roll had been brought in from the stable. That gave him a queer sense of uneasiness at first. Suppose somebody had gone through them and found that huge volume containing the case histories of every man of the five?

Babel had compiled the histories slowly and painstakingly as Aven Larson, whom The Five hadn't known back in the old days, lived unknown among them and made his weekly reports by letter: every cattle deal, every rancher driven out, the name of every homesteader burned out—it was all there in that big volume whose outlines he could see in the saddlebags piled in a corner.

"I'd last about as long as a poisonous rattlesnake found in the house," he muttered to himself, "if they knew who I am—that Tom Kent is here to settle an old, old debt of murder and robbery."

The door—it was a big double door painted white—opened, and a man came into the room. Dr. Emmons came over to the bed and smiled a professional smile.

"Feeling better?" he inquired.

"There have been times when I've felt much better," Babel replied.

"You'll be all right in no time at all. The bullet plowed along your ribs and then entered the *latissimus dorsi*, coming out the back. It'll be rather painful for a while, but you'll be up and about in no time. Meanwhile, you never came out of it because I gave you a heavy opiate to help ease the shock of your wound. You've been asleep for over twenty hours. And now let's have a look at the wound before Martin comes up. He's at breakfast."

Babel rolled over on his left side and Emmons skillfully removed the upper bandages. The wound had closed and showed no signs of infection. A Negro servant came in with a breakfast tray converted into a medicine chest, and Emmons bathed the wound carefully, applied a salve that would prevent the fresh pads from sticking, and swathed Babel's chest again in fresh strips.

"How is he, Doctor?" a cheery voice said, and Martin Jennifer, freshly shaven and sleek, came into the room. "Well, well, Babel! Man, this whole section of the cow country is talkng about you this morning. That thrilling gun fight single-handed against the worst gang of outlaws in the state will go down as an epic that will never be forgotten. Why, man, you're a hero! Our paper—I decided we ought to have a daily, though the town's population doesn't warrant one yet—is filled with nothing else but accounts of the fight. Our staff artist ran down there and, right on the very spot, while they were still lying there, mind you, drew pictures of the whole thing. It was the most magnificent sight a man ever witnessed. Ah, I tell you, Babel, there's nothing you could ask for this morning that you couldn't have. Nothing, I tell you!"

"Sometimes," Babel said from the bed, and it was fortunate for the cattle baron that he was too jubilant to see what lay deep in those ascetic eyes, "sometimes a man wants something he can never attain. Sometimes he wants something out beyond his reach."

Jennifer laughed a hearty laugh, his elation taking on a high note.

"Well, my boy, I'll tell you this much: if it's anything in this country, you can have it. A dozen proposals have come in to make you town marshal. Others want you to become a deputy sheriff. Ben Johnston is even talking of getting kind of old and wanting to retire to take life easy, and suggested that you be appointed in his place. But none of those things for you, Babel. We'll show you that Partridge can be appreciative. First, what do you want more than anything else this morning that I can give you?"

Babel said softly, "That corner lot where Alveraz had his dive and the lumber from the two wrecked buildings."

"Done! Say no more, Babel! Lots and the wreck of

both the saloon and church are yours. But what do you want with them?"

"I'm going to build a club there, a quiet saloon with music and soft lights. I'll call it the Tower Club, the Tower of Babel."

Jennifer's freshly shaven face lost some of its jubilation and was replaced by a look of disappointment. "But good heavens, man, my associates and I had something far better, far more useful in mind. That fight yesterday, in addition to making you a powerful figure in this section, made Ben Ferguson an open outlaw with a price on his head. Ben put a flat ten thousand reward on his head yesterday afternoon and a thousand a head for each of those scurvy, rustling riders of his. With the—ah—bonus the bank's grateful board of directors has added, I'm putting ten thousand in cash to your account this morning."

Emmons picked up his bag and turned to Jennifer. "I think I'd better go in and see if we can let Mary get up today for a while."

The ex-gambler let out a peal of laughter. "Up?" he said, laughing the harder. "The moment she woke up this morning and found out this man Babel was in the house, she came out of that bed like a shot. His name is magic to her. The man has her hypnotized, I tell you."

Emmons gave a slight grunt that showed no appreciation for the humor of the situation and went out. As he opened the door, Judge Calhoun, Bonner, Alden and Sheriff Ben Johnston came in. They advanced upon the bed, and skinny old Judge Calhoun pulled at his white goatee and rubbed his hands together until the white of his palms squeezed out like the belly of a catfish.

"Ah, and how's our man Babel this morning?" he queried, beaming benevolently.

The judge didn't know it, but in that moment Babel sealed his doom. He thought of Calhoun—pictured him in his pew on Sunday mornings with his beady old eyes rolled benevolently heavenward while he sang piously;

and Babel knew that the old robber befouled the very air in which he stood. So George Babel, lying there in bed, marked him off as the first man on his list.

"I'm beginning to think he's out of his head," Jennifer answered. "I just told him we'd voted him ten thousand in rewards for the wonderful civic job he did yesterday, and the man actually acts as though he doesn't *want* the money!"

"All I want," Babel said a trifle wearily, "is the lot and the two wrecked buildings."

"You see," Jennifer said, throwing up his hands in an expansive gesture after explaining what it was all about. "The man's not human, I tell you. But—very well, George, you shall have your wish. We'll take the reward money we voted you and buy the property from Alveraz."

The thought made Babel smile: this building his Tower of Babel on a foundation of blood—blood money. He remembered the words of the Greek and the restaurant man's prophecy that it would be wrecked in violence. But then Babel knew he had come to do a terrible job and that, after yesterday, he had ceased to become a mere man: he was an instrument of destruction to the empire these foul five had built upon the same foundation. They had built their empire on it; it would be destroyed the same way.

"Frankly, George, my boy," the banker was saying in that sirupy tone of voice Babel had come to abhor, "we're a little disappointed in this determination of yours to go into business. You see, Ferguson has declared open war on us, and the cattle he's been rustling have been nothing to what he will do now. He'll drive them into the brakes by the hundreds, and we'll be able to do little more than establish line camps and armed riders and try to keep him out. But some will get through, and with the New Mexico Territory line so near he'll put them across over into a country filled with other small groups of rustlers we drove out during the past few years. God knows we've been losing enough as it is, in spite of Alden and Bonner being in personal charge with armed riders, but it's nothing to what we'll lose now unless you help us."

"The pay," Alden broke in hastily and a little uneasily, "won't be too much—"

"Shut up, Alden!" Jennifer snapped in a freezing voice, each syllable dripping with ice; he was having difficulty controlling himself in that moment. And to the man in bed: "You mustn't mind Ed. He's a penny pincher. What we thought, George, is that if you'd give up this foolish idea of going into business and sign on with us, we'd make it five hundred a month and sign over to you a small block of stock—say one hundred shares—in the company. That would really make you a working partner."

"Well," Babel said, appearing to ponder the proposition, "it seems to me that I could work better undercover, using the club as a blind."

"Say, Martin," Bonner broke in in feverish excitement, his small, hard eyes glittering, "I think the man's got something there. If he goes out in the open, even a man as deadly a kill—ah, as deadly with a pair of Colts as he is might not be able to overcome such odds as Ferguson and his whole crew. Why couldn't he pick them off from cover one by one? Think of the effect it would have upon Ferguson as day after day one of his men after another showed up missing and were left in a place where that murdering outlaw would be sure to find them."

"Well, now, yes," Judge Calhoun put in, pacing back and forth at the foot of the bed, his skinny hands clasped behind him and his head bowed as though he were deep in the midst of an important court decision. "Yes, there can be no denying what the effect upon Ferguson would be. Think what the effect would be upon *you*, Martin, if you found *me* murdered mysteriously. And then the next week Bonner. And Alden. Think what the effect would be upon you."

"That's all nonsense," the ex-gambler growled in irritation. "The very thought is preposterous. Anybody murdering *us!* No, I'm now in favor of George going right out in the open and living on the ranch, shooting them down on sight. All he'll have to do is hide down in the brakes with a good Winchester and a pair of field glasses and watch the main trails. We'll have all our riders wear something to identify them so there will be no mistakes. When he spots one of those scum, he merely can ride out, accost the man, identify himself and wait for the rustler to draw."

Alden intruded himself into the conversation, taking from his protruding purplish lips the cigar which he had kept turning in his mouth.

"I'll have one of the men at the company ranch do nothing but take care of supplies and horses for him," he said. "He'll establish a good hidden camp down on the edge of the brakes and come in with supplies and fresh horses by a hidden trail."

Babel had been lying in bed listening to it all, noting that they had completely forgotten him. They were working out details.

"I might immediately sell the place and leave," he reminded them. "I merely came to settle up some—ah—personal matters down in this country. Kindly bear that in mind, gentlemen, while making plans. The new club is a whimsical idea that I'm sure you wouldn't understand."

"Oh, of course, of course," at least three voices out of the five acquiesced.

"I've got it all figured out," the wounded man said, his ascetic eyes staring up at the white ceiling, a dreamy look in them. "A very quiet little place with the best of furniture, rugs, and a big piano at the back where we can have music afternoons and evenings. I've got just the person to play, too—a nice, refined young woman named Kitty Derril—"

If a bomb had been exploded in that room it couldn't

have caused more shocked consternation. Babel saw them staring at him and at each other, and in Judge Calhoun's bearded face was a look of absolute horror. The judge almost shuddered.

"Mr. Babel," he half whispered as though the name had been a blow at the sanctity of the very room in which they stood, "do you realize what you're saying? Why, her presence there automatically would prevent any decent man or woman in this town from patronizing your place. Surely you must be joking. Why, haven't you heard how she forced herself into Emmons' house one night and stayed with him? It's common knowledge."

"What he means to say, old boy, is that the Derril woman is a stench in the nostrils of the decent element in this town," Martin Jennifer put in. "She's been—ah—suspected of a—er—lot of things, if you get what I mean?"

"Perfectly, Mr. Jennifer, perfectly. We'll forget it for the moment."

After they were gone Babel lay there filled with such loathing disgust for those precious five, as he liked to term them, that he was tempted to get up then and there. He didn't because presently Mary Jennifer came in to see how he was, her right arm now in a sling. She wore a white housedress of some flimsy material that appeared to be a sea of ruffles. The locket still gleamed at her soft white throat. And her sweet presence in that room after the five had gone was like opening the window and letting in the fragrance of the warm morning air outside.

No matter what she was, in spite of the fact that she was a complete stranger in his life, he couldn't keep his heart from jumping a little with a strange kind of pride and joy every time he caught sight of her.

"Ah, you're feeling better!" she cried out, and forthwith seated herself on the edge of the bed, to the shocked surprise of her outraged "Mammy." Mammy's eyebrows made an angry signal and her eyes flashed in indignation. The idea!

"Yes," Babel said, smiling at her. "I feel much better now that you've come. I'll be able to be up in a couple of days, I think."

"I hope so, I truly do," Mary said. "I was terribly frightened when I heard about—that."

"It's an unpleasant subject, Miss Jennifer."

"You may call me Mary, George Babel," the girl said. "Call me anything just so long as it isn't a bashful 'Ma'am,' such as the riders do when we're at the ranch. We usually spend a few weeks there during the summer."

He listened while she told him about the great buildings and barns and corrals—though he had it all blueprinted in his mind from Aven Larson's letters. The main headquarters where all the five had their summer cottages were about eight miles from town, west and a little north. Babel had, in fact, crossed some of the range when he came on Black Boy toward Partridge. He had hoped to drop by and get a glimpse of the spread through the long range binoculars he had bought, among other things, in Austin; but the rain prevented it.

But he was more interested in this lovely young woman who was—or had been—his daughter.

"Tell me all about yourself," Babel said to her. "Do you ride?"

"Ride?" She laughed openly at him. "Good heavens, what a strange notion you must have about me! I was raised on the ranch. That is, in between tutoring and music studies."

He found out that she played the violin and the piano too, and that she liked Kitty Derril.

"I lost my violin in the flood, coming back from Aven's church where he'd given a party for some of the children in the lower side of town," Mary said. "I'd been forbidden by Dad to go anywhere that night, as he said he was afraid the dam might break and flood the town, and he wanted me to stay up on higher ground. But I slipped off anyway. In doing so I lost my violin and almost lost my life, had it not been for you."

"I merely found you," Babel said to his daughter. "As for the loss of the instrument—wait until my baggage comes in on the stage."

"It done come, Mistuh Babel," Mammy, who had been standing aloofly nearby, intruded. "Stage driver done brought it right up to the house this mawnin'. I'll have that no 'count man of mine, Booger, git it."

She had it brought up by two husky Negro stable hands, one of whom was her red-coated spouse. Under her scathing orders they meekly placed the trunk near the head of the bed, giving it a final shove back against the wall.

"Now you two git outa here wid dem nasty feet," Mammy ordered, almost shooing them away. "Shame on you two men, comin' in here widout fust cleanin' yo' shoes. I'd oughta bust yo' fool haid fo' you, Booger."

"Just a moment, Mammy," Babel said, smiling in spite of himself at her belligerent bullying of the other servants. "I want to see Booger a moment."

"Well, don't keep him in here too long. It gonna take a week to git de stable smell outa dis house."

Booger came over and stood respectfully by, his red cap in his hand.

"It's about my horse, Booger," the bandaged man in bed said. "I'd like you to take special care of him. He's pretty much of a one-man horse."

Actually, it was more because the black, having been born stone blind, had to be reassured by the sound of a voice. And Babel knew that the Negro, loving horses, undoubtedly had become a trusted friend by talking to the intelligent animal.

"He's sure somethin', all right," Booger answered, grinning his embarrassed grin. "Mistuh Jennifer try every way he kin to make friends with that hoss but he won't have nothin' to do with him. So I tell them other stable boys to stay stri'tly away from him, 'cause he's my charge. I turn him out to graze a couple of hours yesterday and you know what, Mistuh Babel? When I goes out to get him all I had to do was yell, 'Come here, you black devil,' and I swear if he don't come right to me when I talk with him. He's the dawg-gonest hoss I ever see."

After he was gone Mammy obediently opened the trunk. Under Babel's directions she dug down and brought out a violin case.

It was an old case, a very old case, and the instrument she removed was as mellow looking as a roll of aged cheese.

"Give it to Mary," Babel directed. "I want you to have it as a special present to remember me by, should anything ever happen."

Mary Jennifer took the mellow old instrument in her good hand and carefully looked it over—and then a strange little cry broke from her.

"Why—*it's an Amati!*"

"I found it in a second hand store in Austin."

"An Amati!" she cried out again. "Oh, I can't wait until I can play again!"

She hugged the brown instrument to her breast, an instrument that had survived its maker by nearly two hundred and fifty years, and her clear eyes sparkled in a way that made Babel's heart beat faster still as pride in his lovely daughter rose up within him. Whatever kind of murderous, blackhearted scoundrel Martin Jennifer had been, the ex-Mississippi steamboat card shark had instilled in this stolen girl a love of the finer things in life.

And in that moment the wounded man knew that his job of wiping out in blood the man who had killed his brother had doubled. For this girl now had come up as a barrier to bar that vengeance. She loved her "father," whom Babel had come to kill.

What would she feel toward this man she had never

known when he revealed his identity to her? When she learned of his terrible mission to Partridge?

Babel put the thought from his mind and began talking music with her. In his library in prison had been many books on music of all the ages. The great Franz Liszt had scarcely been in his grave a half dozen years; his immortal scores already had flowed across from the Old World. Both Schubert and Beethoven, whom the starving younger man worshipped, had been dead about sixty years. And among Babel's letters in prison was one written in shaky but legible German, in answer to one he himself had written with the aid of his English-German lexicon. Brahms was indeed a kindly old man, though his answer to Babel had taken months.

Mary Jennifer sat on the edge of the big bed, and now he saw for the first time that she was staring at him. On her lovely face was that same look of wonderment and puzzlement he had seen once before.

"What kind of a man are you?" she whispered slowly. "Yesterday down there in the street you—you fought a gun fight with outlaws who were robbing my father's bank and destroyed them alone. Today you give me a rare violin made by a genius who died in 1684, and talk of men whose music has made them immortal. And there's something far back in your eyes—"

She didn't finish, but got up suddenly and fled out of the room, Mammy following with the empty case containing the bow. After they were gone, the man with the gold-rimmed glasses lay there alone, a strange battle raging deep within his soul; a battle with himself to decide whether he must follow unswervingly the course he had laid—or give it up and thus not destroy his daughter's happiness.

"I've got to get out of here," George Babel said, half aloud. "I've got to get out of here before I weaken."

TWELVE

On a morning three days after he had regained consciousness, the wounded man in the upstairs room of Martin Jennifer's great white mansion got up out of bed over Dr. Emmons' quiet admonitions. Another man might have been unable to walk about with a painful furrow along his ribs and a shallow hole through the heavy muscle back of the armpit. But Babel was no ordinary man, and his years of frugal eating, careful exercise in his cell, and a five-day fast each month had built up an amazing stamina. Emmons shook his head when the patient got up and dressed and walked out of the house.

"Babel, the more I see of you the more you become a mystery to me," the young surgeon said. "You're no ordinary man, and I—to be quite frank in a friendly sort of way—cannot believe that you just drifted in here. You're here for some strange reason I—again to be quite frank—wish I knew. However, that's your affair. But I do wish you'd come over and visit me during your convalescence. I'm quite a big game hunter, you know, and I'd like to show you my gun collection."

Babel nodded in his quiet, agreeable way and walked down the slope toward town. The physician was not unaware that there was beginning to form in the patient's brain a few unasked questions of his own. For there was something about Emmons Babel didn't like. As a man who had spent many years in prison, he had met bad men, dangerous men, sullen killers, quiet, cold-blooded ones, and those with warped minds. And he was not fooled by Emmons. That husky, sun-browned younger man whom Babel knew to be a drunkard and a smoker of the weed was dangerous.

Babel walked on, his arm in a sling made of a black

silk neckerchief Mammy had tied for him, and he saw respect in the eyes of all who passed and knew they had turned to stare. He astounded Jennifer by walking into the bank, but almost the first thing the ex-Mississippi gambler told him was a story of his failure to buy the corner lot and crushed saloon from Jose Alveraz.

He swiveled around in his chair and clipped off the end of a cigar, tossing the discarded tip into a cuspidor. "I sent one of the clerks here in the bank down to see about it yesterday. The breed's living with a Mexican woman in a 'dobe shack on the lower edge of town and wouldn't even talk to him."

"That's understandable," Babel said. "Word is floating around town that the dam which broke and wiped out Alveraz's place didn't break but was blown out. Naturally Alveraz thinks you had a hand in it."

Jennifer was rolling the cigar length through his lips to wet it, his eyes speculative. "Hmm," he said thoughtfully, reaching for a match on his desk, "I had forgotten that Ferguson was a friend of the man. In fact, Ferguson practically supported the place, since few other people patronized it on account of there being so much brawling among that tough crew."

"In other words, Alveraz figured that you wiped him out of business in an effort to keep Ferguson out of town."

This was the nearest thing to a slip that Babel had made; and hardly were the words out of his mouth when he could have bitten his tongue. He inwardly cursed himself for an imbecile. He knew he was a loud-mouthed fool when Jennifer's next words came, almost sharply suspicious:

"And just why should I be interested in keeping Ben Ferguson out of town, or give a damn what he does?"

Babel smiled and said: "You're a civic leader, aren't you, Jennifer? Wouldn't people naturally look to you to want Ferguson away from Partridge?"

The cattle baron-banker settled back in his chair again, relaxing. A cloud of tobacco smoke encircled his head, ballooning toward the ceiling.

"Why, yes, come to think of it, that's right, Babel. And whatever damage has been done to the town, part of it has been worth it because it wiped out that breed's tough dive. And I'm not going to give him a chance to rebuild. I'm going to have Johnston take those two *very capable* deputies of his, Thorpe and Sistrom, and pay the Senor Alveraz a visit. I think we can dispense with that gentleman's presence in our little community. Thorpe and Sistrom are good men. In fact," Jennifer said, his eyes on the visitor's face in open frankness, "they've been hinting for a try at Ferguson's scalp."

Babel had seen the two deputies: heavy, pistol-weighted fellows who were more personal bodyguards to the sheriff than anything else; especially hired to back him on dangerous jobs. Or so had said Aven's reports.

Thus George Babel had written in his book in prison:

Supplement to Sheriff Johnston:
Two deputies the past year, Thorpe and Sistrom.
Former prison guards. Gun packers and very dangerous. Thorpe has boasted of killing five men. Both heavy drinkers.

"From what I've heard of Alveraz, coupled with what he said the day we had the little argument," Babel suggested, "Ben Ferguson would smash open any jail Johnston locked him up in, even though yours here in town is now tipped up on one side, due to the water washing out a bank and dropping it fifteen feet into the creek bed."

But Jennifer was not to be drawn out on his intentions concerning Alveraz whether the man was to be shot dead by the two deputies or merely driven out of town. So Babel rose and turned to the man whose empire he was going to undermine and smash.

"Whatever you do, I'd like to see Alveraz first and try persuading him to sell."

"Ah! So you've decided to settle here in Partridge after all?"

Babel shook his head. "No. It's just that my business down in this section is going to take a bit longer, perhaps, than I had anticipated. So I might as well invest. By the way, you say there's ten thousand to my account here?"

Jennifer shifted the cigar to the other corner of his mouth and rose, slapping him heartily on the back. "Ten thousand and as much more as you want, old fellow. Twelve thousand, if you want to include that black horse of yours in the deal."

"Thanks. I'll just take a checkbook instead."

He left the bank porch and crossed the street, half tempted to drop in at Aven Larson's now righted store and reveal himself. But he preferred to wait until he could be sure of things. It might not be best to be seen with Larson yet. He was certain of it when he saw Thorpe, the bepistoled and booted deputy, come out of the bank and with a casualness that was too studied to be natural stroll off down the boardwalk across from him. He had either been hidden in the bank listening, or had gone in.

The main street of the town formed a perfect cross where a cross-street intersected it in the middle. It was on one of these main corners that the bank had been built. Babel went down the boardwalk past four or five business establishments, ducked into a three-foot opening between two buildings, ran down the alley and came out on the cross street not far from the corner. There he pulled up short.

Two minutes later he heard sounds of a man making hurried progress, and then Thorpe appeared out of the alley's mouth. He pulled up, flustered.

"Why—" he began.

"I don't like being followed," Babel said in his gentle way. "Not by amateurs anyhow, Thorpe. And if you're going to do much more of it, I might suggest that you remove your spurs."

The flush on Thorpe's face deepened. For a moment he appeared nonplussed as to whether he should bluster his way out or take the tone of a martyr. He did a fair job of mixing the two.

"Hell," he half sneered, "you gun-throwin' gents are all alike. Touchy. A man tries to help yuh an' yuh gets all riled. I was only doin' my duty. Martin figgered that breed might try to take advantage of yore bum wing an' maybe throw a gun on yuh. He's poison, that gent. Martin's only sent me along to keep an eye on things."

Babel had no way of knowing that Jennifer, spotting Thorpe nearby almost as Babel left the bank, had hurriedly called him in. Had, in fact, ordered him to follow Babel to Alveraz's and wait until the deal was closed. He then was to shoot the man dead from a window and claim he'd *thought* Babel was in danger.

It would be an excellent way of getting rid of Alveraz.

And thus, though the man who called himself George Babel had no way of knowing what had occurred in the bank after his departure, he was certain that something out of order was in the wind. Nor did he like it.

"You can go right back and tell Jennifer that I'm quite grateful for his thoughtfulness but that I need no bodyguards," he said.

Thorpe shrugged and gave in with a half sullen growl. "All right, Mister Short Gun Artist, it's yore funeral."

He turned and slouched off up the street, toward the bank on the opposite corner, and Babel waited until he had disappeared inside its wide corner doors. Then he made his way toward the lower end of town, where a 'dobe shack had stood hard and fast against the flood waters that had swirled three feet deep around and through it.

THIRTEEN

He found Alveraz down in a Mexican shack on the lower
side of town. When Babel offered to buy Alveraz took
one look into those ascetic eyes and hurriedly closed the
deal. For several days more he loafed around town while
men the banker hired swarmed over the two wrecked
buildings and salvaged what lumber they could use. On
the spot rose a new one-story building as square as a box,
with a deep interior to receive the new furnishings and
curved bar—something new in Partridge—being shipped
from Austin to the nearest railway point and then brought
in by freight wagons. Babel no longer lived in Jennifer's
home but had two rooms in a hotel. Yet it was noticeable
that more and more young Mary Jennifer was seen with
the older man, both wearing their right arms in slings.
Emmons noticed it too and drank more and more; and
then one day Babel, visiting the girl at home, walked
across the big lawn, crossed over steps topping the fence
dividing the grounds of the two big homes, and knocked
on the front door. He rang the knocker again.

It was the doctor who answered it. Emmons' face
flushed a trifle, but he forced a cheery greeting.

"Come on in, Babel," he said heartily. "I've been looking forward to this visit for days."

He closed the door and picked up a big single shot rifle
he apparently had been carrying just as Babel knocked.
His riding clothes and boots were dusty.

"I just got in a moment ago," he said as he led the
guest into a big room on the south wing of the house.
"Been out back of the Sunset Ranch. How is the wound?"

"Very good. So you've been out back of the Sunset.
I've heard there's some very interesting country down
there. Been thinking I'd get my horse and ride over that

way. The rascal's getting lazy eating his head off in Jennifer's stable. And I'm afraid Booger is spoiling him."

He took the proffered chair that Emmons waved him toward, his eyes roaming around the walls packed solidly with gun cases. There were, Babel judged, about sixty different rifles and pistols of various calibers and sizes in the collection.

"Yes, very interesting country—and dangerous, so I hear," Emmons said, bringing decanter and glasses and placing them on the table that also appeared to be a work bench. Gun tools of various sorts lined one side in neat racks. There were bullet molds, a stack of bar lead, and a powder measure that could be adjusted to dump any required amount into any empty shell.

Babel picked up an instrument used for punching out fired caps and crimping new ones into place. "Professional call?" he asked idly.

Emmons poured the brownish liquid to the halfway mark in both glasses and recapped the container. He replaced the decanter in the cabinet.

"No, though I've made two or three down in that country—at gun point. The latest was only last week. There's a young rustler down there named Jed Berber—a rather murderous young devil from what I hear, and the latest in that Derril woman's long string of lovers. I believe he rustled Sunset cattle, he and his father, until Alden and some of his riders got the old man. Young Berber got away and went into the brakes. Anyhow, he shot one of Ferguson's riders at long range the other day, and in the middle of the night I was taken down there, blindfolded, to extract the slug. A .44-.40. Here it is."

He reached into a drawer-like compartment of the table and brought out a small chunk of lead. "Well, let's drink to health and a long prosperous life. This is, incidentally, good sherry."

"Salutations," agreed Babel, lifting his glass. The stuff

warmed him with instantaneous fire, for his system was not used to liquor in any form.

"You should do pretty good here, being the only physician, with no competition," he said, setting down the glass and examining the bullet.

Emmons had drained his own glass in a single long swallow. He picked up the huge Sharps Special and laid it lengthwise on the table, reaching for cleaning rags strung on a wire between the end legs. He went to a case and came back with a can of imported cleaning solvent.

"Frankly, Babel, I wish there was another man here, for I don't wish to be bothered with practice. Why should a man, when he's plenty of money?"

"It's a good argument," smiled the visitor.

"I've been hoping that another man would come in and take over. You see, Mary and I are getting married one of these days—soon, I hope. We're going to settle down on the Sunset spread where I can fish and use these guns to my heart's content. The one real passion in my life are these guns. Why, do you know that I can tell you the grain weight of every standard caliber bullet used in all American and European weapons? Take this bullet here—which also has gone through human flesh. It's a 550-grain Sharps."

He extracted a much bigger chunk of lead from the drawer and rolled it over toward Babel.

"Like to hunt, eh?"

Babel had been watching the younger man's powerful hands as they handled the great rifle with the expertness of a man as used to a gun as he was to a scalpel. He had been noting Emmons' eyes too, from the time the physician had opened the front door. They were narrow, the pupils contracted almost to pin points. The man with his arm in the sling remembered the cigarette the medico had been smoking when he opened the door and the cigarette's peculiar but familiar fragrance.

Prisoners with money had smoked that same kind of

cigarette. Kitty Derril had been right about Emmons' drug habit.

Marijuana.

"Actually," Emmons was saying as he fitted rag to the cleaning rod, preparatory to inserting it down the long barrel of the huge single shot, "I am not a cold-blooded man, Babel, despite some ignorant opinions about surgeons to the contrary. The five antelope I lured into range this morning, using a red handkerchief on a cleaning rod, and then dropped at four hundred yards, died because a superior brain triumphed over their wild instincts. That's what I love about hunting—the stalking of the game, the pitting of my knowledge against their instinct. I'm a pretty good trailer, too, Babel. You'd be astonished at what I can do when I put on a pair of moccasins and hit into the wild country afoot, with just a pack. I've killed Rocky Mountain grizzlies and Wyoming Territory moose. I came out here in the beginning looking for new animals to hunt."

"Some men," Babel said in his quiet way, "like still bigger game—the biggest of all. Man."

Emmons paused, with the gun across his lap, and looked at the visitor, admiration glinting in his drugged pin-pointed pupils. He nodded his head slowly.

"Babel, what a really great surgeon a brilliant, cold-blooded devil like you would have made! I believe you're a man possessed of the power to read another man's mind. Do you know—I'm going to confess something: I've been tempted several times to join Ben Johnston's force and start stalking Ferguson's outlaws. God, what a game that would be—down in their country with a pack on my back and two rifles: this .41-.125 Sharps Special and a good repeating Winchester for closer range work."

His eyes were glinting as he picked up the oil can now containing an imported cleaning solvent and squirted a few drops into the barrel of the great gun. "Of all the guns I've ever used, both American and imported, this

Sharps is the grandfather of the bunch. Let me give you an illustration of what one of these 550-grain slugs will do. Up on the Kansas plains a number of years ago when the buffalo were still plentiful, two hunters were out one day skinning their kill. As you probably know, they shot from crossed sticks, which they held erect with one hand. These sticks were about three feet high and the hunter simply knelt with his cartridges piled beside him and kept firing. They'd drop a cow, wounded, to get the bulls milling and goring her, and then pile up one bull after another. Well, there was a Sioux medicine man up in that country who had been making plenty of trouble for the whites. These two hunters caught sight of him in the distance, waving his hands and making obscene gestures. The younger man lined his Sharps over his crossed sticks and let drive—they stepped it off later—at exactly one thousand yards.* He caught that Sioux medicine man right above the belly and tore him almost completely in two. Think of it, man—a 550-grain bullet hitting a man from that distance!"

"Rather a funny thing, in connection with the subject of Sharps," Babel nodded. "In that fight in front of the bank, after I dropped the Winchester, I still was facing six men with my Colts. At the far end of the street was another man, down behind his horse, which I had dropped with the last shot in the repeater's magazine."

"No doubt about it, you were in a tough spot," Emmons said slowly, busy with the Sharps.

"Very tough. I was facing six masked men, including Gorman, who had jumped off his horse. He had been left outside to guard them. But when the shooting started three of those men ducked around behind the bank to try grabbing the reins of the now stampeding horses. That left three other men—Duval, Gorman and another—facing me. I downed those three men, using up all my car-

* This actually happened.

tridges in both guns. Yet, when it was all over, those three other men who had run around back of the bank also were dead. And so was that guard at the end of the street, lying sprawled behind his horse. Four men whom I couldn't possibly have shot."

Emmons was very quiet now, sitting there with the ramrod halfway down the long hex barrel of the gun. But his drug-narrowed eyes were fixed upon Babel's calm face in a strange gaze.

"I'm listening," he said. "Go on."

"The supposition is that I shot those three men and that they then ran around back of the bank and fell. That could have been possible, though it isn't true. However, everybody thinks that's what happened. But there was still that man lying barricaded behind his dead horse at the end of the street, a good hundred and fifty yards distance away. Anybody should know that I couldn't have used a Colt on him effectively at that distance. The idea is preposterous. Yet such has been the excitement that even Jennifer and the others, standing in plain sight, don't know that some *other man* killed four of those men with rifle fire."

He got up from his chair and went to the window cutting the east wall of the room. It looked out over the front veranda and down the slope into the heart of Partridge. There was a marred place in the white paint on the window sill, and Babel ran his finger along it.

"That was damned good Winchester work at four hundred yards, Emmons," he said slowly.

The surgeon had come over and was standing beside him, though Babel made sure it was on his right side, where he now wore no gun.

"I was repairing one of my favorite pistols when the shooting broke out," Emmons said casually. "I jumped to the window and watched you using that Greek's worn out gun, which I've examined. Don't see how you ever hit anything with it. Anyhow, I saw you use up the last shot in the .44-40 to drop the guard's horse at the end of the street. He was just crawling behind it and yanking his carbine out of the scabbard. So I snatched up that Sharps there on the table. I rested it across the sill here in lieu of crossed sticks. The three who ran behind the bank and tried to get horses I dropped with a French gun bought from a maker in Paris. It's rather lucky for you, Babel, that I happened to stop in."

"Very fortunate. But there's one thing I'd like to know."

"What?"

"Why did you deal yourself a hand?"

"Why?"

"Yes, Emmons, why? Certainly not from altruistic motives. Why should you, a respected professional man, risk getting mixed up in such a mess? Why did you risk Ben Ferguson finding out about it and taking the proper kind of retribution for helping me to wipe out eleven of his men?"

Frank Emmons smiled that twisted smile that Babel had come to recognize as that of a man with a slight warp in his soul.

"I didn't do it to help you, Babel. I'm not that kind. And I *was* a little uneasy that Martin and the others might hear the firing from up here and find out the truth. No. It was that man back of the horse—the guard, getting ready to kill you, who interested me most. I caught him just under the right armpit as he leveled the Winchester at you across the horse, and the autopsy I performed to check the results of the 550-grain bullet at four hundred was most enlightening. I showed you the bullet."

"Which means that I owe you my life," Babel said.

Emmons shrugged and put down the window he had slid up. "Think nothing of it, and we'll never let the secret out. You'll keep your new reputation and I—ah—shall keep my present one."

"Then we understand each other perfectly," Babel said, and he meant it in more ways than one. Here was a dangerous man and he knew, when Emmons replied, that he had judged him right the first time. For the medico turned and walked away, half leaning against one of the gun cases. He fixed his eyes upon Babel, and his voice suddenly was edged with steel.

"Not quite, Babel. There's one other little matter I think we could settle between us while we're on the subject. One day I shall expect to be master of the Sunset Ranch and to own it in its entirety. Calhoun, Bonner, Alden and Johnston have no wives, brothers or other direct relatives. It has been agreed among the five partners that upon the deaths of each the fifth share that each holds reverts to the others. It means that one day my fiancée will inherit it all."

"Ah," Babel said softly.

"I'm glad you understand, my friend. Because right at the moment you're the kind of legendary figure who can capture the imagination of a young girl and turn her away from—let us say—the right man for her. I don't exactly fancy her falling in love with you, since she's too sensible for that and realizes you're much older than she. She also owes an obligation to her father. In plain, cold English, Babel, keep away from Mary Jennifer with your gifts of rare violins and talk of music and your air of mystery, or I'll kill you. I'll hunt you down like I hunt down the other animals. Do I make myself clear?"

Babel bent from the waist in a half mocking bow that brought a flush to the other's face "Perfectly, Doctor, perfectly. And I'm afraid that this makes us enemies, because I have a modest knowledge of medicine, especially drugs, and I'm not letting that clean, innocent youngster discover to her horror she's married a drunkard and a marijuana addict. Which means, 'in plain, cold English,' that on the day you announce your wedding date, on that day I, too, turn man stalker. Good day, Doctor, and thanks for an enlightening visit."

He backed toward the door, not daring to turn his back on the man whose face was a mask of black, overwhelming rage, his left hand near his Colt.

"You fool!" half snarled Emmons, following him as he walked slowly back through the hall with its luxurious rugs, and pointing a trembling finger. "You fool, you wouldn't have a chance—not a Chinaman's chance, do you hear?"

"Remember our bargain, Doctor," Babel reminded him, smiling his enigmatic smile. "We both have our reputations to keep." The mockery in his voice brought an angry curse and a slam of the door.

Babel went back to his hotel to find Kitty Derril waiting for him.

"I've been trying to find you," the young woman said breathlessly. "Babel, I need your help. It's about Aven Larson. Everybody thinks he's a little crazy, but now he seems to have cracked completely, for yesterday he spread a story that has swept the town this morning like wildfire. About a man burning to death up north in a prison fire two or three weeks ago, whom Calhoun, Johnston, Bonner, Alden and Jennifer framed into prison after murdering his brother and robbing him of about seventy thousand dollars in gold. They've got him in the courthouse for a quick hearing. Babel, you've got to do something, do you hear? You can't let them hurt him!"

FOURTEEN

"No, I wouldn't wish harm to come to him, Kitty," Babel said. "He seems a rather nice old man."

"Nice?" she said. "I've known Aven Larson longer than people think. He's been good to me."

"Then you believe this story of his—about the Sunset bunch?"

"If Aven Larson told it, then it's true," the girl said, her eyes flashing. "It all fits in with what I think about the whole bunch. It's only Mary Jennifer I'm worried about. She loves that father of hers. I can't imagine what will happen to her if this thing proves true."

Babel himself turned cold at the thought, as he went toward the courthouse up on the hill. For twenty-one years he had planned to take his revenge upon the five men who had murdered his brother and framed him into prison. He knew that hell was about to explode in Partridge, and that he must now come out into the open against them.

Yet what would Mary Jennifer—his daughter—think when he, whom she had never known, shot Martin Jennifer dead?

Babel put the thought from his mind, and presently he became aware that the banker himself was hurrying up the graveled road the short distance to the courthouse. The tall man with his arm in the sling turned and waited.

"Morning, George," Martin Jennifer said. "How's the arm?"

"A little stiff but otherwise all right. I think I'll take a ride down in the rough country on Black Boy for a few days to limber it up. I'm not used to such luxuries, you know," he added, smiling.

"Good idea. But don't be gone too long or Mary'll be after you. She thinks you're the finest man that ever lived. Oh, by the way, about that black horse of yours—"

"He's not for sale," Babel cut in quietly.

They were walking side by side now, and the banker turned toward him, shaking his head.

"Every man has his price, George—even a cold devil like you. I want that horse. I've never seen any animal I wanted so badly. For days while you were recovering, I've been going down to the stables and pasture just to look at him. But do you know, there's something strange about him."

"Strange?" Babel said, wondering if the banker had discovered the black's blindness.

"Very strange. He's the only horse that ever lived around me I couldn't make friends with. I've tried everything in the book, Babel, but that black devil won't let me get near him. I even had Booger put a halter on him, but the moment I got the rope in my hands he bared his teeth and reared. He actually slashed out with his forefeet."

"Black Boy's strictly a one-man horse," Babel said, putting it off that way.

Actually he knew better. He knew that the intelligent animal had recognized the true worth of the man, as only an intelligent horse can do.

"Well, it only makes me want him all the more," Jennifer said. "I'm offering you five thousand cash for him, George. If that isn't enough, I'll give you ten thousand. If that won't bring you around, I'll have my daughter to work on you."

"In connection with that rather unsavory story going around, I heard a slight postscript this morning," Babel lied casually. "It's to the effect that Mary is not your daughter, but the daughter of a man named Tom Kent, who died in that prison fire up north."

Jennifer had been walking beside him with a free-muscled stride that told of a man who kept himself in good physical trim by much time spent in working cattle on the big ranch west of town. And now he wheeled with something definitely pantherish in his movement, a half choked sound breaking deep within him. His eyes were blazing with a strange intensity.

"Where did you hear that?" he half whispered.

"Why, it's floating around town," Babel lied again, watching the murderer of his brother almost writhe. "You were said to have married Kent's—"

"It's a lie," Martin Jennifer said hoarsely. "It's a lie.

Mary is my own daughter. And if word of this ever gets to her ears it will ruin her life. Aven Larson must repudiate that story. And, by God, he will or pay with his damned life!" he suddenly almost shouted, clenching his fist.

The courthouse was a two-story affair of red sandstone construction, with a fence one hundred yards square around it. Steps led up over the fence, and these the two men ascended. As they approached the tunnel-like passage that cut through the center of the building, the door on the right, with Judge Calhoun's name on it, opened. There was the curse of a hard-faced deputy, a flurry of bodies, and then Thorpe and Sistrom struggled out, holding between them a manacled Aven Larson.

Larson had been badly beaten. The old man's white beard was streaked with blood that ran from his nostrils and lost itself in his beard. One eye was streaming water, and there was a big swelling rising higher on his left cheekbone. His shirt was half torn off.

And jammed savagely into his mouth, held tight with a leather belt, was a balled bandana handkerchief that served effectively as a gag. Sight of the storekeeper did something to Martin Jennifer. A cry broke from him, and he leaped straight at Larson, slamming blows at his gagged face and cursing in helpless rage.

Gone was the suave banker and civic light of Partridge. Beneath his thin veneer of a gentleman the Martin Jennifer of old had come to life again. It was the same man who had pressed his thumbs against a dying Jim Kent's bashed-in skull in an effort to make him reveal the location of the hidden mine.

"Spread a story about us, will you?" he almost panted. "Ruin my daughter's life with such a wild tale—"

From seemingly out of nowhere a hand with fingers of steel caught him by the shoulder and spun him away, and even in his incoherent rage there shot through Jennifer the realization that this man Babel had used one hand to handle him as a child is handled. The banker half reeled away, and he heard Babel's cold voice saying:

"Take off that gag!"

And then it grew deadly quiet there in the concrete way of the courthouse. Jennifer recovered, his rage forgotten as he saw the bespectacled face of a man he had thought of as a friend turned into a block of ice.

"Take off that gag!" the man known as George Babel commanded again, addressing the two deputies.

Alden, he of the powerful frame and penny pinching habits and purplish lips, stepped forward, his hand lying close to his right hip and the holstered Colt there.

"Ain't you kind of horning in where you've not been invited, mister?" he queried coldly of Babel, as the two hard-eyed deputies stepped back to side him in gun play, should it come. After all, this fabulous and legendary gun fighter Babel now had one arm in a sling.

"For the last time," came George Babel's deadly quiet voice, "take off that gag before it's too late to stop something I don't want to start if it can be avoided."

Just what might have happened then had not Jennifer interfered would be hard to conjecture. But the leader of The Five saw something in Babel's icy eyes that perhaps even Alden didn't see, and he leaped in between them only a moment before Colts would have been drawn and the affair ended in the roar of pistols at close range.

Bonner had come alive and now was standing with Alden, making four against one. Johnston, whose ruffled clothes showed that it had been he who had beaten up Larson, stood motionless. Judge Calhoun stood rigid in the door leading to his office.

It was Martin Jennifer who spoke, his voice breaking up the deadly tension among them all. In a flash he was the banker again, smooth and suave.

"I'm afraid I do owe you an apology, George," he said smoothly, himself removing the belt cutting into Larson's mouth. The balled-up bandanna fell free. "But the thought of what this crazy old fool's story might do to my daughter—cast a cloud over her life—caused me to see red for a moment. I guess I lost my head."

"Well, I didn't," grunted out Alden snarlingly, his gaze upon Babel. "I'm mad. I'm damned mad! Who the hell does this gent think he is anyhow—this common hired gun fighter? Who's he to tell us what we should do about Larson?"

"I'm only telling you," Babel reminded him gently, "that there's much difference between a Western cattle baron and a medieval baron of the Middle Ages. This man is a free American—not a serf. Yet he's been tried, beaten up, convicted, and now being taken away with a gag in his mouth so he can't even talk."

"He's caused enough trouble as it is," Judge Calhoun put in. "We gagged him because he's violently insane. I've just committed him to an institution—"

"I'm not the law," Babel cut in shortly, remembering how, twenty-one years before, he too had been sentenced by this same judge. "But the law doesn't gag a man when it sends him to prison. And besides, if his accusations are so preposterous, what have you all to fear?"

"That's just the point, George," Jennifer said quickly. "The Sunset outfit has been successful through hard-headed business practices while some of these smaller fry have gone under. Consequently they're angry, disgruntled, and ready to believe anything bad about us. Such a story as this—wild as it might sound—will be pounced upon by them and seized as the gospel truth. It can cause trouble, raise them up against us. And right now, with Ferguson and his outfit to think about, we can't afford it. Of course it's all a lie," he finished.

Aven Larson had stood quietly, a calm dignity in his bearing. Now he turned his honest eyes upon them all.

"No, it is not a lie, as I know and you all know," he told The Five. "Every word I spoke was the truth. Twenty-one years ago I sat in the courtroom and watched you send that innocent boy to prison after murdering his own brother. For twenty years I've been here among you, hoping and waiting against the day when he would find freedom and come back to exact a just punishment. I am a religious man, but there are some things that must be settled here between men. I waited patiently for Tom Kent to come back and make that settlement. But he died in that prison fire up north and I did what I could to repay the debt by spreading the truth. You've beaten me and yet you haven't beaten me, for as surely as I believe in a just higher power so do I believe that at this very moment *the spirit of Tom Kent is present here among us.*"

"Take him away," the sheriff ordered angrily.

They took him away, walking manacled between the two deputies, and the others filed into Judge Calhoun's chambers. Babel was the last to enter.

" 'Spirit of Tom Kent here among us!' " guffawed Bonner, looking around at them all. "If we ever needed any proof that old Larson is crazy, this is it. He's preached about spirits so much he *believes* that stuff."

"There are many people who believe in such things," Babel said in his quiet way. "They say that unbounded faith is a wonderful thing."

"I don't care about anything except my daughter's happiness," Jennifer cut in sharply. "I'd kill Larson or anybody else in cold blood to prevent her life from being upset. I could see the whole business go to pot—"

"Well, I couldn't!" half snarled Alden, still very angry. "We've worked hard to accumulate our holdings—"

"And saved every penny," jeered Bonner, winking at the others, for Alden was notorious for his pecuniary habits.

"—and I'll fight just as hard to hang onto them. That's why, Mister Babel, gun artist or not, you'd better never again stick your nose into any private affairs in which I'm concerned. After all, you're a hired gun fighter and nothing else, as far as I'm concerned. We don't know anything about you. Thorpe, who's been a prison guard, swears you've got the color of a man who's done time. Whatever you were in for, that's your business. And you damn well better let us take care of *ours*, see?"

"Perfectly," Babel said. "As you say, Mr. Alden, you know nothing about me. And as Aven Larson's story hinted, even a man such as yourself can quite possibly have a past. That, too, is *your* business. Good day, gentlemen."

When he was gone a dead silence settled over the judge's chambers. Five men looked at each other, and then Judge Calhoun's eyes watched Babel's tall, black-coated form return down the slope toward town. The man had removed his right arm from the sling and was flexing the elbow.

"I'm beginning to get a little uneasy about him, boys," Calhoun said.

"You reckon he might have been hired by Jed Berber and those other small fry to sneak in here and spy on us?" asked Bonner.

"Sounds kind of far-fetched to me," Ben Johnston said, wiping at a damp red spot on his sleeve. "Right now I'm not thinking about Babel. It's Larson I'm worried about. I couldn't believe my ears when that story burst."

Calhoun shifted his bony weight in the chair and tugged reflectively at his white goatee, his gaze far away and speculative. He appeared to be gazing at the bottom leg of the big iron safe in the opposite corner.

"Hmm," he said absently, after a moment's silence in the room. "Amazing."

"What?" grunted out Alden.

"Larson. He's been here nearly twenty years, a permanent fixture in the town. Ran his little store, attended to his own business, and gathered his little flock around him to preach because the town was too small then for a regular minister to bother with it. Later, when the town grew, Larson kept on with his small congregation, holding weekly prayer meetings and preaching short, unpolished sermons on Sundays. I used to go listen before my own church was established here. But as the years went by Aven Larson was one man who wouldn't kneel to us. Did you ever stop to think of that, boys? I recall that I went into his store one day some fifteen years ago and asked to see a hatchet for splitting kindling. I can still remember the look in his eyes when he said to me, 'You can buy nothing in my store, Judge Calhoun. I do not sell to rogues.' "

Calhoun broke off to laugh, a slightly shrill cackle that didn't appear amusing to the others.

"I know," Alden growled, reaching for one of the cigars. "Last time I was in there was four years ago. He had a sale of cattle salt—two carloads that had been smashed up in a train wreck. He'd bought it at salvage prices from the railroad, hauled it in and piled it back of his store. He was selling it cheaper than our own store across the street could *buy* it!"

Bonner began to snicker. "Hee-hee! I remember you *trying* to buy it. He not only wouldn't sell you a pound, but we didn't sell a single pound of our *own* as long as that salt was in Larson's back yard. Haw haw haw!"

"That's just the point," Calhoun went on. "Larson is a solid fixture here in this community. Any time there were any sick to be taken care of, Larson did what he could. He's given many a man grocery credit, knowing quite well the man probably wouldn't be able to pay the account. That's why people are going to take his story at face value. They'd believe every word of it—even if they all didn't hate us."

"They've got good reason to believe it, because the man spoke the truth," nodded Jennifer from where he had sat down on the edge of a second, older desk no longer in use. "When we put private deposit boxes in the new vault, Larson brought in several bags of dust, real gold dust. From time to time he exchanged it for gold notes. I didn't ask where he got it, because that wasn't any of my business. But there's no gold like that in this section of the country. In fact, I never realized it until this moment, but it was the same kind of dust that we got from the Kent boys twenty-one years ago."

They looked at each other, and there again came a silence pregnant with grim forebodings. Calhoun finally looked at Sheriff Ben Johnston.

"Ben, when that prison fire broke out up north a few weeks back, I had you contact the authorities on the pretext that Tom Kent was wanted down here. Were they *positive* that he burned up in that fire?"

"Beyond any doubt," Johnston answered. "His charred body was found in the locked cell. Kent died up there, all right."

"Well, perhaps it's coincidence, but I'm worried about that man Babel all of a sudden. He's been in prison. Why did he come to Partridge? Why has the name of Tom Kent cropped up since his arrival?"

"Expect I'd better have Thorpe search his rooms," Johnston said, "just to be on the safe side. He doesn't like Babel anyhow. He's some riled over that fish-eyed gun thrower callin' him an amateur trailer. Thorpe's been plumb proud of his ability to foller tracks."

"Who *is* the best trailer in this country?"

Johnston took off his hat and scratched his shaggy head. "Duval was until Babel downed him in that gun fight in front of the bank. That leaves but one other gent."

"Who?"

"Hell, you'd never believe me if I told you."

The judge jerked his head in an impatient gesture. "I never did like riddles, Ben. Get to the point. Who is the man?"

"Doc Emmons. And he hates Babel's guts because he sees him a rival, I got a hunch."

"Rival?" snapped out Martin Jennifer, coming erect off the desk. "Good God, Ben, has the sun cooked your brain? Mary fall in love with a man old enough to be her father! Take any precautionary measures concerning Babel that you wish, but I'll have no part of this silly business. I'm going back to the bank."

After he was gone Calhoun said to the sheriff:

"Martin certainly worships the ground that girl walks on. Anyhow, we can't hire a man like Emmons to trail Babel when he leaves town. Nor would I dare trust Thorpe to do the job after he blundered once. Who else, Ben?"

Again Ben Johnston scratched his head. Suddenly his face brightened. He replaced the hat and slammed his hand down on his thick thigh. "Well, by Godfrey! Why didn't I think of it before? Alveraz is the man!"

"That breed? Good heavens, man—"

"Hold it, boys," the sheriff said, his palms out at the others to stop any further objections. "It's made to order. That Alveraz is as slippery as an eel, and poison with a knife. I oughta know how slippery he is—I tried to trail him a couple of times when he skedaddled out of town and made for Ferguson's hideout. I've allus been afraid that outlaw would cross us up some day, and I ain't been asleep. I figgered that if he ever broke with us, the first thing he'd do would be to bust the bank—which is exactly what he did do. Ten to one Alveraz knew right to the minute when it opened and everything else about it. Anyhow, we can use Alveraz now instead of having Thorpe blow off his head some night."

"I'm not so sure," grunted Alden sourly, twisting his cigar stub. "We not only couldn't trust him, but it'd probably cost us a pile of—"

"Oh my gawdlemighty," groaned Bonner, putting both hands to his cheeks and rocking them from side to side in mock agony. "Here we go again. *Money, money, money!*"

"Shut up, both of you, and let Ben finish," Judge Calhoun said with unjudicial bluntness. "Go on, Ben."

"Hell, it's all simple," the Sheriff said to the other three. "The morning after the flood Babel tangled with Alveraz, and if all reports are true he just about used him as a mop to wipe all the mud out of the street. Couple of fellers who saw it said they still don't know how it happened. About all they saw was Alveraz spring with a knife and then get it took away from him. Said Babel handled him like a child and that the breed went off down the street half screeching his head off, he was so mad. He was mumbling something about getting even with Babel or having Ferguson do it. Then, to add insult to injury, Babel bought him out when he didn't want to sell. You get it?"

"Quite simple, Ben," the judge said, tugging at his beard. "The breed knows he's through here in town and would jump at the chance—for money—to get even with Babel. All we've got to do now is set him after our friend. And I think I know how to find out all that's necessary."

His kind eyes had regained that benevolent look that masked a cold and cunning soul within. The others recognized it, too. Calhoun said:

"We'll have Larson imprisoned in the cellar under my house tonight, guarded by Thorpe and Sistrom, the jail being unfit for occupancy. Ben, you instruct the breed to be on the lookout somewhere outside. Give him certain—ah—orders what to do should Babel show up to effect a rescue. If Babel doesn't show up, then we'll know that his business here in Partridge is strictly impersonal and that his interference here this afternoon was merely from a sense of fair play. Do I make myself clear, boys?"

FIFTEEN

At about the same time that the five men were having their conference in the judge's chambers and Babel walked back down the slope from the courthouse, Dr. Emmons came out of his main bedroom, dressed for riding. Paradoxically enough, and in contrast to custom, he wore moccasins more often than boots while riding; this because of the fact that most of his trips had to do with hunting game.

He wore moccasins now, though the impending ride was merely a jaunt with Mary Jennifer, out for exercise after her curtailed activities.

Emmons came into the gun room and took down one of his favorite weapons, directing his Negro servant to hand him one of several cartridge belts on a special rack in the corner.

"I might get a shot at a coyote or jackrabbit," he said.

The Negro brought him the lead-studded belt, which he slung around his waist and buckled snugly. Very seldom did he ever pack a pistol. As he picked up the weapon and took several shells from the loops, sliding them into the magazine, buggy wheels creaked on the gravel driveway in front. Emmons looked out through the front window and cursed under his breath at sight of the lady and her fourteen-year-old son. Her name was Mrs. Dunham and she was the rather addlebrained wife of a stock buyer of some means. Being the small town counterpart of the social climber had not only made her a general nuisance to Martin Jennifer and his friends, but Emmons, being the town's handsome bachelor, had been her especial target.

The result had been that every time Junior Dunham pricked his finger with a mesquite thorn or stepped bare-footed on a "goat head" sticker, the good lady, gushing and prattling, came to Emmons' office.

He cursed again as she got out of the shiny buggy with the sullen Junior trailing her skirts.

"Robert," Emmons called sharply to the servant moving toward the front door in the hallway. "Get rid of her! Tell the simpering fool that I'm not in."

"Yas suh, Mistuh Emmons."

He went to the door and opened it, but the beaming Mrs. Dunham beat him to the punch, waving a purse in his face.

"Now, now, Robert, don't tell me he isn't home again, because I know different. I saw him through the window just now. And he's simply *got* to see Junior. He's very sick."

"I ain't!" snarled Junior in rebuttal, his words slightly slurred due to the fact that one cheek was badly inflamed and swollen. "I don't want that horse doctor cuttin' on me with no knife."

"Junior! Dr. Emmons is a *wonderful* surgeon. Stand aside, Robert; I'm going to see the doctor."

She saw him, too. Emmons almost gritted his teeth as she came down the hallway and entered the gun room. He slipped the empty sherry glass among the tools on the work table.

"Ah, there you are, Frank!" beamed Mrs. Dunham. "I simply *had* to see you, and you're *never* at your office any more. Say good morning to the doctor, Junior."

"Don't you cut me with no knife," Junior greeted the doctor, glaring at him.

"I'm sorry, Mrs. Dunham, but I've an engagement to go riding with Mary," Emmons said, half curtly. "No, I'm not at the office any more, because I'm resting up after taking care of so many victims of the flood. I've been going night and day." Which, in a measure, was true.

"But Frank," protested the good lady. "Look at my baby's face! I think he's got the mumps!"

Controlling his anger, Emmons bent closer and examined the lop-sided Junior's cheek, while its owner eyed him with surly wariness. "It's only a bad boil coming to a head, Mrs. Dunham. Not a thing to be done until then."

"Boil? Heavenly day! Why, I'm sure there's no reason for my baby to have a boil, Frank. It must be something else."

"It's a boil, nothing else."

"Don't you cut me with no knife," Junior warned.

"But what could have caused it, Frank?" demanded the victim's mother.

Emmons shrugged, his lips tightened. He'd been ready to roll a marijuana cigarette to quiet his jangled nerves when Mrs. Dunham had forced her way in, and now her talk, plus the desire for the weed, was maddening.

"Anything might have caused it. A batch of green apples upsetting his stom—"

"I ain't et no green apples," snarled Junior.

"Too much greasy food piling up poison in his system that couldn't be thrown off normally. That plus the age of puberty causing a change—"

"What's puberty?"

"Junior!" tittered his mother, simpering at the inwardly raging medico. "That's a medical term. Now, Frank—"

"I'm sorry, Mrs. Dunham," he interrupted curtly, picking up the repeating Winchester. "But I've already kept Mary waiting too long. You'll excuse me, I'm sure."

When she was gone, he rolled a cigarette, inhaled deeply, and immediately felt better. For his plans concerning the girl were, like the now departed Junior's affliction, in the process of coming to a head. A part of it was caused by the recent letters received from his fashionable parents in New York; insistent letters that he hurry up and marry this girl he had mentioned, because he owed that much to his fashionable parents in return for an expensive European education and other things.

It had not been Emmons' intention to hurry about mar-

rying Mary Jennifer. Drugs have a way of sapping a
man's vitality in such a manner that he loses interest in
women and is not attracted to them. Drugs had done that
to young Dr. Emmons. Thus for three years he had been
content to play the part of the patient but attentive lover,
waiting until she finished her music studies. He would
have been content to wait still another two years—but
when one's fashionable family is down at its fashionable
heels—

Thus Emmons had made his plans of late, and one aspect of them took into consideration a strange man named
Babel. Babel not only had seen through the mask, but this
terrible gun-master who had shot it out single-handed
with Ferguson's men had to be removed.

Emmons thought with bitter irony how simple it would
have been had he not saved the man's life by taking a
hand with his Winchesters. It would have solved everything. Unfortunately, marijuana may arouse the murder
instinct in men, and Emmons had been "high" on it when
the fight occurred. The drug, plus his natural desire to
hunt men with a gun, had proven too strong. He had shot
down men whom it was to his advantage to let live.

He left the house by the back way to get his saddled
horse, and by the time he mounted, the red-coated Booger had opened the gate of the corral seventy yards away
and Mary came trotting through astride a slim roan. She
waved with her sling-held elbow and galloped over.

"Good morning, Frank. I saw a patient leave the house
a little while back. What's the matter with Junior *this*
time?"

"Frankly, darling, nothing except so much orneriness in
his system his body can't control it."

" 'Orneriness'?" she ejaculated, and burst out laughing
as she chopped her impatient mount around and fell in
beside him. "What a strange word to come from you.
Why, you're beginning to talk like a cowpuncher."

"Just as long as it suits you, Mary," he answered, and

once again he was the gentle, considerate suitor. "The arm feeling better?"

"Much. I see you brought your kit with you."

He nodded, adjusting his black Stetson a little more to compensate for the rays of the morning sun. "I've got to stop by a flood patient's house on the lower edge of town and see how she's getting along. You can wait for me at the bank. I'll only be a few minutes."

She let her clear, intelligent eyes rest upon his rather tanned face. "You know, Frank, sometimes you're so gentle and considerate of people I feel a sense of shame at the way I've kept putting off our marriage these past couple of months."

" 'Sometimes?' " he queried, shooting her a sharp look that he was careful to keep veiled. "You act as though I might have been inconsiderate of you at one time or another."

"Well—not inconsiderate. Just a couple of little things. There was the night we gave the big dance last month and Roddy Underwood from over at Deep Wells—his father buys cattle from Dad every year—asked me to sit out in the buggy with him."

"He was drunk and trying to make love to you."

"He was not drunk. He'd had two drinks from the barrel that was placed on a bench out by all the surreys, such as we always have out there. He was trying to put his arm around me and we were both giggling a little because it was all in fun. I felt terribly embarrassed the way you almost demanded that I come in the house."

"I thought he was getting rough. And, darling, I *did* apologize for misunderstanding."

They were dropping down the slope from the great houses on the hill above, coming into the end of the street that stopped sharply against the slant of the ground, not far from the bank. "I know, Frank," she smiled. "Let's not quarrel about it. Well, you run along and see about your sick lady and I'll wait for you at the bank."

He reined up close as she stopped at the hitching rail and then bent over in the saddle, balancing her with a strong arm as she dismounted and tied the reins with her one good hand. Jennifer appeared in the door and threw up a hand in greeting.

"You two make a striking couple, kitten," he said to the girl.

"Always a pretty word for the ladies," she chided, ducking under the rail. She went up the three short steps to the porch of the bank, and the man with the gray at his once black temples slid an affectionate arm around her.

"You look more like your mother every day, Mary," he said, sobering, his eyes on the tall, black-coated figure of Babel moving along the boardwalk a hundred yards distant. "By the way, there's George Babel."

And he told her of the near clash between Babel and Alden backed by the two deputies, only a short time before. Pain came into the clear depths of her eyes, and they were suddenly troubled.

"I'm glad he stood up for Larson. Poor Aven. Those two deputies of Johnston's came by the house with Aven a few minutes ago. He's been badly beaten up and was trying to talk, but they gagged him. I saw them take him to Judge Calhoun's cellar. Dad, I've a feeling that something terrible is going to happen here in Partridge."

SIXTEEN

As for Emmons, he too had spotted the gun fighter's figure, and the sight brought a savage glint into his eyes. He would have given much, at that moment, for a chance to use the Winchester. But perhaps the other way he had planned—the mission now taking him to the flood "patient"—would be better.

He made his way in and out of narrow alleys and pulled

up at last in front of an adobe shack, getting down with his bag in hand. A surly Mexican woman eyed him in open hostility.

"W'at you want?" she demanded.

From inside the 'dobe came a sharp crackle of command to the woman in Spanish, and then Jose Alveraz himself appeared in the doorway. His face broke into a smile of welcome.

"Ah, Mister Emmons, so glad to see you. Come on in."

Emmons looped the reins over a rocking chair made from green willows bent into shape, and lashed hard by rawhide thongs. He bent and entered the house. Alveraz waved him to a chair. He rapped out another command in staccato Spanish to the woman, and presently she returned with glasses and a bottle of choice Scotch.

"About the last of my best stock, bought especially for our good friend Ben Ferguson," he smiled, breaking out the cork. "It's about all I salvaged out of the wreckage of my place."

Emmons took off his hat and laid it on the surprisingly clean and cool floor, lifting the glass. He drank it straight, without a chaser.

"Yes, too bad about the flood," he said. "And now Babel is building another building on the spot. Nice place, too. A man ought to do good business in that new building, eh Alveraz?"

Alveraz set down his partly empty glass and smiled, shrugging his wiry shoulders. "So?" he said carelessly, and then: "But surely you have not entered my humble home for the first time to talk generalities. Why did you wish to see me?"

Emmons jerked his head toward the Mexican woman. "How much English does she speak?" he demanded.

"Much. But she does not *talk* it."

"Good. Have you seen Ferguson lately?"

"Yesterday. He sent word he's getting ready for the first drive. Not too big, because after the owners of the

Sunset are all out of the way the cows will only have to be driven back anyhow. This is just to frighten them and per'aps make them follow him down into the badlands. There, with some of the Sunset riders working with him, he'll be able to complete the job that will make you and him owners of the Sunset spread."

"That's all very nice," grunted the medico, reaching for the bottle again and pouring himself another drink. The brown liquid splashed into the glass. He corked the bottle and leaned back again, his eyes upon the breed's face. "But there's just that one little item Ben seems to have overlooked—that man Babel."

"Ah, yes, Babel. A dangerous and very mysterious man."

"He's too dangerous. He's got to be put out of the way. How much do you want to do it, besides getting your new place of business back when we make the cleanup?"

Again a careless shrug of the shoulders. "A thousand dollars will be needed to restock the place with liquor."

"It's a deal, Alveraz," Emmons said at once. "But there's still another job connected with it. There's something about that man Babel that I want to know. Who is he? Where did he come from? Why did he come to Partridge at this particular time? So I want you to slip down to his rooms in the hotel right now and make a search. Get everything you can that might identify him or his business. Bring them to me at once."

Jose Alveraz grinned a feline grin and scratched his swarthy chin, looking across the low table at the visitor. "Very well. But you are not the only one interested in Babel, Mister Emmons. Less than five minutes ago I was given another certain job concerning this strange man. I am to hide outside of Judge Calhoun's house tonight and see if he shows up to rescue Aven Larson. If he does, I am to *skkkt!*" And he jerked his hand across his throat.

He told Emmons about the concern the owners of the Sunset felt after the near clash between Babel and Alden.

"If he doesn't show up," he finished, "or does not try to free Aven, I am to do nothing."

Emmons leaned forward, his eyes almost shining with a new inspiration. "This is made to order, Jose," he breathed softly. "We've got to get rid of him. So whether he shows up or not, *you get George Babel tonight!* Understand?"

A shrug.

"Good. Now get on down there and search his rooms. They're on the back side. You can get in through the window by climbing upon the buggy shed of the hotel corral."

He rose, put on his hat, and tossed off the rest of the glass's contents. A warm new glow ran through him. He'd now insist upon an immediate marriage and immediately thereafter they'd wipe out the men who owned the Sunset, leaving him its master by virtue of his marriage to Mary Jennifer. Ferguson then could have the breed shot to preclude the possibility of his ever talking, Emmons would get the outlaw a pardon, and the the two of them would reap the profits of the Sunset land and cattle empire.

Emmons jogged back to the bank to pick up the girl, and on the way he built in his mind a new town house in New York City. It would make a proper setting to introduce his new wife to his fashionable friends.

He caught sight of Babel's figure coming out of Aven Larson's store with what appeared to be two boxes of .45's weighting his hand. The man on the purebred horse grinned thinly.

"So you'll turn man stalker at the announcement of my wedding, will you, mister?" he sneered. *"Sic transit gloria mundi."**

---

*So passes the glory of the world.

SEVENTEEN

As for the man known as George Babel, he made his way back toward the hotel rooms, a terrible conflict going on within him. He had come back with but one thought in mind: revenge. A thousand times he had lain awake nights in his cell picturing the meeting with The Five, and the looks on their faces when he revealed himself as Tom Kent.

But something had come up to sour that revenge: the girl Mary Jennifer. The certainty that in destroying The Five he also would destroy the happiness of his daughter seared into Babel's tortured soul.

Yet his iron code demanded that the death of his brother Jim be avenged and The Five made to pay with their lives for both the murder and the twenty-one years Babel had lived behind cell bars.

He shook his head and again unconsciously removed his arm from the sling, flexing the muscles. The movement brought a slight twinge of pain from the still tender wound, but Babel scarcely felt it.

A movement off to the north caught his eye, and he saw a big bay horse, sweat-streaked, come loping into the opposite end of town, carrying a shaggy-haired young rider of twenty-four or so. There was something magnificently strong and wild about the rider which told Babel that he was out of the brakes to the west.

"That's Ferguson country," muttered Babel to himself, his eyes on the rider. "Might be one of the outlaws. But he's burning the breeze, or has been. Looks like something's up."

The bay trotted up the street, as the shaggy young puncher's eyes darted here and there, and Babel saw then that the reins were draped around the horn and that both hands of the man in the saddle lay close to his hips.

Then the rider caught sight of Kitty Derril coming along the boardwalk and kneed his horse over, grinning as he half leaped from the saddle.

"Kit!" he cried out joyously, and that one word identified him.

The rider of the wild brakes was Jed Berber.

Any other girl but Kitty Derril might have hesitated, or been embarrassed, but not that spirited miss. She gave a glad little cry and went hungrily straight into his arms—thereby causing several ladies emerging from the Emporium Modeste (fine things for fine ladies) to pause with shocked eyebrows slightly askew. One of them was Mrs. Dunham, with the swollen-faced Junior in tow.

"Well, of all things!" Babel heard one of them gasp, outraged. "Right on the street in broad daylight."

"I kissed Cissy Baggott once," Junior informed Babel.

"Something ought to be done about that young hussy, don't you think so, Mr. Babel?" Junior's mother said indignantly, though not without a slight coquettish drop of the eyes.

"Quite, madam," he replied. "Quite. Men are notorious for marrying homely women but still having a bold eye for the pretty ones. That's why I'm hiring her to take charge of my new Tower Club. I'll get the business of all the married men in town. Good business principles, you know."

He strolled on past them, surprised that he could be jocular when he was so beset by conflicting emotions. For his direct plan of revenge had gone all wrong. The man who overnight had become a legend in Partridge was uncertain for the first time in his life.

"Babel!" cried out Kitty over Berber's broad shoulder. She released herself, her face flushed. "Babel, I want you to meet Jed Berber, my future husband," she said, actually blushing. "Jed, this is the man everybody in town is talking about."

"Howdy," Jed Berber said, sticking out an iron-fingered hand. "Been hearin' a lot about yuh. We've been down in the brakes, bidin' our time and waitin' for yuh to get well enough to ride. We don't know what yuh've got against the Sunset outfit, but Kit says yuh're on the level, and that's good enough for us. We've been rustled clean and driven out of our homes, Babel. Some of us—including my own dad—have been murdered by Sunset riders, half of which belong to Ferguson's outlaw pack. That's why I burned the breeze in town—to hunt yuh up. Hell's started to pop."

"We'd better go to my rooms in the hotel," Babel said. "We can talk better there."

Berber draped the reins of his sweaty mount over a hitching rail and the three went together up the street to the square, boxlike building on the corner, where loungers already had started their daily game of horseshoes on the cross-street side. The three went upstairs to the second floor and along the hallway toward two corner rooms, the carpet muffling all sound except the jangle of Berber's big spur rowels.

"Listen!" snapped out Babel suddenly, and held up a hand.

Then, key out, he leaped toward his door. He jammed the key in the rusty lock and twisted savagely, aware that Berber, a six-shooter in each hand, was close behind. The door crashed open and both men lunged into the room.

"That window—he went out that window!"

Babel leaped across the room and looked out. He was just in time to see a man's leg disappear around the corner of the horse shed. A moment later Jose Alveraz's figure darted out, crossed an alley at a run, and then disappeared down its bottle and tin can littered length.

He carried a square, paper-bound object in both hands. *Babel's case history of The Five!*

"See anything?" asked Berber, sheathing his guns.

"No," George Babel said. "I didn't see anybody."

"Probably some sneak thief after a few dollars' loot," Kitty said, settling herself on the bed. "Hope he didn't get anything valuable of yours, George."

Babel took off his glasses, reaching for his ever present handkerchief. He polished the lenses, set them on his nose again, and turned to the boy and girl.

"You were saying—" he reminded Jed Berber, who sat beside Kitty rolling a cigarette, the tobacco bag dangling from the strings gripped between his teeth. He returned it to his shirt pocket, licking the brown paper.

"Plenty," replied the rider, reaching for a match. "First of all, I've found Ferguson's hideout and been staking it out for the past few days. There's been a big bustle of activity goin' on there, with plenty of Sunset riders comin' and goin'. Looks like they're getting set for a big drive of Sunset cattle. Everybody allus thought it kinda funny that Ferguson was careful to rustle everything but the Sunset iron. Some said it was because he was afraid of so powerful an outfit. We small ranchers know better now. It's because he's been in cahoots with them all this time. Now he's turned against them, looks like."

Babel saw no reason for withholding from them what he had seen and overheard in the library that morning, when Ferguson turned on his cronies. He told Kitty and Berber about it, and the young puncher out of the brakes went cold with rage at the revelation.

"It all fits," he said grimly. "It's all beginning to take shape. Ferguson rustled them into power and wealth while Johnston made a show at tryin' to catch him, or pinned his crimes on us small ranchers. Johnston hung Ike Slauson for a killing that Ferguson's bunch committed. Hung him after a farce of a trial presided over by Judge Calhoun. All because Ike didn't fear man or devil and threatened to go gunning for the whole Sunset outfit. Tommy Corson was a wild kid not more'n twenty who was chased off his own homestead by Alden and some of his tough riders. When he came to town to gun Alden he was arrested by Johnston."

"And—" Babel queried softly, as Berber's face went pale with rage that was mounting to the bursting point.

"He was shot dead by the sheriff for 'trying to escape,' " ground out Berber. "Yep, it's all beginning to take shape. But there's more than that to it, Babel. There were other visitors to Ferguson's shack down in the wild country. Doc Emmons and that breed Alveraz rode in together the other day."

"Emmons!" gasped out Kitty Derril. "How would *he* be mixed up in it?"

"I don't know," her sweetheart replied. "That's what I'd like to find out. I thought at first he'd been called in by Ferguson to doctor up one of that outlaw gang who suffered an—er—accident when my .44-.40 went off at long range the other day."

"Maybe Alveraz, who's a friend of Ferguson, was sent to bring him to the hideout to fix up a gunshot wound," Babel suggested.

But Berber only shook his head, dropping the cigarette stub to the floor and grinding it out with his boot heel. "He's been there before, lots of times. But I can't figger why a man who's getting ready to marry Mary Jennifer would be mixed up with an outlaw gang like Ben Ferguson and his men."

"In the first place, he's not going to marry her," came the quiet voice of the man known as George Babel.

Something in his words changed the whole atmosphere of the room. It was as though a sudden gust of cold wind from a Texas norther had swept down across the prairies and blasted an icy path into the room. Kitty Derril looked at the ascetic face of the strange man wearing the gold-rimmed glasses, and because she was an intelligent young girl with an intelligent girl's intuition, she saw something that even Babel himself did not know was in his countenance.

"George," she half whispered, her eyes wide with a new understanding, "you love Mary Jennifer, don't you, George Babel?"

"Yes," he said in a low voice. "Yes, Kitty. From the first moment I saw her in the water that morning."

He didn't tell her anything more then, for all the raging fires shooting conflicting points of flame through his tortured soul burst out anew, and he got up and began to pace the floor. His tall, black-coated figure seemed to tower in the room; and had it not been for the lead-studded cartridge belts encircling his lean waist, he might have been taken for some noted professor struggling with a difficult problem in physics.

"What is it, George?" Kitty asked him. "Why should you be so upset over it all?"

He didn't answer, but she saw his iron hands clench and knew that some great battle was going on within him. And she sensed much more.

"Who are you, George Babel? Where did you come from? Why did you come to Partridge?" she whispered.

"Why did I come to Partridge, Kitty?" he replied, wheeling at the opposite side of the room and facing her with a stony countenance. "To kill five men: Calhoun, Alden, Bonner, Johnston—and last but not least to take the life of Martin Jennifer."

"Ahhh! Now I understand. And now you've fallen in love with Martin's own daughter!"

"I fell in love with her twenty-one years ago," came the strange reply. "You see, Kitty, her name is not Jennifer but Kent. And my name is not Babel but Tom Kent, the man who supposedly died in a prison fire up north a few weeks ago. *Mary Jennifer is my own daughter!*"

"My God!" Kitty Derril cried out. "Oh, my God! You Mary's own father! What are you going to do?"

He had reached the open window, through which the

breed Alveraz had fled with that damning book, probably to carry it to—whom? Now he turned and looked at both the girl and the silent young rider out of the brakes.

"I don't know, Kitty," the man known as Babel said. "I don't know. But I'll know tonight at ten o'clock, if Berber will meet me at the blown-out dam at that time. I'll have Larson with me to be taken into the lower country for protection from those five he has exposed."

As Kitty and young Berber rose, there were a thousand other things the girl wanted to know. Yet she asked but one question:

"About Emmons, George Babel: you'll not let him marry her?"

"No, Kitty, I won't let Emmons marry her," was the reply.

Overcome by some strange impulse she couldn't understand, the girl went to him and took both his cheeks in her hands. She pulled his ascetic face down and kissed him gently on the lips.

"We'll be waiting for you," she said.

EIGHTEEN

The rest of the day passed slowly; so slowly that, to Babel, pacing the floor in his hotel rooms, it seemed a year long. But at last the sun went down and dusk set in. By then Babel had eaten supper. And he had made up his mind too.

He made it up while cleaning and reloading his guns and filling the belts with fresh shells from the boxes he'd bought from Larson's clerk.

"She's spent her life with Jennifer and therefore never knew of my existence until I arrived in town," he reasoned. "And if she had to choose between the two of us, it would be Jennifer."

So the die had been cast; and the fact that that case history stolen by Jose Alveraz now might be in Jennifer's very hands—for a cash price—had something to do with the decision to carry out his original plan.

He went to the closet and got out the spurs he had not worn of late, placing a boot on the chair while he buckled each on. An extra pair of moccasins went into the slicker roll back of his saddle cantle. Just as it got good and dark Babel left his rooms, saddle slung over his good shoulder. He carried the heavy .45-.90 repeating Winchester in his right hand. He left by the back stairs, slipping down into the alley into which the breed had fled. Once there he set off, circled town, and a half hour later became a shadowy figure that crept up to the back of Martin Jennifer's stables.

He found Black Boy in the special stall that the banker had ordered reserved for him, and the great black horse, sleek and complacent under Booger's care, followed him out on the lead rope. Babel saddled him, slipped the Winchester into its boot beneath his left leg, and set off through the darkness just as the upper edge of the moon thrust its crescent above the distant horizon.

Twenty minutes later the moon was a round white ball above the skyline, and in its bright glow Babel peered through the bars of a jail now sitting aslant, its lower side down in the wash where the bank had given way against the flood waters.

"Aven!" he called sharply, for the third time, "Aven, it's Tom Kent. Where are you?"

No answer; only a dead silence. A bat flew by in undulating circles, on the hunt for its especial prey, the great tailed stinging scorpions, and it seemed to Babel then that a sudden chill came to the air. He felt cold with a rising apprehension for Aven Larson's safety. Perhaps they already had done away with him.

Had he already been started toward the "asylum" only

to have been shot in the back while "attempting to escape," as that young boy homesteader had been shot?

Grimly Babel swung Black Boy around and set a circular course for Judge Calhoun's house up on the hill. In a brush clump two hundred yards from the judge's small private stable, where he kept a surrey team and one saddle horse, Babel reined up. Lifting a booted foot high in the saddle, he removed the spurred boot and slipped on a moccasin. The second followed, and when he slipped out of the brush and began fading into the night as noiselessly as a black panther, it was not Babel the mystery man of Partridge but Tom Kent the mountaineer who approached the big white house.

There were lights in some of the other homes, though he noted that neither Bonner nor Alden was at home. They either had sensed the impending storm coming and were at the ranch, or some of the Sunset riders, remaining faithful, had tipped them off about Ferguson's impending drive.

But there was a tenseness in the night, in the very air Babel breathed, and when he saw the white-clad form of Mary Jennifer come out on the porch after supper he sensed by the way she went to the porch railing and stood there alone that the girl was troubled. Again the door opened, and this time Martin Jennifer appeared, smoking his after supper cigar. The glow of it lit up his face in basilisk relief before it descended in a circle to his side.

"What's the matter, darling?" His voice came quite clearly to the prone Babel, outstretched on his slab-muscled stomach in the shadows of the white picket fence that cut the grassiness of the tree-studded yards between the houses. "You hardly ate any supper at all."

"I don't know what's the matter, Dad," came her weary voice. "It's just that—well, I've a terrible feeling as though something were about to happen."

Jennifer's sleek form crossed to her and an arm went around the girl's waist. "Mary," he said to his daughter, "is it because of that wild fable Aven Larson spread around town, the poor demented old man?"

"I don't know what to think," she cried out. "I've known Aven for so long. I've been to his church. He's kind and gentle and intelligent. He's not crazy. I know it."

"Good God, girl!" snapped her father angrily, tossing away the cigar and half stepping back. "You mean you actually believe—"

"I'm too confused to believe anything, Dad. All I know is that many times in the past you've taken mysterious rides while we were staying at the ranch, and come back tired and dusty. All these past three or four years there have been accusations by the smaller ranchers that the Sunset brand was growing too fast. I wouldn't believe a word of it. I shut my ears to it. And then on the morning after the flood swept through the town I had just been put into bed with this arm when I saw from my upstairs window a horse being tied in the trees and a rider cross the lawn. Dad"—she turned and faced him squarely—"what was the outlaw Ben Ferguson doing in the house that morning? Why did he storm out in a rage, cursing you and the others?"

For a moment Jennifer was too taken aback by the revelation to reply. Then he regained his composure and a short laugh broke from him.

"So that's what has been preying on your mind, kitten? Good heavens, why didn't you say so? Ferguson has been after us for months to use our influence with the Governor to get him pardoned. He threatened that if we didn't he'd steal the Sunset spread dry—him and the thirty or forty outlaws he leads. He finally grew impatient and rode in here to demand action, even threatening our lives. When we refused he stormed out of the house, swearing to get even. But I think we can take care of him."

"You mean—George Babel?" she asked slowly.

He nodded, though there was uncertainty in the nod. "Yes, darling, you might as well know the truth. This

George Babel that you've almost come to worship is a hired gun fighter for the Sunset spread. He's a cold-blooded killer whom we've put on the payroll to extermi-nate Ferguson."

"Then that—that terrible gun fight in front of the bank was a part of his job?" she almost whispered.

"It was," he lied smoothly to his daughter. "I'm sorry to bring your idol tumbling down off the pedestal in shambles, kitten, but that's the way it is. So you'd better forget this Babel with his cultured manners and gifts of rare violins and air of mystery and concentrate on the man I've picked out for you. Emmons comes from a fine New York family. He'll make you a good husband."

"Dad," the girl answered in a low voice, turning to face him, with the moon playing full on her lovely white face, "I shall never marry Dr. Emmons. I give you one good reason why."

Then she was running swiftly across the porch, leaving a stunned Martin Jennifer staring after her, his mouth sagging agap. She disappeared inside and fled up the stairs, and Martin turned slowly. He did not speak as he saw the tall man in the black coat and gold-rimmed glasses standing at the corner of the house twenty feet away.

"You heard?" Jennifer got out slowly.

"Yes," Babel said in a low tone. "I heard. I sensed what was coming and came to stop it before the words were said. And it's got to be stopped, because my name is not George Babel. It's Tom Kent come back to claim his daughter and to kill five men."

Jennifer half fell back against the wall as though struck in the face by a thrown fist. A hoarse whisper broke from him, and his face blanched.

"*You—Tom Kent!* I—I can't believe it—George Ba-bel."

"You will soon enough. Right now, we've got to think of that girl's happiness. It means even more to me than vengeance for the murder of my brother that day twenty-one years ago. What are you going to do about my daughter, you murdering scum?"

Something akin to a crazy laugh broke from Jennifer then. His face began to twitch, and for a moment the man known as Babel thought he *was* a little crazy.

"Oh, my God!" choked out the banker of Partridge. "And you came here thinking Mary was—why, damn you, Kent, I got rid of your wife and child a week after the gang of us got settled here. Divorced her and sent her away with the child and never heard of them since. I'd met an English woman here. She was cultured, educated—the kind who could give prestige to my home. I married her, and Mary was born to us within a year. And now you come back, thinking you can spoil my daughter's happiness by exposing us—"

Babel never knew how it happened, but he saw Jennifer's hand flashing inside his waistcoat and he heard the noise behind him. He half wheeled with a heavy .45 Colt in his right hand as Alveraz, creeping up from behind, sprang with knife out. The Colt roared spitefully, lashing out an orange tongue of flame. It roared again—and still again; and Alveraz seemed to pause almost in mid-air, half turning as he fell flat and limp on the well kept grass, never to rise again.

Babel spun out, and the big weapon's black muzzle almost lashed fire. It didn't, but it stopped Jennifer's hand, half drawn from inside his dinner coat.

Thus they stood, these two men, with death between them, and then the man with the ascetic face back of the gold-rimmed glasses half lowered the big six-shooter.

"I can't do it, Jennifer," he said in a low voice. "For the sake of that girl I can't do it."

NINETEEN

He wheeled and sprang completely over the sprawled body of the dead Alveraz, lying face down and crumpled, with arms outspread. The former dive owner who had stolen Babel's case history of The Five still had the long knife clutched in one hand. But Babel had little time or thought for Jose Alveraz. He was not certain whether Martin Jennifer would attempt to use the gun in his waistcoat or not; but Babel took no chances.

Hence, instead of bounding straight across the lawn toward Calhoun's house to find out Aven Larson's whereabouts, he ducked toward the back of Jennifer's great residence, his moccasined feet flying.

And in this he used good judgment, for two things happened almost simultaneously:

Jennifer opened up with the six-shooter, its snapping reports whipping out on the clear night air. And the two deputy sheriffs, half drunk on bottled beer, came roaring up out of the cellar where they had been guarding the bound prisoner, shouting to know what happened.

They saw Jennifer on the porch, his arm quite visible as it made short chopping motions and lanced out orange flames that split the moonlit night. A great black-coated figure that seemed to run with the speed of a sandstorm shot out from behind the house and disappeared toward the stables. In one mighty bound Babel cleared the fence of the back yard, ducked from sight back of a surrey shed, and ran at top speed, cutting a circular course for the back of Calhoun's house.

As for the judge, he had been in his library most of the evening, nervous and waiting to see if Babel would show up. Now he heard the heavy roar of the .45 slugs that smashed the life out of Alveraz, followed by the lighter crack of another gun. This he recognized as the .38 with a two-inch barrel Jennifer carried nights. Calhoun heard the banker shouting something about Babel killing Alveraz and ordering the deputies to get the man at all costs. He stood there with his head and skinny shoulders out the raised window, calling out, "What is it, Martin? What is it?"

But Jennifer either did not hear or completely ignored him; for Mary had come downstairs and the banker had some explaining to do. And even in that split moment of action the former gambler and murderer of Jim Kent found it ironical that only a few moments before it had been the man in the black coat who had been worried about his daughter's happiness. Now it was Jennifer himself who had suddenly been shouldered with the same problem—the same girl.

For the suave man now knew that his own daughter loved that terrible gunman who had come back to kill the five of them.

Calhoun, however, knew nothing of this. He heard only the confused shouts of the half drunk deputies as they blundered about in the moonlight back of Jennifer's white-washed, red-topped stables. With a worried frown, the judge withdrew his head, lowered the window, and turned.

Then a half strangled cry broke from him at the sight of the tall, black-coated figure standing, menacing and grim, on moccasined feet just inside the doorway of the library. There was a heavy Colt six-shooter in his left hand.

"Good evening, Judge," the man known as Babel said softly.

"What do you want?" Judge Calhoun demanded weakly. "How did you get in this house—"

"Quiet, Judge; I used to be a mountain man, you know. Learned it back in the rugged country of a certain territory up north before I was framed into prison by you and four others, because you hoped to get the Kent brothers' gold mine. Why, Judge, you look pale. Why, you're shaking!"

"Don't!" whispered the judge, cowering back and finally sinking weakly into a chair. "Don't say any more. I knew from the first that you were more devil than man. But Babel—or Tom Kent—I'm an old man—I'm not well—" He was trembling with a strange kind of terror and swallowing hard as though choking.

"Where's Larson?" snapped out Babel.

"In—the cellar. We were keeping him here until—"

He couldn't go on. He, who had sentenced this other man to a living hell and taken his share of the prisoner's loot, was shaking as though with the ague. He swallowed hard, twice.

"Come, come, Judge, you're in no condition to ride."

"Ride?" gasped out Calhoun, new terror filling him. "Where are you taking me?"

Babel's answer was to step swiftly to a glassed-in cabinet in the corner of the library and return with a large decanter of imported wine. He poured the Chablis into a large goblet, noting, as he handed it to the man, that it was decorated with the judge's own initials.

Calhoun drank it greedily, and the liquor brought new life into his terror-stricken limbs. He moved ahead of the grim nemesis with the ascetic face and gold-rimmed glasses, and they descended into the cellar.

There, bound to a chair in a corner, sat Aven Larson. Scattered about were a dozen empty beer bottles, and on an upended box lay scattered playing cards, where the two deputies had been passing time playing poker.

Babel crossed the room on noiseless feet and, flipping open a jacknife, started cutting the prisoner's bonds.

"Don't talk, Aven; just listen," he ordered sharply. "It's Tom Kent speaking. Your prayers have been answered, Aven, for I didn't die in that great prison fire up north. I substituted another man's dead body for my own and then went over the walls during the confusion. I should have taken action before now, but there are certain things that sometimes a man doesn't take into consideration beforehand—"

"Say no more, lad," old Aven answered, pushing free of the several bonds and getting to his feet, half stiff and stumbling. "I understand everything. And you underestimate me sadly, Tom. Remember the day that chunk of quartz fell from overhead and caught you above the temple as you lay on your side in the tunnel, digging with a pick? It left a small crescent-shaped scar just above your left eyebrow. I saw the scar that morning when you stood beside me on the street—the morning Alveraz tried to attack me and you dumped him in the mud. I knew you'd reveal yourself at the proper time."

"Then why did you spread that story?" queried Babel, surprised.

"Because I saw something in your eyes as you strolled the streets with Mary Jennifer. You imagined it to be love of your own daughter. I saw that an instinct you never realized existed was telling you it *wasn't* your daughter. I was afraid you would weaken in your vengeance upon these five murderers. So I had to shake you out of it by spreading that story—before it was too late. Listen!" he cried out, holding up a hand. "It sounds like those deputies coming back. What do you want me to do, Tom?"

"Take Calhoun to the stables and saddle two horses, one for him and one for yourself. We're meeting young Jed Berber at the blown-out dam three miles above town. Your life won't be safe now in town, Aven."

"And Mary Jennifer?" queried the old man softly.

"Get going!" Babel ordered gruffly.

He gave Larson one of his Colts to protect himself, and the friend of old left by the back way, slipping through the night toward the shed. Inside the house, Babel went through the rooms with their luxurious rugs and antique furniture from Europe. Paintings, mellowed with age and looking shiny under their coats of preserving varnish, lined the walls; paintings bought with profits from a murdered man's gold dust.

Babel returned to the kitchen, neat and clean as the judge's Negro housekeeper had left it before returning for the night to her own home. In a cupboard he found a square five-gallon can of kerosene, and the colorless liquid spilled a wet trail through the kitchen, into the dining room and on through the library. It cut a great wet path in the thickness of the Persian rugs all over the lower rooms of the house. That done, the man known as Babel tossed aside the empty tin in the kitchen and struck a match to the beginning of the wet trail.

Silently he watched the flames grow. They did not leap wildly but burned slowly, increasing their pace as they crawled through the doorway and began eating into the thickness of the rugs. Smoke welled up against the wallpapered ceilings, and the varnished paintings grew still more mellow looking, smudged by smoke that pushed up and boiled in rolling columns against the rooms, seeking escape.

Then, for the first time, the man in the kitchen seemed to become aware of the shouts as the flames lit up the yard. He heard bellows from the deputies and slipped out the back way, running toward the thicket two hundred yards distant where he had left Black Boy. The great black horse could not see, but his ears told him of the oncoming runner, and then Babel hit the saddle. He loped westward into the moonlit night.

Three hundred yards farther on he reined up beside Aven Larson and Judge Calhoun, sitting their horses on a slight rise, watching the billowing pillar of flame that had been the judge's big home.

"It was a fine home," Aven Larson said in his quiet way. "I wish you hadn't burned it, Tom."

"It wasn't a home," the man with the ascetic face said harshly. "It was a part of a Tower of Babel—bought with a murdered man's gold. I'll never have peace until the others are burned to the ground with it. Come on, Jed Berber will be waiting."

TWENTY

They struck out for the upper country, and it was noticeable that only Judge Calhoun, sitting dejectedly in the saddle, looked back at the night glow in the sky. But the glow soon fell farther behind, the moon rose higher, and after a time the broken dam showed up like a giant mouth with one front tooth missing. Several figures suddenly emerged from the thick screen of the surrounding cedars. The forms of Jed Berber and Kitty Derril took shape out of the gloom. With them were several cowmen.

The two little groups met and the girl reined her horse over against Babel's. "What's that glow in the sky? What have you been up to, Babel?"

He told her. She looked at the judge.

"What are you going to do with him?" she asked.

"Have Aven look out after him until such a time as he can sign a confession that will clear the name of Tom Kent," was the reply.

She nodded her worldly young head and introduced him to the others: Olaf Anson, Jim Kerry, Buck Tory, and Ed Frobar. Each leaned from the saddle and stuck out a horny hand. They had heard much of this man Babel; Kitty Derril and young Jed had told them more. They understood.

"We're kinda spokesmen for the rest of the little fellers driven out by the Sunset spread, Babel," Ed Frobar said hesitatingly. "We were all set to start rustling Sunset cattle until Kit here told us the truth about that—er—Kent business. And, I dunno, but somehow that kinda seems to put a different face on the matter."

"Why?"

"Well, if it's all true about these five yaller coyotes starting up their empire on seventy thousand in gold dust robbed from yuh and yore brother—why, to our way of thinkin', that makes *you* the sole owner of the Sunset spread. How about it, Judge? Now that yuh're out of the picture and on the way to the penitentiary, what's yore honest opinion on the subject?"

Calhoun shrugged his bony shoulders disinterestedly; yet a sigh of relief that it was all over came from him.

"Why, I believe such a contention would stand in court, Mr. Frobar."

"In that case," Babel cut in shortly, "we'd better get going. But I don't want the cattle or any part of the Sunset holdings. My plans for the future are made. Come on."

With Babel and Kitty and Jed Berber leading, the little cavalcade set off again. Presently they left the creek, working toward the rougher country which, on the southwest, bordered the lower part of the Sunset range. Here left off the great cattle company's holdings; here began Ben Ferguson's outlaw domain, through which they were going to pass. Babel's plans were simple. He knew that Sheriff Johnston would be on his trail with every available man he could lay hands on, with orders to shoot on sight the man who had struck at them out of the night and then disappeared with Judge Calhoun a prisoner. Johnston and the others, especially Jennifer, would be frantic at the thought that their whole great financial empire was in danger of being smashed down around their feet, with death the end for some of them.

It was now a fight to the finish, with the grim and mysterious figure of outlaw Ben Ferguson looming up dimly in the background.

The party of riders worked a few miles more to the west, skirted a line rider camp on a knoll, and then took a well traveled trail deep into the cedar-choked brakes.

Now and then a crash broke out in the underbrush as a wild-eyed cow fled from the oncoming riders. There was little talking among the group. There seemed little enough to say. Now and then Kitty and Berger pointed out things that Babel wanted to know: mountain ranges and the location of waterholes and springs.

"About how far is it from here to Ferguson's hideout?" he asked Berber, after a particularly long silence.

"Roughly, fifteen miles west," the younger man replied. "But if you're figgerin' on—"

Ed Frobar, riding close at the rumps of their horses, suddenly called out, "Whoa! Hold on a minute, men!" and held up a hand. The others reined up. Then Babel caught it too—something ahead that looked like a faint haze of smoke in the night sky.

"Looks like fog to me, kinda hangin' low over the tops of the ridges," Berber said, peering. He stood stiff-legged in the stirrups.

"Fog, hell!" Jim Kerry burst out. "It's dust! It's dust from a big herd bein' pushed deeper into the rough country."

"Ben Ferguson!" breathed out Kitty Derril. "He kept his word. He said he'd steal them by the hundreds, and he has."

She turned questioning eyes upon the man they all recognized as their leader. His eyes, flat and emotionless behind the gold-rimmed glasses, did not change as he realized that that wholesale stealing of an entire herd was, by rights, the theft of *his* cattle.

"That herd of cattle," Babel said slowly, "is part of what one day will belong to all of you, depending upon how many head each of the small ranchers lost to the Sunset raiders under Ben Ferguson, plus a natural increase in the calf crop. Now that I have no daughter, Kitty, I'm assigning to you and Berber any interest I might have. I want none of it. Which means that Ferguson is stealing your own cattle, men. Come on, let's

head him off and stampede them back toward the range
they were rustled off."

"What about Judge Calhoun?" somebody called.

Babel reined up Black Boy's head and turned to Kitty
Derril.

"Look after him until we get back—" he began, but
never quite finished it.

For out of the night two hundred yards distant came
the throaty roar of a heavy Winchester, and something
struck Judge Calhoun in the breast. He toppled out of the
saddle without a sound, and even as the others slammed
dull steel to their broncs and broke away Babel leaped to
the ground and bent over the fallen man.

One glance at the great gaping hole told him all that
was necessary.

*Calhoun had been killed by a 550-grain bullet fired
from a .45-.125 caliber Sharps buffalo gun!*

TWENTY-ONE

Back in Partridge that night the girl Mary Jennifer
had, in a matter of moments, been transformed from a
nineteen-year-old girl into a full blown woman. The
change had been brought about by the terrible roars of a
.45 caliber Colt whose bullets had killed Alveraz.

The next ten minutes or so ever afterward were to remain a blur in her memory. She was aware that people
were running and shouting, that a white glow had lit up
the sky to the brightness of daylight as Judge Calhoun's
house burned down.

She stood and watched it from an upstairs window, behind panes that grew hot under the touch. Sometime she
became vaguely aware that Booger was shouting half hys-
terically about Babel's great black horse being gone; that
Mammy, his strong-handed spouse, was shouting to her

husband, "You git outa dis house an' stop dat shoutin' befo' I whacks yo' over the head wid somethin'!"

Mary stood there, dry-eyed and calm, like some frozen image, until the fire in the next yard died down into a mass of glowing coals. Presently she became aware that Mammy had her by the uninjured arm and was trying to lead her away.

"Heah, now," Mammy said determinedly. "You can't go on dis way, chile. What is yo' father goin' to think?"

"Where is he?" she asked dully.

"Downstairs," Mammy replied. "Mistuh Alden an' Bonner an' Johnston done come arunnin'. They's all in the library talkin' somethin' awful."

She descended the curving stairs with their thick plush carpeting of wine red color. Through the big dining room window could be seen crowds of townspeople standing in the light of the glowing mass of coals that had been Calhoun's house. The terrific heat that had made the upstairs window panes hot to the touch also had turned the white paint on that side of the mansion into ugly, browned blisters.

Voices came from the library, and Mary Jennifer recognized them as those of her father's three remaining partners. Alden, he of the purplish lips and penny pinching habits, was cursing steadily.

"So Calhoun's suspicions were founded on something after all?" he was saying. "Kent did escape and come back to exact vengeance. I never trusted that man from the beginning. I felt in my very bones that he might want to cut himself in for a part of our holdings—"

"Shut up. Goddam you for a penny pincher, shut up!" came Martin Jennifer's voice, and the shaken girl realized that it was the first time in her life she had ever heard him utter an oath in their mansion.

She stepped to the partly opened door and looked in. Ben Johnston, Alden and Bonner were dressed for hard riding; grim and gun-belted. Edson, the Negro butler, was holding riding clothes for Mary's father, who hurriedly was changing from his after dinner vestments. The servant had a gun belt slung over one arm.

"Did you send out a posse after him yet?" Bonner asked the sheriff.

Johnston reached for the quart of bonded Scotch whiskey on the library table and poured himself a stiff one. "What kind of a damned fool do you think I am?" he demanded half angrily of his crony. "We're sitting on the edge of a powder keg. It's ready to explode right under us unless Babel—and Ferguson too—can be wiped out pronto. And you're asking if I swore in a posse of citizens, nine out of ten of whom suspect we blew that dam to get control of the property on the lower part of town; nine out of ten of whom suspect the real truth about our operations—our connections with Ferguson—that we're rustlers and murderers on a grand scale. Don't be a jackass, Bonner! This is a job for us alone. It's a job of the kind we did in the old days, when we depended upon nobody to do our dirty work for us."

Martin Jennifer had finished dressing, all except his spurred boots. These he tugged on with grunts. He straightened and took the lead-studded cartridge belt from the inscrutable Edson, slinging the heavy Colt into place against his hip.

"Ben is right, boys," Mary Jennifer heard her father say. "This is a job for us to do alone. It's either sink or swim—and I don't intend to sink without putting up a fight to hold what we've built up on a murdered man's gold. Ferguson has got to be wiped out tonight, and so has Babel—or Kent rather. Come on, men—let's get going!"

At the partly opened door the girl suddenly turned away, too filled with horror to think coherently as the whole crushing truth came down and beat its way into her mind. Her father was a murderer and robber! Martin Jennifer—banker, horseman, newspaper owner, rancher—he of the kind ways and cultured manners—he who had instilled in her a love of good music and good books—

Blindly she half stumbled back toward the curved stairs leading to her room above. She heard the heavy tramp of boots and the jangle of spur rowels; heard them lope away into the night a few minutes later while she herself was changing into riding clothes. It was an awkward job, one arm still being in a sling and splinted, but she dared not let Mammy know. She crept downstairs again and made her way to the stable—and then she saw Booger's form loom up in the moonlight.

"Why, Miss Mary, where you-all goin' dis time of night?" he demanded.

"Shh! Saddle my horse, Booger," she commanded. "That big roan Dad bought for me last month. Hurry!"

Booger hesitated long enough to take off his cap and scratch his curly-thatched dome. "All right, Miss Mary, Ah'll do it. But if Mammy ever find out about dis, I gonna git my head broke. Yo' don't know dat woman lak I does." He was already moving toward the long red-topped stable with its rows of horse-filled stalls. "Everything sho' gone wrong tonight. Dat breed done gittin' himself kilt right by the porch, Judge Calhoun's house gittin' burned down, de boss ridin' off wid a gun on—"

"Stop talking and hurry," she commanded. "Quick!"

Five minutes later he led the big, deep-chested roan out of the opposite end of the stable, held the bit chains until she settled herself firmly in the swell fork saddle, then opened the pole gate to the corral.

"Remember, Booger," she admonished. "Not a word about this to anyone."

He looked up at her, cap in hand, his faithful face a map of worry. "You sure don't need to worry about that, Miss Mary. If my wife find out about me helpin' in this foolishness—good night, boy!"

It apparently had never occurred to the servant to ask

where she might be going, nor did she herself know. All she was certain of was that something strange and terrible had come up and torn her way of life asunder; and that the old life as she had known it was gone. No, Mary Jennifer didn't know where she was going, but into her mind came a picture of the one person she had always called friend: Kitty Derril. True, her father had frowned upon the friendship between Mary and her former music teacher, yet now Mary found herself hurrying toward Kitty's rented house.

It was then, passing Emmons' own stables, that she saw the rider. He rode out of the corral and loped over to her, chopping his mount in beside hers.

"Mary!" he cried out, obviously relieved at sight of her. "I just got back in town and heard the news. Was just getting ready to hurry over. You poor darling. What a blow this all must have been."

He, too, was dressed for hard riding in the country, wearing moccasins he used in the stalking of game, such as antelope, deer and the Mexican pumas he loved to hunt. She noted that he carried not one Winchester but two; one under each saddle skirt. These she recognized as a heavy repeater and the great Sharps Special he was always boasting about.

"Don't, Frank," she said wearily. "I'm not a hothouse flower to be coddled. I can stand anything but sympathy."

"But these stories, darling—"

"They're not stories, Frank, but the bald and brutal truth. My father is a robber baron and a—murderer. Let's not talk about it."

He reined his horse in beside hers as she moved on, and it was fortunate for Mary Jennifer that she could not see what lay in the man's glittering eyes. For Emmons had been increasingly aware of late that the girl was colder than ever toward him, and probably would never marry him, at least not willingly. And this man whose socially prominent family had scores of creditors at its fashionable heels—this man who himself expected the girl's fortune to replenish the Emmons family coffers—saw now that the action he had planned must be put off no longer.

No, it was forunate for Mary Jennifer that she could not see what lay in young Dr. Emmons' drugged pinpointed eyes. She would have been horrified.

"But you surely don't know what you're doing, Mary," he said. "Where are you going, honey?"

"To Kitty Derril's house first. After that I'm not sure."

"Kitty Derril! She's not your equal. She's no good. I forbid you to see her."

The girl jerked up her horse's head sharply and half wheeled in the saddle.

"You *what?*"

He saw he had made a blunder and made an immediate attempt to cover it. "But she's not your equal—"

"I'm the daughter of a murderer and still not her equal?" she cried out bitterly. "And now you try to tell me what I can or cannot do. You've always had certain masterful habits that I didn't like, Frank. One apparently is the idea that a wife is a piece of property, bought like a horse. So let's get it all settled now, Frank Emmons: I tolerated you because my father wished it that way. But that's all in the past. I'll never marry you."

He leaned over in the saddle and snatched the reins of her horse, wrapping them around the horn. She felt his fingers sink into her still splinted arm, and because the healed break in the bone was still tender a cry of pain broke from her.

"Don't! You're hurting me!"

"Will you come quietly?" he demanded brutally. "Or shall I be forced to apply a gag?"

"Are you mad?" she shot back at him. "Don't you know that my father, no matter what his past, will kill you when he finds out about this?"

"He's not going to find out about it," Emmons callously replied. "You might as well know the truth now as later, my darling, since you brought it upon yourself just now by casting the die and refusing to marry me. I need the Sunset fortune—all of it—to keep up my family prestige and my own too, for we're about broke. I played the game carefully for three years, but of late we've been rather desperate for money. So I hooked up with Ben Ferguson recently in a deal to wipe out the five owners of the Sunset. You and I are hurrying to a rendezvous with Ferguson now, to tell him we're ready to complete the job tonight. Come on, and don't fight that horse with your spurs to make him hold back or I'll shoot him and take you up behind me."

They set off westward at a mile-eating lope, Emmons pausing now and then to let the horses blow and get their second wind. As for the girl, the whole thing seemed to be some horrible dream. It was unreal.

But the reality of it all came back to her some hours later when, with the high moon making the cedar-studded country almost as bright as day, Emmons suddenly flung his horse over against her led one and forced it into a brush clump. He reined around and came up with the huge single-shot Sharps Special.

"Not a word—not a sound out of you!" he warned sharply. "It's riders—a group of horsemen."

She turned toward where his glittering eyes were directed, and then she saw them, crossing a clearing. The figures of Judge Calhoun, Kitty Derril, Jed Berber and several others took shape. But the girl's horrified gaze was riveted upon one and one only: that of the gun fighter who had called himself George Babel. Mary heard Emmons mutter, "I can get Babel any time. He doesn't count. But I can't get the Sunset spread until the five pardners are wiped out."

She turned in the saddle with a cry of horror, trying too late to strike at the gun barrel of the great Sharps. But it gave off a terrible roar and recoiled against his shoulder,

and even as he spurred away, crashing through the underbrush, she saw that Calhoun's saddle was empty.

Judge Calhoun had rendered his last decision. Fate had
seemed to render one in *his* case, and the judge had lost.

TWENTY-TWO

As Babel's party broke for the cover of a nearby knoll
he himself jumped back into the saddle and buck-jumped
the great black horse for protective cover. Babel didn't
look back; he didn't need to look back.

He knew from the caliber of the bullet and the deadly
accuracy with which it had found its target in the center
of Calhoun's bony breast who the shooter was: Emmons.
And that it would be death to come within his sights.

Thus Babel, spurring Black Boy for cover, never saw
the girl with the doctor and had no way of knowing she
was being taken on to Ben Ferguson's outlaw hideout, a
prisoner.

He rejoined the others and held up a hand for silence.
All listened, and to their ears came faint hoofbeats drumming away in a distant gully.

"He's burnin' the breeze outa here, the dam' bush-
whacker!" growled Ed Frobar. "Wonder who he was?"

"From the size of the bullet hole I could make a fair
guess," Babel replied. "Calhoun appears to have been hit
dead center with a Sharps Special."

"Emmons!" gasped out Kitty. "I always knew he was
bad clean through."

"There can be little doubt but that he fooled a lot of
people," was the reply. "Come on, follow me and keep
your eyes open. Some of Ferguson's outlaw riders might
have heard that shot above the sound of the drive."

He swung Black Boy around and set off east and to the
south, to circle the drive ahead. Behind him the others

loped along in pairs. In and out of gullies they pounded on, working through patches of timber, skirting the brighter moonlit spaces that would reveal their presence.

Gradually the low-hanging dust cloud above the bobbing backs of the rustled herd passed to the west of Babel and his party and eased on north. In a little clearing a mile to the south of the oncoming herd, Babel pulled up. They sat there for a few moments to let the heavily breathing ponies get their wind again, and then Babel spoke.

"I've no idea how many men are with that herd. Perhaps a half dozen, perhaps two dozen. But this looks as though it might be the beginning of a fight that will decide the future for all of you. And we're heavily outnumbered."

"There's quite a number of the boys hid out not too far from here," Jed Berber broke in. He grinned a bit embarrassedly. "We didn't figger it right to let Sunset steal all our cows, so we've been stealin' a few back and brandin' them with our own irons."

"Does Kitty know where they are?"

"Of course I know where they are, Babel," Kitty replied at once. "For months I've been riding down there once a week with a few worn out school books trying to give a dozen kids some school learning along with some lessons in group singing."

"Then you'd better burn the breeze after them."

"And you?"

"We'll turn the herd, stampede it right back in Ferguson's face with slickers and gunshots. Once it gets running they'll never be able to stop it this side of the Sunset range again. I doubt if they'll even try."

"And then, George Babel?"

"If any of them know where Ferguson's hideout is, have them wait about a half mile south of it. There'll be no peace or hope for any of you until Ferguson, along with the Sunset crowd, is wiped out. It might as well be now."

He suddenly leaned over and stuck out his hand to the girl, and there was surprise on her face as she took it. "I think you'd better not come back with the men, Kitty, so this looks like good-bye."

"Good-bye? You're leaving us?"

"As soon as I settle a debt with four men now probably heading down in this country to settle one with me."

The other men had turned and jogged away, sensing that Babel somehow could say his farewells much better alone. Only Aven Larson remained, sitting silent and inscrutable in the saddle. Now, as the girl reined her horse over and rode off in a southerly direction, old Aven spoke.

"You're a strange man, Tom. You don't think or act like other people. Another man would want to stay here among friends and relatives."

"You're talking in riddles, Aven," the other said sharply. "I have no relatives. I had thought that perhaps Mary Jennifer—" He looked at the other man accusingly. "Aven, why didn't you tell me the truth about Jennifer's family all these years? Why did you stick only to business details and say nothing about his private life?"

Old Aven tugged reflectively at his beard. "Well, Tom, you loved that vain, no-good creature who bore you a daughter and then left with the gambler when you entered prison. I knew news of her would only hurt you. So all those years when I sent you the rest of the money taken from the mine before I covered the tunnel with a blast, I kept away from such details. All I ever told you was that, after leaving Jennifer, she died. I never mentioned your daughter at all."

"And then I came back, saw Mary, and jumped to the conclusion that she was mine. But my own daughter, Aven—what became of her?"

"Well," Aven Larson said slowly, "she was less than a

year old when her mother died, so I never told her the truth. I put her with a good family up north, sent her to school back east, and then brought her west again. I was afraid to tell you about each other, not knowing for sure if prison had kind of—well, warped you because you lived only to kill. Then three years ago I brought her out here and she got a job as music teacher to Mary Jennifer, until Emmons gave her a bad name with his lies. Kitty Derril is your own girl, Tom."

For a moment the man once known as Tom Kent sat there like a stone statue. He did not speak. His eyes were on the figure of the girl disappearing into the mouth of a cedar-choked gully two hundred yards to the south.

Then, slowly, he reached up and removed the gold-rimmed glasses from his ascetic looking face. There was something automatic in the way he polished them with the handkerchief, placed them back on his nose, and returned the handkerchief to his pocket. Something like a tired sigh came from him.

"I think we'd better get going after the others, Aven," he said, and rode away.

They caught up with the others, and while the cattle-men untied their slickers from back of the cantles, Babel borrowed back his gun from Aven Larson and told the other man to stay out of the fight. Up ahead the bawl of cattle was coming nearer, and mingled with it now came the *whup-whup-whup* of the riders' voices, urging greater speed. Three of them riding at point suddenly broke into view, and a snarl broke from Ed Frobar as he recognized the mustached figure in front.

Ferguson the outlaw!

"Hell's fire!" yelled out the rancher, and his Colt came out and up.

It lashed out a flame spurt, but the distance was far too great for accurate Colt shooting, nor had Frobar ever been considered in the category of a short gun expert. The slug smashed a steer in the side, and then hell broke loose as the group of men led by Babel spurred straight at the head of the herd.

Babel heard a yell of rage and surprise go up from Ferguson as he recognized the man who had killed one of his henchmen in the Greek's place that morning, and later wiped out several of the others in that terrible gunfight in front of the bank. His Colt began to roar, but there was too much confusion for that kind of shooting. The wounded steer had let out a bawl of pain and run amuck into the herd, going and slashing with its horns; and what it had started to do was finished up by yells, shots, and the nerve-shattering rustle of whirling slickers.

With one accord the leaders of the herd sheered off, doubled back, and the stampede was on!

As for Babel, he spurred Black Boy staight at Ferguson in the hopes of cutting him down, but the outlaw was too wily. He had shot away on his horse just as the stampede broke and turned back, thus putting the cattle between himself and his pursuer. All up and down the line men were yelling and guns going off. Because of the great black horse's blindness, Babel had to guide him with one hand and keep to the more level spots in his pursuit of Ferguson.

He soon lost track of all the others, but not the outlaw leader. Ferguson had swept back alongside the running herd bellowing orders to his men. And the farther back he went the more he collected.

"Let 'em go, let 'em go!" came his terrible roar of command to his wild bunch—not that anybody could have stopped them. Those cattle had started back toward the home range. They were angry and tired and thirsty. Not even a canyon wall could have stopped them for long.

They swept back in a long, rumbling thunder that shook the ground with its passing and filled the air above with a fog of reddish dust that roiled and hung low and grew thicker.

Somewhere out of this Babel heard voices and mistook

them for the ranchers he was leading. He swung the black over—and too late ran smack into Ben Ferguson and nearly a dozen of his gun crew.

"Black Boy!"

Just that one cry from its rider accompanied by a left swing of the rein, and the great black horse acted. He wheeled, spun on hind feet toward the right, and lunged straight ahead into his own particular world of darkness. He could feel every move of his rider's body, and those moves told him as much as his eyes could have told him. He felt Babel's left hand flash to his hip, felt him wheel in the saddle, even felt the concussions as the freshly reloaded Colt .45 began to crash under Babel's thumb.

One, two, three times fire spurted from the vicinity of Babel's waist, back over the black's running rump. Then one, two, three again. Two Ferguson riders fell from saddles. Another gave a sharp cry and then slumped over his horse's neck, clasping a hand to his right shoulder. Lead drummed all around Babel as the welcome cloud of dust closed in around him.

He knew he was outnumbered, and because there still remained the matter of killing four certain men, he took no chances. He fled at headlong speed, northward through blinding, choking dust, almost on the tail of the herd. The great black horse flattened out and its sleek belly came still lower toward the ground. Its mighty shoulders surged in powerful rhythm as it carried its master headlong at a thundering run through its world of blackness.

Three hundred yards farther on Babel came out of the dust, off to one side of the still running herd. He pulled the black to a halt to let him blow and to look back. For just a few moments while Black Boy's deep barrel heaved hard beneath the cinches, he sat there while the rumble of the running cattle grew fainter and fainter in the distance.

From down below came sounds that told him the outlaw leader was ordering a search for the rider of the black horse; was ordering his men to get him at all costs.

For it was obvious that Ferguson the outlaw still believed Babel to be a gun fighter hired by Jennifer and the others to wipe him out. And it was equally obvious that all too fresh in his memory was that Colt battle in front of the Partridge bank, in which Babel had come off winner.

As for the man who had come back from prison to exact a toll from The Five, he now urged his mount off in the general direction where the herd had gone.

"If I know Jennifer and the others right," he muttered, "they'll burn the breeze straight toward this section of the country, and the sound of this herd can be heard for miles. It'll bring them running."

And he knew then that could he but have the good fortune to run into them, he could wind up his mission of death this night—at least with The Five.

Touching the black's sides with dull moccasin heels, Babel set off into the eerie moonlit night again.

And, three hundred yards to the south, Aven Larson made out his dim figure and watched him go. It was his imagination, quite likely, but Aven would have sworn that all of a sudden Babel had grown old and gaunt.

With a shake of his head he turned his own mount and set off to try and catch up with Kitty. For Aven was worried about the man to whom he had remained faithful for twenty-one years.

TWENTY-THREE

As for the four remaining owners, they gave blooded horseflesh almost more than it could stand in a race westward the eight miles or so to the great Sunset spread. In an incredibly short time after leaving town they loped on foam-flecked mounts into the yard of the ranch.

It hardly could be called a ranch, since it was more like

a small city. Once upon a time there had been a ranch house; but this long since had been converted into a storage room for grain. Jennifer and the others now possessed carefully landscaped homes not far from the sprawled area of barns, sheds, storehouses, commissary trading store, bunkhouses and corrals. A private railroad spur, nearly four miles in length, tangented off the main line and ended up at the Sunset's own private loading pens on the flats a half mile below the main buildings. Their whitewashed squares gleamed that far in the brightness of the moon.

The four loped down the lane that was more like a street, and the hounds Jennifer kept in kennels to run coyotes on moonlit autumn nights set up a loud baying. From somewhere ahead, near the corrals, a bunkhouse door opened and a rider's bareheaded length appeared in the opening. The four slid to a halt in a cloud of dust.

"Why, it's Mister Jennifer!" cried out the hand.

"Where's all the men?" snapped the banker at the man in the doorway. "The whole ranch looks deserted. Where are they?"

The hand hesitated.

"Out with it!" bellowed Ben Johnston, his hand on his gun. "What the hell's going on around here anyhow?"

"Well, it's like this, Mister Jennifer," the puncher said. "I tends to my business, savvy? I let other people tend to theirs. And if them gents wants to go ridin' off down in Ben Ferguson country nearly all the time of late, I figger I better keep my mouth shut or mebbeso git it shut for me. So the same I figger tonight. If they wants to saddle up 'bout sundown an' hit for the south range, I ain't the gent to try stoppin' 'em. I'm strictly neutral, I am. I tends strictly to my own—"

"Dirty double-crossing scum!" Alden broke in savagely, tearing his cigar stub from its mooring in a corner of his mouth and slamming it to the ground. "Pay them good wages—"

"You never overpaid them," Bonner simply had to cut in, from force of habit.

"—and then they turn around and steal the very profits under your nose. All the time we've been blaming those small ranchers for rustling our stock, when I'll be damned if I don't think Ferguson had a hand in it all the time. Ferguson and those riders of ourn."

"We're wasting time," Martin Jennifer said coldly to his penny pinching partner. "We'll get fresh horses and hit south after them. Somewhere down there we'll find this man who called himself Babel. And I've a strange feeling that where we find that cold-blooded devil we'll find our cows—and Ferguson. Hey, you!" to the hand.

"Yes, sir."

"Saddle us some fresh horses," Jennifer ordered.

"Yes, sir, Mister Jennifer. Pronto!"

He dived back into the bunkhouse and jerked on his boots by the table where he had been reading. There was a saddle dumped on the floor beside the door, and the hand grabbed up his lariat from it. He set out for the horse corral, running awkwardly in high-heeled boots through dust left by the others as they loped on.

Ben Johnston had opened the corral gate and was now inside, swinging his lariat. The hand roped a good horse for the banker, and by the time he had Jennifer's saddle on, the others of the partners were already swinging up.

"Yuh wants that I should go along?" he queried.

"No," gritted Alden, half choking with rage over the thought of possible lost profits on the herd stolen that night. "You stay here and watch the ranch. After what those dirty rascals have done tonight it wouldn't surprise me if they came back and hauled off all the barns and the rest of the buildings."

They reined over and spurred away into the night, drumming away from the ranch. A half mile south Bonner got down and opened a wire gate, remounted, and the four were off again. After a time the flatter terrain near the ranch began to give way to the rougher country on the south range. Once they came out onto a level stretch of open plain a mile wide, and the cursing Alden cursed anew at sight of its bare loneliness.

There wasn't a single head of cattle in sight.

"Shut up, Alden," called back Martin Jennifer. "All you've done is whine about losses. Won't you ever get it through your head that there are other things more important tonight?"

"What, for instance?"

"My God!" bellowed the sheriff disgustedly, half throwing up both hands. "We stand a good chance of going to the gallows—of being hunted down by the Texas Rangers we've always shied away from here. We stand a chance to lose everything unless Babel is stopped cold tonight. And you set there and bellyache about losing a few head of cattle to Ben Ferguson, who rustled half of them in the first place. I give up!" he groaned.

The going got slower when they hit the rough country, and once or twice they stopped to argue as to which direction they next should take. But it wasn't long afterward, when the moon was a great white ball riding a majestic path across the sky, when the decision was settled by the coming of the now tiring herd itself. The four rode up on top of a grassy knoll and sat their horses, watching the scene far below. About three hundred head of cattle had lumbered into view in a wide swale, breaking through the brush at a weary sharp-paced trot. More came on straggling through the gullies and draws, and then after a time they were all gone, heading toward their familiar feeding grounds.

"Headed back for the home range," muttered Alden, staring his disbelief but obviously heartened by the sight. "Ganted out from a long hard run. Boys, mebbe things aren't so bad after all. I've got a hunch that that man Babel—or rather Kent now—ran into Ferguson and busted up the drive. That means that somewhere down there we ought to run into——".

"Shh! Hold it!" cut in Jennifer sharply. "Look! Over there coming into view around the end of that ridge."

They looked and saw the dark moving blot that was a black horse and black-coated rider, coming at a walk and apparently trailing the herd. They had no way of knowing that Babel was following that herd in the hopes of running into them; nor that not far back of him was an enraged Ferguson who still thought Babel had been hired by the Sunset owners to wipe him out.

Thus the four murderers of long dead Jim Kent sat there, Alden grinning a hard and cold grin of expectation, as Kent came on.

"Get set, men, and remember—take no chances," Alden ordered. "All right, *let's go!*"

He slammed spurs to his blooded mount, and the four of them shot off down the side of the knoll, guns out and at a dead run straight for the rider of the black horse. Babel jerked up in surprise—or so they thought—and then wheeled his mount around to flee. He began spurring back the way he had come with the four in headlong pursuit.

"I always had a feeling he might be yellow when it came to a showdown!" yelled out Alden joyfully, as they began shortening the distance separating them from the fleeing rider on the black horse. "Look—we're closing in! We've got him!"

"Not as long as he's astraddle of that black horse, you haven't!" snarled back Martin Jennifer. "Not unless it's played out. And remember about your shots. Aim them high. *I don't want that black horse hit!*"

Alden was the first to try at long six-shooter range. They were running down a long, flat-bottomed draw that was carpeted with thick grass, their horses' flying hoofs seeming to skim the vegetation. He brought out his long-barreled Colt, swung it high over his head in a circular motion, and then whipped it down in a chopping motion, the barrel's muzzle lashing fire.

Nor was he shooting at Babel. He was trying to bring down that black horse and thus seal Babel's certain doom. Jennifer could get a horse anywhere. But this man Babel who had come back—

Alden swung the Colt around his head again, to make another try.

He never quite knew just how it happened—and for a moment he thought he had hit the rider. For Babel seemed to fall forward in the saddle. He went down low over the horn, came up almost at once, twisted about; and then the bright rays of the moon struck a white glint from the metal of a heavy .45-.90 repeating Winchester. Alden saw the weapon go up, heard its ear-shattering roar, and that was about the last thing he ever heard in life.

For the 300-grain slug of lead caught the blooded horse he was riding squarely between the eyes and almost blew open its head. It went down in a flying somersault, carrying Alden with it, and when at last it rolled to a stop Alden's body was little more than a mass of broken flesh with not an unbroken bone left in it.

Two of The Five were gone.

But not the three others. They spurred on without stopping. It had to be now or never. As far as Alden was concerned, his passing left them with no regrets. He had been a grumbler, a nickle squeezer who had even tried to juggle the credit books of the riders at the ranch, adding extra items to their accounts to get back part of their wages.

No, they were thinking of themselves now.

"I've got to down that hoss, Martin!" Ben Johnston bellowed out to the banker.

"No! By God, no! We can run him down. That shot was just luck. Don't kill that horse!"

Up ahead of them Babel swung the repeater over and slipped it into the boot again as the draw made a slight

curve. He had come up this same draw not long before
with Ferguson and his riders not far behind, and if his
calculations were right he should be running into them
again.

And then he did run into them as he rounded the
curve. He caught a brief glance of seven or eight outlaws,
heard a yell from Ferguson, and swung hard to the right,
spurring toward the thicket close by. With Ferguson's
slugs drumming about him, he crashed Black Boy head
on through the green screen just as the three Sunset men
rounded the turn and found—too late—that the grim man
they had been pursuing had led them into a death trap.

The next two or three minutes lived for a long time in
Babel's memory. He saw the two parties run almost into
each other, heard a confused chorus of curses, yells, and
accusations about double-crossing, amid which guns were
roaring at short range—at ranges too short to miss.

Bonner was the first to go down. He went out of the
saddle, still firing, and was trampled to death beneath the
hoofs of a half dozen plunging horses. Johnston didn't
wait but dived out; and that cold-faced man sitting up
there on the ridge watching it all with eyes blank behind
the gold-rimmed glasses felt a tinge of admiration for the
sheriff, fighting alone as Jennifer fled to safety.

The sheriff was staggering forward with a half dozen
bullets in his huge girth, guns spouting, and he brought
three outlaws down with him before he fell. He tried to
get up, rolled over, and wagged his great head from side
to side like a wounded range bull. He was still wagging it
when Ferguson got down from his horse, walked over
with a reloaded six-shooter in his hand, and bent down.

Ferguson shot him three times as he lay on the grass,
wallowing convulsively, and when it was over Johnston
only quivered.

"There, damn yuh!" grunted the outlaw leader, his eyes
flaming. "That puts you and Bonner out, and unless my
eyes fooled me just now I saw Alden's horse go down.

That's three, and Doc Emmons will take care of Calhoun when he gits a chance. That'll make four."

He went back to his horse, mounted, and sat there for a moment looking at the scene around him.

"Yep, that leaves only Jennifer and that Babel gent. When we git them, Doc Emmons will own Sunset spread outright until I git right with the law, and then we'll own it together. Unsaddle them hosses, boys, and dump the gear on the ground for the buzzards to sit on. We're headin' for the hideout to meet Doc Emmons and mebbe wait for Jennifer to foolishly stick his nose in the valley. After seven years, Ben Ferguson is comin' into his own!"

TWENTY-FOUR

Quite a number of hours later the same moon that had witnessed the sudden turmoil that was to change the course of several lives that night lay far over on the opposite horizon from which it had started. Its rays were a hazier yellow now, as though the long night's work had dimmed them somewhat. But they still shone bright enough to reveal a long valley, running north and south, where Ben Ferguson had his headquarters.

Almost beneath the west side of the valley Ferguson had built his house. Here Martin Jennifer had come in secret to plan the various deals that would mean another small rancher rustled and driven out, his holdings added to the great Sunset spread. Here the others had come at various times for many different reasons, but always with profit for themselves. Here Ferguson lived and from it led his outlaw band, his crimes either pinned on somebody else or never solved by Sheriff Johnston.

It was a surprisingly comfortable place for an outlaw home. The ceiling, of slab pine supported by cut cedar posts, was low and smoke begrimed from the tobacco of a thousand poker games, though Ferguson lived in the house alone. At one end was a fireplace, built of the red sandstone common to the section, in it the dead ashes of last winter's fires. There were books on shelves; who would ever have guessed that Ben Ferguson the outlaw leader was an omnivorous reader of Dickens?

He sat at the big table in the center of the room now, a pair of reading specs on, absorbed in the pages of *Oliver Twist*—though he knew the book almost by heart. Across from him Emmons was busy with rags and cleaning rod, working on the Sharps Special. On the table between them lay the hand-bound volume that the dead breed Jose Alveraz had stolen and delivered to the doctor's home. Emmons had read it through, almost gasped at its full import, then brought it with him to show to Ferguson.

They had spent an hour going through it.

"I take off my hat to that man Babel," Emmons finally said, breaking a rather long silence. "Maybe I should have dropped him instead of old Calhoun."

"What you should have done," Ferguson said, putting down the book and reaching for the whiskey bottle, "was use that repeater you carried and got both of them. Never could figger out why you wanted to lug that cannon around when there's plenty of good repeaters handy."

"Looks like all the use I'll have for it now is to hunt antelope," Emmons grunted. "Wonder how Mary's making out in her room?"

"She'll have to make out whether she likes it or not," said the outlaw, yawning. He pulled a battered watch from his pocket. "Hell, it's two-thirty. I'm turning in. Coming?"

Emmons put down the cloth, closed the breech of the huge single shot and laid it on the table. He shook his head, got up and began to pace the floor in his moccasined feet.

"If you're worryin' about that gal not marryin' you, forget it," Ben Ferguson advised. "She'll marry you, all right. If she don't, you can keep her here and have her anyhow. And if you're worryin' about somebody slippin' into this valley, forget that too. My guards know their business."

"Yes, but they don't know that Babel is first and last a mountaineer. You're not dealing with any blundering cowpuncher stomping around in high-heeled boots, Ben. You're dealing with a man who's as noiseless as a panther—and as dangerous. I think I'll look around a bit."

He got up and, making no sound, crossed the room like an Indian. At a chained and padlocked door he paused, noting the light still beneath it.

Mary Jennifer still wasn't asleep.

Emmons unlocked the chain and went in as she half rose up off the bunk. Had not his continued use of drugs reduced most of the passion in him, he would have been affected by the loveliness of her white face. But he thought of her only in terms of money.

"What do you want, Frank?" the girl demanded.

"Thought I'd take a look at your arm after our hard ride, Mary. Forgot all about it until now."

"The arm's all right. Please get out."

He sat down on the edge of the table and looked at her casually through his drug-inflamed eyes.

"We might as well be sensible about this whole thing, girl. I'm not marrying you because I want to. I'm marrying you because you're practically the sole owner of the Sunset spread. There are only two men standing between me and it now."

"Two?"

He told her then of what had happened since he had killed Calhoun earlier in the night on their way to the hideout. Bonner, Alden and Johnston were dead. "Your father got away, and Ben's got a little reception waiting for him now. That leaves only one other man: this gent Babel. And I'm taking care of him now. I've got a hunch he's prowling the country around this valley, and I'm going out to hunt him. Sleep tight, darling."

She almost shuddered at his callousness and turned her back upon him. He chuckled, went out and closed the door, locking it once more. "My fiancée's most unreceptive to a visit from her future husband," he informed Ben Ferguson, who had stripped off his clothes and was sliding a white woolen nightshirt over his head. "And thanks for the look, Ben."

"Look?" queried Ferguson, his mustache appearing over the top of the garment.

"At that nightgown. If there's anything in the world that could kill romance in a young bride, it would be to see her husband in one of those things on their wedding night. I'll make it a point not to get one." He reached for the rifle.

Ferguson grunted as Emmons took up the Sharps and left the house, crawled into bed and blew out the light on the table beside his pillow, but not without the thought that Emmons either had a warped sense of humor from smoking those marijuana cigarettes or was a little crazy.

He rolled over in the darkness, kicked his feet comfortably in the covers, and dropped off to sleep.

TWENTY-FIVE

At about the time that Emmons left the hideout and the valley, after stopping to talk to the guard on the south entrance, a group of grim-faced men sat around a low fire some three miles to the south. The fire was built under a ledge, so that its rays were not visible from any great distance. The fifteen men were grim and coldly determined as they examined weapons and talked in low tones. These were the ones that Kitty had gone after. She had changed to a fresh horse, and then hurried back with them.

She sat apart some distance with the others, and with her sat Aven Larson, who had showed up shortly after the party's arrival. The girl slowly shook her head from side to side, staring out into the silent night's black fastness in the canyon below.

"I can't believe it," she whispered in a low, tense voice, for about the fifth time. "I simply can't believe it. Babel—or Kent—my own father."

"It's true enough, Kitty."

"Why didn't you tell me?"

"Because prison sometimes does the wrong things to a man," old Aven replied. "Warps his mind. Suppose I had told you long ago? You might have gone to see him and found him a surly, bitter, snarling convict. It would have cast a shadow on your life. So I decided to wait until the day he might be free. Then, had he been the wrong kind of a man, you would never have known."

"But he wasn't," she half whispered. "He was the right kind."

"He came out of it all one of the greatest men I've ever met," Aven nodded softly. "And despite the injustice and suffering—depsite the more than twenty years in a cell—I think he'll now get more out of life than he would have got being an ignorant mountain man with no appreciation of good books, good music, and many of the other finer things he has learned about. He's still a young man."

"How old is—my father, Aven?"

The bearded man thoughtfully stroked his hirsute chin. "Let's see now, Kitty. He was eighteen when you were born, going to prison shortly afterward. That makes him thirty-nine now."

Up on the ridge above them there came a sharp command from the rancher on guard. Around the fire men leaped to their feet, hands reaching for Winchesters. It might be Ferguson's men, or perhaps Babel. They were taking no chances on the grim job that was to start some time around daylight: the wiping out of Ferguson's stronghold. There was to be no quarter asked and none given.

Now, as the command came again, there were voices, a startled oath from the guard, and two men began to descend the declivity from above. One rancher after another froze as he saw Martin Jennifer's figure step into the firelight.

"What're yuh doin' here, mister?" snapped Ed Frobar coldly to the cattle baron. "Don't yuh know we're gettin' set for a clean-up try, with every man who's taken prisoner due for a rope around his neck?"

"That's why I'm here," came the quiet reply.

Jennifer looked anything but the suave banker they had known. He was booted, gun-belted, and very haggard-faced. He spoke very quietly, telling them of the fight with Ferguson—of how Babel had led them into the death trap.

"Well, what're we supposed to do about it?" demanded Jed Berber belligerently. "Cry on yore shoulder?"

"No," Jennifer said. "I'm not the crying kind, as most of you losers have good reason to know. I'm here to talk business—to make all of you a proposition."

As leader for the group, Jed Berber stepped forward, backed by Ed Frobar. "Any time *you* talk business somebody else gets skinned," the younger man grunted contemptuously. "So we ain't talkin'. Yuh're stayin' right here until we clean out the valley. Then we're swingin' yuh with a rope, along with any others who are foolish enough to give up. But we ain't goin' to give 'em a chance. We're goin' to surround that valley and sieve the buildings with Winchester slugs, startin' at daylight."

"That's just the point: you mustn't do it that way," the banker said wearily. "Tonight after the fight I headed straight for the hideout to beat Ferguson there and kill him. But my horse stepped in a gopher hole and he got into the valley ahead of me. I'd lost my gun in the darkness, too and couldn't do a thing. But I got near enough to recognize a roan horse in the corral as belonging to my daughter. There's another with it, a prize bay belonging to Emmons. So that told me all I wanted to know. My daughter would never willingly go to Ferguson's hideout. She didn't know where it was. But Emmons did. So it looks like that swine has taken her there as a prisoner. And that's why you can't wipe him out. She'd be killed in the rifle fire with the others. Oh, I'm not asking any favors for myself," he went on passionately. "I took my chances in life and I'm not whining now that I've lost. But that girl of mine has no reason to lose her life because of my own crimes. So I'm offering you a bargain."

Kitty Derril had come forward, and now she stepped past the fire to lay a hand on Martin Jennifer's arm. "If you know a way into that valley, Martin Jennifer, and can lead us to it past the guards, I'll see that when it's over you have a horse and a chance to carry you to freedom."

"Thank you, Kitty, That's what I came for. I do know a way. It's an emergency exit and entrance Ben prepared should the gang ever be cornered. I'll take you down it at daylight. And now, if I may, I'd like a cup of that coffee. Somehow I feel very tired."

It was the girl herself who got him the steaming tin cup and brought it to where he sat on a rock gazing moodily into the fire. She sat down beside him and gave him the coffee. While he sipped at it, she told him the whole story of how Aven had taken care of her after Jennifer rid himself of the former Ellen Kent.

"It's amazing how things turn out," she said. "I'm Tom Kent's daughter. I was your stepdaughter when you first brought me here when I was two months old. And now—"

"And now," Jennifer cut in slowly, his eyes still fixed upon the flames, "justice has overtaken us all. God, Kitty, what a heartless, greedy, power-mad fool I've been. I think I knew instinctively all along that Emmons was lying when he said that you stayed with him in his house that night."

"I've never stayed with anybody but Jed," Kitty answered simply. "Aven married us a few days ago."

"How I regret that I didn't raise you and Mary together," he murmured. "All this might never have happened. And now Kent—"

"When did you see him last?" she asked.

"Right after the fight with Ferguson's men there in the gully. I broke away and fled west through the cedars, but soon discovered that Babel was after me. I suppose he was, too, for I don't believe that even his love for Mary could have made him spare me a second time tonight. Then my horse stepped into a gopher hole two miles this side of the valley. I ducked into the underbrush on foot and got away. When I last saw Babel he was heading in the direction of the hideout. If he kept going that way, he was due to hit the valley squarely on the east rim."

Kitty jumped to her feet and looked at Jed Berber.

"Jed, did you hear?" she cried out. "He—he's going into that valley alone."

TWENTY-SIX

At the south entrance to the valley Emmons, the great Sharps slung over his left arm, moved up the steep trail that wound out on top, where a trusted man was on guard. Fifty yards from where the man was stationed the medico dropped his cigarette, ground it into the dirt with a moccasined foot, and then faded on through the night as noiseless as a fox. The first intimation the guard had that anybody was anywhere within miles was when Emmons' sarcastic voice came from four feet behind him.

"It's lucky for you, Thorpe, that my name's not Babel."

Thorpe wheeled with a startled curse, half bringing up his repeater.

"Whadda you mean sneakin' up on me like that?" he grunted. He had been pretty drunk on beer all that day, up until the time he and Sistrom made their fruitless search for Babel around the grounds of Calhoun's now burned down home. And beer has a way of leaving a man loggy, his brain befouled, and with a vile taste in his mouth.

Thorpe was in a savage temper.

"For a man who deserted what he thought was a sinking ship and fled down here to join Ferguson tonight, you're a hell of a fine specimen of a guard," grunted the medico, setting the rifle down and leaning against the rock. "I could have got you a half dozen times had I been Babel."

"I was busy thinkin'. And no man gets me a half dozen times when I'm on the alert. You just remember that I walked a prison wall for many a long night with a carbine, on the lookout, in a damned sight more darkness than this. No man ever got over the wall on me yet; and no man ever will ketch Lurt Thorpe off guard."

"Yes, I hope not," Emmons replied sarcastically. "But you keep your eyes open from now on while I circle the valley. Babel is on the prowl. And because he knows what kind of a man you are, he'll kill on sight."

He picked up the Sharps again and cradled it across his left arm. "I'm going to circle the valley before the moon goes down. Keep your eyes peeled and listen for the hoot of an owl—twice. That will mean that I'm back. At daylight Ben's going to get all the men together and sweep south to comb those small ranchers out of the brakes. We figure we might as well make a clean sweep of it in one fell swoop."

"Sounds good. Looks like you'll also need the right kind of man for a new sheriff, see? I always did think Johnston was overrated."

"Johnston was underrated. It's just that at the final moment he was outsmarted by a better man. He made just one mistake, and that was enough."

"You ain't said that I get his badge."

"We'll see. And keep on your toes."

Emmons disappeared into the underbrush and set off toward the east side of the valley, working his way northward along the rim. He went as noiselessly as a night owl soaring through the darkness, aware that Babel probably was prowling somewhere in the vicinity. He certainly would have been surprised had he known that Babel already had found the place and was still looking for Martin Jennifer, who he thought was down below.

Emmons moved on, pausing now and then to let his keen eyes pierce the darkness. His eyes kept going to the moon, low on the horizon. It was going down much faster than he had anticipated, and this caused him to set a more hurried pace. He finally reached the north end, cut down across the bottom of a draw where another guard was on station with a repeater, spoke to the man, then set out southward along the west wall.

After a time the tops of the hideout buildings, snuggling almost beneath the perpendicular west wall, showed up. The medico cursed as he saw the two lights twinkling down there. One was from the wing of the house where Mary Jennifer was a prisoner, and still awake. The other came from a sort of community bunkhouse some distance away, where the outlaw Babel had shot in the shoulder was cursing the bandage Emmons had put on him.

He moved on for some two or three hundred yards, heading back toward the guard at the south entrance. Then he jerked up sharp, and a muttered exclamation came from him as the moving blob of black showed up in the darkness on the valley floor below. He peered again, and this time he cursed at sight of the black horse.

Babel was in the valley!

Emmons swung up the great Sharps Special, and then lowered it again, realizing that its roar would carry across the country for miles and thus reveal the hiding place to the ranchers who undoubtedly would be hunting it. He turned and set off at a dog trot toward the south entrance, covering ground like an Indian runner. After a time he approached the south entrance and the rock where the guard was stationed. The call of a night owl went eerily through the darkness.

"Thorpe!" he whispered into the night, for the moon now had gone down and it was pitch black. "Thorpe! Don't shoot. It's Emmons."

There was no answer, and he called again. Still no reply. Putting down the rifle, Emmons wriggled forward on his belly, and his eyes soon made out the supine form of the guard. He rose, went forward, and risked all to strike a match. The deputy, his face black, had been garroted from behind.

Cursing like a madman, Emmons ran back and got his rifle and almost loped down the winding trail into the valley proper. A half mile to the north the lights still gleamed. And somewhere nearby, like a great wolf scenting a kill, was the man who stood between Emmons and the Sunset ranch.

The medico ran the faster.

And out there not far from the ranch Babel was indeed on the scent of a kill. He had figured from the terrain that the main entrance to the valley would be on the south, and his mountaineer instinct had been correct. After dispatching the guard, he had gone back and got his black horse and ridden down the trail. Now he swung into a clump of cedars nearby and faded into the night, toward the light in Ben Ferguson's house.

Flat on his stomach, he wriggled toward it, and after a

time he came up beneath the window, a Colt .45 in his left hand. He peered in, and a short hiss of surprise escaped him at the sight of Mary Jennifer. She lay on the bunk with wide eyes looking up at the ceiling, and the tear streaks on her face indicated that she had been crying.

"Not that she can be blamed," he muttered. "Must be a terrible thing for a girl to find out her father is a murderer. But how did she *get* here?"

A cold warning shot through him at the thought. Something was wrong!

Risking all, he tapped gently with his forefinger on the pane. She didn't seem to hear, or her senses were too dulled from shock and grief. He tapped again, louder. And this time she turned her head. She saw a face that she had never expected to see again, with fingers to its lips, below a pair of gold-rimmed glasses; and the sight brought a quickly stifled cry. She got up and slipped to the window, tried to raise it. Then she looked helplessly at him and pointed to the big spikes driven in to prevent its being raised. Emmons himself had nailed them down.

His fingers were still to his lips, but he kept motioning toward something at the opposite side of the room. His lips framed the one word *paper*. There was an old copy of a stockmen's paper there, and she got it. Again his lips formed the word: *water*. Obeying his instructions, she dipped it into the pail of drinking water and then pressed it against the window pane, learning a simple trick of burglary he himself had learned in prison. When she pushed out the pane there hardly was a sound of broken glass.

She could hear him plainly then.

"I'll have to break in the whole window frame. When it breaks, dive through into my arms. My horse is a hundred yards from here in that big clump of bushes. Run hard for him, but remember to call him by name and to guide him with words for Black Boy was born stone blind."

"But you, Babel—"

"I don't matter, Mary. Just get free and ride hard for

the south entrance, where the guard has been removed. I killed him."

Before she could reply further—before she could tell him that no matter what happened she loved him—his blackcoated shoulder crashed against the pane and the whole lower part of the window caved in toward her. The crash of splintered wood and glass rang out loudly.

"Quick—through the window!" he cried.

She plunged through, trying hard to protect the arm still in a sling, and then several things seemed to happen all at once. From within the house proper a bellow came from Ben Ferguson, and he hit the floor with a gun in each hand; the bunkhouse spewed surprised and yelling outlaws; and Mary Jennifer caught a brief glimpse of something that looked like a catamount launching itself at Babel from the corner of the building.

"Emmons!" she screamed, and that word saved Babel's life.

He half dropped her and wheeled, only to go down beneath the snarling medico's hundred and seventy pounds of drug-crazed weight. This drug turned Emmons into a human tiger.

But he had forgotten that Babel had learned many things in prison and that his fingers, twisting a cell bar for years, were like steel bands. Emmons struck once, futilely, with his gun barrel before it was torn from him as though he had been a child. Babel's clawlike thews sank deep into his neck on each side and he shook him as a wolfhound shakes a limp jackrabbit it has caught. He shook him with an inhuman savagery that broke every bone in Emmons' neck; and he dropped him just as the night-shirted figure of Ferguson came roaring off the front porch and around the corner of the house with a Colt in each hand.

Ferguson saw Babel's face in the light of the broken pane, and a great roar came from him as his guns came up. But fire and smoke spurts enveloped Babel's hips just

as they had that day in town when he had killed part of
the outlaw crew, aided by the now dead Emmons, whose
murder lust had made him join in against men who were
supposed to be his friends.

Ferguson gave a horrible gasp of surprise as the lead
tore at him, ripped him through and through, shook him
as Babel's terrible fingers had shaken the life from the
mad medico's body. He went down and rolled over on his
face, and on the back of his white nightshirt dark stains
that would show red in daylight began to spread.

Just what might have happened to Babel—and the girl
too—had not another factor intervened, would not have
been hard to envision. The outlaw pack were coming on
the run, yelling questions, and Babel had half backed
toward Ferguson, hoping to get the leader's still loaded
guns. But at that moment firing broke out anew from another direction, where Jed Berber and a dozen other
ranchers ran forward on foot, after working their way
down stone steps cut in the canyon walls.

It had first been necessary for Jed Berber to slip forward and dispatch a guard stationed exactly where Martin
Jennifer knew he would be stationed. And after they were
all down onto the valley floor, the young cowman had
said, "All right, Jennifer, because of this and the fact that
Kitty thinks so much of your daughter, we're squaring accounts. When it's over you're free to leave the country."

Then the fight was on, and Ferguson's men, stunned
that outsiders had got into the valley past the guards,
broke for the protection of the bunkhouse. There weren't
many of them who were now surrounded. Babel and Emmons had wiped out seven of them in the gun fight that
would go down in history at Partridge. Others had returned to the Sunset spread, where they would be taken
care of in due time.

And upon the rim several others on guard saw the gun
flashes below and quietly sought their horses. They rode

away and kept right on going until once again they could find men of their own kind.

Ben Ferguson's day of dominion was done.

For two more hours slugs from a dozen different quarters drummed into the doors and windows of the building where the cursing raiders flattened themselves on the floor and tried to fire back. But the walls, though fairly solid, couldn't stop the bullets from a couple of .45-.70's, one .45-.90, and a Sharps Special that Jed Berber had picked up where Emmons had dropped it, and with it was methodically ripping great gaping holes at the floor line of the bunkhouse walls.

Thus when daylight broke two hours after the attack began, five men came out with a white handkerchief held aloft, hobbling and cursing. But if they had expected anything but cow country retribution for their crimes, they were doomed to disappointment. Jed Berber jerked his head toward several saddles piled against the corral, and men took the lariats from them before saddling more horses. Twenty minutes later a little cavalcade of grim men, with five bound punchers in the center, disappeared toward a group of hackberry trees growing at the north end of the valley. One of the men had a deputy sheriff's star on his shirt.

"Well," Sistrom grunted with grim humor, after learning what had befallen his crony, "I allus figured I'd take a fast trip to hell some day, but I never figgered I'd be racin' Thorpe to see who gits there first. Looks like I lose."

But back at the buildings it had been found that two men were gone. One was Martin Jennifer. The other was Tom Kent.

All during the terrible gun duel the banker had lain back of the horse corral watching it all, and now in the confusion he decided it was time to slip away. He knew that the old rule of The Five was over; that a new kind of life—a cleaner life that Lad begun when the flood hit Partridge—was coming to the country. In it there would be no place for him or his kind.

And strangely enough, he was content. He knew that his daughter Mary loved Kent, though there was little chance the man ever would reciprocate that love. But Kitty and her strong young cowman husband who were destined to rule the Sunset ranch would see that she was taken care of. So Jennifer slipped quietly away toward a big thicket where he had caught a glimpse of a great black horse.

Time would heal Mary Jennifer's grief, and some day, somewhere, she would find happiness.

He ran straight at Black Boy, unaware of the big animal's blindness, and the black's nose told him of the coming of the hated man who had tried to make friends with him. Black Boy reared high, and too late Martin Jennifer saw the rapier hoofs slashing down at his head. He went down with his skull smashed in, hardly knowing what had hit him.

Thus it was that Babel, slipping into the thicket to get his mount, found him. He found bearded old Aven too. Aven was waiting for him, looking down at the story Jennifer's crumpled body told.

"So you're going away now, Tom?" he asked the man who never again would be known as George Babel.

"Yes," Kent said, swinging up. "I'm tired, Aven; and for some reason I feel very old. I lived only for vengeance. It kept me going all those years in prison. But like a hungry man who eats too much and becomes ill, that vengeance has now turned bitter. So I'm going to try and get well again by forgetting all this and feeding my soul on hard work and a belief in God."

"You'll come back some day?"

"Perhaps. Kitty and Jed can run the big Sunset outfit and square up with the ranchers for what they lost. See that Mary Jennifer gets a generous share of what's left, for The Five did well—better than I could have done—on the proceeds of that stolen pocket of gold. And tear down those big houses up there on the hill; they'll only rot now."

"Where are you going, Tom?"

Tom Kent's shoulders shrugged dispiritedly. "What does it matter as long as I can be alone to work out my own destiny? As for you, Aven, I want you to have the building I foolishly named the Tower of Babel. Make it into your new church. Tear out the bar and fixtures and put in a big organ with pipes that will carry all over town. And some day, perhaps, when time has made us all forget, I'll come back and play that organ for my grandchildren. Good-bye, Aven, and keep watch over Kitty. She's more your daughter than mine."

He bent in the saddle and shook hands, suddenly seeming gaunt and haggard; then he turned the black's head and rode toward the winding trail that led up out of the valley. And it wasn't until he had climbed out on top that Kitty and Mary, looking for him, saw him up there.

"Why, Aven," Kitty cried out to the old man as he stepped onto the porch, "he's—he's *gone!*"

"It's better that way, kitten," Aven said softly, his arms around them both. "But don't worry. I think that some day—Look!"

They looked up to where he was pointing, to where for just a moment a great black horse and rider were outlined on the east ridge in the rays of a golden morning sun.

Then horse and rider disappeared from view and the ridge was bare.

Tom Kent was gone.

TWENTY-SEVEN

On an afternoon nearly three months later, a huge four-horse wagon pulled by sturdy animals bearing a Texas brand drew up in a clearing far to the north of Partridge.

The faithful Booger turned in the seat and looked down at Aven Larson riding near the front wheel.

"Dis de place you talkin' about, Mistuh Aven?"

"Of co'se it's de place!" Mammy, riding beside him, cut in scathingly at her spouse. "Honest to goodness, man, you is de dumbest—"

"Now, now, Mammy, never mind," Aven cut in, smiling at her. "Yes, this is the place."

He turned to the bright-eyed girl who had constantly kept her face turned northward during the long trip.

"This is it, Mary, the place where Tom and his brother intended to build their great ranch house. The old mine is right down there around the turn in the gully. I'd never forget its location, and neither would Tom."

"Aven," she said a little breathlessly, "you're—you're sure he's here?"

"It's the one place where Tom would come to lose himself in hard work and solitude. Yes, he's here, Mary. There's a wisp of smoke coming up through the trees. That should mean supper. We used to eat about this time."

"You wait here—all of you," she said. "I—I want to go to him alone, Aven."

He nodded and watched her go, directing Booger to get down and set about making camp in the clearing where one day a ranch and corrals would stand. As for Mary Jennifer, she rounded the turn in the gully and saw the newly opened mine in the side of a steep bank.

It was about as Aven had pictured to her—*arastra* pit, the trees, the stream a narrow trickle down below, the partly hidden one-room shack. But the camp itself seemed deserted. She got down from her horse and went to the mine tunnel mouth, turned away to look seeking sight of him.

It was then that Mary Jennifer saw Kent, coming through the trees with a collapsible canvas water bucket dripping in his hands. He was bareheaded, but there was something new and vital and young in the face back of the gold-rimmed glasses. His gray woollen shirt was open at the throat, and the rolled up sleeves showed brawny arms and hands grown horny from wielding a pick. Those guns that had wreaked such terrible destruction were gone.

He didn't say anything when he saw her, nor did she; but the man whose memory had been filled with her night and day set down the pail and came toward the girl he had loved from the first morning when he had taken her half dead body, its clothing torn, from the chill waters of the flood that had helped to cleanse Partridge.

"Tom," she whispered. "Tom, I had to come."

"I know, Mary, because I was—getting ready to come to you."

Yet he somehow hesitated, and she saw in that hesitation a fear and an uncertainty, as though what had happened in the past now lay like a shadow on their souls. She went closer and looked up at him.

"Tom, don't you want me? Are you going to make me throw myself at you?"

"But don't you see, Mary, the past—"

"The past is all forgotten. Only the future matters."

He sat down on a great log with the girl beside him, and the warmness of her as he held her in his arms and kissed her kindled a strange new fire within him; a fire that he had thought was dead ashes.

"I'm thirty-nine years old, Mary," she heard him saying softly. "You're only a girl."

"I wouldn't have it any other way, Tom. I think that right from the first moment I saw you as you came into the room where I was propped up in bed, I wanted it to be this way. Aven is up there with Mammy and Booger. He's got a pardon for you, since Edson told what he had overheard that last night in the library. But that too is in the past. There's something clean and fresh up here in this country that I love. There's work to be done and a new life to build. Aven says—he says it's a wonderful site for a new ranch house."

"Yes, a wonderful place," Tom Kent said softly, his face buried in the fragrance of her hair while his eyes gazed out over her shoulder to the majesty of the surrounding hills; "and here, after Aven marries us, Mary, we'll build it together."

GUNFIRE AT
SALT FORK

Chapter One

Jonathan Carr rode into Marlinville a few minutes
before midnight and fed his saddle and pack horses from
Ad Slocum's stack lot; wondering with grim irony what
the angular deputy's reactions would be at daybreak. Like
the sheriff, Ad, too, was a boot licker who knew which
side of his bread the butter had been smeared on.

The two horses cared for, Carr broke pack and carried
his tarp bed beneath Ad's buggy shed. He faced it toward
the dim outlines of the town and the jail, a hundred and
fifty yards away. He didn't trust Ad any more than he
trusted Bert Burton the sheriff. Ad was a violent-tempered
loudmouth who talked too much. Burton was a fat sloth
who owed his job to vicious old Ples Kendall.

Ples and his sons and the others had known that Carr
was now resigned from the Texas Rangers and taking up
law practice again. They would know he'd head for Marlinville to see his client, who had killed one of the Kendall
sons. Question was what old Ples would do now. Keep his
public promise to kill both of them before they reached
Salt Fork? Most likely. It wouldn't be the first time he'd
made known his intentions, and then followed through.

Carr held no illusions as to whether the old man would
keep his word that the prisoner and his lawyer would
never get to trial in Salt Fork. The jail was a death trap

5

for Jonathan Carr; his prisoner was the bait, and Carr knew it.

But he had given his word.

Right now the place probably was ringed with armed K Cross men, with Bert Burton sitting in the darkened interior with a sawed-off shotgun cradled across his fat lap.

Carr shrugged away the thought. He would have liked a cup of coffee, late though it was. He settled for a cigarette and went to sleep beneath the shed, midnight stars bright in the black bowl above the drabness of the west Texas horizon. . . .

Shortly before daybreak, Carr's Ranger-trained ears caught the faint vibrations of cautiously approaching footsteps. That would be Slocum, normally loud and grumbling, coming in to take care of his customers' horses. Mostly K Cross, Carr guessed wryly.

Carr had been asleep on his left side, six-shooter cuddled in his lax right hand—that much five years of trailing cow thieves and desperadoes in the rangers had done to his former habits of easy slumber.

Now he snapped open his eyes without moving otherwise and lay there with senses fully alert. Almost above him was outlined the angular deputy's gaunt figure. Slocum stood four feet away with a long-handled pitchfork gripped hard in his clamped fingers. For a man who had been creeping, his breath was coming hard in a long, even flow, his nostrils probably quivering as he stood in indecision.

Slocum's mind probably was saying yes, but his hands had refused to obey. He knew Jonathan Carr too well, knew that five killer outlaws were strung out down a relentless manhunting trail of the past five years.

Carr grinned and pushed himself up on an elbow, the .44 Colt aslant at the deputy's thin, elongated belly. He'd been counting upon Ad. A man walking into a death trap to get his client free needed information, and Slocum would supply it without being coerced—Ad, the loudmouth.

The muzzle of the .44 shifted its steady gaze from Ad Slocum's face and lined the bright spot that was a cheap badge pinned to the man's shirt front. Slocum said, *"Aggghhhh!"* and hurriedly dropped the deadly tined thing he'd been tempted to use on Carr. He backed away a step.

"Hold on now, Carr!" he blurted out, and backed up another step. "You got no call to throw a gun on me like that."

"No, not now," came the reply. "You'd have given your soul to have been able to make the lunge and then go running back to tell Ples Kendall how you did the job for him and protected his sons."

"I don't know what'n blazes you're talkin' about!"

"The inference is," Jonathan Carr said, "that I knew you wouldn't hurt me, Ad. I slept beneath your shed for safety. Nobody to get at my back, and an ear against the ground and to the front. What's Ples planning for me, Ad? I got word Duval is riding for him now. Is he one of them waiting around the jail?"

"I don't know what you're talkin' about, I tell you!"

Jonathan Carr came up to a sitting position on his blankets and his voice took on the well-known lash so many people remembered from the past, when he and his father were on a case in the old sod courtroom over in Salt Fork.

"Ad, I'm going to give you some damned good advice. Throw away that cheap, two-bit tin badge Bert Burton gave you. You've no business wearing it. Loudmouths like you who wangle one to bolster up their nerve usually end up getting killed. If you'll do that, and stop playing heel dog to Ples Kendall and his sons, you might live quite a few years longer."

"Look who's talkin'!" the stableman exploded jeeringly, and fell right into the trap. "The whole Kendall family swore they'd never let you take that dirt farmer hand to Salt Fork for trial, includin' Alma. So we'll just see how long somebody stays alive around here today."

Well, Ples Kendall was keeping his word.

Carr shoved the pistol into its sheath inside the cartridge belt coiled beside his pillow. Carefully folding the legs of his black broadcloth trousers, he pulled on soft knee-high boots by tugging at the outside finger loops and rose to his feet, buckling on the belt. One-half of the loops were filled with short cartridges for the .44 Colt six-shooter. The other half contained eight rounds for the .45-70 side-hammer Sharps rifle in his saddle scabbard.

Carr asked, "How are they planning to stop me, Ad?"

"You'll find out," Slocum said, glowering sullenly and fingering the badge on his shirt front as though the touch of it gave courage to the other words forming in his mind.

"Duval, probably," Carr mused aloud. "Even old Ples should be a bit hesitant about killing an ex-Ranger under half a dozen guns. At least I've been figuring that. He wouldn't want his precious sons expended. That leaves Duval and or Dale Hayden, their white-trash cousin."

Ad Slocum found his courage. He sneered at Carr. "Duval, you say? Why, you damn law-book Ranger, young Ed Kendall could let you an' Duval both pull a gun an' kill the two of you. Then we're goin' to take that dirt farmer hand outa jail an' string him—"

Jonathan Carr took two long steps forward and towered over the angular deputy. His mouth turned tight and unfriendly in the increasing light as he grasped Ad Slocum's unwashed shirt front in one hand. With the other he ripped the badge loose and tossed it aside, his brown eyes beginning to smoke.

"Now let me tell you something, you boot-licking son of a bitch," Carr said in quiet fury. "Lee Delaney became my client after he killed Luke Kendall for attacking his wife at my aunt's ranch down on Double Mountain River. I brought him into this country for safekeeping last spring, with a warning to Bert Burton what would happen if anything happened to Lee. You used him to haul your stack lot feed from the sheriff's fields. But I happen to know that his back has been cut to pieces by a blacksnake whip wielded by you and the sheriff. Ad, you'd better be pretty damned careful how you talk and what you do today!"

He pulled the man closer and shook him. "Where is that sheriff? Where are they all?"

He pushed the man away as though the touch had dirtied his hands. Slocum, now certain he was in no actual danger at the moment, found raging courage and gave tongue to it.

"Go find him your ownself, Carr! Ask me, and be damned to you. I'm not afraid of your gun or Ranger's badge any more. Neither will anybody else be after today. You won't git outa town alive with Delaney. If you do, neither of you'll ever make it past K Cross roundup wagons to Salt Fork, because by sundown you an' your preachin' dirt farmer will be dead."

He bent, fuming, and began to hunt around for the badge. He straightened with it in one hand and fumbled to pin it back on, the corners of his mouth quivering. He'd worn that badge of Burton's for almost two months, and loved the mild authority it carried. It had given him courage to tell Carr a thing or two right to his very face —and now he'd do it again.

"Alma Kendall is in town with two of her brothers, Ed and Link," the deputy said, his small dark eyes gleaming with savage satisfaction. "Dale Hayden is with 'em. They've been waitin' around three or four days for you to show up after the client who killed one of their brothers. Duval, you said? Duval, hell! Ed don't need 'im. He don't even need Link and Dale, mister."

Well, that cleared up that part of it anyhow. The jail wasn't ringed, and Carr now frowned at the thought. Old Ples must be pretty sure of his sons to play it like this. And Alma! Carr had no illusions about her, either.

"It won't work, Ad," Carr said softly to the deputy, and shook his head. "If that's the story they sent you to tell, you'd better think up another one. Ples and his men are here."

"But I tell you they ain't!" Slocum cried out vehemently. The man was almost begging to be believed. "He's got the fall roundup crew working on the county line, along the stagecoach road between here an' Salt Fork."

Carr returned the bedroll to his pack and then crossed to the short bench by the office wall, where Slocum kept soft rain water and basins and dirty towels for his trade. So that was how things shaped up? One of several plans came into his mind, one he thought might work. And that was contingent upon the old man and his K Cross crew not getting in on time.

That they would come was almost a certainty. He'd come and he'd bring men such as Duval and Jules Mac-Candless with him.

Carr drank thirstily from the night-cooled tin dipper, bathed his hands and face, drying them with a clean handkerchief. He retied the black string tie at the buttoned collar of his white shirt.

Strange, he thought with fleeting irony, how the years

had never changed his habit of wearing white shirts—
except nights when there was an undercover job to be
done. His father had been like that too. In courtrooms.

Slocum, gloweringly intent and now more uneasy than
ever because he'd been tricked into blabbing information,
shot him furtive glances and wondered how he could get
word to Alma and the others over in the lone hotel. He
threw more armfuls of maize roughage over the fence;
fall cut stuff he'd bought and hauled out of the sheriff's
own fields, aided by the mild-mannered dirt farmer who'd
turned killer when Luke Kendall turned rapist, and
then turned religious in jail. Just let Carr give him a gun
and see what happened! The roughage fell with a rustle
of leaves amid the outlines of converging horses and
Carr, thinking of Alma Kendall, moved away.

Ad had lived up to his reputation as a loudmouth and,
in doing so, faced Carr with a problem he'd never have
counted on: meeting the woman he'd once loved, backed
by two tough young brothers and a gunfighting cousin
named Dale Hayden.

Marlinville's lone café was a dim light in a sleep-
drugged street, the heavy-hipped widow not a stranger.
She was the one who cooked for the prisoner, who listened
to the talk of Sheriff Bert Burton, who had written Carr
regularly of how the man had been treated by Burton and
Ad Slocum.

Carr accepted the coffee cup from her, standing near
the stove, and then moved back from the end of the
short counter to one of three small tables. It put his back
to a wall and his eyes to the front door.

"What time does the sheriff usually come for Lee's
breakfast, Mrs. Long?" he asked the woman.

"Usually midmorning, because Bert is a very lazy man,
Mr. Carr. But lately he's been hanging around the jail
nights, expecting you to slip in and get Lee, poor fellow.
What do you suppose will happen to him?"

He said, "Lee? According to Ad Slocum, Ples Kendall
and his crew will take care of Lee, and me too, on the
way to Salt Fork today."

Leisurely footsteps, about four sets of them, were coming along the hard-packed dirt from the direction of the
town's lone squalid hotel. That would be Alma and her

two cocky brothers and Dale Hayden. Jonathan Carr thought, I'll know in a few moments now, and felt a sudden dread inside.

Mrs. Long was busy carving large slices of ham for breakfast. Carr sat sipping the bitter black coffee and waiting, finding a fleeting thought for the wonders of morning transmutation: a world changing from dark to gray in the drabness of the street outside.

In the dim glow of a lone soot-blackened lamp chimney his eyebrows had become a solid bar beneath a black hat much smaller of brim than the big ones worn by plainsmen who didn't have to run cattle—or wanted outlaws—through south brush country canyons. The hat was four-fingered into a sharp peak on top and the brim didn't quite hide the bleakly thoughtful cast of Jonathan Carr's prominent features. They looked shadowed and grim.

They'd all be saying, of course, that he'd deliberately turned in his badge in order to bait the Kendall clan and settle the thing with gunfire before the trial in Salt Fork courthouse. Like his father before him, he'd go to any lengths to free a client. He'd free a client and, at the same time, settle a five-year grudge old Ples held against him. He'd be fighting Alma Kendall.

He hadn't seen her since that wild day last spring in Salt Fork when he'd taken Delaney out of their kill-crazy hands and slapped Alma down into the dirt, threatening to kill Ed and Link, threatening to shoot their older brother Poke, the sheriff in Salt Fork. Poke, the eldest of the outfit had sat in his office in the courthouse and made no move to interfere as his sister and two younger brothers started in to lynch a helpless man and then riddle his body with lead.

Coffee cup in hand, Jonathan Carr sat waiting as she came in, followed by Link and Ed and the gaunt-eyed figure of their cousin, Dale Hayden.

Link was a dark-featured man of twenty-five, a fiery Kendall to the core and a bad man to meet when he'd had a few drinks. He hadn't been drinking this morning, and no matter what he might have felt at the prospect of throwing a gun against Jonathan Carr, it didn't show. He sat down at the counter and began to read aloud from a calendar on the wall back of the water jar. The picture on the calendar was that of Jesus.

Carr found himself studying Ed first. Ed was younger than Link by a year or two, tawny, blocky-shouldered. Cruel to horses, which he rode with filed spur rowels, Ed Kendall could laugh and joke with Link. Most of the time he was the quiet one who listened instead of talking. He'd be the one to watch if gunfire exploded this morning.

Carr dismissed him with that thought and only then let his bleak eyes cover the woman he once would have married. The change of five years was upon her, of even those past few months since that rage-filled day last spring. He had sensed it in her mannish stride, the swish of her duck riding skirt, the rattle of her spurs, the significantly harsh sound made by the slapping of her gauntlets beside Link's hat upon the counter.

In the determination to kill Lee Delaney, and possibly himself, she appeared to have dealt herself into a man's game; and he wondered if, when the showdown came, she could abide by a man's rules.

"Let's have some coffee here, Mrs. Long," Alma Kendall said, and pushed back at her russet hair. "I had a couple of drinks in my room last night to cut the boredom, and now I need some black coffee to cut their aftertaste this morning."

She'd be about twenty-eight now, Carr thought, and then wondered how he could ever forget. The lines around her once-soft mouth had changed and he found himself wondering if unmarried maturity or her more active role in the Kendall affairs had brought about the mutability of mind now displayed. It wasn't becoming; her mouth once had been soft and passionate and demanding.

Dale Hayden sat leaning forward, elbows on the counter, morose, his long spine curving in the habitual slouch of a tall man in the saddle. He paid no attention to sudden rough laughter between Link and Ed Kendall. He shoved back his wide-brim plains hat with its tall rounded peak that could swallow a man's face and ears. He ran a hand nervously across the sad droop of his sand-colored mustache.

He said to Alma, "He's got to show up here between now and noon. Unless he's got something foxy up his sleeve, he's damn near got to."

"He'll show," she replied in off-hand assurance.

"Sure, and probably with one of his ranger friends covering him with a badge and two guns."

"No, he'll come alone."

"You seem mighty certain, Alma."

"I know Jonathan a whole lot better than you do."

"Hell, you ought to," Link broke in and exploded with laughter. "He used to make love to you plenty." He whacked Ed on the back. Alma didn't appear to be disturbed at the insinuation.

She said quietly, "Lee Delaney worked for the Carr family before the war. He stayed behind with Miss Melissa until Jonathan's father came home. He was working on Miss Melissa's ranch when—well, when this trouble broke. It would be a matter of principle with Jonathan to come back and defend his aunt's hired hand."

"He'd better think about defending himself with a six-shooter," Hayden grunted morosely and patted his own weapon significantly. He looked over at Link for further confirmation of a previous arrangement between the two of them.

Link returned the glance of his angular cousin and laughed. Hayden was the poor white trash of the Kendall clan, and Link possessed a devilish, cruel proclivity for searching out men's weakness and putting the barbs in deep. Hayden, when not accepting occasional largesse at the Kendall ranch headquarters and the big house in Salt Fork, lived alone in a shack down in the Double Mountain breaks. There he had time to drink his raw moonshine whisky in morose solitude and to draw his gun and snap it at imaginary enemies, to brood over Alma Kendall and his own low position in the lordly Kendall clan, and to think of the two men he had killed and the brother that Jonathan Carr had shot five years before.

Link knew of these things and used them as barbs to be driven in cruelly. He laughed again and then winked at his brother Ed.

"Sure he'll show, Dale. When Jonathan pulled off his badge and decided to defend Lee Delaney in court, he pulled his Ranger protection with it. This morning you got a free hand for the first time in five years. But we won't have time to bury you today, cousin. Have to come back and do it later."

He went off into gleeful whoops and Carr thought,

watching Link. He's been getting away with it since he was a cocky young buck of sixteen. He's always known that any time he ever went in over his head he had behind him a crew of Kendall's K Cross punchers to pull him out. I've a hunch that Link is going to be in for a very unpleasant surprise one of these days.

"Link, you stop that kind of talk," Alma said sharply. "I want no killing in Marlinville today."

Link's prodding grin faded and his black eyes went agate hard. He sneered openly at his sister. "Sure you don't. No woman does, not after the gent in question was once engaged to marry her. But we're going to get that dirt farming son of a bitch, and I'm going to kill Jonathan too. You been thinkin' you got Pa and Poke under your thumb. You're going to find out in a damn little while that you ain't got Ed and me by the ear. Not yet, you ain't!"

At the stove Mrs. Long had lifted the frying pan and removed two eggs and placed them on a platter beside thick slices of smoked ham. Studiously concentrating her attention upon the food, she spoke in a barely controlled voice. "I'll have the coffee in just a minute, Miss Kendall," and added four hot biscuits from the oven.

She straightened, hesitated, and then picked up a saucer of butter. Carrying the platter in her other hand she went to the table where, in the dim light, Jonathan Carr sat with elbows on the oilcloth, something saturnine making a cast over his features. Alma turned slowly on the stool, and only then did she and her brothers and Dale Hayden become aware that somebody else was present in the little restaurant.

Link Kendall's nostrils pinched in and then flared warningly. His body went tense, but Jonathan Carr's biting voice stopped him cold.

"Not one move, Link. I always had the feeling that some day you'd talk loud at the wrong time, when the K Cross outfit wasn't around to keep you from getting your guts shot out."

"That's no way for a lawyer to talk, counsellor," Link grinned, his eyes weighing his chances. Carr's elbows were still on the table. "Or maybe you just been away from law books too long."

"A barrister's language level must be gauged by the

subject to whom he's speaking, Link. Mine seems to fit the occasion."

"An even break, Jonathan," Link Kendall said softly. "Just give me an even break and I won't need Ed and Dale, and you won't ever again need them law books."

Carr put down his cup. Mrs. Long had hastily backed away and turned to the stove. Jonathan Carr said harshly, "I never wanted it this way, but that's how the chips fall now. Get over your foolish ambition of trying to gun-rep yourself into a Texas Ranger's job, Link. As I told Ad Slocum this morning, you'll live longer not wearing a badge."

Hayden had stiffened and then slowly let his long curving spine slump again. Carr's right hand was out of sight beneath the table now, and Hayden was glad to let matters rest for the moment. One of his brothers hadn't been content to let matters rest, and he'd been buried over in the cemetery in Salt Fork these past five years. Carr had shot swiftly.

Hayden had waited five years. He could afford to wait a bit longer now.

Carr said, "That's more like it, Dale. Link grew up loud, but you're old enough to know better. You boys just slide those guns across the counter and let's hear them all drop on the floor back of it."

His right hand lifted above the edge of the table, gripping a walnut-handled six-shooter. He laid it on the brown-and-white checkered oilcloth to the right of his plate. It was like the oldtime cowmen who, sitting down to a high-stake poker game, often laid their guns on the table. No direct threat intended; merely a notice to the others that the game was to be played above the table.

That .44 Colt single-action had killed five Mexican and American outlaws during the past five years. It also had killed Dale Hayden's brother in a gunfight that had repped Jonathan Carr into the Texas Rangers against his wishes.

Chapter Two

WHEN THREE PISTOLS on the floor back of the counter had been retrieved by Mrs. Long and taken into a back room, Alma Kendall gave a laugh of relief and astonishment and rose from the stool. Without hesitation she came to Carr, seated herself, and sat there studying his face. She met his eyes with frank approval.

He hadn't been bleak and wary like this in the old days. He'd been the lawyer son of old "Judge" Carr, engaged to marry her, ready to take over the legal and financial ramifications of Ples Kendall's immense land and cattle empire in several counties.

And now it was all buried under hatred, overshadowed by a Texas Ranger's gun reputation.

The onrushing violence of events had moved in like a flood tide in a rocky canyon and left its high-water mark, dark and perhaps lonely, upon him; and also, she suddenly realized, upon her own restless, unhappy and unmarried life.

"Don't look so unfriendly, Jonathan," she laughed, glad to be with him again even on these terms.

"What reason would I have to feel other than wary, Alma?" he countered. "I've never been happy over how things got all twisted up between our people, but never took the time to cry over the spilled milk either. Now I'm here to take a client to trial in Salt Fork, to make certain he gets there alive. You appear to be here to keep a Kendall promise that neither he nor I will make it."

"You never spoke a truer word in your life, Jonathan," came quietly and unexpectedly from young Ed Kendall. He sat with a hand resting upon Link's strong shoulder. "We ain't forgot what happened over in Salt Fork last May: Luke dead on the ground from a shotgun blast Lee Delaney had hit him with; us with a rope around his damned neck; Poke sittin' in his office in the courthouse maybe a little upset about it, but still waitin' for us to

16

finish up the job over one of the bank's new rafters. Then you busted up across the flats on that roan hoss and slapped Alma down and had a gun on us."

How could you handle a man like young Ed Kendall? At Ed's age Carr hadn't killed a man; Ed had already killed one. Carr wondered why young Ed Kendall hadn't tried to throw a gun against him that day, but now he remembered that Ed hadn't yet downed his first man. Not then. But last summer at a Saturday-night dance in Salt Fork—Ed had been cleared in court, of course.

A picture began to take shape in Jonathan Carr's mind. Ples Kendall either was certain young Ed could kill any man before his gun cleared leather, or he was coming in to back up their play.

Ed said gratingly, "Time ran out for you today when you came into Marlinville to pick up your client, Jonathan. You must have been crazy to think you could get away with it. You oughtta know the old man better than that."

Carr answered softly, "I gave Ad Slocum some good advice this morning, Ed. A bit of it won't hurt you either. Wherever your father is, get your horse and ride out to him. Tell Ples I want no trouble because of what happened five years ago, or what happened last May over in Salt Fork. You better stay out there with him, Ed."

"Uh-uh." Ed suddenly grinned. "I'll stay. You can't keep us here all day, not with the old man probably comin' in. You were a fool to come back here, Jonathan, but the old man knew you'd keep your word. You got our guns, but we got you just where we want you."

Alma Kendall spoke sharply. The woman in her had been wondering if Jonathan Carr had changed as much as his appearance indicated. It was hard to tell at the moment, because he'd grown a heavy dark brown mustache that made him look older than thirty-one.

"Ed's right about what they intend to do, Jonathan, but he's wrong about my part of it," she stated. "I came here to try and prevent the very thing they're planning to do to you and Lee. But the only way out for you is to give up this mad idea of taking Lee Delaney back to Salt Fork and defending him during his trial, because I know what is going to happen."

"I knew it," Link Kendall almost murmured, looking

at his sister. "I had a hunch all along, the way she's been acting."

Carr glanced dryly at the three men seated at the counter and said in an equally dry voice, "I can't understand why Poke didn't come along, too. Still in his office in the new courthouse in Salt Fork, or couldn't he stomach this attempt at cold-bloded murder?"

"Poke's prowling the bluffs on the other side of Salt Fork with a long glass," Alma Kendall stated simply. "Pa's not taking any chances that you get through, Jonathan."

Mrs. Long brought their coffee cups, stopping to lean over and blow out the smoky wick lamp. Gray dawn outside filtered in and seemed to lighten the place. A few flies, sleeping on the ceiling, came alive. The street outside was deserted. People were staying inside on this day when the Kendalls were in town, ready for the kill.

Carr hadn't answered Alma's information about Poke.

She said, "I'm not quite sure, Jonathan, but I thought I saw a question in those unfriendly eyes a few moments ago."

"So?" he murmured and began to eat. Mrs. Long was carrying coffee cups to the three men at the counter.

"The drinks in my room last night. Dale wasn't with me, no matter how much people speculate about Kendall's wild, unmarried daughter."

Link Kendall looked at Hayden and nudged Ed in the ribs and haw-hawed, appreciating the unconscious barb. Hayden sighed, "Ah, the hell with it," tiredly, as though his nerves were too finely drawn and he was weary of the whole backwash of expectancy. He was accustomed to drinking alone and brooding, he was aware of the speculation regarding his hopes toward Alma, and as for Link— he knew that one day he was going to throw a gun against his cousin and kill him.

Alma leaned forward intently toward Carr, breasts tight and firm beneath a man's blue shirt, her light cobalt eyes sincere. In that moment, to Jonathan Carr, she was as beautiful as she had been a long time ago—beautiful and in love and not hardened enough to attempt a lynch job.

She smelled of soap and he pictured her in her hotel room, naked to the waist, standing before a mirror and laving herself clean before breakfast. He saw it in his mind, and it stirred up again the hot blood of old memories he hadn't been able to keep buried.

She knew she had stirred him and it caused her to laugh warmly, and she wanted him to know that the old feeling between them had not died. "I know. Laura Beecroft is in Salt Fork with her parents, staying at your aunt's house during court term. You haven't seen her in two years now, have you, Jonathan?"

He put down his fork and looked at her, and the thought came to him that it was better to yank out a bad tooth with a single wrench than to have it start festering again. He said, "No, Alma. But I made a deal with Porter Beecroft. I agreed to resign from the Rangers and return to law practice if he'd come from Fort Worth to Salt Fork and help me with Lee's defense."

"You what?" she cried out angrily. "Porter has been managing Ples's financial and legal interests in Fort Worth, and now he's giving that up to get you as the son-in-law he and Judge Carr always wanted?" Her eyes, so soft and appealing moments before, now hardened in quick fury. She became again the woman he'd slapped down hard into the dirt the day he rescued Lee Delaney from Kendall hatred. "And she's been waiting meekly all this time, hasn't she?"

"I don't know," he shrugged. "I haven't seen her in two years. But I wrote her I'd see her in Salt Fork the day before court convenes. I think she'll be able to read between the lines."

"And I came here to try to save your life!" She drew in a long breath, fought for self-control and grasped it firmly. "I came here to try and save your life, knowing that the whole Texas plains country is waiting for Delaney's wife to go on the witness stand and tell how a Kendall raped her in a moment of drunken lust. And now—"

She came to her feet abruptly, adjusting the blue bandana around her russet hair as she rose, her hands jerking hard at the back knot. Hot fury of the kind he remembered lay naked in her eyes.

"You're not going to get away with it, Jonathan," she said in a deadly quiet voice. "Five years ago your father won a land case against us and broke the friendly ties between our families. I never thought you to be a vindictive man, waiting to take it out on us because I broke my engagement to you. I see everything now."

"You don't see anything, Alma," he answered her harshly.

She ignored him and jerked her head for her two brothers and Dale Hayden to move toward the front door. In front of them she turned and gave him a piercing look. Carr saw Ed grinning slyly.

"If you leave with Delaney today you're a dead man. Well, Jonathan?"

"Keep Hayden and your two brothers on a leash, Alma," Carr answered curtly. "I'm taking my client to Salt Fork and defending him there in court tomorrow. Tell Ples that if K Cross tries to stop me, I'll put guns in the prisoner's hands and help him to do some defending of his own."

Back at Ad Slocum's small livery, Carr laid aside his food package and filled his canteen from the deputy's rain water barrel.

Carr went under Slocum's buggy shed to his only rental hack and lashed bedroll and a metal trunk containing long-unused law books—with certain passages carefully underlined—in the splintery bed back of the spring seat. Slocum came walking by bent upon some errand, his angry eyes whipping sidewise. He nerved himself to explosive protest, remembered his loud talk and two hands gripping his shirt front, and wordlessly went for his span of rental duns.

Come to think of it, it would be better that way. In case of a running gunfight, Carr would have less chance of escaping pursuit with his damned dirt farmer client.

While Slocum harnessed the duns, Carr saddled his own roan and took some extra guns from his pack. He neck-roped the roan to the back of the hack, put two shotguns up in the seat, and slung a repeating rifle in its boot within reach of driver or passenger.

Slocum came back presently with the lines in his hands, made the team straddle the tongue, and went around to hook up the tongue yoke. He saw the guns in the seat and a cold fear came into him at the thought that he himself might be facing those same guns before the day was out. He'd been careful, after Carr went to the restaurant, not to belt on his own weapon, and now he spoke in a surprisingly friendly tone of voice.

"That dirt farmer helped me haul in the feed from the sheriff's fields, all right, Carr," he admitted and raised the hack tongue, guiding it through the yoke ring. "But don't blame me. It was Bert's idea. He said as how Lee was tired sittin' in a cell anyhow."

He went down behind a dun's stifle joints, bending to hook the inside traces, backed out and handed the lines to Jonathan Carr. When the team was fully hooked up and ready to go, Carr, still without answering the man's weak attempt at a lie, stepped to a front wheel hub. He went over into the front seat, tall and almost gaunt, a droopy-mustached man who looked a little tired this morning.

Slocum stood looking up in sudden decision, a crafty glint in his mean eyes. "I'll take two hundred cash from you, Carr, just in case one of them prize duns gits hit today. You can git it back from me when you reach Salt Fork."

"Cut it out, Ad," Carr grunted, impatiently short. "If one of these duns gets hit Ples Kendall's men will do it. Collect from him."

He nodded curtly for Slocum to open the gate and then drove through while the deputy held it and stood glowering.

Carr rode stiffly in the spring seat, sitting a little forward on the edge because of the two shotguns barrel-to-stock in back of him. Behind the hack the chinless roan horse trotted along with still another weapon on the saddle; a long-range sidehammer Sharps equipped with a Civil War sniper's glass sight.

His bleak features held a gravity spawned by the knowledge that Alma and the others undoubtedly were back inside the café, watching, her two brothers and Hayden rearmed. And now that the chips were about to fall, he wondered if she'd raise or stand pat on her hand.

He now knew from Ad Slocum why Ples Kendall's fall roundup was a week later than usual, why the wagons were working in the vicinity of the coach road from Marlinville to Salt Fork. He could pretty well guess what Porter Beecroft, his father's former law partner, would be thinking, relinquishing the lucrative tenure of handling

Ples Kendall's affairs to gain a son-in-law and new law associate in the Fort Worth office. Carr had been amazed when Beecroft accepted his own offer.

That was one thing upon which Carr had not cared to speculate. His father had wanted him to marry Laura, had objected with rare vehemence to his marriage with Alma. But Alma had been all fire and passion and Laura had been so—so damned meek!

Then violence had split apart the respective worlds of the Kendalls and the Carrs, and as an aftermath of that violence Jonathan had killed a man and gone into the Rangers. He'd shut out the other life, drawn a curtain across it and away from Laura Beecroft.

Luck forced a man's reluctant footsteps along a trail he sometimes didn't wish to travel. But when his brain had been deluged enough with the passing of time each month, and the months grew into years, it always made the thought of turning back a little too difficult to attempt.

It had gone on that way until Luke Kendall raped a woman at Miss Melissa Carr's ranch and was killed, and it had forcibly thrown Jonathan back along the road he never would have traveled otherwise.

Carr spun up briskly in front of the crude, flat-topped jail and, feet braced, lifted himself erect with the lines as the trotting duns came to an abrupt halt before the door.

Marlin was one of five newly created counties surrounding Salt Fork on the broad expanse of west Texas; each with its own Kendall-elected sheriff and, sometimes, a slouchy deputy or two such as Slocum. All judicial matters were handled in the newly built two-story courthouse of red sandstone twenty-eight miles west of Bert Burton's makeshift jail.

Ples Kendall's holdings comprised five hundred and forty sections of K Cross land in all five counties, and Burton was another county sheriff who owed his job to the iron-handed old man's largesse.

Burton, his heavy stomach soured from drinking coffee most of the night, was in the small office when Jonathan Carr wheeled up in Ad Slocum's rental hack. Sight of it caused the sheriff to scowl uneasily through red-rimmed eyes. An inherently lazy man, his fields and few head of cattle handled by K Cross men, Burton hadn't been getting his usual amount of sleep these past few nights. He'd been afraid to be away from the jail, knowing that Carr was coming.

He turned his shaggy head and spoke warningly to one of the two tiny cells, to the dim outlines of a big man sitting serenely on a bunk; to the man he'd kept alive since late spring because he himself knew Carr and wanted to stay alive. "You heard what I said before, Lee. One word to that damn ex-Ranger out there about me an' Ad layin' on the whip an' you'll be awful sorry, by God!"

He would never forget the cold, grim warning from Jonathan Carr the day he had brought Delaney, face battered and swollen, from Salt Fork and lodged him in jail for safekeeping away from Salt Fork. He'd gone with a frantic plea to old Ples not to harm the prisoner, and Ples had nodded assent while the crow's feet wrinkled deeper around his piercing eyes.

"We'll wait, Bert. I've got a five-year score to settle with that lawyer and we'll get them both when the time comes."

That time had come today, the sheriff knew, but the cold fear of Carr's words had been etched into his brain for months until they seared deep.

I hold you personally responsible for Lee Delaney's life, Burton. If he loses it to the Kendalls in your jail, then you'll lose yours too.

Burton swung open the slab iron front door, the long months of resentful brooding coming to a barely controlled boil. Hating Jonathan Carr as he had never hated a man, wanting to gloat but afraid to, he'd been expecting Carr every night these past few nights, while Ad Slocum kept a fast horse saddled at his shack to take the word to Ples Kendall at his roundup wagons. But Carr had come in broad daylight to take his man to trial, and something sardonically incongruous about it enraged the red-eyed sheriff all the more.

Could it be possible that all the whispered speculations were true, that the ex-Ranger knew Ples Kendall was out to get him and was going to kill the old Comanche-fighter and his sons? Was it possible this thing could happen and several sheriffs, including Burton, be sent packing?

Ad Slocum, damn his loud mouth, probably had been blurting; Ad talked too much.

Bert Burton reassured himself the thing wasn't possible. But he stood there in the opened doorway of his small jail, the rage of a helpless man in his sloth frame, watching balefully as Jonathan Carr got down and inspected the lashings of tarp bedroll and a metal trunk lashed in back.

The sheriff three-fingered his stomach with dirt-grimed nails and did his best, an outward bluster, to let the tall man know he wasn't afraid of him—not any more.

"Damn it, Carr! I been up night an' day for six nights waiting for you to come get this dirt farmer. You thought I couldn't keep him alive, didn't you? Well," he grunted, "he is."

Carr turned from an inspection of the lashings and let his brown eyes play over the short figure in the doorway. Burton looked as though he hadn't shaved in a week, and no telling when he'd had a bath.

"So I heard," he said and moved forward. "Six days and nights without sleep. Takes a good lawman to stay awake that long to protect a prisoner."

"Damn it, I didn't say that!" Burton shouted at him in helpless rage and yet with the old fear sucking hard at his blustering courage. He'd warned Lee Delaney not to talk, but forgotten the blacksnake whip. It lay coiled beside the cold coffee pot on his desk. "But you didn't have to keep me on edge like this. You coulda sent me word . . ."

Futility hit him hard, and he let the words trail off into a rumble, knowing this man and how much he feared him. He knew Carr hadn't sent him word because it would have meant a night ambush by "parties unknown."

In his mind, a thousand times during the past few months, he'd stood in this very doorway of his jail and shotgunned Jonathan Carr into the dirt as he walked toward him. The same way that damn dirt farmer hand of Miss Melissa Carr had killed Luke Kendall. Now Carr was here and Burton moved back to let the tall man bend his head slightly to enter.

He shook hands with an angry grunting noise through his nose, all he dared muster, knowing Carr read his thoughts and held him in contempt. Through the open doorway he saw Alma Kendall, a bright blue cloth around her russet hair, standing in front of Mrs. Long's café with her two brothers and the gaunt figure of Dale Hayden. The woman held a hand shading over her eyes, looking intently along the road that led away north and west toward Salt Fork.

Burton's heart gave a sudden leap at the implication. He wanted to run out and himself take a look along the stagecoach road, but didn't dare at the moment. But he knew she was expecting old Ples and his dog loyal foreman Jules MacCandless and some of the K Cross roundup crew. The old Comanche-fighting prairie wolf hadn't waited. He had done some figuring of his own and was coming in to see that none of his three wolf cubs got killed.

Burton's hands trembled slightly as he turned from the doorway. Carr was leaning over and picking up a big cell key. He appeared not to notice the coiled blacksnake whip from Ad Slocum's livery on the desk. Distant shouts came from somewhere and both men looked out. The morning sun fingered Ad Slocum loping hard toward the café on his horse, gunbelt on and a rifle scabbard tied on his saddle. Ad wheeled, waved an arm importantly to Alma and her brothers, and spurred away at a dead run along the Salt Fork road. Strangely enough, Burton felt a sneer come up unbidden. Ad, the loudmouth.

Ever since he'd made Ad a deputy, quite a lot of people had been saying with an insight born of long acquaintance, that Ad just wasn't going to be happy until he'd used that badge to kill himself a man. Link Kendall in particular had made life miserable for the fuming deputy with his biting jeers.

Carr went to the cell, in which stood a powerfully muscled man of about forty-three with broad features and a pair of eyes that couldn't be read well at first glance. Delaney's large hands, resting against the upright cell bars, showed as many rope burns as scars from saw and ax and plow handle. Those hands had bulldogged a steer faster than any man in the country. They'd cooked meals for ranch hands and even for Miss Melissa on occasion. And they'd used the shotgun that had put Luke Kendall down into the dirt, dead, right in front of Luke's still unfinished bank building.

Carr opened the door and felt a hand like an iron

clamp grasp his own in silent greeting, but not for a moment had he let his eyes stray from Burton. If the sheriff could summon the courage, he'd kill from behind without compunction. Ples Kendall expected it of him.

"It's good to see you again, Jonathan," Lee Delaney said with a smile that made his eyes easy to read now. "But I've been very much worried about my wife. Is she all right, Jonathan?"

"Hidden but perfectly safe, Lee," Jonathan Carr nodded. "She'll be produced tomorrow."

"In court?" Delaney's eyes clouded. He squared his massive shoulders and shook his uncut locks. He said earnestly, "Jonathan, I'm going to ask a favor of you. I don't want her on the witness stand in my defense."

"She'll be well protected; even Ples wouldn't try anything as rank as that."

"I know, but I'm afraid you don't understand. I've turned Christian since I killed a man."

"Later, Lee. We may have some trouble in a few minutes. I think Ples Kendall and his outfit are riding in from the roundup, and I'll give you one good guess why: they don't want you in court any more than you want your wife on the witness stand. You might go free, and therefore they're coming in to do the job in the Kendalls' usual way."

He looked at the sheriff and said to Delaney, "Lee, step outside and get those two shotguns and rifle out of the hack, while I watch this rotten example of a law officer. Bring in that sniper's Sharps and saddlebags full of ammunition, and the canteen. If Ples and his outfit try to lay siege to this jail I'll drop any man of them who shows his head within three hundred yards."

"Now look here, Carr—" Burton cried, and threw a frantic glance toward the door and escape.

Carr, however, paid him no heed. Delaney's astonishing words came with the calm serenity of a man whose mind long had been made up. "I'm grateful but sorry, Jonathan. I've had time to think these past few months, and it's brought on a change of outlook. I've known since the day I killed poor Luke Kendall that I'd have to pay the penalty here, and then a bigger one after I'm gone. My wife is more than twenty years younger than myself, young enough to take up life again over in Louisiana. I can't let you sacrifice yourself for me here today. Alma Kendall visited me just last evening and told me there'd been too much killing already, and I agree with her. I would have written you these things except that the sheriff has not allowed me to write or to receive mail."

Burton stood in uncertainty within three feet of them, new courage in his eyes, feeding the foul residue of his months of fear. He didn't have to be afraid now.

"That damn' killer is lyin', Carr!" he blustered. "He—"

Jonathan Carr hit him. He slammed a left-handed blow into the sheriff's middle and then another under the chin to straighten him up. He smashed his right hand hard at the man's hated, unshaved face and sent him reeling backward on unsteady legs. Burton fell over the corner of his scarred desk and toppled to the floor. The wicked coils of the bullwhip thudded down on top of him and lay in a tangle of plaited leather across his flabby features.

Carr turned and looked at the calm, resigned face of the big man he had always respected in the past, but more so now. A man had to follow his own trails according to what his conscience told him. Carr had had this in mind when he entered the jail.

He grabbed Delaney by a shoulder and almost ran him at the front door of the jail. "Then get out of here quick, Lee. Get on my horse and run for it. The chinless roan is fresh and there's no horse in this country can catch his dust. Hit for New Orleans and I'll see that Ruby gets to you there."

"You'll never escape this town alive, Jonathan."

"I knew what I was doing. Walking into a trap, with you as the bait. Now get out of here fast, Lee. I guess I never really thought I'd need those law books to buck a man like Ples Kendall."

Delaney went. He ran out into the bright sunlight and snapped loose the slipknot Carr had so carefully tied in the roan's neckrope. He went up into leather with practiced ease. One of his big work-hardened hands reached down and jerked free the long-range Sharps sidehammer rifle.

The weapon described an arc as it soared through the air and fell softly on top of Carr's tarp bedroll back of the hack seat.

The man looked down at Jonathan Carr and his mouth widened in a smile Carr would never forget. "So long,

Jonathan, I'll never again use a gun against one of God's creatures. You'll hear from me."

He wheeled the fresh roan over hard, and it gave a tremendous leap forward. The tail of the man's faded shirt flew up, and upon Delaney's back Carr saw the brutally administered marks of the livery blacksnake whip.

A sudden splash of rapid gunfire began to hammer along the street. Carr heard Link Kendall yelling, his gun out and spanging frantically; it and two others. Of the three, Carr noted that only Ed Kendall was taking his time, aiming over a forearm and squeezing them off methodically. Carr saw Delaney lurch and then straighten in the saddle and pound on up the street, the hard running roan's sleek belly low above the ground. One of Ed's shots had paid off.

Then riders swept by the jail, led by Ad Slocum. They started to pull up. But a leonine figure astride a black horse, white beard flying, close on the heels of Slocum's horse, bellowed another cry for hot pursuit. The nine or ten riders spurred on down the dusty width that was the street. One was the gunman named Duval.

Ples Kendall jerked his panting black to a halt and then moved on toward the café, where his two sons and Dale Hayden stood waiting for him. Alma Kendall was running hard toward the jail where Jonathan Carr stood in the doorway, and her father's piercing bright eyes followed her with something indefinable in their brightening blue depths.

Carr was sitting in the seat of the hack, a cocked shotgun across his lap, when she arrived.

"Jonathan!" she cried, panting from lungs unused to the call of sudden pedestrian exertions. "You've got to get out of here quick. But where could you go now?"

She placed a hand on the front wheel and looked up at him and in her blue eyes, the deep flush of her tanned cheeks, he saw a woman's soul and the revived hopes once smashed along the trail of years. Her eyes, all anger vanished, were pleading with him.

"I told you I came here to try to save your life. But where can you go in a buggy before Jules MacCandless and the others get back? Ed shot Lee and he can't get far."

He said, "Over to Salt Fork to tell Porter Beecroft he

won't have to give up his tenure as legal and financial adviser to your father, Alma. Something," he added dryly, "that I imagine Porter will be relieved to hear."

"You'll never get there alive!" she cried out passionately.

"All depends upon how well Ples remembers the way I used to handle a long-range rifle. I'll get there."

"And after that?"

"To the Army telegraph at Camp Coke," he replied, shrugging. "I've found out within the past three minutes that I've been in service too long to return to law. Captain MacNab of the Rangers will wire me new orders to Camp Coke."

"And Laura? What will she say when you tell her of this sudden decision?"

Carr's shoulders shrugged again. "I'll find out the answer to that one, Alma, when I see her at Miss Melissa's house this afternoon."

He lifted his eyes above her head and shifted the cocked shotgun. The town was still quiet, except for a few people who had thrown aside caution and run out into the street to watch, standing in hushed little groups. There was no movement except three men striding along beside Ples Kendall's walking black horse; coming purposely, Link shoving fresh cartridges into his six-shooter.

"You better get inside the jail, Alma," Jonathan Carr suggested, and rose to his feet with the deadly shotgun crossed over her head. "There may be some trouble here. If there is, and Burton is up on his feet, keep his gun off my back. He's been daydreaming about it for months."

Instead, she grinned up at him and came over the hub of the left front wheel like a man stirruping himself into the saddle. The seat springs sagged lower as she snatched up the other shotgun, sat down beside him, and swung the twin muzzles toward the open door of Bert Burton's little jail.

Carr studied the bearded features of her approaching father. He could have sworn the old man was laughing silently at some joke known only to himself, and something about it made him uneasy.

Ples Kendall had sworn to kill Jonathan Carr when he came back to the Salt Fork country, and the old ex-Ranger was a man who kept his word.

Chapter Three

PLES KENDALL halted his favorite black saddler and sat there with both hands palmed over the saddle horn, a rugged old plainsman of about sixty who fought Comanches before the war, fought Yankees during the war, and fought Jonathan Carr and his father in court after the war, and lost a big land case. A faint breeze had begun to current along the swale on the road to the county seat, and an updraft of it swayed the tip of his white beard. A faint, brittle twinkle had appeared in his eyes. The wrinkles around them deepened as though he were squinting into the sun. A harsh sound came from within the jail and Bert Burton, thick-lipped mouth bloody, staggered into the doorway and stood there with a hand on the jamb to steady himself.

Link, standing warily with legs aspraddle, took one look at him and exploded with jeering laughter, slapping Ed hard on the back. He sobered and his black mustache began to skin slowly back over his white teeth in a grin of cruel satisfaction at sight of the sheriff's hard-hit mouth.

"Ed, I told Pa he shoulda put you in over here as sheriff instead of Bert, but he's got other plans for you and Laura Beecroft. But you just wait until I get my appointment into the Rangers. Then we'll see something."

Ed looked up at Jonathan Carr and grinned the sly feline grin he'd worn in the café, and nudged his distant cousin Hayden, whose morose expression did not change.

So that, Carr thought swiftly, was the way things were shaping up? A woman could change much during two years of waiting, and now he felt like an utter fool for having written Laura that letter.

"Howdy, Jonathan," Ples Kendall said amiably and leaned forward to rest more of his weight upon the saddlehorn. "Been a long time since we met, eh?"

"Five years ago this month," Carr nodded, warily wondering why the old man wasn't making a short, wild fight

30

of it and getting the job over with. He was probably concerned about his sons, waiting for the time when his men were present—including Duval, the ex-Ranger now turned gunman. "In the old sod courthouse over in Salt Fork, fall term of district court. Miss Melissa Carr versus Ples Kendall."

"Uh-huh," the old man said wryly and even grinned faintly. "Cost me forty sections of good land. So you got your client free, huh?"

"It's better this way. If we'd barred ourselves in the jail somebody would have got killed, and I don't want that."

"I recollect how handy you used to be with a long gun. You reckon Lee'll make it on your horse?"

"Hard to say, Ples. The roan might step into a prairie dog hole or break a leg buck jumping into a gully. Lee's a heavy man, you know, and he's been hit. Jules and his men could run him in relays if they could get fresh horses."

Ples Kendall straightened his spare, wiry frame in the saddle and lifted a hand from the round horn to stroke at his white beard. He said mildly, "Jules MacCandless knows all that, I reckon. Plenty of fresh horses at the roundup cavvy, other side of the Brazos. They'll git him. All taken care of just like I said it would be."

Carr's eyes had begun to turn icy from a warning bell whiplashing signals to his brain. Could it be possible, now that Lee was assumed certain to be dead within a matter of time, the old man was going to call off his dogs? Or was he afraid with a pioneer's fear of a shotgun that one of his family would go down in the dirt the way another son, Luke, had fallen?

Carr said almost softly, "You swore I'd never get to Salt Fork alive with my client, Ples. Maybe you kept your word insofar as Lee is concerned. How about the rest of it? Right now?"

Ples Kendall looked down at the twin muzzles now lying almost carelessly across Jonathan Carr's left arm. A yellow-toothed grin enchanced the depth of the wrinkles around the old plainsman's eyes. Something about the way he looked at his daughter rang the signal bell again, but the old man seemed in a sudden benevolent humor.

"Looks like you an' Alma got back together again,

Jonathan, so there's nothin' more to be said. The road's open to Salt Fork. You two git on out in the hack."

He reined over, heading for the café and coffee, leaving his two sons baffled and disappointed. Young Ed turned away like a puma with nostrils twitching.

Carr clucked to the two duns. Dust sprang up and left a faint wake in the breeze as the hack went out of town behind the briskly trotting team. Bert Burton's baleful gaze followed them, murder in the man's small eyes.

The sheriff, too, was a baffled man.

This sudden turn of events had caught Jonathan Carr completely off guard. He'd taken Laura Beecroft for granted, a little ashamed to be sure, but knowing she'd wait for him. Now it appeared that Ed Kendall had begun to pay court to her.

And the one thing that burned hard into Carr's mind was the memory of how Judge Carr had objected to his son's engagement to Alma Kendall, of Ples Kendall's vitriolic rage when he found out about that part of it.

But Judge Carr was dead, and old Ples was almost thrusting his daughter with Jonathan on the trip to Salt Fork—taking a fiendish delight in revenge upon the judge's memory.

Carr's black thoughts at the unexpected situation were interrupted as Alma Kendall tossed the two short-barrel weapons back on the tarp and looked at him, happy, relieved laughter deep in her cobalt eyes. "Jonathan! I'd never have believed it! Pa acting that way after all these years when he's taunted me so cruelly— But it's all past now, the old hatred gone. Let's forget it, and laugh the way we once did."

The hack crossed the swale, harness rattling, and the duns slowed to a walk up the slope coming out on the prairie once more. Carr put them to the trot again, his thoughts far ahead.

Shortly before noon the red sandstone bluffs of the Salt Fork of the Brazos came into view, an ugly red gash showing where building stones for the new courthouse had been quarried. Carr followed the winding road down into deep sand and the tire rims sank in a trickle of gyp water where inch-long fish flashed back and forth. A hundred yards downstream, beyond the opposite bank, a group of chinaberry trees threw a green mushroom of shade over the ground close by the bluff. Carr stopped the lightly sweating duns and let them drink.

The team pulled on up through deep ruts of soft sand deposited by the last rain floods, and Alma, riding beside Carr in silence, suddenly reached over and seized the lines from his hands.

"Dinnertime, Jonathan," she laughed, and swung the span off to the left toward the chinaberry clump. "Don't misunderstand me. I'm not trying to recapture the old days. I'm just so happy at Ples letting bygones be bygones that I could cry. And, besides, I'm hungry!"

She drove over and pulled up by the trees. Carr hub-tied the team and then helped her down, aware of the new hope and the man hunger she couldn't conceal from the old days, and he frowned inwardly in a fight against it. He'd have preferred to eat Mrs. Long's food as they made miles. Miss Melissa would be impatient to talk until at least suppertime.

Alma's strong hands had unlashed the tarp bedroll and spread it in the heavy shade of the chinaberry trees. He brought the canteen and food package, still silent as he had been most of the morning. She'd sensed this mood in him, had respected it, seemingly content merely to be with him once more.

That much you couldn't take away from a ranch woman, even though she should know that a broken and spliced rope never handled the same again.

A cool breeze flowed down the twisting course of the river bed and low above the thin trickle of water a large black buzzard, beaked head peering down and scaly white legs drawn back, soared on the drafts with a rocking motion of motionless wings. Across the shimmering expanse of dry sand, humped and twisted into grotesque mounds studded with dead cottonwoods, the top of the bluff point above the quarry was not more than two hundred yards away.

Alma had sat down on one end of the tarp bedroll cover and removed the blue bandana, shaking out her hair into a mass of russet color. She lay reclining, one long leg outstretched, top of a boot showing. Her breasts were tight against the blue shirt. She wanted him as badly as he fought the fire in himself.

"Why so thoughtful, Jonathan?" she bantered. "You hardly spoke a dozen times all morning. Worried about the boys running down Lee?"

"Naturally," he admitted. "Wouldn't you be, if you were in my position?"

"A few hours ago I would have given you a definite and unpleasantly truthful answer. Now I don't want even to think of anything connected with the past. I wronged you this morning when I accused you of wanting to take revenge upon us, and I knew when I said it I wasn't speaking the truth. I was angry, afraid for you, and I wanted to sting you a bit."

He crossed his booted feet and lowered himself into the sitting position cowpunchers and Texas Rangers always used when eating out in the open. He placed the damp canteen on the tarp between them and slid away the string from cold roast and biscuits wrapped in brown paper.

She said, "Were you serious this morning about going right back into Ranger service again, now that Lee's case is settled?" At his brief nod she asked him why.

"Habit, I guess, Alma," he answered. "They grow less flexible when a man has passed thirty."

"Fiddlesticks!" she retorted spiritedly. "What about your aunt, Miss Melissa? She's running fifty head of cattle to the section on the forty sections you and your father took away from Ples five years ago. Nobody to leave it to except you, since she's never married."

"Is that why you've adopted a go-to-hell attitude toward those who speculate upon your own unmarried status at twenty-eight?" he asked her bluntly. "Are you seeing in my peppery little aunt yourself in another thirty years?"

Her nostrils flared ever so perceptibly and he heard the intake of her breath, faint with warning anger. She pushed herself up to a sitting position, the moment and its invitation gone, buried under the inundation of a broken love of her own doing.

"Don't!" she said sharply, and he saw the edge of defensive defiance come into her eyes to cover the truthful hurt. "It doesn't become you, Jonathan, being cruel that way. When you slapped me last spring in Salt Fork, and stopped me from doing a horrible thing I'd have always regretted, I never hated you for it. The pain in my cheek was something pleasant to remember a long time afterward. So perhaps you have changed a little. Turned brittle and efficiently hard, knowing that no matter how long the time Laura would still be waiting for you because she's one of the meek. God pity her if she ever does marry Ed," she added bitterly. "He's a Kendall all the way through."

She took the cold food from his hand and let it fall laxly in her lap, making no effort to eat. She wasn't hungry now. She looked at him and spoke in the face of his awkward silence.

"All I wanted for today was just to forget everything for a little while, and perhaps to laugh in the carefree way we once did a long time ago."

"Things change, and cause people to change too. Five years is a long time, Alma."

"I know, Jonathan, and I'm just now beginning to see in you some of the fine-drawn cruelty I've witnessed in Link toward women who wanted to marry Kendall money and cattle. The way he led them to believe; the way, when he'd had all he wanted from them, he put the barbs in deep and twisted them with pleasure."

"What's this about him wanting into the Texas Rangers?" he broke in abruptly.

She didn't appear to have heard. She stared out across the river water and sand dunes. "It's not like the way Ed bloodies up the sides of a good horse with filed spur rowels, or wrenches their mouths into bloody foam. Ed's a horseman who demands everything from the mounts he rides. He does it without thinking, and hurts only a brute animal without the power to remember too much."

"But he's a Kendall, and you're already feeling sorry for Laura Beecroft. Shall we forget it? I'm truly sorry for what I said."

"I wonder," she mused and then smiled at him and tossed aside the food.

It was her invitation to come to her and before he could think he felt the blood begin to pound through his temples and the memories of that past came back to strike fire inside him. He put aside his own food and rose with a single cross-legged motion of his knees, forgetting Laura and the letter to her, forgetting everything except that he was back with Alma. Then he paused and looked away.

One of the duns had raised its head and stood with ears pointed, looking off downstream toward the bluffs above the quarry. Carr caught a quick glimpse of a rider dismounting from his horse, rifle in hand, as several others appeared. The man was Ad Slocum, and he was already dropping to one knee to steady his left elbow and get in a first shot ahead of the others.

Jonathan Carr made a twisting leap toward the hack and the Sharps rifle in the bed. Slocum's repeater cracked bitingly from the distance, and he heard the angular deputy's wild yell. Slocum had waited impatiently for weeks for this big moment, when he could use the protection of his badge to kill himself a man. Now he was in his glory.

His rifle smashed a second time as Carr leaped aside and a jagged yellow splinter whizzed through the air from a garish hole in the left sideboard of the hack. But Carr was already diving into the protective cover of the chinaberry trees. He rolled over twice and came up behind a small shrub mounded around the roots by the relentless hands of wind and water shifting the sands.

He caught a glimpse of Bert Burton, Link and Ed Kendall, Dale Hayden, and the massive form of Jules MacCandless, K Cross major-domo.

From the looks of things, Jules had caught up with Lee not too far out of Marlinville, and had returned with his men in time to pick up a vindictively raging sheriff.

Carr suddenly remembered the brittle twinkle in old Ples's bright eyes there in front of the jail, and he knew now that the Kendall patriarch must be laughing up his sleeve at both Carr and his own daughter. She'd mentioned something about her father taunting her. . . .

He turned to look for Alma and saw her just as, the other rifle in her hands, she fell prone beside him, her cobalt eyes ablaze with cold anger.

"Damn my father!" she cried out bitterly. "Damn him! He planned it this way the moment he saw me get into the hack with you, Jonathan. For five long years he's taunted me about the way Judge Carr never thought his only son should marry a Kendall woman. It's been gall to his soul, eating away at him like a malignant disease. Now he wants you dead in front of me so he can taunt me some more. Now you know where Link's cruelty comes from. Now you can see how bad Kendall blood really is!"

She snapped the repeater to her shoulder and began to lever it. Dust spurts jumped high from the edge of the bluff and drifted away like thin smoke from a dying campfire as two of the shots ricocheted. But the others were higher and a scream came from Ad Slocum's horse. Another scream, one of rage, came from the liveryman as the animal fell kicking. Slocum stood shaking his rifle above his head as Jonathan Carr caught him through the sniper's sight and drove a slug through the cheap tin badge wheedled from Bert Burton—a chance center hit, salted with the bitterness of irony.

Slocum crumpled across the writhing, kicking remains of his horse and for a few awful moments, while Link Kendall laughed jeeringly and big Jules MacCandless ran forward and grabbed at the dead man's booted ankles, the three small figures were one at the sharp edge of the river bluff. Then Jules MacCandless suddenly leaped back to get clear and save himself, just as the writhing horse toppled.

Horse and man went over, down sixty feet to where the great blocks of red sandstone had been pried out to build the new courthouse in Salt Fork. A thudding, rumbling crash welled up from below, followed by the void of a shockingly terrible silence.

Carr lay there with the suddenly warm barrel of the huge weapon in his hands; not sick—because this kind of thing had happened other times in the past when it was kill or be killed—yet with a dark question in his mind as to why. A loudmouth and a brutal man with a blacksnake whip, a tinsel-star deputy anxious to kill—yes. But had it been really necessary? Was there a slight chance that Ad actually had intended using the pitchfork?

He would never know the answers.

He felt Alma's ungloved fingers on his forearm and turned. She was searching his eyes for something, and she seemed to find it. She said softly, "Jonathan, Ples's men's horses were winded this morning when your roan fresh when they went after Lee Delaney. But Ad's horse was fresh too, and Lee was wounded and unarmed. Ad probably was the one who stretched out ahead of the pack and killed him while he was helpless, and then hurried on here to get himself a second dead man this morning."

"He's still down in that quarry under his horse," Carr said tonelessly.

"He shot at you first! And if it will make you feel any better, Jonathan, hitting Ad's horse was an accident for me. I was trying to kill him."

He twisted and reached down to the left side of his cartridge belt and the eight rounds of .45-70's there for the huge Sharps. He extracted nearly four inches of bright brass and dull lead from a loop and the breech clicked hard as it closed upon the long cartridge.

"Thanks," he said dryly, his eyes on the now deserted bluff. "I was aware of that, Alma."

"What's your next move? They'll circle you, and Poke should be somewhere close enough to hear the shots. I can't help you any more with a gun, Jonathan—not against my own kin."

"No," he answered and turned to look at her, "you can't fight your own people with a gun. But I can. Get in the hack and whip out of here and keep going to Salt Fork. Ples struck back hard at you this morning, and you can't stop your brothers and Jules now."

Strangely enough, Carr wasn't worried too much about them at the moment. He was thinking of Captain Mac-Nab. MacNab had warned him before leaving Austin that if he got into gun trouble such as this his previous service as a Ranger would mean nothing if they had to go after him.

He'd gotten into that trouble. He'd spilled a lawman's badge over the ragged edge of a red sandstone bluff, a full quarter-mile inside the Salt Fork County line, in Sheriff Poke Kendall's bailiwick.

Chapter Four

HALF A MILE west of where Jonathan Carr lay under angrily futile, sporadic gunfire near the stage road crossing, the Salt Fork of the Brazos made an abrupt bend northward toward the Spur and Matador range country higher on the plains. On the west side of the river, about nine miles due east of the new courthouse, the K Cross outfit, with chuck and hooligan wagons, was busy with roundup on that particular area of Ples Kendall's vast land holdings. Beef stuff was being cut out and thrown across another quicksand free ford about two miles above the stagecoach crossing. As always, each year, it would be held on Marlin county graze until time for the drive to Fort Worth, consultations between the old man and Porter Beecroft during Ples Kendall's semiannual week-long spree in the parlor houses.

The roundup, several days later than usual because of Jonathan Carr's expected appearance in Marlinville, was almost done. The vicious old man had played his cards carefully, drawn to a straight flush of triumph, and was getting ready to rake in the pot.

He could forget the forty sections of range pre-empted from under his beaked nose by Miss Melissa Carr; a small legal loophole overlooked by his lawyer Elmer Gibbens, now prosecuting attorney, but discovered by Jonathan Carr and his father. The land was lost these five years to Miss Melissa by virtue of a court decision, and that had been the end of the matter—at least for the time. Ples Kendall was a man who knew how to wait.

Carr was Miss Melissa's only heir, and Laura Beecroft was her godchild. If Carr could with impunity be killed outside of Ranger service, and young Ed should marry Laura, then, by hell, he'd outlive Miss Melissa another twenty years and *still* see that forty sections back in the Kendall clan! Such were his thoughts that morning.

The old man's black saddler was wet around the neck

39

and flanks from hard riding when he crossed the north ford of the river, past some of his own cattle, and spurred out on the plain again. He gigged the tired black into a fast lope toward the two wagons a quarter of a mile away.

Only three men were present in camp when he arrived and threw off. The aproned cook, busy in the shade of a large canvas fly stretched out back of the chuckwagon, looked up once and then went on mixing cornbread batter for a string of Dutch ovens already on glowing coals. The Mexican night wrangler, his long nocturnal vigil with the cavvy lost in dreams, slumbered in his tarp roll in the shade of the smaller hooligan wagon.

The third man was old Ples's eldest son by a first marriage, Poke Kendall, the sheriff of Salt Fork county. Poke was a heavily muscled man with a sweeping brown mustache, just passing into middle years, his temperament that of a milder man slowing down as his wild Kendall blood was cooled by the relentless hand of time. He sat on a canned-goods box with his broad back against the rim of the chuckwagon's left front wheel, holding a tin cup of unsweetened black coffee in one hand.

The sheriff's deep-set eyes went once to the black saddler and then returned, frowning, to his cup. It was bad enough the way young Ed cut the sides of his horses with filed spurs until old Pete the night wrangler sometimes had to doctor them for fly blows that turned into screw worms. But the old man usually almost babied that favorite black horse. The fact that he had left hours before daylight with Jules and the others and ridden to Marlinville, and was now back again, indicated that one and possibly two men were dead over there this morning.

Poke frowned again, not having liked any of this business from the very beginning. He had no stomach for planned murder.

The sheriff said nothing as his father's figure strode through the grass, spurs rattling. Sixty years old and as hard and tough as the day the two of them had migrated from Kentucky, where the Carrs also had lived a long time ago.

Ples took the clean tin cup the cook handed him and went to the blackened two-gallon coffee pot suspended over live coals, tilted it forward on the pail hook and poured. Poke knew his father too well. He'd ridden with him since he was a child, and he'd seen that look too many times on the old man's face. It had been there most of the time since Jonathan Carr had sent Ples word that he was resigning his commission in the Texas Rangers to defend Lee Delaney.

Since you were eleven you remembered these things, Poke Kendall thought moodily; when you stood before a porthole in a sod shanty not too many miles from this very place, blasting away at Comanche horsemen circling the corrals at a run and pin-cushioning cows and calves with arrows—blasting away with an old .69 Flintlock muzzleloader longer than an eleven-year-old was tall.

You remembered these things, and maybe that's why you grew up blindly devoted to the old devil, no matter some of the brutal things you'd had to help him do to build his cattle and land empire.

Poke sipped at his coffee again and wiped at his long mustaches as his father straightened and came toward him. He got up from the box and leaned against the side of the wagon box. Ples sat down with a sigh of relief and stretched out his long, leather-covered legs.

"That horse ain't used to rough handlin' like that, Pa," the sheriff finally spoke up. "You have to ride him *hard* that way to run down Jonathan?"

"Never mind," grunted his father and swallowed scalding coffee that would have seared Poke's mouth. "I'll ride my own horses."

"Jonathan get back this mornin' after Lee?"

"He got back. Why in the hell ain't you out ridin' the bluffs above the road with that long glass like I told you?"

"You had nine men with you—not countin' Jules, who don't pack a gun." Poke said to his father with a sharpness alien to his usual slow way of speaking. "What was Ed an' Link an' Dale doing all that time?" the sheriff demanded swiftly, dread of family tragedy hanging upon every word.

Old Ples grinned and wiped at his mouth and the sheriff relaxed. "Ed done all right. He put a forty-four in Lee's arm when he got away. That young one's more like me every day."

"Got away?" Poke's face was incredulous.

"Jonathan pulled one on us slick as any Comanche

horse thief. Brought that blue roan horse of his to the jail an' made Lee run for it. The boys cut down on him in the street, but Ed was the one who scored, shootin' slow an' easy across his arm like we used to do against Injun bucks."

Poke pushed his shoulder away from the boards of the chuckwagon and stared down at his father. "Well?" he snapped impatiently.

"Jonathan had already bashed up Bert's face for usin' a blacksnake whip on his client, an' then when Lee hit out of town he was ready to barricade himself in jail with a couple shotguns an' Winchesters."

"Lord!" Poke Kendall snorted disgustedly, vastly relieved, and yet the Kendall in him aghast at the way Carr had got his client away and then made the whole outfit back down.

He threw the contents of his cup on the grass and tossed it into the wreck pan near the tail box. It fell with a hard rattle and under the hooligan wagon Pedro Viejo—Old Pete—came out of his dreams and then lay perfectly still, listening. Everybody had really been on the short tempered edge these past few days.

Poke sneered openly and then went to his father's sweaty black saddler. He jerked almost savagely at the cinch buckle, loosed it, and then shook the saddle hard to free it and allow air circulation beneath the sweat-drenched blanket.

"Lord!" he snorted again, angrily.

The mess warping his father's mind was supposed to have been executed over across the county line, in Bert Burton's bailiwick, and let Burton have to answer to Captain Mac-Nab of the Texas Rangers. Now it would have to be done over here in Poke's own county. And Captain MacNab only recently had stopped by with a cold warning to all concerned in case of gunfire in Salt Fork.

Poke went back to the shade of the wagon fly and stood beneath it, hands on his hips. "Ride the bluffs, you say. I told you I wanted nothing to do with that dirty job over there, in case you bungled it and Jonathan got over into my county. Now just where in the hell is he, anyhow?"

Unruffled, the old man sat relaxed on the box and drank his coffee. "I waited around town till Jules an' Ad

Slocum got back alone. The boys are runnin' Lee in a slow circle, down toward Double Mountain breaks. I figure he's headin' back for Miss Melissa's ranch. But he didn't have no gun an' he was losin' blood. Jules told the boys to bury him down there, if they caught him before we can git back with some fresh horses from the cavvy here."

"Damnit," Poke fumed angrily. "You still ain't said what happened to Jonathan Carr!"

Old Ples rose to his feet and grinned, bearded lips skinned back over a paucity of front teeth, something malevolent in his blue eyes. He explained the part Alma had played and added, still grinning, "She's with him, horsin' around like a damned filly, an' Jules an' the rest of us are waitin' for him along the bluffs above the road. Go git your hoss, Poke. I'm goin' to settle an old score with Jonathan today, unless it's already settled. I want that damned daughter of mine to see him stretched out dead! I'm goin' to put the hooks into her today like no headstrong woman ever got 'em before!"

Poke Kendall swore again, obediently went for his horse, his brooding face dark. As the eldest son by many years, he'd always been closer to his father than his half-brothers and sister. But he could see now that the old man's long span of hard, often brutal way of fighting to exist and to build now was turning into something warped and twisted.

He mounted his big sorrel and, still scowling, rode back and sat waiting while his father retightened the girth and swung up. Ples led off through the grass, dry and brown. Poke rode in gloomy silence for a while and then finally spoke what was on his mind.

"Don't get me wrong, Pa. I've always backed you to the limit and I always will, no matter what comes up. I—"

"Glad you agree with me," his father cut in dryly.

"But," the sheriff went on doggedly, "you've made life hell enough for Alma the past five years without doing this to her now. And you've got to get it through your stubborn damn head that things are changing in Texas. Jonathan Carr alone has run down and killed five Texas outlaws who rode roughshod the way you're setting out to do. If you're not careful, you're going to get our whole Kendall family busted up and scattered or dead."

He knew as he spoke that it was useless to point out

these things to the leonine old man. Ples was blind to the encroaching shadows of things such as the new courthouse in Salt Fork, to men like wiry little MacNab of the Rangers, to the deadly qualities of Jonathan Carr's gun hand.

They rode south along the line of bluffs and circled around the bend to the east, the grim old man in front, heading toward the coach ford below.

Poke reined his horse over sharply to clear a large patch of prickly pear and then closed into position again like a cavalry sergeant following his commanding officer. He'd never wanted to be one of his father's menial sheriffs, any more than Luke, the playboy, had wanted to run the new Kendall bank, never finished after his death last spring. Link was different. He felt that a man wasn't a real man until he'd killed himself an hombre or two and served a hitch in the Rangers. His father and Elmer Gibbens had been trying to swing it, Poke fully aware it was solely for the purpose of allowing Link free rein to do Kendall killing jobs.

As for young Ed, Poke thought now, he hadn't needed any urging to play up to pretty Laura Beecroft on his many contrived trips to Forth Worth the past year. With Jonathan Carr out of the way today, once Ed and Laura were married they'd eventually inherit Miss Melissa's forty-section ranch.

Poke spat sour taste from his mouth and looked at his father and thought, He never gives up, never goes back a step once his word's been given. He never climbed the stairs to his invalid wife's room any more. But just let him get to Fort Worth after calf roundup in the spring, and beef roundup in the fall! Among the young girls in the parlor houses he was worse than many a sprier, more peppery man.

Ples Kendall suddenly jerked up the head of his tired black saddler. Rising to full height in the ox-bow stirrups, he lifted his left hand. "Listen. Hear that shootin' down there? I guess Jules an' the boys cornered him all right, just about the way I figured the time. C'mon, Poke!"

The black grunted as the spurs gigged in and set it off at a long swinging lope, Poke's own horse pounding along behind, the hoofbeats muffled in the grass. Ahead of them the stagecoach road bisected up a long incline from a quartermile gap in the bluffs, and down this they flung their horses. Poke recognized his brothers and the others, but noted that Ad Slocum was missing. The damn loud-mouth was probably sneaking around in the brush below, trying for a back shot.

He saw Alma come to her feet from among the china-berry trees, shout something to the men on the bluff, and then point toward him and old Ples. It caused the firing to cease at once.

Jonathan Carr got to his feet and began brushing sand from his dark broadcloth trousers. Instinctively, he shifted the Sharps to his left hand and let his right drop to the deadly Colt at his hip as Ples Kendall and his sheriff son rode up.

"Yore timing was a bit off, Ples," he informed the cattle baron harshly. "They didn't quite make it, and Ad Slocum is already dead. He went over the bluff into the quarry with his horse. Now call off those kill-crazy damned fools or I'll drop you out of the saddle. Call them off!"

Ples Kendall raised in the stirrups and sent forth a howling cry. Then he slumped down and palmed his hands over the horn and grinned at Carr. Carr glanced at Alma. She was looking up at her father, hatred reflecting from her cobalt eyes. Ples got down and loosed his saddle and began leading the panting black through soft sand to where ox and mule teams had struggled to haul out the crudely shaped blocks of red sandstone.

Poke Kendall had dismounted heavily and now stood with booted feet deep in the soft sand, his eyes reading a message in the unrolled tarp bed. They said, also, that he didn't give a damn what might have taken place there, one way or the other. His half-sister had never gotten over her romance with Jonathan Carr.

But if Carr had made love to Alma here, and now died at the hands of this tough bunch, the hellish taunts she'd suffered from her father would be small compared to what the old man would do to her in the future.

Poke spoke to Carr, being careful to keep the reins of his sorrel horse in his right hand. "Jonathan, Captain MacNab was through to see me a time back and he laid it on the line. If there's any shooting over this court trial, he's going to get the man responsible."

"There's been some shooting this morning, Poke," Carr pointed out.

"I know," the sheriff admitted. "Porter Beecroft will probably have to start earning some of the money the old man has been paying him. But you've just admitted killing Ad Slocum, a duly sworn deputy sheriff. I've got to arrest you."

"Now?" Carr asked him almost too softly.

"You think I'm a damn fool?" Salt Fork's sheriff snapped back, flushing. "You know I wouldn't take your gun now."

"No," Jonathan Carr agreed. "You won't be taking my gun now." He turned and tossed the heavy rifle over into the bed of the hack, and it broke the glass sight. Carr said harshly, "All I wanted, Poke, was to see that a man got a fair trial and wasn't shot dead through the window bars of your jail before he had a chance to get into a courtroom. Nothing more, and he'd have gone free when I put his wife on the witness stand. But you Kendalls knew it and were out to keep old Ples's promise that Lee would never stand trial. Now there's been some killing, and from the looks of things there'll be some more. This is a showdown, Poke, and you've got to decide which side you're on—the law's or your father's."

"I warned the old man," Poke Kendall almost murmured, shaking his head. "I told him he wasn't bucking a lawyer any more, that you've changed into a gunny who'd kill at the drop of a hat. I got enough worries on my mind about the hate between Alma and the old man, plus a sick step-mother in the big house at Salt Fork. Now I got to worry about Link. If five years in the Rangers has changed you into a hardcase, what do you suppose is going to happen to Link when *he* gets his appointment?"

His sorrel, neck outstretched against the pull of the reins, followed him toward the mutilated rubble of the quarry where another horse and a man lay dead among the rocks.

Poke Kendall had not made a direct answer to Jonathan Carr's blunt question. It meant that, come hell or flood water, he would stand or fall beside his father.

Carr stood in tight-lipped silence as Poke led away in the tracks of his father's horse. Jules MacCandless had found a way down, and now half-slid his horse into the river bed, followed by the others. They were coming back upriver to the quarry, Bert Burton riding in front beside the huge unarmed major-domo. Burton knew he had a job to do, and he was sick inside at the mere thought of doing it.

Carr had picked up the bedroll with its waterproof tarp covering, and put it back in the hack bed with the small metal trunk containing his law books. He saw the morose figure of Dale Hayden at a distance of eighty yards and noted a white piece of paper sticking out of the man's shirt pocket. Ed Kendall was laughing about something, and Carr made a note of comparison between the two. Hayden would kill sneakily now, he thought, and young Ed had certainly proved his quiet mettle that morning while Link and Dale Hayden shot wildly.

Carr remained by the hack in the shade of the chinaberry trees, waiting to see what would develop. The repeater Alma had used was in the hack bed, empty, and she looked as though she'd never touch a weapon again. There seemed to be some kind of a terrible dread inside of her and that she was helpless, in the face of her brothers and father, to do anything about it.

Carr held anything but a pristine desire to go over on the heels of the others and see what lay among the boulders that had tumbled down from above after the courthouse job was finished and the quarry abandoned. He'd shot to kill from instinctive reflexes because self came first and a man wanted to go on living. But the backwash of regret was there, and it could not be denied.

He turned, feeling Alma's cyes studying him. He again saw understanding, and also a faint hope that this terrible morning had brought them closer together.

She seemed to read the thoughts of a man who had killed almost ruthlessly because Texas law and conditions demanded that it be that way, and who now was feeling a remorse alien to that of a manhunter carrying a badge. With a gentleness he remembered from the past, she said, "Jonathan, you couldn't have done anything else. Deep inside of him, Ad Slocum was a shriveled little man making his one big attempt to be big in the eyes of Ples Kendall. He was kill-crazy; the same way Link is openly, the same way Ed is secretly, the same way Dale is. Put it out of your mind."

"He would have been scared weak afterward, enough to

give back that two-bit tin badge to Burton," he answered
her in harsh self-recrimination.

"Would he? In his mind you were as good as dead today and he wanted one big moment, one thing he could
brag about for the rest of his life. I heard little else from
him during the four days in Marlinville before you arrived. If you hadn't shot him today, the family of some
inoffensive man eventually would have been left to shift
for themselves. You know men like Ad. You've been ar-
resting them for five years."

Bert Burton had been sitting his horse at the mouth
of the quarry, cringing at the task facing him, aware that
he could expect little aid or sympathy from this hard
bunch as he nerved himself for what had to be done.
Alone, he'd have turned and ridden away. In front of the
old cattle baron who had put him into office, there was
no escape.

He'd given Ad the badge more to be rid of him than
anything else. But the big-mouth had talked loud to Carr
this morning, boasted about it all the way to the crossing,
jumped to get in the first shots, and now the fool was
there under his horse among the boulders.

Burton gave a final glance at Poke Kendall for succor,
but the sheriff stared back at him stonily while Link canted
his head at Ed and closed one eye in a wink. Burton gave
a tired sigh and swung his flabby weight to the ground.
He picked his way past a broken wagon, left abandoned
by Pedro Viejo and Ples Kendall's other Mexican team-
sters when the rock-hauling contract was finished and the
new courthouse a monument to judicial progress on the
plains.

One front wheel was down, smashed by a falling boulder
around which pack rats nested, the broad tire rim rusted
and twisted. And the weatherbeaten tongue had slewed
around and shoved its long, work-strained length up aslant
at the scarred face of the bluff, like a skeletal Indian's
half-buried finger pointing in accusation to the handiwork
of the Great Spirit desecrated by invading white men.

To the sound of suppressed guffaws between Link and
Ed, Burton worked his way up among the rock rubble,
balancing here and there with a hand on the side of a
boulder, reaching forward with a strangled grunt to tear
loose the badge, which once before this morning had

been jerked from the dead man's shirt. The fetid odor of horse blood choked into Burton's nostrils, and when he came down again his face was icy from sick sweat.

He sank weakly to rest on the base of the askew wagon tongue, toppled forward at the middle, and retched. It brought the tears to his eyes and for a moment it looked as though the fat sheriff was crying.

Link spurred over closer and sneered down at the abjectly shaking figure. "You and that loud-mouthed bastard up there! You was the gent who, when you got a few drinks, was goin' to shotgun Jonathan at the jail when he come for that dirt farmer, wasn't you? Ad braggin' all morning about how he nearly got him with a pitchfork—only he didn't. Dale talkin' loud and patting his six-shooter!"

He spat past the shoulder of his mount and wiped at his cruel mouth in disgust. He looked over at his father, at his older brother the sheriff, bold black eyes turned agate. "Well?" he almost snarled at them and jerked his head in the direction of the hack.

"No," Poke Kendall spoke up. "I won't have it, Link. If Jonathan goes down he'll take at least two of the family with him, and us that come out of it will be hauled into court by the Rangers."

Carr couldn't hear the rest of it. He saw the old man, ignoring Poke's coolheaded argument, speak to Jules Mac-Candless and then swing aboard the black. Whatever the decision, old Ples had made it for them all.

Jonathan Carr stood waiting as three sons and Dale Hayden followed Ples Kendall. They left Burton still sitting motionless on the wagon tongue, a bullet-smashed tin badge in one fat hand. The man had control of himself now.

"I'll get him for this," Bert Burton was saying ominously in the manner of a man who'd just discovered a long dormant courage. "If Carr gets out of this alive today, I'll get him if it's the last move I ever make in my life!"

Chapter Five

J ULES MacCANDLESS reined in close beside the old man he'd served long and faithfully. He heard Ples say, "Never mind that thing sittin' back there, Jules. I guess I shoulda put Ed in his place over in Marlinville last year except that I had other plans for the boy. You savvy what to do now?"

Jules nodded and pulled at his left ear. The whole left side of his dark face was whitened and scar-twisted from a fire; and though it had come from an oil lamp explosion, it was said around Texas that the huge quarter-breed Frenchman got it when Ples Kendall ordered him to ride through the wall of an Indian-set prairie fire blazing on a forty-mile front.

MacCandless lived only for the old man's orders and never carried a gun. He wore a dirty cap and light coat summers, and his shoes were awkward things of rawhide he himself cobblered. He'd once killed a man with a single blow of his mighty fist, and his past reputation as a fighter made the gun-packers keep out of his way; a big, quiet, human mastiff who never looked for trouble, never made a move without first getting the nod from the old man.

They rode up and Jules dismounted. Carr stood with his back to the hack, waiting, near Alma. Dale Hayden he dismissed for the moment, and he already knew that Poke wouldn't use a gun. Not today, anyhow. The buzzard came back again, up-current, still hunting, and Link Kendall saw it and laughed harshly.

"He's thankin' you for fixing up his dinner, Jonathan. But before we get through with you maybe he'll start thankin' us, too."

Alma said sharply, "Don't talk so stupidly, Link. It becomes you too much."

Carr looked up at Ples and spoke with no uncertainty edging his voice, his mind made up and ready; clicked into place and then locked tight like the breechblock on the side-hammer Sharps.

"You're a very hard man to convince, Ples," he said quietly.

"Could be," admitted the old man without moving his palmed hands from the saddlehorn. "If I hadn't been down to Fort Worth that day last spring when you took Delaney away from Alma an' my boys, you'd a knowed it a whole lot sooner, damn you!"

"Your son got exactly what he deserved. You'd have done the same thing in Lee's case, and under different circumstances you'd be the first to admit it."

"He was a Kendall, an' she was only a dirt farmer woman," the old man said with relentless malevolence. "She woulda got over it."

"Until the next time Luke got loaded up on Dale Hayden's raw whisky down in the breaks and rode by again. It cost him his life. It cost Ad Slocum and perhaps her husband their lives this morning. If that still hasn't convinced you, it'll cost you yours and another son or two right here, Ples!"

The deepened twinkle of crowfeet appeared around the old man's glittering blue eyes. Carr had seen them that brittle once before this morning and now waited, coldly alert. Ples rocked forward in the saddle and laughed, and except for the scattering of remaining teeth it might have been Link's lips skinning cruelly back.

"Wasn't I had my eyes open, I'd swear I could close 'em an' be listenin' to you an' your paw in court five years ago when you took my land for Miss Melissa. Same meanin'. Me makin' my own laws all my life. Well . . . "

"Poke," Carr spoke up, turning to appeal to the gloomy sheriff's common sense. "Can't you—"

"Jules, take him!" old Ples yelled piercingly.

Jonathan Carr spun back with his right hand flashing to his hip. His mind unlocked briefly, a flash that told him the vicious old man had counted upon Jules, knowing that Carr couldn't, and wouldn't, shoot down a gunless man.

Jules was already leaping with arms outspread, a big mastiff flying in to smother Carr down with his weight. Two hundred and twenty pounds of Frenchman and Indian and other mixed bloods smashed Carr back between the front and rear hack wheels, knocking his hat flying. The small of Carr's back struck the edge of the sideboard where Ad Slocum's rifle bullet had whistled in and splintered through, and the pain of it was like a man struck across the spine with a two-by-four.

Jules said, "Easy now, Jonathan," and almost broke Carr's right arm as he twisted it up behind and carefully shook the .44 Colt loose from Carr's paralyzed fingers. It dropped into the sand and Ed Kendall stopped his sister's dive as she grabbed for it. Carr heard her screaming and kicking as he held her and, above it, the cruel laughter of Link.

Poke Kendall dropped his hand to his own hip. He started forward and then saw Link, still in the saddle, bring forth from his saddlebag a pair of cavalry mittens and slip them on his hands. Poke relaxed and stepped back as Link lifted his right leg up over the saddlehorn and dropped lightly into the deep sand.

Link tightened the mittens, pulling them hard against the ends of his fingers. Jules had both arms locked behind Carr now, holding him as easily as a man working spring calves at a roundup fire. Carr stood quietly.

He said up to the old man astride the black saddler, "So it's going to be like that?"

"You heard what Poke's been sayin', ain't you?" Ples Kendall laughed dryly in satisfaction. "You oughta count yourself lucky he represents the law, because twenty year ago we didn't let 'em off so easy. Poke an' me—we just run 'em down an' strung 'em up an' let 'em kick. Link, git at him, boy!"

Link laughed and, measuring the distance with his eye, stepped in and swung a vicious blow against Jonathan Carr's stomach. It landed against hard, suddenly constricted muscles. It gave Carr the opportunity to raise his knee and lash out straight with a booted foot. The toe smashed into Link's crossed forearms and drove him backward four steps and finally down upon rump and hands in the sand.

"One final warning, Ples," Carr called coldly. "If Link lays another hand on me I'll kill him!"

"Will you now?" Old Ples grinned. "Go at him again, boy!"

Link pushed himself up out of the sand, all laughter kicked out of him, the uncontrollable, raging urge to kill blazing in his black eyes. He dived in and began to hammer Carr about the face and head, and now he knew fully what Alma had meant when she spoke of her brother's inherent streak of cruelty.

Carr tried to roll his head aside while the stoical Jules held him. He could hear Alma's screams while Ed held her, but he couldn't make out their meaning because pain was beginning to bunch his senses and herd them down into darkening caverns in his mind. He knew he was bleeding at the mouth and nose, and when Link, panting hard, finally stepped back and lashed forward with a boot into his midriff he hung like a grain sack in Jules MacCandless's big arms.

Carr tried weakly to straighten his knees, but gave up the effort. He sobbed in breath that was part red liquid and then chocked out a mouthful of blood upon the sand. He felt Jules shift his grip to another around Carr's middle, and he knew vaguely that the big man was looking up over him at Ples with a further question in his eyes.

Link had tossed aside the gloves and now stood breathing heavily and wiping at his face with a sleeve.

Ples Kendall gigged the black saddler a few steps closer and pulled up. "Can you hear me, Jonathan? Now I've got something to tell you, an' you damn well better listen close. I come into this country an' fought Comanches, me an' Poke, time you was born, him an eleven-year-old younker sidin' his old man. I got my land, an' we held it against Injuns an' cow thieves, until you an' your lawyer paw took forty sections of it away from us. Can you hear me?"

"I can hear you," Carr answered thickly.

"Good, because I ain't through. It was me got these new counties surveyed after the Injuns was druv out, helped float the bonds to build the new courthouse, an' then I put up the new red stone school without no outside help. But I still run what I own an' I don't give a damn about laws. Now you've threatened to kill my boy. I'm turnin' you loose, Jonathan, but with a warnin' that if you'll get on outa the country you can go. But if you ever set foot in Salt Fork again, you're a dead man!"

"He'll come back," Poke Kendall said with conviction.

"Sure, he'll come back." Link laughed. "But I'll fix that, Pa."

He reached down and withdrew his six-shooter from the sheath, tossing it into the air with a flamboyant gesture. It turned over twice and came down again with the long barrel grasped in Link's right hand. "Jules, put his right hand on the tire rim of that front wheel!" he ordered, suddenly harsh.

Jules ignored him and again looked a question at old Ples. Alma stood rigid in Ed's grip, her face beginning to change color. Nobody paid any heed to Bert Burton, sitting his horse a short distance away, plans forming in his mind.

"Well, Jules?" snapped Ples Kendall at MacCandless. "You still got one good ear left, ain't you? Do what the boy says! He'll make us a good rip-snortin' Ranger come one of these days."

Jules shifted Carr's sagging body around and obeyed. Carr felt the first blow of the square butted weapon on the back of his right hand and screamed once.

Link said, "I'll fix that," and struck him a glancing blow on the side of the head; and after that Jonathan Carr felt nothing more.

He came out of it to find himself stretched full-length on his back on the tarp bedroll in the deep shade of the chinaberry trees. His head was propped up, but he was too numb to open his eyes for a few moments. He heard the sharp, violent sound of cloth being ripped apart and he twisted his face to look. The place was deserted except for Alma Kendall and the dozing team of duns. She'd tossed aside her duck riding skirt and now stood only in white split petticoat, tearing part of it away from one of her long legs.

He saw her only in that part of his mind hazed by the brutal beating he had received. But the dark caverns were opening again. Carr turned his numbed face to the sky and closed his eyes in utter weariness. Her father had ordered this savage beating for the personal enjoyment of witnessing it, not to intimidate. He'd warned Carr never again to set foot in his home town, knowing it would make him all the more determined to return. Link had known it too, and smashed his gun hand.

Alma stepped into her riding skirt once more and belted it at her slim waist and came to him, kneeling, with the canteen in hand. He saw the compassion and sorrow in her eyes as she let him rinse his mouth and then drink.

"It's all right now, Jonathan," she told him softly, dousing water upon a strip of her underskirt. "They went on to the roundup wagon to eat dinner. Burton has gone back to Marlinville to send out a wagon to get Ad's body—he said."

"You didn't have to stay, Alma," he said thickly.

She began to bathe his face and the bruised spot where her brother's gun had struck the glancing blow. A bitter laugh broke from her.

"I'm glad you weren't able to hear it, Jonathan," she said.

"When I broke my engagement to you the day you and your father won the land case against us, Ples was quite proud of my loyalty. But in the years which followed he vented his hurt pride on me by taunts, knowing why I never married afterward. He told it all to me again just before they left, in front of Poke and the others, and told me to stay with you. He disavowed me, and he'll have Porter Beecroft draw up a new will leaving me nothing."

He struggled to a sitting position and sat with hands braced behind him. "He'll get over it. No man could do that to the only daughter in the family."

"You don't know my father!" she said with the same bitterness in her short laugh. "He means it. I'm taking the team on to Miss Melissa's house tonight while I get my things, and then tomorrow I'll take the morning stage out to Fort Worth. What are you going to do?"

He struggled to his feet and steadied himself and looked down at her. She seemed to know the answer before he spoke. "I'm going on in to see Miss Melissa and Porter Beecroft. I don't know what Ples is going to say or do when he finds out that Porter had agreed to leave him and help me with the defense. He might need some help from me."

Later, sitting beside her while she drove, they pulled out upon a small rise in the endless prairie and saw the red courthouse over there on another rise, square white cupola pointing up sharply into the cloudless sky.

Half a mile east of town she swung the team to the left, skirting the new schoolhouse to the south side, working them down a road knifed through a growth of young mesquite bushes. Alma drove on west again, down a lane to where a red barn and sheds sat back from the white house where Miss Melissa Carr lived alone.

Laura and her parents were there, and he thought again of the letter he had written her, of finding out later she was being paid court by Ed Kendall. Two years now; you couldn't blame a woman like her for not waiting any longer. Not even a meek woman such as Laura Beecroft.

At the white corral gate Jonathan Carr got stiffly down with the aid of his good hand, the other hanging bandaged in a sling hung from his neck. She would take the duns and hack and go on home to pack her things and then come back to Miss Melissa.

He said slowly, "Alma, I never thought that such a thing as this could happen. Ples knew I'd come on here because I'm another man who doesn't break his word. But I'm going to break it this once and disappoint him. Instead of killing Link as I said I would, I'm going to get hold of a horse and get out tonight to Camp Coke and let things gradually quiet quiet down again."

"You won't have to, Jonathan."

"Leave? Of course I shall."

"Get a horse, I mean. Look over there under the shed!"

Carr turned and glanced to where she pointed. Under Miss Melissa's barn shed, the saddle bloody, stood the played-out figure of the chinless roan horse Lee Delaney had ridden at a hard run out of Marlinville eight hours before.

Carr stood by the white swing gate for a few moments, holding between thumb and forefinger a brown paper cigarette, one of many she'd been fashioning for him on the drive from Salt Fork crossing. He watched the faint dust wake of a dead man's hack and team as the duns trotted up the lane north past Miss Melissa's comfortable home. The straight-backed woman driving them knew that things never again could be the same between them as in the past. Time and events had changed them both too much.

He dropped the butt of the cigarette and, with the instinct of a ranchman, automatically ground it deep with a boot toe; then he went on inside the small corral where

Miss Melissa's ranch hands usually left their mounts when they remained overnight in town.

Lee should have put that roan out of sight in the barn, Carr reflected, and then remembered that the man probably had been completely done in. Carr led the weary animal inside to a stall and pulled the saddle, noting the absence of his aunt's two pet buggy blacks. Knowing her as he did, Miss Melissa likely was up at Elmer Gibbens's office in the courthouse, giving the district attorney uncomfortable hell for ever having filed an indictment in the first place.

Carr went along a hay-strewn passageway, peering inside two small rooms with empty makeshift bunks, not surprised at finding no sign of ranch hands. That, he guessed, would be the work of his shrewd aunt. She'd ordered her men to stay out of town and trouble when her farmhand went on trial for killing Luke Kendall.

Carr came out of the opposite side of the red barn and went along the well-worn foot path, past Miss Melissa's prim privy and woodpile, and he opened the back gate of a white picket fence. In the sling his bandaged right hand was burning, and the sheathed Colt, butt forward at his left hip, bumped awkwardly in its unaccustomed place.

He remembered wryly that his possessions were still in the back of the hack Alma had driven away. Not that it mattered now. All he wanted to do was to get hold of Porter Beecroft and have him, as a very religious man, spirit Lee away in the darkness that night until he was well and a change of venue into a far county granted. Ples Kendall had sworn that the man would never get to trial, and Delaney would be a dead man the moment they found out where he was hiding.

Thirsty, Carr bent slightly to step up on the back porch. He saw the back door open and his aunt come out and stand for a moment looking at him.

"Well!" she finally said tartly and eyed the white, frilly sling and bandage. "I saw Alma Kendall rattle by in what looked like Ad Slocum's rental hack. I peer at people, you know." She was peering at him over the top of her gold-rimmed glasses. "I don't suppose she could have used your shirt instead of her drawers!"

"Here, now!" he grinned back at her reprovingly and

used his one good arm to advantage. She stepped away and stood looking him up and down, a handsome, slender woman of fifty-eight

She went to the cistern, slid back the rusty metal cover, and lowered the tin pail, letting the water-bleached pulley rope slide through her fingers. "Well, go on, Jonathan," she commanded him. "I'm listening."

He told her in brief detail what had taken place in Marlinville that morning—which she already knew from the wounded man—and then at the river crossing. "Where's Lee, Melissa?" he asked, then.

"In the cellar with his wife. He came crawling to the back door weak from loss of blood, but he's been fed and will be all right now. If you could get some protection for him between now and the opening of court in the morning, he'll be a free man by noon. People still remember you and your father, and they're getting pretty sick and tired of Ples Kendall's high-handed methods. Him and his sheriffs and his own district attorney!"

"How'd Lee get away from them?"

"He hit out in the direction of my ranch down on Double Mountain and then cut back through a bunch of my cattle to blot his tracks." She pulled hand over hand on the pulley rope.

"Well," Carr said thoughtfully and frowned, "that gives me some time, but not much. Your punchers will tell them he didn't show up there, and after they cut a circle around the other side of the ranch the rest won't be hard to figure. Knowing I'm his lawyer, they'll know he came here to wait for me."

"I hadn't thought of that, Jonathan," she said and lifted the dripping pail over the edge of the cistern top. She unsnapped the harness bucket from the tin bail.

He followed her into the cool kitchen with its clean fragrance of soap and a fresh cake she'd baked, and hunger bit into his lank stomach. He said, removing his hat, "I've got to get hold of Porter right away. No telling what's going to happen when Ples learns his lawyer has switched to our side to help me. Where is Porter?"

"Just where he should be," she said snappishly and handed him a mail-order glass dipper with a wooden handle. "He went to the courthouse in my buggy after helping bandage Lee. He went to tell Elmer Gibbens nobody but a fool would bring that case to trial tomorrow, after what the Kendall outfit did in Marlinville this morning."

He shook his head. "Elmer won't deal, Melissa. Ples put him into the district attorney's office, and he'd wet his prissy pants at the thought of quashing the indictment."

"Plus the fact he's a politically ambitious jackass dreaming of braying his opinions in Congress some day. Sit down while I get some hot water on to soak that hand. Dinner is still warm in the oven."

Pain fingered through his back and stomach muscles as he obeyed; pain and a terrible letdown of tension into weariness. He glanced down at his blood-spattered white shirt and then began removing the frilly sling and unwrapped the bandage. He gritted his teeth as his bruised fingers slowly closed, but they were not broken. He worked loose the buckle of his cartridge belt and laid it on the checkered oilcloth and pulled the .44 free of the sheath and put it into the band of his pants.

"Alma said that Laura and her mother are staying here," he remarked.

"Humpfff!" she sniffed over her shoulder and went on poking short lengths of mesquite wood on top of half-dead coals. "So you finally asked? They were to leave Porter at the courthouse and then drive down to see poor Mrs. Kendall. Poor thing can't talk any more."

He thought with a strange dismay, Laura will be there when Alma drives up in Ad Slocum's hack and breaks the news.

He said angrily, Dammit, Melissa, I wish Porter would remember he's not connected with the Kendalls anymore! If Ples comes on in town from the roundup wagon and talks with him—"

She slammed the lid of the stove with unnecessary vigor and turned, a deceivingly prim-looking woman who wasn't prim at all and whose white lace collar above the black dress appeared, right now, ready to bristle.

"Maybe that part of it was Laura's idea, young man! Maybe she wanted to go because she got good and tired of waiting for you. And I don't blame her in the least!"

She brought roast and potatoes and vegetables canned from her own garden and put them on the table. She used a long sharp knife to cut almost furiously at the meat in order that he could eat it with a fork. She brought him cool milk from a terra cotta crock. As she started to sit down he heard the front door open and light footsteps crossing the living room carpet.

He turned as Laura Beecroft stood in the doorway.

Chapter Six

LAURA HAD UNTIED and removed a lace-fringed bonnet which, except for its severity, would have given her a peek-a-boo attractiveness. She was twenty-five, and she'd been in love with Jonathan Carr ever since she was sixteen; partly because he was a brilliant young Texas lawyer, and partly because her severe mother and her father and Judge Carr had expected it of her.

In the old days when her father had been here in Salt Fork as law partner with the elder Carr, she'd "kept company" with Jonathan until the night of the big dance at the Kendall ranch headquarters. That was the night Jonathan Carr and Alma Kendall had been found standing at one end of the long front gallery, locked hungrily in each other's arms. There had been hell to pay, of course, with Laura's outraged mother the most recriminating of them all. But fire had been struck and there was no denying it between the two.

Young Carr wanted Alma and intended to marry her over his father's objections. Mrs. Beecroft had sent Laura away to relatives in Fort Worth. When Miss Melissa's big land case against Ples Kendall came up for trial, Porter Beecroft had bluntly refused to take part in it and ended the law partnership between two long-time friends.

Carr and his father had won the case and Alma had broken the engagement and then begged forgiveness, but it was too late. Judge Carr had been shot in the back that night, and Jonathan had trailed Dale Hayden's brother into the Double Mountain breaks and killed him and then turned Texas Ranger.

Porter Beecroft's domineering wife had forced him to move to Fort Worth, set up law practice there, and take over the handling of Ples Kendall's financial affairs.

And now, after five years, Laura Beecroft's father had recanted and come back to Salt Fork to help Jonathan Carr. He might have done it because he was sick of the ruthless old cattle baron's ways of killing men, or because the ghost of Judge Carr haunted him. It might have been that he wanted to get back his self-respect. A few people said that it was because of Laura. Beecroft still wanted Jonathan as a son-in-law and a partner, as his father had been in the old days.

Whatever the motive, Jonathan Carr had written to Laura and expected her to read between the lines. He had not expected to run into Alma again, except as an enemy in a family of enemies.

He looked at Laura there in the doorway of Miss Melissa's kitchen and he remembered so vividly how he had felt when he got up and started for Alma there on the tarp bedroll, hot blood pounding through his temples.

He rose to his feet with a feeling of slight embarrassment. She was studying his battered features and red-stained shirt much as Alma had studied him that morning across the table in the little café in Marlinville.

He said, "Laura, it's good to see you again after such a long time."

"How are you, Jonathan?" she asked simply in return and took his left hand.

"Won't you please sit down? I just got in."

"I know," she answered and went to a place beside Miss Melissa. "I saw Alma just now as she drove home. She told me. I'm—very sorry about everything, Jonathan."

Miss Melissa cleared her throat and rose from the table. She went to a cupboard, took down an old bonnet, and came back with a small tin of grain. "Quail feeding time out by the woodpile," she announced briskly and smiled. "I'll see if I can get us a big mess of them for supper."

She went out and Carr began to eat hungrily after a brief apology to Laura. Her light-brown hair, parted in the middle, had been pulled down tight and coiled flat over her ears in the severe manner demanded by her mother. He remembered Alma's russet hair that morning as she had shaken it out, sitting on the tarp at the river, and a strange kind of anger flared through him.

Meek, she had said. Laura was the meek kind. But damn it, she was!

In that moment he hated Laura's mother for what she had done to the girl. Hair coiled down like the "chongo" on an Indian woman of the Southwest tribes, he thought angrily. Only a sharp point of a thin shoe toe visible under a skirt hem so low it probably collected dust; and beneath her bodice her breasts looked as though her mother had laced them so flat Laura hardly could breathe.

"Jonathan, I have something to tell you, and I hope you will try to understand," she said, her gaze unwavering in the face of the sudden question in his own eyes. "Alma told me a few minutes ago what happened today. Everything."

"Well, she should have," he said. "I almost made love to her."

"I wonder. I have known for a long time what happened between the two of you when you were so much in love; what might have happened again today if fighting hadn't broken out and you killed another man. That's seven now, isn't it? Dale Hayden's brother, five outlaws wanted by the Texas Rangers, and now Ad Slocum this morning."

He felt himself grow a little cold inside. This smacked exactly too much like the way her mother had ranted about the shooting of Hayden and then, doubly horrified, sent her away to Fort Worth. It was too much like a younger edition of Mrs. Beecroft, cut from the same mold.

He said quietly, "Go on, Laura. I'm listening."

"Thank you, Jonathan. That is why I came, because I won't be seeing you again after today. You've thrown your gun against seven men and in order to survive, when Ples Kendall gets back in town, you are going to kill again. These things I've always understood despite my mother's harsh opinions. But Porter has grown independently wealthy off Ples Kendall and an ever-widening reputation as a successful barrister, just as your own fame has grown as a manhunter. He and mother have been painfully aware that I should have married several years ago, just as they are now aware of what your name could do to the firm in Fort Worth."

"In other words, you've been led out here and you view the letter I wrote you as a mere formality?" he asked her quietly.

She nodded and a slight flush crept into her smooth cheeks. "I—this is so hard for me, Jonathan, but such words have to be spoken. I—I came here to tell you that I can't marry you."

She rose and picked up the bonnet, and a smile fought its way into existence at the corners of her generous mouth. "I'd better get back to the Kendalls and get Mother. I don't think Mrs. Kendall is going to live through the night, although she's under the good care of a widow named Mrs. Deen. We'll go on up to the courthouse and get Papa."

He stood up and through him came a strange kind of loneliness he had never before been aware of. That was what happened when you took a woman too much for granted, when you kept on going along a road that each day made it more difficult to turn back. He'd traveled too far; he had come back a year or so too late.

"Are you going to marry Ed Kendall?" he asked her.

"I might," she admitted with amazing calmness. "I've heard that if a woman makes the life of a mean man hellish enough it often tames him. At my age, and with not too much choice in the matter, it might be worth a try."

He went with her to the living room and opened the door. Out beyond the picket gate the blacks dozed, hooked to Miss Melissa's shiny black buggy. Laura was at the edge of the porch when he called her name

"Yes, Jonathan," she answered and turned.

"You'll do," he said briefly and smiled. "I've the feeling that cracks are beginning to appear in the mold."

"What—" she asked, startled.

"You'll do," Jonathan Carr said, and meant it.

Miss Melissa's footsteps vibrated hard in the kitchen and she appeared in the dorway. "Jonathan! Come here, quick! Riders are coming down the lane from Double Mountain way. They've trailed Lee here!"

He hurried back into the kitchen and looked out the rear window. They were a hundred yards south of the barn, seven or eight of them, heavily armed, riding horses stumbling from exhaustion. Poke Kendall and Link led them, and Carr surmised that the sheriff and his brother had got fresh horses at the roundup wagons at noon and then made a hard ride south to catch up with the K Cross men still trying to trail the wounded fugitive.

Jonathan Carr stood there watching through the window pane, tall and gauntly weary himself, dried blood still splotching the front of his white shirt beneath the crescent droop of his dark mustache. He was unaware that

Laura was back in the kitchen, that his aunt's bright, prideful eyes were upon him and she remembering how much he favored his late father.

He saw Link throw up his hand in signal to the others to halt and then, head far down along the right shoulder of his horse, move slowly forward, studying the ground. Here Alma had turned the corner of the corral and Link was reading the tracks. At the gate he swung from his horse and squatted to study Carr's boot marks beside those made by the hack tires.

He straightened grimly, and his own toe disturbed the place where Jonathan had scuffed out the cigarette butt.

Link was suspicious, wondering why Carr had stopped at the corral instead of having Alma drive him on up the side gate facing the lane.

In sudden decision, Link Kendall dropped the reins of his horse and moved to open the gate and take a look inside. He stopped cold in his own tracks as he heard Carr's piercing voice from the back porch fifty yards away.

"Better not go in there, Link. He might meet you with a shotgun the way he met Luke."

"It's all right, Jonathan!" Poke Kendall called out hastily. "He's my prisoner now. I'll go take a look."

He came out of the barn almost immediately and swung up, shaking his head at Link's sharp question.

"But, damn it, we followed them tracks—"

"I said he's not in there!" the sheriff snapped.

"Of course he ain't," Link sneered. "He was hit, wasn't he? They got him in the house. Come on!"

At a walk they broke into movement and went on along the line of barbed wire strung between Miss Melissa's barn and a corner of the white picket fence surrounding the yard. Miss Melissa was conspicuously absent from the back porch; so was her long-barrel, smallbore quail gun from its usual place inside the kitchen doorjamb.

Link drew up in front of them and grinned at sight of Carr's blue-marked features. In a gesture so much like his father, he palmed both hands over the saddlehorn and sat with saturnine amusement on his dark face.

"Where is he, Jonathan? Hidin' under Miss Melissa's bed?"

"You were always loud, Link. You tell me where he is," Carr answered coolly.

"Talk up, damn you!" Link Kendall cried, his face flushing darkly. "There's ten of us here, and the old man warned you!"

Jonathan Carr already had counted them, and two he knew by name and reputation; Duval, who'd killed four men in a wild shootout in a Corpus Christi saloon and then had a six-shooter explode almost in his face, leaving it scarred and powder blackened; and Evans, another spoiled son of a wealthy rancher who, like Link, hoped to shoot his way into the Texas Rangers—these and six others of the K Cross roundup crew.

"Link, you shut up for a minute," Poke Kendall said angrily to his younger brother. He rode closer to the fence and rose in the saddle, resting his weight on a stiffened leg.

"Jonathan, I reckon you know how I feel about this whole business. But I'm still sheriff with a job to do, and the old man is still my father. If you'll get hold of Lee —wherever you figure he might be hidin'—bring him up to the courthouse and surrender yourselves, I'll guarantee both of you protection until court opens tomorrow."

Carr laughed shortly without humor. "You mean you'd try—and then salve your conscience afterward, when Ples kept his promise. No soap, Poke."

"Will you come up to the courthouse and talk with me?" the sheriff insisted doggedly.

"I'm going to Camp Coke tonight and get in touch with MacNab."

"You're stalling!" Link blazed at his brother, eyes flashing. "You're afraid of him."

"I just don't want you to get your damn fool head shot off right here," Poke replied calmly. He said to Carr, a vast relief flooding his tired, worried face. "You do that, Jonathan. But wherever Lee is he's my prisoner, bound over to trial tomorrow."

He reined back and said shortly, "All right, you men, let's rack 'em on up town. I'm good for one drink around and then I've got official business to take care of."

Carr heard a distinct *thump* as the butt of a light quail gun was dropped to the floor inside a kitchen window. The little cavalcade of dusty horsemen rode off with Link gesticulating ragingly with his hands to Duval and Evans and the others, and Miss Melissa came out.

"Heavens, Jonathan!" she exclaimed in relief. "That easy? Poke would be a good man if he wasn't a Kendall."

"Too easy, Melissa," Carr murmured. "And he's still Ples Kendall's son."

"He saw the roan horse in the barn and blood on the saddle, of course?"

"He saw it, and Link can track a bobcat across red sandstone. He knows, and he'll tell his father. I've got to see Porter right away. I've less time now than I thought."

Chapter Seven

PORTER BEECROFT was still deep in heated conference in the office of district attorney Elmer Gibbens, pacing nervously back and forth behind the locked door. Elmer Gibbens, sitting behind his desk with crossed feet on a corner and hands clasped on his head, made an impatient grimace of annoyance. "Sit down, Porter! We've got to get this thing thrashed out right here and now, and there's no sense in working yourself into a lather."

It was said in Texas that a good jackleg lawyer had to be a hungry one; Porter Beecroft didn't look the part. He'd grown heavy with wealth and a small dewlap of skin hung prominently beneath his clean-shaven chin. Dressed flamboyantly in gray, he held his hands beneath his coat tails as he paced.

A wealthy man through Ples Kendall's largesse, he had, in turn, cleaned up a huge fortune for the old cattleman by investments in railroad bonds; and it had been upon this premise he had made the decision to come back to Salt Fork. He'd been certain he could convince the old patriarch to drop the whole matter for the sake of a woman's shame as well as that of the Kendall family name.

Now he wasn't so sure; Gibbens was adamant.

"Shame, my eye!" he had laughed at Beecroft moments before. "You think that old hellion gives a damn? How many women do you think he's grabbed in his day? He wants the man who killed his son—and we're going to get him."

The man annoyed Beecroft. He wore high, stiff collars and had developed the annoying habit of pinching at the tabs with thumb and forefinger, leaving perennial dirty smudges. In the opinion of Porter Beecroft, he'd been merely another jackleg Texas lawyer who'd lost the land case to the two Carrs, and was now back in the good graces of the old man as district attorney. He'd been promised a seat in Congress in another two or three years.

Beecroft stopped pacing and jabbed a finger again,

switching his attack. "But I have hopes of breaking down Jonathan's determination to go through with this case and put Ruby on the witness stand. I—"

"All right, all right!" Gibbens grinned and lowered his polished shoes, adjusting the instep straps attached to the cuff of his pants. He straightened and pulled his chair forward and adjusted false white cuffs under the sleeves of his brown coat.

"I agree with you on that part, Porter. Keep her off the witness stand. We can select a jury panel in two hours, have the evidence in by midafternoon, and a jury verdict by dark, all cut and dried. That is, providing Carr does show up with a prisoner—already a dead man if Ples finds out he's hiding in Miss Melissa's cellar."

Beecroft pulled a handkerchief from beneath his coat tails and mopped at his sweating face. He hadn't counted on anything like this, and he was more afraid than he cared to admit.

He'd frowned upon young Ed's attentions to Laura, still hoping that Jonathan one day would give up ranger service and settle down with him in Fort Worth as his son-in-law and legal associate. He had gambled much of future success upon this decision, and run into a brick wall.

"Jonathan will get here somehow, that you can be assured of," Beecroft said to the district attorney. "But that's just the point. He's going to make some kind of legal history in that courtroom tomorrow by getting Lee off, if you bring this case to trial."

"And when he does there'll be six-shooter law in Salt Fork before the crowd even gets downstairs."

"Precisely," exclaimed Beecroft with a nod of triumph at a point gained. "And when it happens, I'll lose more than the man who is slated to become my son-in-law. You'll lose Ples and about two more Kendalls—plus the only hope you'll ever have in this world to get into Congress, Elmer. Men in our position must think of these things."

Filed spur rowels made hard rattling sounds on the mortarfloored hallway outside, coming through the north entrance. Somebody tried the knob and then banged on the locked door. Beecroft glanced uneasily at Gibbens, a prayer in his heart that it wasn't old Ples. He still didn't know how he would be able to summon the courage to tell him of his decision when the cattle baron returned to town.

Gibbens rose from his chair, slipped the latch and opened the door. "Why, come in, Ed," he invited genially. "How are things with you, boy?"

Ed Kendall came in, removing his hat. The band left a dampish plastered area of dark blond hair around his temples and, without the kind of mustache affected by Link, he looked boyishly handsome at twenty-four. Despite the man's wild family background and the way his right hand unconsciouly hung above the butt of his pistol, Beecroft found himself admiring Ed's clean, youthful good looks. Of course, he'd been in his share of dancehall fights, and he'd shot a man dead in a rough fracas when Link had been caught off guard.

Beecroft knew too that Ed was no stranger in the parlor houses when K Cross was delivering cattle to the stock pens in Fort Worth. But then—well, what young fellow hadn't? He'd taken quite a few whacks at it himself when he was Ed's age.

Ed had a way of sleepily narrowing his boyish eyes, cat-like, something Jonathan Carr long since had noted and catalogued in his mind. It had been that way the day Carr had taken Lee Delaney away from them just west of the courthouse square. Ed had stood there beside his brother's body, his face pale, his eyes half closed, catlike.

They were veiled now, and Ed grinned thinly. "I just saw Laura and Mrs. Beecroft pull up on the north side of the square, Porter, and they said you were in here with Elmer. You two seen the old man yet?"

He knew they hadn't. Ples Kendall had sent him. He had found out that Porter Beecroft was in town, and why.

"I thought he was out with his roundup crew east of here the past few days," Gibbens answered, and held out a cigar box.

Ed bit off the end of the cheroot and spat. "His played-out black horse is down in front of the saloon back of the hotel, where Link and the boys just went. You heard the latest news since this morning?"

"Only about what happened at Marlinville," Gibbens answered quickly. "That was good work you did over there, boy! Too bad you didn't get him dead-center and save us all this trouble."

Ed lit the cigar and blew out a stream of smoke, his lids dropping again. "They was some hot hell over on the Salt Fork of the Brazos today. Jonathan Carr killed Ad Slocum in a gun fight."

"Good God!" cried out Porter Beecroft in horror, and threw both hands ceilingward in a dramatic courtroom gesture. "Ad Slocum, you say? Wasn't he a Marlin County deputy sheriff for Bert Burton? This is terrible!"

Ed Kendall puffed on his cigar and told them with relish his one-sided version of the story, including how Carr had seen them first and stopped making love to Alma, grabbed up a rifle, and then fired the first shots.

"The old man had figured for months," he went on, grinning, "that there was only one place that Delaney woman could be hid out—in Miss Melissa's big cellar where she used to feed us kids canned wild plums. Link said Lee got away on Jonathan's roan hoss, all right, but they were pretty sure they cut his tracks, and trailed him back to Miss Melissa's barn. But Jonathan was on the back porch and Poke wouldn't let the boys take him. Porter, I suppose you know what this means. If the old duck gets a few drinks in him, me and Poke won't be able to hold him down. He'll tear that place apart. He told Jonathan he'd kill him if he ever set foot on Salt Fork again. Now you know what's going to happen."

He put on his hat again, tugging at the front of the brim, and shifted the cigar to his other hand. He said, importantly solemn, "The old man is really sore about you takin' Jonathan's side is this business, Porter, but I'll do my best for you. Nothing Jonathan can do. Link busted his gunhand with the butt of his sixshooter, like I told you."

He went out, closed the door behind him, and the filed spurs he used to bloody the sides of Kendall horses rattled again.

The old man, he thought with a grin, had told him just what to say—and he'd done a pretty good job of embellishment on his own. He'd put the fear of God into Porter Beecroft.

In the office, after Ed was gone, Elmer Gibbens got up and stretched as though he wanted an afternoon cup of coffee over in the hotel. He grinned lazily at Beecroft.

"Well, Porter?" he asked the visibly shaken visitor.

"I wash my hands entirely of the whole affair," Laura's father murmured gloomily and wagged his head in sorrow. "How could Jonathan do this thing to me . . . " He almost added, Making love to that shameless Kendall woman, when I thought . . . "I must go tell Ples that I've been a fool and that I withdraw completely from the case."

"Good, that's fine," Gibbens said heartily and thought, How could a man with Carr's cold courage ever have considered you as a father-in-law, and how could a man like you ever fathered a woman as pretty as Laura? "Let's go over to the hotel and get some coffee. Old Ples will be very happy about this, no matter how he roars."

He removed his hat from a wall hook and held the door open, then closed and locked it.

They went out the north entrance of the breezeway and down two steps to the walk leading to the new box-shaped hotel beyond the courthouse.

At the corner stile Miss Melissa's shiny buggy, drawn by the blacks, had pulled up with two fluffily dressed figures, identical in color and design, in the seat. Standing on the ground by a front wheel, idly slapping the tire with the ends of his reins, Ed Kendall was trying to make serious talk with Laura. Around the corner of the hotel from the saloon in back, Ples Kendall was coming at a slow walk on his exhausted black saddler.

Beecroft and Elmer Gibbens went up the steps of the stile and down again as old Ples came to a halt, big hands palmed over the saddlehorn. He stank of sweat and tobacco, and he'd never tipped his hat to a woman in his life.

Beecroft glanced at the frigidly set face of his wife and then at Laura. Unaware that Alma had told his daughter of what had taken place between her and Jonathan, and not knowing Laura already had been to Miss Melissa's house, Porter wanted to get her aside at once and tell her the family would all be leaving on the Fort Worth stage first thing in the morning. Carr was being revealed as a cold, implacable man who'd kill at the drop of a hat. Ed looked more boyish and handsome than ever standing there talking to Laura, and—well, a man had to think of these things.

Beecroft looked with misgivings at the twinkling eyes of the old man in the saddle. "Good afternoon, Ples," he greeted with forced cordiality, and then waited for the roar of angry denunciation to come.

"Howdy, Porter, howdy. Nice of you city folks to come back home to visit with us plains people again. How's my business goin' down in the office?"

"Fine, Ples, fine," Beecroft said heartily, and had trouble controlling the relief in his voice.

"Good! We got a couple thousand head throwed across the Brazos into Marlin county past week or so. I'll be down with 'em in a few days, first shipment of the year. Got some more money matters I want to talk over with you. Nothin' like a good lawyer to help a cowman handle his business, eh?" and old Ples laughed ingratiatingly, the twinkle bright in his eyes.

Gibbens glanced at Porter Beecroft and noisily cleared his throat. "Ples, there has been some small talk that Porter here might aid Jonathan Carr with the defense when court opens tomorrow. But he has just reassured me there is absolutely no truth in the rumor; that a man of his loyalty and integrity can't afford to be mixed up in such an unsavory affair. I agree with him. Carr will have to conduct the defense by himself."

The crow's feet deepened around the old man's eyes and the twinkle became satisfyingly brittle. "That's fine, Elmer. Now I want you to go back to your office an' swear out a warrant for Jonathan's arrest for the murder of Ad Slocum this mornin'. I'm goin' on down to the house to tell Poke. He'll deputize Duval an' Evans an' some more of the boys to serve it. Git along with it now."

In the living room of Miss Melissa's comfortable home Carr threw in his hand, five cards face down, and watched his prim-looking aunt triumphantly rake in an eighty-cent pot of chips. He'd gone out to the barn again, after Laura departed to get her mother, to rub down the roan and feed it. Miss Melissa had stubbornly insisted upon shaving him and then brought him a white shirt from the stock always in the bureau in his room. And she'd combed his damp hair as fussily as she'd done twenty years ago, after his mother died.

Miss Melissa reached over and picked up the cards Carr had tossed in. She sniffed and began to put away deck and chips. "Lost your gambling nerve, have you? You might have filled that straight if you'd tried." Her face softened perceptibly as she racked the chips and placed them in a box. "I'm just a selfish, lonely old woman, I guess. But I thought I could get your thoughts away from things. Jonathan, you've a legal mind trained by your father to sift facts and to weigh them. Use it and forget about Ad Slocum."

"I wasn't thinking about Ad at all," he said.

She rose and went to the front window, drawing aside the brown lace curtain and glancing up the quarter-mile slope toward the courthouse and the buildings scattered around the square. In the chinaberry tree, called an umbrella tree by plains people, a bird began to trill, and she heard an answer from quail out in the mesquites across the lane up which the Kendalls and two gunmen and other K Cross riders had ridden.

The blue quail, top knots bobbing, were coming in for their evening grain.

"I do declare, I wish Porter would come on back," she said impatiently and let the window curtain drop. "Perhaps I'd ought to fix some coffee for them."

He handed her his tobacco sack and papers and leaned back in the chair, watching as she built the cigarette. As her heir, he knew the secret hopes she'd always had for him; that some day he'd give up Ranger service and come home to Salt Fork to her and the ranch, and end up with the judgeship that "Judge" Carr had never attained before his death.

He said, "What's done is done. Melissa, and I have put Ad out of my mind. Alma was right; he was kill-crazy."

She licked at the brown paper and then leaned across the table to put it into his mouth, smiling as though she still couldn't get used to her nephew wearing a long mustache. He used his right hand, off color from soaking in hot water doused with salts, to strike a match. He could flex the fingers quite easily now.

"I can read you better than Alma Kendall, Jonathan. And I know almost every thought that goes through old Ples's black heart. Do you remember the night after the land case when your father died on the way back to my ranch on the Double Mountain? You followed the tracks to the Hayden shack down in the breaks, killed the man who did it, and then joined the Rangers for a while to escape possible trouble with the law and not put a blot on your future name."

"All over with and forgotten, Melissa."

"Yes—by you. But not by Ples Kendall. You knew the Kendalls were responsible but you sensibly said nothing or did nothing more about it. Yet for five years old Ples has lived in the fear that, behind Ranger protection, you would some day come back and take vengeance upon him and his sons. Texas Rangers have done it before."

"But I didn't," he pointed out.

"That's just the point—as your father would have said. Today you did come back! You came back without a Ranger's badge to defend Lee for killing a Kendall, and because old Ples is afraid for himself and his mean young sons, he'll strike first. Now Alma will be back pretty soon with her belongings, coming to you. It is my one hope that it will stop Ples long enough for Porter to get Lee away tonight, and for you to get out safely and go to Camp Coke. I see no other bloodless solution. Do you?"

He sat looking down at the cigarette, one black boot resting high across his other knee, as gaunt of face as she ever remembered seeing him before.

He got up from his chair without answering and went to the same front window and drew aside the lace curtain and stood looking broodingly up across the flats to the town square. He saw the afternoon sun shining on skeletal beams of the frame bank building, now turning weatherbeaten, just west of the courthouse fence and in plain view from Poke Kendall's office. On the ground beside the unfinished building, a small black dot from where Carr stood in Miss Melissa's living room, was the rusting bank vault.

Carr looked over a shoulder at his aunt. She sat prim and straight with the knitting needles she'd taken from a basket now clicking away. A little too straight, and the needles clicking just a little faster than usual.

You couldn't fool a woman like her; she'd lived in this country too long. She knew the promise Ples Kendall had made, and that he had never yet broken one. He'd sworn to kill Carr if he ever came back to Salt Fork, and then left Alma with him at the river as a reminder that he could take her and then make his own choice.

Movement up there in the town square caught Carr's

eyes. He saw Melissa's buggy pulled by the fast blacks swing around the courthouse fence and speed by the skeletal bank building. He could make out Porter driving, squeezed in under the top with his wife and daughter. From the way Porter sat rigidly upright, whip tip flicking those black pacers at a sizzling trot down across the flats toward Miss Melissa's house, it was pretty obvious that he'd heard of the fight at the river crossing.

Mrs. Beecroft would again be frigidly horrified, and the thought gave him no sense of regret except a sympathy for Laura. Her money had educated Porter and then her same uncompromising will had molded him into the kind of practicing attorney she'd thought a husband should be.

The same effect had not been lost upon Laura either, but Carr had to admit that she might have more spunk than he had thought. Except for her mother, he and Laura Beecroft probably would have been raising a family by now.

Carr said to Miss Melissa, "Here come the Porter Beecrofts at a fast trot. I guess that word is all over town by now that I'm back."

"I'll fix some coffee." she said, rising and putting aside the knitting.

She disappeared into the kitchen and Carr waited for them to tie up by the front gate. Looking back in retrospect, he'd always known that some day he'd go back to her and set up a law practice of his own with no aid or influence from Porter. But there had always seemed to be just one more tough manhunt for Captain MacNab to pass along; always just a few weeks more that never ended.

He'd ridden just a few too many, and now Laura had begun to break the mold.

Carr went to the front door and opened it.

On the front porch Porter Beecroft removed his soft felt hat and mopped at his forehead, as though he dreaded meeting the son of his former law partner more than he had dreaded the meeting with Ples Kendall. His graying hair was rumpled and he looked beat out. He saw Carr in the doorway and hurried toward him.

"Jonathan, I've just come from the courthouse. I saw Ples. You've got to get on your horse and get out of here in a hurry. They're coming to arrest you for murder and two of the men are gunfighters."

"Is Ples coming with them?" Carr inquired.

"I don't know!" Beecroft cried wildly. "And does it matter? They're coming and you know why. To kill you and drag poor Lee out of the cellar."

He hurried on inside to the kitchen to get a drink of water and his wife followed with her frigid gaze straight ahead. Carr heard her accusing voice talking to Miss Melissa. He found himself alone with Laura and was astonished to find her smiling.

"You look much better now, Jonathan. Almost the same as when I used to see you in the courtroom, except that you wore no mustache and your face was unmarked. Much better."

"So would you," he said almost roughly, "if you'd throw that damned bonnet in the cistern and unwind those Indian braids. What's Porter so upset about?"

"He's concerned about us. The family, I mean. He's about to tell you that after you killed another man today he's withdrawing from the case—washing his hands of it all. Mother is making us move up to the hotel at once."

"Laura!" came her mother's strident voice. "Come in here and start packing!"

Chapter Eight

Hot water left over from what she had heated to soak Jonathan's hand was still on the stove and Miss Melissa, poking the fire into life again, didn't look up as Porter Beecroft's wife swept in from the living room. Miss Melissa did glance out through the rear window of the kitchen. In single file another stream of blue quail, top knots jerking, was coming across the road of the lane and under the wire fence of the woodpile.

"Too bad you're running out on us so soon, Belinda," she remarked and set the pan over the lid opening with a clatter. "We'd have had the first fall quail supper tonight."

Belinda Beecroft made no reply. She'd removed her own severe bonnet to lay it on the table, and then almost snatched it up again as though for the first time she saw the gunbelt and ominous looking six-shooter on the oilcloth. Carr had left them there when he and Miss Melissa sat down to the session of draw poker.

Mrs. Beecroft started to say something but caught the look in Miss Melissa's eyes and clamped her mouth tight.

"Go ahead and say it, Belinda. That gun has put Tom Hayden and five other murderers in their graves. There may be others before this night is out. But just remember that except for you and your money, Porter Beecroft might be wearing one tonight in the interest of decency and justice instead of being in there babbling his indignation to Jonathan."

"And just what is he, Melissa?" Mrs. Beecroft challenged sharply.

"A man more afraid of his wife and Ples Kendall than his conscience."

"I made Porter what he is today!"

"Yes, and you did a pretty good job of ruining Laura's happiness while you were at it."

"What's she got to do with all this rape and killing

and death hanging over this whole town right this minute?" demanded the other heatedly. A slow flush came into her stern cheeks.

"Put the cups on the table while I grind the coffee," Miss Melissa answered and went to the cupboard.

Porter Beecroft's voice, haranguing and defensive, came from the front room; and the faint vibrations of Carr's even steps could be felt as at intervals he crossed the carpet and watched for activity outside. No sound came within the bedroom where Laura had gone to pack their portmanteaux.

"Melissa, I don't think you'd better bother about the coffee," Mrs. Beecroft said anxiously. "I won't stay in this house another minute with those men coming. What is Jonathan going to do—stay here and wait for them?"

"Knowing the Carr blood as I do, I don't think so, Belinda," Miss Melissa replied softly. "He never had a wife to lead him around by the nose."

"I won't listen to another word, Melissa!" Mrs. Beecroft stormed and swept out again. She went into the west hallway and opened a big bedroom door. She stood there, surprise turning to outraged indignation as she saw that Laura still had not packed.

Laura stood before a bureau mirror with the braids uncoiled from her ears and hanging loose, cocking her head from side to side like a girl of sixteen and smiling at some inner secret.

"Well, I never . . ." Mrs. Beecroft began grimly.

"I rather like it, Mama, don't you?" Laura smiled. "But I'll have to keep the bonnet. It might taint Melissa's drinking supply."

"What on earth are you talking about?"

"My bonnet. Jonathan told me to throw the damned thing into the cistern."

Miss Melissa left the coffee in the grinder and picked up Jonathan's belt and six-shooter. She carried them into the living room and laid them on the card table. Carr was at the window again, watching the flats. No sign of them coming yet, and he guessed that old Ples figured they had plenty of time. Porter Beecroft got up agitatedly from his chair and looked at her as though he now knew what Carr intended to do; settle this thing away from the house.

"Melissa," he said heavily, "I've done all in my power to make this madman see the light but he won't listen."

"Good," she snapped tartly.

"Have you got a drink of whisky around here? I need it badly."

"There are two dusty bottles of Judge Carr's toddy whisky in the cellar, Porter. Go down and bring them up."

"No, no," he said hastily and raised a protesting hand. He looked sick.

"I don't think you had the gumption. I wanted you to see a big man down flat on his back and helpless from Ed Kendall's bullet this morning. I wanted you to see a woman who for months has lived hidden like a wild animal and afraid to come out except in the small hours of the night. They were put there by the man who made you wealthy, Porter. I had hoped that the sight of them would arouse something in you that Belinda has smothered. Has she done so much to you that you won't drive them out of the country tonight to stay alive until Jonathan can ask for a change of venue?"

His face turned an unhealthy color from her waspish sting, and she went toward the kitchen again. But, as was her wont, she paused in the doorway for a final thought, the white lace at her throat seeming to come alive.

"When you get packed and moved into the hotel, send my blacks back at once. I'm taking Lee and his wife out of this country to safety tonight, and I'd like to see Kendall, damn him, try to stop me!"

She remained alone in the kitchen when the Beecrofts left. Mrs. Beecroft, a portmanteau in each hand, her face set in its usual grim lines, nodded curtly without speaking as Jonathan Carr held open the front door. She swept past him with long skirts brushing the porch planking.

He found himself looking at Laura in surprise. Something in her face had changed, and he'd never seen her amber eyes so expressive. It probably was pity, an awareness that she was seeing him alive for the last time. Then he saw her fighting to control a faint quiver at the corners of her mouth.

"When you and Ed get married, give him hell, Laura," he said, smiling. "I don't think I ever really knew you until today, and now I guess it's too late."

"Don't pity me for what I am, Jonathan," she answered

softly. "Alma told me things today I never realized. If you sense any change in me, thank her. I always thought I hated her because I knew that you two were lovers when you were engaged, but I find she's quite likable."

"Allowing for the Kendall blood," he commented dryly.

"Yes, but have you really any right to speak so?" she asked without rancor. "Have the Kendalls done worse, in some ways, than you?"

He said soberly, "No, I guess not, Laura. Allowing for old Ples, who in the early day Texas Rangers used to kill Comanche women and children, I don't suppose I'm hardly in a position to criticize."

Holding the bonnet in one hand, she put out the other to him and looked up at his gaunt height, at the long drooping mustache that made him look so much older at the moment than he really was.

"Good-by, Jonathan. We'll be taking the Fort Worth stage out first thing in the morning. Would you mind telling me what you plan to do now?"

"I've never seen the new courthouse inside, Laura. I'm going to ride up and have a look."

"Of course," she murmured almost inaudibly. "Because of Miss Melissa, isn't it? I . . . I am very sorry for you, Jonathan."

She left him and moved toward the end of the porch. He saw the twin braids hanging down back of her shoulders and he thought, what a poker-faced cuss she is, and all these years I never suspected. Must be a throwback of blood a generation or two, and it's just beginning to show.

He closed the front door, shutting out the view of them squeezing in under the buggy top, and he went to the card table where his gun and cartridge belt lay. He stripped the thorn-scuffed sheath from the belt and laid it aside. His fingers handled the buckle easily as he strapped it on, but the split-second co-ordination was not there in his right hand. Miss Melissa came noiselessly into the room.

"That Belinda," she said grimly and shook her head. "What a price Porter paid when he let her money buy him, shove him through law training, and then forced him out on the plains to begin cutting his legal teeth on cow-thief cases. No backbone any more."

Smiling at her words, he picked up his worn .44 Colt

and extracted a cartridge from a loop. He put it into the empty chamber that had been under the hammer, closed the loading gate, and shoved the barrel of the weapon into the waistband of his pants.

"You going uptown, Jonathan?" she asked, as though she didn't know.

He nodded and picked up the narrow-brim hat with its pinched-in sharp peak. "Thought I'd bring the team back. They'll have to be watered and grained before you leave tonight."

He followed her into the kitchen. She said, "All right, Jonathan. But let me step out on the back porch ahead of you."

She reached down and lifted the quail gun by its long, thin double barrels. Miss Melissa eared back both curved hammers and made sure of the copper percussion caps. She stepped through the doorway and crept along the back porch wall. Beyond the low top of the white picket fence about forty blue quail had bunched, pecking at grain while others ran around and called. Miss Melissa lifted the long weapon to her shoulder and steadied it.

It sounded more like a pair of light rifles going off, and a cloud of powdered dust rose from half a dozen objects fluttering there by the chop block where others lay still. More burred up like bullets and shot over the road and were gone.

"There now, Jonathan," Miss Melissa said briskly and leaned the weapon against the kitchen wall. "First quail supper for us. I'll have them ready by the time you get back."

She walked in her energetic stride out through the gate with him and grabbed up fluttering objects and pulled off their heads in the timeless manner of the hunter. She left them on the ground and straightened. She raised on tip toes and kissed him and then stood watching as his tall figure moved along the path to the barn. Her eyes had become unnaturally bright.

Then she took a white lace hankerchief from her black sleeve, sat down on the chopping block, removed her gold-rimmed spectacles, and buried her face in the cloth. Her shoulders shook uncontrollably.

On the point of entering the red barn, Carr caught a glint of sunlight on a distant object. The rider was four hundred yards to the west of him and so was another. Nor was the object a rifle. Contrary to general belief, sun rays didn't glint from the barrel of a long gun. This was from polished brass.

"Poke Kendall's long glass," Carr muttered as he saw the second rider emerge from the mesquites and join the first.

They'd had the house under surveillance, waiting for him to make his move, and now he'd come into the open. He thought of the broken sniper's sight on the Sharps. At four hundred yards he could easily have dropped both horses and, riding up to see Elmer Gibbens, let it serve notice to Ples Kendall and the others not to close in on Carr. He carried only his pistol.

He went inside the barn.

The roan stood as though half asleep, hip-shot and resting, its belly rumbling gastric content from the grain. Carr curried the rough from its sweat-dried back and laid on the blanket, still soggy from the wounded man's desperate ride to escape.

Carr led the saddled animal out under the shed to the gate. The roan followed him through and, in obedience to the bridle reins across Carr's arm, spun on its four feet and waited. He closed the corral's gate and stirruped into the saddle. Link Kendall's boot tracks were there in the dirt.

Carr trotted the chinless roan up the lane past the house. Miss Melissa, her apron filled with quail, had gone ir 'de and was nowhere in sight. No waving to him from the ~k porch. His aunt wasn't the kind.

Haa Carr been aware that his moving up to town was merely another facet of his own singular nature he would have been surprised. Had Miss Melissa, watching unseen as he rode away, ever told him so he would have denied it.

He was riding up across the flats to see Gibbens about something special, but mainly to wait for them to make Ples Kendall's play.

Carr turned in the saddle and glanced to the west—two riders closing the gap to three hundred yards and less, Duval the ex-Ranger and young Evans. Kendall didn't consider his sons expendable. The barrel of the .44 Colt pressed deep into the lean muscles of Jonathan Carr's stomach as he rode to the southwest corner of the town square.

He noted with not too much surprise how deserted the town was. Only a few horseshoe pitchers between the blacksmith shop and a big former mercantile store building now a Saturday-night dancehall. But the horseshoe pitchers, too, had been watching Miss Melissa's house, and now six shoes lay where they had fallen; scattered wide around the rusty stake as though all interest in the game suddenly had ceased.

They stood watching in poker-faced silence and with their eyes on the two men following, now only two hundred yards away. The whole bunch of them are hostile, Carr surmised. Hostile because although they might hate Ples, they're afraid of him, afraid of what might happen if he dies. Carr pulled up by the corner stile.

He unstirruped his right boot and kicked open the gate beside the steps over the fence. He rode through and kicked the gate shut once more.

Only two saddle horses had ever been inside the courthouse grounds in Salt Fork. Ples Kendall had ridden one and crippled it to death by a gunshot through the head. Jonathan Carr rode the other one at a slow walk to where Elmer Gibbens, seeing him coming, hurriedly went inside his office and shut the door and stood with his back to it, pinching nervously at the tabs of his white collar.

Carr got down and his own four-prong rowels rattled hollowly against the mortar as Ed Kendall's had done. He turned the knob and went in to find Gibbens seated back of his desk. Gibbens knew full well that Duval and Evans were coming after Carr, while Link and Ed had been ordered to stay out of town until it was over; and the prospect that a shootout now might take place right in Gibbens's office had the district attorney terrified.

As old Ples's former lawyer, he'd defended Duval and others who'd done killing jobs for the clan patriarch, but he'd never seen them at work close up before. His throat felt constricted.

Carr said sardonically, "Don't get impatient, Gibbens. They'll be over in a few minutes. That's what Ples pays them for, to avoid the risk of Link and Ed's necks."

"I . . . Carr, I don't know what you're talking about," the district attorney cried nervously.

"No use to call a man like you a liar, Elmer. You already know it. I came up here to tell you to quash that indictment against Lee Delaney. I'm taking him and his wife out of the county tonight until request for a change of venue can be filed. I want you to go tell the man whose boots you lick that I hold no grudge against him for anything that happened in the past, that I want no more trouble with him in the future. There has already been too much killing in this county for one day. There won't be any more of it if he's got sense enough to stop those two gunfighters and leave things as they are."

"I don't tell Ples Kendall how to run his business."

"You can tell him what I said. Where's the indictment?"

Gibbens grabbed frantically for a sheaf of papers on the desk before him, but Carr picked them up first. Over the district attorney's vociferous protests, he began to thumb through them. Elmer Gibbens tried again to snatch them but an outspread hand with long fingers, the back of it swollen a bit and discolored, took him in the chest and slammed him back against the wall. Gibbens's hat with its rakishly curved brim, dislodged from a wall hook, glanced off his shoulder and tumbled softly to the floor.

"You can't do that, it's against the law!" shouted the man as he straightened with his hat and put it back on the hook. "This is an outrage—"

"So is this," Jonathan Carr interrupted and his voice turned cold from anger. "You didn't miss a thing, did you, Elmer?"

Alma had said that morning that Ad Slocum was a shriveled little man inside. The thought came back to Carr now. His face turned into a mass of controlled fury as he ripped the papers to shreds and flung them at the district attorney.

"You shriveled up little son-of-a-bitch," he whispered. "Briefing in here the inference that Lee's young wife was kept on my aunt's ranch for the pleasure of the other hands. Why, you damned bastard, this makes Miss Melissa about the same as the madam of a ranch bawdy house! Elmer, who helped you think up all this rotten inference?"

"You're finished, Carr!" Gibbens almost shrieked, his face livid with anger despite the fear of this tall, deadly man. "This finished you with the law in Texas. You'll be disbarred, I'll guarantee you that!"

"I wouldn't know at the moment," Carr said savagely.
"I'd have to look into my law books, and Alma still has
them in the hack."

Gibbens had become like a cat backed protectively into
a safe corner, spitting and snarling defiance; unafraid now
as long as it remained there and didn't come out until the
enemy cornering it had gone away.

He leveled a rigid forefinger at Carr and it began to
tremble. It was the first time in the man's life he'd ever
been manhandled. "I'm not afraid of you shooting me
here, Carr. So the very moment you leave this courthouse
I'll write up another indictment against Delaney and
another charging you with Ad Slocum's murder."

"Maybe I'm not going to leave this courthouse for
a while."

"Makes no difference to me. I've no use for that black-
eyed little squirt MacNab—"

"No, I expect you haven't," Carr murmured his contempt. "He ignored every letter you wrote demanding a
Ranger commission for Link Kendall in order for Link
to do his killing behind a badge."

"Never mind that!" Gibbens yelled, and actually shook
his fist. "This new courthouse is a symbol of how the old
order is changing in Texas. It represents the law and
order you've smashed today by freeing a prisoner from
jail and killing a deputy sheriff trying to recapture the
man—"

"Oh, shut it off, Elmer," Jonathan Carr grunted at
him. "Get out of here and go tell your master what I
said."

He closed the door, leaving Gibbens fuming speech-
lessly. He stood there for a few moments, looking out the
entrance of the breezeway, aware that a dozen pairs of
eyes were riveted upon him. Two leather-chapped riders
were with them now. One had a long glass thonged to
his saddlehorn.

Carr turned and moved along the breezeway to the
last door on the left, the one leading into Poke Kendall's
office. He opened it and stepped quickly inside.

The girl in the office was not more than seventeen, a
thin little thing Carr vaguely remembered as a child
whose widowed mother, a Mrs. Deen, had taken in washing to support them.

"Why, Mr. Carr!" the girl cried in crimson-faced confusion, and dropped the small mirror into which she had been peering. She'd been in this office that day last spring when Carr had brought his rescued prisoner in and then threatened to kill the sheriff. She looked at Carr and a slight shiver of anticipation went through her thin young body.

He said, "Hello, Ides Lou. How's your mother?"

"Oh, fine, but—Poke ain't here. Him an' Ma are down at the Kendalls' house lookin' after Miz Kendall. She had some kinda stroke an' can't talk. Is there something you was wanting?"

He said, "No, I guess I'll wait around a bit and perhaps Poke will be up."

The two shotguns he'd seen last spring were there in the rack. Carr sat down at Poke's desk and looked out the window. The girl had almost fled along the path to the walled security of the women's outhouse in the courtyard. Carr's cold gaze went down across the flats toward the big two-story Kendall home.

Nearly a dozen horses down there, stomping away heel flies and switching their long black tails. Ples would be sitting in the spacious kitchen, drinking coffee spiked with whisky, awaiting the kill. . . .

Carr shook off his dark thoughts and got up and put on his hat. He couldn't wait any longer for Poke to come up and perhaps stop what was certain to happen. The sheriff was keeping his promise to side the old man, no matter what took place.

Carr took down one of the shotguns and gave a final glance out the west window of the office. Down there, clipping past the church at a fast trot, Ad Slocum's duns and hack were leaving a dust streak as they sped in the direction of Miss Melissa's house.

Alma, too, was keeping her word; she was leaving her home and coming to Carr—if he wanted her.

Something like a sigh went out of him. A long road he'd ridden these past five years, Jonathan Carr thought. A road leading into the maw of a dark canyon with the wind and its lost echoes shrieking their mocking laughter.

Carr shifted Poke Kendall's shotgun over to his left hand and went out into the breezeway again. Duval and Evans were jogging their horses along the south side of the

courthouse fence, heading around it either for the hotel
or the saloon in back of it, near the jail.

They probably didn't want to brace him in the building. They were guessing that he'd come after them, and
then get him braced in a two-way crossfire.

Chapter Nine

JONATHAN CARR went up the steps of the stairwell to the second floor, opened double doors and came into the emptiness of a courtroom. It was much larger and higher inside than he had previously pictured; so huge and impressively dignified compared with the old sod-wall courthouse of pioneer days. That had been Ples Kendall's first ranch.

He stood looking around him and thought, My father would have loved this. He would have belonged here, up there in the judge's chair back of the bench. He wanted to serve his people.

To his mind as Carr stood there came all the essence of the many letters his peppery little aunt had written; a remark here, a suggestion there, slyly hidden, buried deep in her hopes for his future. She'd laid out the picture for him piecemeal, and only now was he seeing it as a whole for the first time. He hadn't allowed himself that in the past.

She held no briefs for Porter Beecroft's successful, carefully fashioned way of life in his law practice in Fort Worth. The cultivation of only those people who were important, parlor games and proper small talk over cigars and Benedictine; singing reedy baritone in the choir of his wife's imposing church while collecting wealth from a bloody cattle empire on the plains.

Jonathan Carr had known for a long time that some day he would return to the way of life taught him by his father. His lack of enthusiasm for Porter's plans for him had made him sure of it.

And now the crowning irony. Possessed of a spunkiness none of them ever suspected, Laura had refused to accept her part in a cut-and-dried situation. She'd broken with Jonathan and, in doing so, repudiated further parental dictation. Maybe she'd nursed secretly the same dream as her godmother, Miss Melissa. A home here in Salt

Fork and a judgeship for Carr . . . All gone now in her words that morning, and two Kendall gunfighters circling the courthouse yard.

He'd idly had dreams himself, being equally sly with Miss Melissa, and now they were gone just when he really wanted them so badly.

Carr walked between the rows of long benches with slanted back rests, and he went over to the jury box on a raised dais, with its twelve empty chairs and six new brass spittoons. He looked down through a window at Duval and Evans, now jogging their ponies along the east fence toward the hotel; he saw Miss Melissa's shiny buggy racked in front of the hotel.

Prominently displayed on their shirt fronts were the deputy sheriff badges that Poke Kendall had given them.

Carr laid Poke Kendall's short-barrel shotgun on the polished rectangular table assigned to the district attorney. He put his hat beside it and brushed back the hair Miss Melissa had so fussily combed. He heard the dull echoes of his own boots as he treaded over to the witness chair beside the judge's bench—where his father would have been at home, where he himself couldn't ever be.

He lifted a boot to the small witness stand where the chair rested and put his left elbow upon his knee. He bent forward and said, the words sounding strange to his ears, "Mrs. Delaney, I want you to tell this jury exactly what happened the day you were alone at the ranch house last spring when Luke Kendall came by after a three-day drinking spree with Dale Hayden down in Dale's shack in the Double Mountain breaks . . ."

Later, he walked over to the jury box and placed his left hand on the railing. He turned to the bench, "Your Honor, Judge Carr, and you twelve men of the jury . . ."

Sound strained into the emptiness of the big courtroom and brought him back to reality. Some damned fool was shouting down below somewhere. Carr looked through a window at the hotel porch and saw figures there. Porter Beecroft and his wife and Laura, and other people Carr neither knew nor remembered, vague faces in the late afternoon sun. The two horses of Duval and Evans were tied at the northeast stile of the courtyard, but Carr saw no signs of their riders.

Terrified footsteps came running up the stairwell and he

turned as Ides Lou hurried through the doorway. She flung a look back over her thin shoulder and pointed down and her eyes were large in a face gone white.

"Mr. Carr—Jonathan! They're coming after you. Men with guns. Elmer Gibbens is with them!"

He said gently, "Thank you, Ides Lou. When I come back again, and there is a dance in town, I'd like you to save one. Go down and tell Poke I'm sorry he didn't come up here."

To his surprise, Elmer Gibbens came into the room alone. The white paper he held in front of him was like a peace flag, but back of it his mouth was twisted in malicious satisfaction.

Carr said with strange quietness, "Men who hell-dog for Ples Kendall also seem to have to learn the hard way, Gibbens. You should have done what I told you."

"I've done what I should! Take a look at them, Carr! And now, damn you, here come two deputies to serve these papers!"

Carr didn't have to be told that part of it.

He could hear their steps coming up the stairwell to the second floor; heavy and even and without haste, in the confident manner of men with the law at their backs and gun speed below their swinging hands.

Elmer Gibbens's face had changed color as though his vitriolic outburst had drained him dry and left the residue of fright biting at raw nerves. He took two steps backward and flattened his back against the wall beside the open double doorway. His eyes were in a queer awe and fascination upon Carr, standing there in the aisle between the benches.

And as long as he lived Gibbens would never forget Jonathan Carr's next words to him, dry and sardonical.

"You'll never know whether I made love to Alma out there at the river today, Elmer, because neither of us will ever tell. So put it out of your mind. She wouldn't ever have let you marry into Kendall money even if I hadn't come back."

He knew by the man's expression that that spade had gone down deep and turned up into words the hopes in the district attorney's heart. Gibbens's thin nostrils began to flare wildly, and then there was no more time to look.

Duval came in first, although the shorter and younger

one, who reminded Carr of Link Kendall, appeared to be pushing forward as though in fear he'd arrive too late. But Carr's eyes were mostly for the ex-ranger. His sandy complexion and sandy mustache made startling contrast with his scarred left cheek.

They knew each other by reputation, these two Texas Ranger gunfighters, but only Duval knew that had it not been for Jonathan Carr's smashed right hand he'd have turned down cold Ples Kendall's orders for the kill. That spoiled pup beside him, Duval was remembering, was worse than Link when it came to trying to gun-rep himself into the Rangers. He wouldn't last long enough to become cagey in a game where a man never lived past the first mistake.

Before Duval could speak, however, Evans cut in with a twisted smile at the corner of his own hard mouth.

"You know why we're here. Poke Kendall wants to talk with you."

"Where?" Carr asked and smiled faintly. "In the jail or down at the house?"

"We didn't come here to talk, we came here to get you. You can walk out on your feet or be carried out feet first."

Carr spoke coolly to Duval, giving a brief cant of his bared head. "Where'd you pick him up, Duval?"

The scar on the gunfighter's left cheek contorted as a sneer broke beneath the sandy mustache. "Link met him in Fort Worth. Same age, two of a kind, their guts aching to git into the Rangers. They'll both learn, if they live long enough. Like you an' me learnt."

"Evans, you get out of here before it's too late," Jonathan Carr said, suddenly harsh. "Get on back home and stay there while there's still time."

"Hell I will!" Evans bawled, telling Carr split seconds ahead of time what he was going to do, and then he made the fatal move. He clawed wildly for his gun.

The move, made in the face of the ex-Ranger's previous harsh orders to the younger man, caught Duval completely off guard by a second. But the die was cast and his own right hand streaked to his hip.

Carr's .44 was out in his left hand and spouting fire, the spiteful crashes of the weapon deafening in the courtroom. Under the shocking impact of two bullets Evans went down and Carr, body and mind in lightning co-ordination, didn't hesitate. Duval's gun was coming up in a lightning blurr when the stony-faced man they'd come to kill drove two more bullets into Duval's chest.

Duval's gun flashed fire once, a convulsive reflex of his thumb as it slid off the almost cocked hammer, and when he fell the six-shooter thumped loudly to the floor and skidded against the leg of a long plank bench.

Carr came out of a crouch, behind his flaming eyes that instinctive regret—always that instinctice regret when he saw a man die. And Duval was dying. He lay curled on his right side, the black scar twisting on his left cheek as his lips began to work.

"Goddlemighty," came in a choking whisper and then a fleck of red appeared at the corners of his mouth. "To think I had to git killed on account—of that spoiled young pup—" He broke off and began to cough.

"Duval, I'm sorry for both of you, sorry for why you came," Carr said, bending over the man. "But there's nothing I can do for you now."

"Did you . . . kill him?" the man choked out.

"No, but I don't think he'll ever use his right arm and shoulder again."

"Then—kill him for me, Carr!" Duval urged, and then broke it off and died quietly. His long frame relaxed and the leg that had been partly curled back slowly straightened.

Carr's fingers automatically went to the loading gate and the ejector plunger under the warm barrel of the .44. Four brass commandmants tinkled oddly as they flipped to the floor. Carr reloaded and looked at Evans, down on the floor near Duval's body, hat off, blond hair rumpled and shining. All the sneering toughness had gone out of Evans's young face. He lay whimpering and moaning softly like an overgrown boy who wanted his mother.

A choking sound of a different kind came to Carr's ears and he saw Elmer Gibbens. The district attorney was apoplectic from the shocking, death-dealing violence he had just witnessed, and a new rage he couldn't find words to express.

"You . . . you'll pay for this, Carr. You'll . . ."

Jonathan Carr was upon him like a panther. One hand got Gibbens by the back of his coat collar. The other went under the district attorney's coat tail and grasped him by the back of his belt. Carr rammed him through the doorway and to the head of the stairs. He lifted a booted foot and placed it above the small of Gibbens's narrow back and sent him crashing down the stairwell end over end. Gibbens gave a strangled bawl as his face skidded against the mortar of the breezeway below and he miraculously scrambled to his feet unhurt.

"Go tell Ples what I said, Gibbens," Jonathan Carr called down. "Same as before. I still don't want any more trouble with him and his sons."

Gibbens fled from view, shouting at somebody as more running footsteps came from below. Carr turned back to the whimpering sounds in the courtroom. Evans's eyes looked up at him, pleading.

"Do something for me," he moaned over and over again. "Do something, Carr—I'm dying."

"You're losing some blood and you've got a smashed shoulder because I had time to shoot for the shoulder socket. But you won't die."

He started to kneel, to tear away the man's shirt, but the steps were coming up the stairs again, fast, and Carr turned. He was standing with booted legs braced, stony cold, the deadly six-shooter cocked in his right hand when Laura came running through the tall doorway.

"Jonathan!" she cried, and then horror suffused her face at the crimson trickle working away from Duval's body and pooling on the new gray paint. "I thought . . . are you all right?"

"Thanks to him there," he said and indicated young Evans. "See if you can pad his wounds and then get a doctor. He's bleeding bad, but he'll pull through."

"But this killing? Where will it end?" she said.

He shoved the .44 inside the waistband of his pants once more and turned. "It probably won't now, ever," he said harshly.

He went up the aisle to the district attorney's table and put on his hat. He picked up Poke Kendall's shotgun and went back to her. She looked at him, her face white.

"Where are you going?" she asked, although she knew. "Out to get the rest of them? To splash this town with the blood of more dead men when you could get your horse and ride away from it all?"

"It has been in my mind for a long time that when a man travels a certain road long enough, he reaches a point where there's no turning back. I reached that point a few moments ago, Laura. Thanks for being honest with me today. I don't expect we'll meet again."

He went down the stairs and came to the north end of the breezeway and stood there, a tall gaunt figure in black and white against the red stone block walls of the two-story courthouse built by Ples Kendall's money. The sun threw long shadows along the side, but the glare of it was full on the hotel porch where Carr saw Porter Beecroft and his wife and Gibbens among others. Gibbens was gesticulating wildly and shouting, his face livid with mixed emotions of fright and indignation. Men were shouting all over town and a few of them from the south side were running through the courtyard.

Carr turned and looked at them, and they came to a halt, and then all moved slowly at a cautious walk. The word was that Carr had killed both men, shot them so fast that neither had pulled a trigger.

Hoofbeats floated up across the flats from the northwest part of the town and Carr saw Poke Kendall and Link and Ed coming at a lope.

He cocked both hammers of the shotgun and with the short weapon dangling in one hand he walked on the graveled pathway to the stile and over it. He was unaware that Laura was following behind.

Carr stood there in the street in front of the hotel's porch with Poke Kendall's double barrel in both hands as the sheriff and his brothers loped up and pulled to a halt. Poke swung down fast for a middle-aged man, his eyes going to the two saddled horses ridden by Duval and Evans and then flicking to the courthouse.

Link and Ed sat in wooden silence, and for once neither of them was grinning. Link's black eyes were upon the bruises he'd put on this deadly man's face at noon while held by Jules MacCandless.

"What's going on here, Jonathan?" Poke demanded.

"I thought you knew. Duval was carrying your long glass. Didn't you hear the shooting?"

"I heard Elmer yelling all the way down across the flats, but couldn't make out what he was babbling." He cleared his throat. "Where are they, Jonathan?"

Carr jerked his head toward the courthouse. "Upstairs. Just inside the courtroom doors."

"Dead?"

"One of them. Evans needs a doctor."

"By God," Poke Kendall said softly. "You beat Duval. You killed Duval with a crippled gun hand!"

Laura's skirt hem rustled as she hurried unseen to the porch to where her parents stood. Carr didn't move his cold eyes from the three brothers. He would have liked to see, but he could pretty well guess the emotions on the face of Porter, and of Mrs. Beecroft, and Laura.

He'd always taken her for granted, but only against an unreal background against the real feeling of having Alma Kendall's passionate body in his arms; picturing her as coming obediently to Salt Fork in answer to her parents' wishes. A woman like that, one you thought you could have through the mere formality of asking, didn't mean much to a man—not until you suddenly realized she now was out of reach, that something unbridgeable had come between you.

His trailing down and killing five murderous Texas desperadoes probably had been made indistinct to her, by the vagueness of time and distance. But now, even after she'd repudiated him, she'd seen first-hand more of it in shocking ugliness.

Carr spoke to Poke Kendall. "I told Gibbens to take a message to your father. Now, I want you three to take it. Tell Ples that five years ago I got the man who killed my father, and then called it finished without getting the person who ordered it done. I still feel that way. It's all finished. I want no more trouble with the Kendalls."

For some unknown reason the sheriff flushed uncomfortably. It might have been remorse. Carr couldn't fathom a guess at the moment.

Poke asked slowly, "Where you goin'?"

"To Camp Coke tonight, as I told you. I've got to wire a report of this whole affair to Ranger headquarters, and then wait to face the consequences."

"If you do that, Jonathan, there won't be any to face," the sheriff answered harshly. "The old man won't wait that long. He warned you not to come to Salt Fork, and he never broke his word in his life. Go get that roan hoss and ride out now!"

"I've got a badly wounded man lying in Miss Melissa's cellar and with him his wife. Miss Melissa is taking them out tonight in her buggy because Porter Beecroft didn't have the courage to stand by his convictions. When they go out under cover of darkness I go with them. But not until then, Poke."

Ed Kendall's hard young face broke into normal lines. He looked over at Link and grinned. "Alma is over there at Miss Melissa's house with Ad Slocum's hack. Maybe she'll take 'em out for you, Jonathan."

Carr's icy eyes and the shotgun muzzles swung in Ed's direction. "Maybe she will, Ed," came the grim reply. "But you get out of here. If this thing still has to be settled after what has already happened today, then I might as well start now."

"Get out of here!" Poke roared at his two brothers. He ran at their horses, hands outflung. "Get out of here before you get your damned bellies full of buckshot the way Luke got it from Lee Delaney. Git!"

They got. They whirled their horses and spurred back down across the flats and the sheriff, breathing heavily, turned and came back to his own horse. He swung into creaking leather and looked down at the grim man standing with the sheriff's own shotgun in his hands.

A sigh went out of him and his big shoulders seemed to droop. He said, "It's been a long time since me and the old man come into this country with two wagons and yoked bulls. Just the two of us, and him treatin' me like I was a grown up man. There's been somethin' different between him and me, and the rest of the family. I'll do what I can to stop him, Jonathan. But you just remember this: I been sidin' him all my life, and if he comes after you I'll be sidin' him again."

He lifted the reins and necked over his horse, and as it turned he called to Mrs. Beecroft. "Much obliged for comin' down today to see Ma, even though she didn't recognize you. I expect she'll be going most any time."

He rode away at a slow walk to go back to the big white two-story house, back to where an old man sat drinking coffee spiked with whisky. He knew what the old man's answer would be.

Carr uncocked the two hammers and, in a strange silence blanketing the entire town square, went back alone to the courthouse. He returned without the shotgun, led his roan through the still gate, and hooked the reins to the back of Miss Melissa's buggy. If he was aware of a hundred pairs of eyes watching him in silence he paid them no heed. Without looking at Laura or her parents, he got into the buggy and picked up the lines. He drove around the northwest corner of the square.

Halfway down across the flats Jonathan Carr looked back just once at the upper windows of the courtroom where one dead man and another wounded one lay in their own blood. He thought again, My father would have liked it up there. More than anything in his whole life.

And, heaven help me. so would I.

Chapter Ten

DISTRICT ATTORNEY Elmer Gibbens was the first to speak after Carr left. His face was raw but not skinned from contact with the mortar flooring and he was still badly shaken from witnessing the deadly violence that had erupted in front of his eyes. He placed his left hand over the cap of his right shoulder and worked it with a grunt of pain.

"Well, Porter, there's nothing more we can do now. I've done my level best and I want no more to do with it."

"No, I would imagine not," Beecroft answered with a measure of grim satisfaction. "I expect you'll be quite content to let Jonathan alone now, Elmer."

"He's the most brutal man I ever heard of!" Gibbens cried out wildly. "He—"

"I know, I know," Beecroft interrupted impatiently and waved a deprecatory hand. "I have eyes of my own, Elmer, I saw what happened here. But my conscience will never rest easy unless I go down and make a final attempt to stop this terrible thing."

"How?" snapped the district attorney. "You tell me!"

"I have some measure of influence with Ples," his lawyer replied stiffly.

"Ahhh! You heard what Poke said just a few moments ago. You ought to know better than that."

"It will do no harm to try."

He turned to his wife, noting the set, stubborn cast of her mouth. A stubbornness of his own, long dormant in the face of her uncompromising severity, rose within him. In Porter Beecroft's mind was exactly the same thought which had been in Jonathan's that same day: He'd quit his partner in the land case against Ples Kendall and become wealthy, and then quit again today. He still had his life where Judge Carr had died because of his convictions and creed. He had his wealth and his position in Fort Worth. But he had paid for it all with his self-respect.

Gibbens eyed him with a small man's malicious satisfaction, and he thought almost savagely, No, it won't
hurt you to try. You can't afford to see the murderous old
prairie wolf get himself killed the way Duval did. It
would cost you another fortune—and it will cost me a
future seat in Congress, too, unless this whole matter can
be hushed up.

"I guess it wouldn't hurt for us to go down and try, at
that. Because Jonathan Carr is finished, Porter. After what
he did today in the face of MacNab's warning to Poke,
the Rangers will take care of him. Let's go."

"Porter!" Mrs. Beecroft spoke stridently to her husband
as he stepped heavily from the hotel porch. "You get
right back here. You're not leaving this hotel until the
stage takes us out to Fort Worth early tomorrow morning."

Beecroft ignored her and looked at his daughter, sensing
the change in her. His wife had almost exploded when
Laura broke away and ran to the courthouse. She'd broken
their engagement before it was announced, but she'd gone
running to Carr when guns began to explode.

Porter Beecroft left the hotel with the district attorney
and began walking just as Poke looked back.

Poke pulled up and waited, his unhappy eyes suspicious.
He sat his saddle, listening briefly to Beecroft and finally
nodded assent. He swung to the ground and the three of
them walked on with the led horse plodding behind.

Seven or eight pairs of curiously quiet eyes were upon
them as they came up on the front porch, men who'd
helped finish up the Salt Fork part of several fall round-
ups. Some of them had never used a gun and were afraid;
others among them were of the Duval stripe; but all had
the belief that a Texas cowpuncher's loyalty came first
to his outfit, right or wrong, come hell or high water.

One of them, a man of thirty-five with a half-inch
scrubble of dark hair on his face, came up off long haunch
muscles and spoke to the sheriff.

"Link said Duval got killed, Poke," he said casually.

"He did," the sheriff said curtly.

"But, hell, wasn't that Carr we just seen in a buggy
headin' down across the flats?"

"You got good enough eyes, I reckon," Poke Kendall
replied coolly. "But my long glass is still on Duval's saddle.

Go up and bring down their two horses. Keep your mouth shut and come on back right away."

"Shore, shore. Evans goin' to cash in his chips?"

"I don't know, and at the moment I don't give a damn."

He avoided the eyes of the two waiting lawyers and then followed them inside and closed the front door.

Nobody but three of them, plus Link and Ed, knew that it was Alma Kendall who had instigated the death of Judge Carr the night after the trial was finished. She had sent a Hayden after the hack on the way to the Double Mountain ranch—and then lived in an agony of remorse for five long years, taunted by her father.

That was the reason why the old man had repudiated her today at the Salt Fork crossing. It was why she was at Miss Melissa's house now with her personal possessions. The years that had softened up Poke and changed him showed no effect of the same kind upon his father.

A loud burst of laughter came from the kitchen as Poke and the two Kendall lawyers went in. Old Ples sat alone at a small table with a tin coffee cup in one hand, spiked from a bottle in front of him on the table. Link and Ed stood with legs aspraddle, grinning, with all the cockiness of youth and wealth in their hard young faces. Jules MacCandless sat humped on a low stool like a huge mastiff awaiting the orders of his master. Dale Hayden's angular frame was in a chair tipped back against the wall by a rear door, the brooding, morose mood still upon his bony features. The piece of paper Carr had noticed that morning was still tucked in the breast pocket of his shirt.

Poke looked a question at his father and old Ples laughed again and put down his coffee cup. "I just found out from the boys, Poke, that that Delaney woman is goin' to have a baby. You reckon it's Luke's kid?"

Porter Beecroft winced visibly, outraged at the coarse old man. He said placatingly, "I don't think there's any doubt of it, Ples. They never had any children during four years previous to the day last spring when your son—ah—"

Link and Ed went off into howls, pointing scathing fingers at the lawyer, and old Ples leaned back in his chair and roared.

Beecroft, his face flaming red, went to a cupboard and returned with a small white cup. He poured himself a drink and then watered it from a pail dipper on a stand near the kitchen door. The laughter subsided and old Ples looked at Elmer Gibbens.

"What happened to your face, Elmer? Did a horse kick you?"

Gibbens, his voice beginning to quaver again, told what had happened in the courtroom when the two Kendall fighters had closed in on Carr and braced him for the kill. He made no bones of the fact that Carr had flung him down the stairs and again told him to take a message. He cared nothing about who had ordered the death of his father; he wanted no more trouble.

Ples Kendall thought of his daughter down at Miss Melissa's house and something vicious began going through his mind. Poke saw the familiar look.

He left them and went upstairs. At the head of the landing he saw Ides Lou come out of a room and softly close the door. She told him what she had seen of Carr in both the office and upstairs and the sheriff nodded. It enabled him to piece things together in his methodical way and pretty well tell what had happened.

Another burst of laughter rolled up from below, seeping through the floor cracks like the slam of a distant door, and a chair crashed as though somebody had tipped too far back. The door to the sickroom opened again and Poke, hat in hand, saw Ides Lou's mother. He could see in her where Ides Lou got her gangling thinness.

"Any change, Miz Deen?" he asked in a whisper.

"All that noise goin' on downstairs. Can't you put a stop to it?"

"I'll try."

"And, Poke," the woman added, "you'd better go after Alma. Tell your father if he wants to see *her* again he'd better come up now." She indicated the closed door.

"I'll tell him," said Poke and went down again. He knew it wouldn't do any good. Old Ples hadn't been up inside that room in nearly a year.

Gibbens was still talking excitedly. The old man was listening with both elbows on the table. Porter Beecroft stood motionless, cup in hand.

"So that's how things have shaped up, Ples," Gibbens

was adding as though summing up the prosecution's case for the judge. "Carr is finished with the law in Texas. All you have to do is sit back and wait. The Rangers he once served will never let him get away with this."

"Nor you either, Ples," Porter Beecroft reminded sharply. "One of the men Jonathan Carr killed was Bert Burton's deputy in line of duty. All you have to do is let him go on to Camp Coke and wire Austin, and then let them take care of the rest. The same thing holds true for Lee Delaney. Let the law try him for murder."

Old Ples wiped at his mouth and picked up the tin cup. "Well," he said, "I ain't got nothin' against the woman. She ain't the first as ever got throwed on a bed; been quite a lot of others. They all got over it. So there ain't no harm goin' to come to her tonight."

In the silence that followed he leaned back and shifted at the loopless gunbelt around his waist.

Porter Beecroft broke the silence, clearing his throat again. "What about her husband, Ples? You know by now where he is and his condition after Ed's bullet caught him high in the arm. He rode for hours with that wound. He had to crawl on his knees and one hand to get from Miss Melissa's barn to her back gate."

Link looked at Beecroft with his black eyes burning. He sneered. "He killed a Kendall, Porter, and people don't do that and live. Miss Melissa or Alma can take the woman out of the county tonight, if they want, and us Kendalls'll see she gets a few hundred dollars from you to tide her over. But Lee Delaney gets finished off, damn him! That job belongs to me and Ed."

"Now, now—" Gibbens began soothingly, but was cut short by the old man.

"I want every damn one of you to shut up an' stay shut up. I'm still running things around here. Porter, you're right."

"About the prisoner? Fine, fine! I knew I could convince you that—"

"You ain't convinced me of nothin'," the old man growled harshly. "I'll tell you what I'm going to do. Delaney can go. I want him outa the county on account of his wife. Far as I'm concerned, we're all square. I don't want it said that Ples Kendall makes war on women an' crippled men. Fair enough, Porter?"

"Very generous of you, indeed, Ples." Beecroft's face was alight with sudden pleasure.

"But what about Jonathan Carr?" Gibbens's question came almost as an objection.

"He can go," old Ples said with finality and rose to his feet. "Poke," he ordered brusquely. "Go back uptown with Elmer an' squash the indictments an' the warrant for Jonathan's arrest. I guess I been all wrong. Jules, tell them punchers outside to hit the breeze outa here to the roundup wagon on Salt Fork. We're startin' the drive to Fort Worth in the mornin'."

After they were gone Link Kendall still stood there in the kitchen with booted feet apart, his mouth curling in a half sneer as he looked down at his father. Jules Mac-Candless had stepped outside, called a command to the riders, and then returned. He saw a brittle grin come into old Ples Kendall's face and a slow one of sudden understanding change Link's features.

Link chuckled and relaxed. "You had me worried for a minute there, Pa. Thought you'd grown old and maybe soft."

"Not yet, I ain't, son," Ples Kendall said.

He jerked a horny thumb to indicate the departure of Poke and the two lawyers. "Poke's the one who's grown soft. He'd still back me like he done all his life, but chances are he's so relieved no Kendall is goin' to risk gettin' shot tonight he'll go straight to Jonathan with the news. That's what I aimed for him to do."

His malevolent glance went to the huge figure of Mac-Candless. "Jules, now that Poke is outa the house, slip out an' git them men of yours. Have 'em strung out on the east side of town after dark, somewhere around the school-house, because Jonathan will come that way on the way to Camp Coke."

"All right," Jules MacCandless nodded without moving his big body.

"This is one night you better have a gun on, after the way you held Carr for Link to beat up today."

"I never carry a gun."

"You damn well will tonight!" snapped the old man. "I don't want Jonathan Carr to git away because you didn't have to have one."

"I use my hands. If Carr try to shoot me, I break his

neck with these." He held out his huge paws, palms up.

Dale Hayden stirred and got up from his chair. "Where do I fit in, Ples?" he asked quietly. "I've had a score to settle with Jonathan Carr for five years, though I never did know who it was sent my brother after the judge that night after the land trial." He sensed that he would now find out, and he was right.

"Time you found out, Dale," old Ples replied, "because after tonight it ain't goin' to make much difference no-how. It was Alma."

The morose expression in Hayden's eyes changed, and for a brief moment something savage came into them.

Jules MacCandless got up and followed as Hayden went out the back door to the kitchen porch. The sun was almost down, blood-red across the flat drabness of the plains.

Ples Kendall rose to his feet.

"I told Jonathan Carr to keep outa Salt Fork an' never come back here! I gave my word, an' I never broke it in my life. He's got to learn what some of them sodbusters learned a long time ago—what it means when Ples Kendall warns a man!"

He stalked toward the stairs he hadn't ascended in more than a year. No sense of premonition impelled and guided his steps. He felt instead a tremendous surge of relief, like a man riding out of a prairie rain into endless bright sunshine again. The passing of a final dark shadow obscuring complete peace he had never known.

That shadow had been Jonathan Carr these past five years; the fear that because he himself was a vengeful man, so would Carr be in avenging the death of his father.

He turned and bellowed back through the living room. "Link, git hold of Pedro Viejo for me."

Young Ed was getting to be more like him every day, and he'd given in and let the boy go to Marlinville, certain that if a showdown came there would be no doubt about the outcome. Jonathan Carr was a manhunter, not a gunman. Ed would kill him before his gun cleared leather.

Ples Kendall went on up the stairs to the top, a cold fear he had never known in the past biting at his vitals. In the old days he'd have settled this thing in a hurry with twenty men. No fussing around, just run the man down and kill him.

But he'd been an early-day Ranger himself, and Poke's repeated warnings about MacNab had stung because subconsciously, as an ex-Ranger, he knew them to hold truth.

Chapter Eleven

CARR LEFT the team of blacks and his roan horse in front of Miss Melissa's gate and went inside the yard. The tip of the setting sun struck with a copper fire along the tops of the mesquite brush over across the lane down which Alma Kendall and, later, her brothers and their men had traveled that day.

Now Duval was dead, and Evans was up in the courtroom being bandaged by a doctor. But Ples Kendall would keep his promise to Carr even if it meant the risk that apparently filled Poke's mind with dread: the loss of any member of his own family.

Carr saw no signs of Ad Slocum's hack and the two duns. He guessed that Alma had put them into the barn until Bert Burton could send over a man to get them.

Out there at the Salt Fork of the Brazos today the old hunger, and the long years of loneliness, had made him forget everything for a few moments. But he knew now that this thing was over and done with between them. And he realized that in Laura he'd lost a woman he'd never really wanted until now.

Carr went up on the porch where she'd stood that day, and looked again at the sun going down across the tops of the mesquites. Meeting Laura today was like meeting a beautiful stranger, a new person he'd never known existed within the frowning shadow of her stern, intolerant mother. The thought caused a wry grin to break over his face.

Miss Melissa opened the front door and came out, her eyes unnaturally bright and curious and filled with unasked questions. He removed his hat and asked, "Where's Alma, Melissa?"

"What happened uptown?"

"I didn't see the hack and team out here."

"I heard shots and a lot of yelling."

She listened as he briefed her, and although her eyes shot him a sharp look when he mentioned Laura's presence, she made no comment.

"Alma's in the kitchen, just taking the quail out of the frying pan; I knew you wouldn't be gone very long, Jonathan. Alma's going to take the stage out to Fort Worth with Porter and Belinda and Laura in the morning."

She led the way into the kitchen and Carr, putting his hat on the card table, followed. Alma Kendall was placing plates for three on the table. She'd put on another clean shirt, and she wore one of Miss Melissa's white aprons.

She looked up at him and smiled without speaking, her cobalt eyes holding a quiet unhappiness, an uncertainty of thought.

He mistook that thought, unaware of the remorse that had been haunting her for these past five years because she'd been a misguided, hotheaded Kendall woman then. He knew she must have heard the muffled sounds of gunfire uptown and was asking him an unasked question about her father or brothers.

He said, "None of your family were uptown, Alma. Ples sent Duval and some young fellow named Evans. They didn't make it."

She paused, and he could feel the relief that flooded through her.

"Thank God for that, Jonathan," he heard her murmur. "As you said a little while ago, nobody ever could have realized how things can change. Before you leave tonight I've got something to tell you. It's been on my mind for five years."

He went to a glassed-in cupboard in a corner of the kitchen, where Miss Melissa's gold-edged chinaware reposed upon the shelves, and he rolled its castored legs aside. Removing a small rug, he lifted a trap door leading to the huge cellar where long ago Miss Melissa had taken the Kendall youngsters to feast upon sweetmeats. He went down the musty steps into living quarters for a woman living like a hunted criminal for several months. He saw a big man who'd been in the jail that morning in Marlinville, bandaged and on his back in a bunk, features pale from months indoors and a loss of blood from Ed Kendall's bullet.

Ruby Delaney sat on the bunk beside her husband. She was not more than twenty-two, a young girl who had married a much older husband because he had meant security and kindness. Carr was glad of the loose shawl wrapped around her body, but Ruby Delaney, who'd always wanted a child, didn't appear to be embarrassed at all.

"Hello, Ruby," Carr greeted her, and smiled. "How is he?"

"A lot better'n you'd think, Mr. Carr. Miss Melissa gave him some whisky an' then he ate."

Carr bent over a face that was strong despite planes of suffering and exhaustion.

"Feel strong enough to travel, Lee?" Jonathan Carr asked.

Delaney managed a weak nod and an answering smile. "As long as Ruby goes with me. I have a double responsibility now to keep alive, Jonathan." The smile on the man's drawn face turned wry. "If I hadn't changed my views about many things while in jail in Marlinville, I'd have lived out my life in shame over this. I don't feel that way now."

"That's fine, Lee, because tonight you're going out of here in Ad Slocum's hack. There's been more trouble uptown, which just about makes me an outlaw, but if I can get you away safely I'll see to it that another lawyer gets you a change of venue. It will mean a fair trial away from Ples Kendall's seat of power, and it will get you a complete acquittal, I'm certain."

Delaney was silent for a few moments; then a sigh went out of him as though he viewed the long future. He grasped his wife's hand and closed his eyes.

"Thanks, Jonathan. But in doing this for Ruby and me you're destroying everything for yourself. You never fooled Miss Melissa for a moment; she always figured in her mind that some day you'd come back here to take up where your father left off five years ago."

Carr went back upstairs to the kitchen and replaced the rug and cupboard. The sun was down now. He'd have to eat hurriedly.

With an equally spare appetite Alma Kendall ate with him and Miss Melissa in a strained atmosphere made somewhat warmer by Miss Melissa's sprightly attempts to carry the conversation away from the thought in the minds of all of them. Once or twice Carr caught Alma's eyes studying him, uncertainty still in their depths. Five years ago, she'd said—when his father had died.

When the meal was over Miss Melissa began fixing up food packages for the fugitive and his wife. Carr put on his hat and went out front to put up the blacks. He heard Alma's footsteps and the creak of the gate behind him and saw her coming to him in the darkness. He untied the lines, looped them in one hand, and she fell in beside him as he led the team and buggy around the corner of the fence and down the lane toward the barn.

Around them the night lay in stillness except for the soft plod of the two blacks and the roan behind. The mesquites west of the lane threw ragged patterns against the sky like a piece of fine lace against the black of one of Miss Melissa's prim dresses. He thought he heard another horse somewhere out there, but couldn't locate the sound. The old familiar wary chill came into him then and through it came the first words the woman walking beside him had spoken.

"Jonathan, what made you almost love me today when you were on your way to Laura?"

Some of the old harshness rose up in him, sub-conscious antagonism toward Laura's mother. "I wasn't thinking of Laura then," he said.

"Would it have made any difference if Ples and the others hadn't shown up?"

"All in the world," he answered her frankly. "I'd have told Laura. It would have saved her the painful duty of breaking our engagement before it had time to become an actuality."

"And now?" she asked gently.

"I'm leaving," he said shortly. "I'll never be able to come back home after today."

"Neither will I, Jonathan," came her low reply. "One part of my life was cut off today. I'm starting a new one, and I want it to be with you as it was in the old days here. I want to drive that hack out of here tonight and meet you at Camp Coke. But it has to be a clean beginning, and there's something you've got to know first."

They were at the gate now and she left him and opened it and came back, holding it. He made no effort to move inside. He stood waiting.

"What is it?" he asked her.

"For five years my father has lived with the secret uneasiness that some day you'd come back to Salt Fork just
as you did today, in the violence of gunfire. To his way of
thinking, you'd never rest easy until you'd found the person who sent a murderer after your father that night after
the land case. He's used it as a club over my head. I was
a lot younger then, Jonathan, fiercely proud of the hot
Kendall blood strain, thinking it was wild and arrogant,
not knowing that in reality it was all bad."

"But why?" he asked her, and wondered that he felt no
anger and hatred now that the truth had come to light.

"I wanted your father hurt, but not killed, Jonathan,
hoping to hurt you. But like so many other men, a poor
Hayden wanted to be big in the eyes of Ples Kendall.
Your father lost his life, you killed the man I sent after
him in his buggy, and my life hasn't been worth living
since. If it will make you feel any better, I've lived in hell
ever since."

"I feel no anger, Alma," Jonathan Carr answered, and
lifted the lines to bring the blacks into motion. "Nothing
but a deep regret." He wanted to say, "You were all
wrong about my father. He objected, but he would have
accepted you into the family, and all this hatred and killing would never have happened."

In silence he unharnessed the blacks, turned them loose
in the lot, and backed the buggy beneath the shed beside Ad Slocum's hack. That hack contained his law
books.

Alma was silent beside him as he filled the empty loops
in his belt. He reached over and picked up the repeater
she had used against Ad Slocum's horse, shoving shells
into the magazine from a box of cartridges. He could
hear the telegraphic message of the mesquites, telling him
of riders out there. Somebody was closing in.

He heard the creak of a door and saw the glow of a
lantern coming along the passageway between stalls and
feed room. In the light of the lantern he saw his aunt
and a man.

"Why, it's Poke!" Alma cried out sharply.

"Get inside," Carr ordered quickly and followed her in,
closing the shed door.

"Poke, where are they?" Alma Kendall demanded of
her stepbrother.

"Who?"

"Pa and the others, of course!"

The tired lines of his face relaxed and he managed a faint smile. He didn't look like a man bent upon arrest; new tragedy ran stark lights through his eyes. But he told Carr that for the first time in his life Ples Kendall was breaking his word. Carr and the Delaneys were free to leave town.

Carr remembered the sounds out there in the brush, and his face tightened. Poke had warned twice that day he'd side his father to the end if need be, and now the sheriff had stooped to treachery. He's come with this message when Carr's own ears had told him differently.

Carr said, "I was hoping he would, Poke. I'm relieved." No use in putting the sheriff on guard; he'd lull him into thinking Carr believed him. Let him take the message back to his father.

"Where is Ples?" Alma asked.

Poke shrugged disinterestedly. "Uptown, I guess. I sent him word to come back to the house. And you'd better come on back too, Alma."

"I'm driving Ad Slocum's hack out of here tonight for Jonathan. I'll never again set foot in Ples Kendall's home as long as he's alive."

"You'll have to change your mind for a few days." Poke looked down at Miss Melissa. "I sent word to the Beecrofts to come too, an' stay over for Ma's funeral tomorrow or the next day. Will you come too, Miss Melissa?"

"You know I will, Poke," Carr's aunt replied with briskness. "Jonathan, I think—"

"I know, Melissa," he nodded. "We'll leave Lee and Ruby where they are for a few days until I wire the Rangers from Camp Coke to come get them."

"All right," she said. "You hurry along about your business now, and next time don't be gone from your aunt so long."

She led the way out of the barn again, followed by Poke, and Carr found himself alone in the darkness with Alma. He felt her arms go around his waist and she buried her head against him. To his astonishment he heard her crying softly.

She lifted her head, finally. "I guess the cards were

stacked against us right from the beginning, weren't they, Jonathan?"

"That's what I tried to tell you today, using other words. I wanted you out there at Salt Fork today. I might have tried to be noble about it afterward. I'm glad now it didn't happen."

He was thinking of those riders out there in the brush. No telling what would have happened had she gone out driving Ad Slocum's hack, he accompanying it for a short distance.

"Are you?" She wanted an answer with finality.

"Take the hack and go home to your family, Alma."

She drove out and turned down the lane again, and almost immediately he heard the crashing of horses through the mesquite, heading toward her. Carr led his roan out.

As he swung up into creaking saddle leather he could hear Alma's voice in angry denunciation of three or four men on horseback now surrounding the hack in the lane. Bert Burton's rage filled voice came back in reply. The sheriff of Marlinville had ridden hard to Salt Fork to deal himself a hand of cards in the biggest game of Jonathan Carr's life.

Chapter Twelve

Jonathan Carr eased himself through the mesquite where quail slept squatting in protective circles on the ground, heads out and senses alert for predators even in sleep. Long habits of years in the brush were upon him now, making him keenly sensitive to his surroundings.

He didn't know whether Poke really had lied, but he did know that a raging sheriff and at least three or four men had closed in on the hack, and no telling how many other Marlinville men were scattered elsewhere.

Carr rode low over the left shoulder of his horse, blending his body with its protective bulk; hoping that if shots came they would be taken solidly by the chinless roan.

Poke had said he thought the old man and his bunch were somewhere uptown, away from a house where death had mercifully ended a Kendall family problem. It might cause old Ples to forget any plans he had made, at least for the present.

And that would have been just fine, Jonathan Carr thought almost savagely, except for Bert Burton. The damned fool didn't have brains enough to stay home. He'd come to flush out the quarry and kill it for his master.

Carr worked the roan cautiously through the night and finally came out a hundred and fifty yards west of the Kendalls' big house. Lamps were on, but an eerie silence reigned. No lights shone at the town dancehall tonight, either—an odd thing the day before court when many people usually came to town. Everything seemed dead, deserted. As on past occasions when Ples Kendall went on the rampage, Salt Fork had locked its doors and waited for the dread reports of gunfire in the night.

A new sound from the west intruded upon Carr's ears. He heard the distant rattle of harness and saw the baggage-humped outlines of the stagecoach rock by, the driver talking loud to his teams. Another one, Carr thought bitterly with a hand over the warm muzzle of the roan, who'd known he was bringing Delaney from Marlinville for trial tomorrow, and recognized the dark silence hanging over Salt Fork for what it was. From Salt Fork to Marlinville to Camp Coke to Fort Worth. The driver would leave the trial judge at the hotel and perhaps another passenger or two, but he'd have no new passengers for the final run tomorrow, since the Beecrofts would be staying over.

Carr circled the north side of the town section and, at a slow walk, worked the roan up toward the rear of the hotel stables. Near them stood the town's only saloon, small and box-shaped like Ples Kendall's hotel, and fifty yards apart from the low outlines of the red sandstone jail.

There was one lone light inside the saloon and one lone horse in front. Carr had never been inside the place during the ten years since it was built. He dismounted and dropped the roan's reins back of a mesquite clump. The stock of the reloaded .44-40 repeater he'd taken from the hack and shoved into his saddle scabbard stuck up past the roan's neck and gave him a small measure of comfort. Allowing for six cartridges in his Colt and five in the Winchester, plus the filled loops in his belt, he had about thirty rounds of ammunition.

Having discharged passengers and baggage, the empty stage came rocking around the east side of the hotel. It moved in back of the saloon and pulled up at the lot gate of the hotel's livery. Carr was inside the stable shed when the driver came walking in behind his unhooked six tired horses. Carr's tall form materialized out of the night and his voice came in low warning.

"Easy, friend. I want some information."

"What—"

"Keep your voice down," Carr commanded. "I'm Jonathan Carr. Who'd you bring in on the stage?"

Five horses loped out of the night around the same corner of the hotel, from the front, and pulled up before the saloon. Carr caught the bulky outline of Bert Burton swinging down with the others. Whatever Alma had told them, they'd come here. They disappeared inside.

The stage driver said, "Carr? Man, I ain't heard anything else for the past week. The whole plains country has been waitin' to see how things shape up. What did you say you wanted to know?"

"Who were your passengers?"

"Judge Tullock, from Brownwood. You asked for an impartial judge, an' you got one. Two other fellows, drummers, from their looks."

"You sure about these last two?"

"Hell yes!" protested the driver. "One fat man an' one little one, talkin' hardware an' groceries all the way."

And that was strange, Carr thought. Any time a trial came up where feeling ran high, two Rangers usually were sent in as a silent reminder that there would be no trouble. Carr himself had served in that capacity on many occasions during the past five years.

They hadn't showed. Yet MacNab had warned him in Austin that if he got in gun trouble during court session in Salt Fork he'd be considered in the same light as any others.

He was in trouble, bad trouble. If he failed to get free of Salt Fork tonight, he'd be in handcuffs tomorrow morning.

"Just what did this small drummer look like?" Carr asked the stagecoach driver.

"Hmm. Let's see. Small man. Black eyes an' hair. Black mustache an' goatee—"

MacNab! There couldn't be any doubt of it! He'd come in on the quiet to take personal charge of this case himself.

"Let me give you a hand unharnessing," Carr said to the driver. "I've a little more time than I thought."

"You goin' to talk to the judge?"

"Not permitted," Carr answered. He bent and unbuckled a belly band on one of the wheelers, his face planed in cold lines. If MacNab tried to arrest him . . .

They finished unharnessing and turned loose the tired horses, giving them a chance to get down on their knees and roll in the corral before being watered and fed. Carr moved alone to the corral gate and stood there with his eyes on the back of the saloon a hundred feet away.

The darkened jail windows gaped at him and he felt a cold caution uncoil itself inside him. To a gunner sitting in there with a repeater, he'd make a perfect target at the saloon's front or rear door. But he had to move now.

He'd just spotted the black-coated figure of the trial

judge, tired from the long stage ride up from Brown-wood, coming toward the ramshackle saloon to get himself a quick one.

He couldn't under law discuss the case with Tullock, a fair man. But he could, in one bold move, set the wheels spinning for Lee's acquittal and dismissal of charges that he was an escaped prisoner. Bert Burton and some of his men were in there, hunting him. He'd killed Burton's deputy, and Carr wanted no more trouble before leaving town. He had to see Judge Tullock and smash this thing wide open in Ples Kendall's face.

Carr closed the corral gate behind him and strode boldly through the night to the saloon's back door. It was warped and stubborn and when he shouldered it open and stepped inside every eye in the place was turned his way. He saw the bar along the left side, and Lennox, the owner, on duty. Bert Burton and his men stood at the near end, and Pete, the Kendall night wrangler, was sound asleep and snoring at a rear corner table.

Carr saw Judge Tullock at the front end of the bar, being served from a special bottle. Tullock was sixty, white-mustached and goateed—another Texas lawyer who had played it square and honest and attained his goal in life.

Burton was in the act of lifting a shot glass of whisky to his lips, still swollen from Carr's blow that morning. He put down the glass with a half-strangled cry as Carr, his fingers loosened up from unharnessing, stood poised with his right hand above the deadly Colt at his hip.

"Don't make one damned move, Burton—you or your men," Jonathan Carr warned softly. "I've already been pushed too far today."

His cold eyes burned into those of the heavy-set owner, Lennox. "Keep your hands above the bar, Lennox."

Lennox shrugged his heavy shoulders and said, "All right. I know you." He held up the bottle, but Carr shook his head, moving past Burton and the others to Tullock. He couldn't turn his back upon them. Facing them, his back was partly to the open doorway of the porchless frontier saloon. That couldn't be helped, either.

He said, "Good evening, Judge Tullock. I believe you know me."

"I do; You were on Ranger duty in Brownwood during

court term there last year. I knew your father. Fine man."

"Did Captain MacNab of the rangers come in on the stage tonight?"

Tullock stiffened and his keen eyes became unfriendly. "That's a matter for Captain MacNab, wherever he might be."

"I suppose you're aware that I'm defending lawyer for Lee Delaney in the killing of Luke Kendall last spring?"

"I am aware that as a barrister you should know that I cannot discuss anything concerning the defendant except in due process of court."

A voice spoke up from the open doorway behind his back.

"No more discussion, gentlemen. I'm in charge here now," MacNab said.

Carr turned slowly and saw the little black-eyed man he'd served under for five years. MacNab was the worst outlaw scourge in Texas—a small chunk of dynamite who lived by the rule books. Back of him appeared Elmer Gibbens and Ples Kendall.

MacNab wasn't a man to discuss his business in a saloon, but neither was he one to waste time and words. Carr saw only duty in the icy black eyes. It wasn't difficult to read from the triumph spread across Gibbens's face that he'd babbled out the whole story of the fight at the river crossing and the death of Duval. Carr wondered with grim irony if the prosecuting attorney also had told of being kicked all the way downstairs from the courtroom. He saw old Ples grinning calculatingly, his piercing eyes brittle.

MacNab said, "Carr, I've heard the whole story. Looks like you've disregarded my warning of what would happen if you got into gun trouble here. I want to talk to you."

"I'm afraid it's a little late for that, isn't it, Captain?"

"Don't crowd me, Carr," MacNab warned softly. "You'll come talk with me."

"Sorry, Captain. I'm on my way to Camp Coke to wire headquarters and wait for arrest there."

"You're under arrest here, my friend!"

"I'm not getting shot through the window of a Kendall jail tonight by one of Ples Kendall's dogs. I'll take my chances in court later. You just take care of my client in Melissa Carr's house."

He turned to Judge Tullock and his voice lashed out. "My client was shot and wounded early this morning by one of Ples Kendall's sons, and is in no condition to appear in court. No arrest has been made in the case, of course. Neither can I appear and ask for a change of venue."

"I'll remember this violation in court, Mr. Carr," the judge said coolly.

It was then that Jonathan Carr threw his bombshell. "There will be no trial tomorrow, sir. With due respect to you, I am asking you to disqualify yourself as trial judge on the grounds the defending attorney believes an impartial trial here in Salt Fork is impossible."

In the stunned silence that followed, Carr moved toward the back door, past Burton and the others and the old Mexican night wrangler.

MacNab snapped, "Carr, if you go out that door under Ranger arrest I'll run you down if it's the last thing I ever do in my life!"

"Captain MacNab," Jonathan Carr said softly, "the trail is a straight one between here and Austin."

He closed the door, jerking it hard to shut it, knowing no shots would be fired through it. He went through the night, hearing the rough laughter of Ples Kendall.

No doubt about it now; he was an outlaw. He could defend himself in court and probably clear himself in the shootings of Ad Slocum and Duval, but the Rangers would be after him. MacNab would never sleep easy until Carr was rearrested, tried, and put behind bars in Huntsville Prison.

In the silence following Carr's closing of the back door MacNab turned, his blazing black eyes on Burton.

"Who shot Delaney this morning, mister?"

"Why, now—" Burton began uncomfortably, and glanced at Ples Kendall for succor. Into the old man's eyes had come a look promising death to the Ranger.

"My boy Ed shot him when that damn Carr turned him loose!" Ples Kendall cried. "What are you goin' to do about it, Ranger?"

"Arrest him!" snapped MacNab promptly.

"Like hell you will! They was deputies, wasn't they, Bert?"

"Sure, sure," Bert Burton said hurriedly.

"I still want him," shot back the Ranger. "Will you bring him to me, or do I go after him?"

"You come after Ed," the old man said ominously, "an' I'll kill you, MacNab. This is my town. I run it. I own it! Git on a hoss an' leave this town tonight."

His leather shotgun chaps rustled and his spurs made rattling sounds as he strode out into the night. Bert Burton and his men followed.

MacNab looked over at Judge Tullock and smiled. "If you've had your nightcap, Judge, let's get on over to the hotel," he said quietly. "I'm hungry and need a good night of rest. I imagine we'll both have quite a bit of work to do tomorrow."

When they were all gone Lennox still stood with both hands on the bar. Pedro Viejo, the best night trailer on the plains, was no longer feigning drunkenness, and waiting for Carr to show. He'd vanished, and nobody had seen him go.

Chapter Thirteen

PLES KENDALL strode angrily around the northeast corner of his hotel and stepped into the dim glow from lamps in the deserted lobby. He paid no attention to Gibbens, who had followed at his heels, nor to Bert Burton and the four men who'd come with him to Salt Fork.

He stood on the porch scowling across the flats to the lights in his big home. The old woman was dead and they were blaming him for it, claiming his bellowing had brought the final, merciful shock. He could still see the accusing look in that Deen woman's eyes.

In Kentucky he'd lost his first wife from the fevers the year before he and Poke came to Texas. As soon as he and Poke claimed their first block of land he'd gone to Austin and got this prim spinster, with little choice on either side. He'd wanted a brood of tough sons and the woman quickly found out he intended to have many. She'd given him three, and Alma. Luke was dead, and Poke, damn him, had turned soft. He'd driven Alma out, forcing her to go to Carr—he'd hate her more than ever if the damned lawyer married her. It would give Carr a claim to part of his holdings after he, Ples, was dead. Instead of taking back Miss Melissa's forty sections as he had planned eventually, Porter Beecroft and Carr would see to it that Ples lost more!

Ples Kendall turned as Burton dismounted heavily and came onto the porch. His eyes bit at the pudgy sheriff he'd put in office over in Marlinville.

"I asked you before, what'n hell brought you here?" he snarled at the man.

Burton brushed his swollen lips with a tender hand, "Why," he began awkwardly, "Carr turned loose a prisoner of mine today, and killed my deputy. I thought I'd come over and help square up. More law around, make it look more legal."

"Law!" The old man spat out the word. "We got too

much damn law around here. Goin' to arrest my boy, MacNab says. You git on down there in the mesquite with the others. I got Pete trailin' Carr. If he gits through Pete will come runnin' an' tell you so the trail can be picked up."

He turned his back again, hiding the worry raging through him. He hadn't eaten since noon over on the Salt Fork of the Brazos, and now fourteen cups of scalding coffee spiked with whisky were tearing at his nerves. Of all his sons Ed, the youngest, was the favorite. Gettin' more like him every day, Ed was. Stood there with his gun leveled over his forearm and shot at Delaney as cool as they come, while Link and Hayden pumped at the breeze. If the boy showed up and MacNab tried to arrest him, there'd be a dead Ranger in Salt Fork.

Kendall turned slowly, his eyes plainly baleful, as the judge and MacNab stepped upon the porch. In the dim yellow glow from inside, the old man's eyes gleamed. They were going to kill Carr tonight, quite likely within the next few minutes, and this little black-eyed squirt would either do some wholesale locking-up in Poke's jail or die trying.

"I want to talk to you, MacNab," the old man snapped.

MacNab paused, quiet and wary. "Yes, Mr. Kendall?"

"How come you turned down Link for a commission in the Rangers?"

"Sorry, can't discuss it," came the curt rejoinder.

"You think he wasn't good enough, eh?"

"We have certain requirements, Mr. Kendall. With no offense meant, Link didn't qualify."

"No, but Jonathan Carr did, didn't he?" Ples roared.

"I've no desire to discuss it further, sir," the Ranger replied. "Let's go inside, Judge."

The cowman's eyes followed them as they went into the lobby and then on into the dining room. One horny hand clamped itself around the butt of his pistol. He'd killed enough Comanches and Mexicans and whites with it during the building of his land and cattle empire.

The old man turned and looked over at the dark outlines of the courthouse. He'd taken cattle money and huge profits from Porter Beecroft's successful venture in railroad bonds and subscribed to county bonds that had built that building. Now came the shocking realization that he'd made a terrible mistake; created something whose symbol could destroy him.

Elmer Gibbens stirred and cleared his throat nervously, as though he read what was going on in the old cattle baron's mind.

"Ples, I think—" he began.

"Git!" the old man growled. "Git outa my sight!"

He clomped into the big lobby and through it to the dining room. MacNab and Judge Tullock had seated themselves at a table in a far corner. MacNab's back was to the wall, his face toward the lobby. His right hand was at his gun under his short coat.

He didn't appear to look up as Ples entered and sat down and flung his hat across the room. The light from wall bracket lamps shone on a balding head and stringy white locks cut straight across the bottom at the lower tips of his ears.

He bellowed for the woman to bring him some grub and then sat there staring at MacNab.

Long minutes went by; no firing sounded.

Ples Kendall was bent low over his plate, shoveling in stew, when a horse loped up out in front and a rider got down. Kendall heard the familiar rattle of spur rowels and knew their wearer because the rowels always were filed sharp. He heard Ed say to the woman who'd served the food, "Where's Pa? Jonathan musta got away."

"Ed, come in here!" the old man shouted.

He came to his feet as Ed's youthful face, hat at a jaunty angle, appeared in the doorway. He pulled the old cap-and-ball and leveled it at Captain MacNab.

"All right, Ranger!" he roared. "This is my boy Ed you was goin' to arrest for shootin' Delaney. Now go ahead an' arrest him!"

Chapter Fourteen

HALF A MILE north of Salt Fork, Carr turned east, working deeper into the protection of more of the dense mesquites surrounding the base of the town. Below him lay a wide, shallow gully, rocky and choked with brush and stunt cedar. A low dirt dam two hundred yards in length had been thrown across the gully by ox teams pulling plow and scraper, and broad, well-beaten cattle trails led through the mesquites to water.

Carr was following one of the trails when he suddenly pulled up and clamped a hand over the quivering nose of the chinless roan. Riders down there ahead, a quiet splash in the night silence as a watered horse turned away to the bank and blew loudly. Carr heard Ed Kendall laugh and Link's voice in reply.

"We better be gettin' back to the others along the road. I don't aim to miss anything when Jonathan rides out toward Camp Coke."

Fury took hold of Carr. Poke had said the road would be clear when Carr left Salt Fork. Had Poke lied, or had the old man duped his son? Well, it made little difference now.

Carr eased the roan forward at a walk and came out on top of the dam, following the wagon road across the top. On a rise beyond lay the town cemetery. He had never yet come home to Salt Fork and gone away again without first visiting his father's grave. That alone had prevented him from walking squarely into Ples Kendall's trap.

The cemetery plot was fenced with barbed wire to keep out Kendall cattle and Carr left the roan near the skeletal outlines of the double-gate brace poles. He walked through into where old headboards and stones stuck up in the tall, ungrazed fall grass. This was one infinitesimal part of the surounding country not owned by Ples Kendall.

Jonathan Carr, moving through the grass, felt a quiet

relief come over him, a let down of tension built up since daybreak this morning.

His father's grave was over near the west fence, neatly ridged and not a blade of grass growing inside the lonely square of fence. That was the work of Miss Melissa.

Carr stood there in the darkness for a few moments with his hat off; then he walked over twenty yards to still another ridged mound and he thought, I wonder how many others ever come back to the graves of men they killed.

This grave, too, had been cleaned recently by Miss Melissa. The plain headboard was weather-split and Carr stopped beside it. Into the split he saw a folded white object somebody had placed there. Curious, he bent to pull the paper free but heard a faint rustle in the tall grasses behind his back. He whirled but the voice had already come.

"Don't move, Carr! I can see you. Lift your hands!"

Carr obeyed. He saw Dale Hayden's angular figure come toward him in a crouch, cocked rifle in both hands. The muzzle pressed against Carr's lean stomach, and even in the dark he could see the man's eyes burning.

"Easy, Dale," Carr spoke softly. "The two men resting here have been dead five years."

"I'll do the talkin'!" A hand reached forward and extracted Carr's .44 and shoved it into Hayden's belt. He stepped back a pace, rifle still ready.

"If you'd a touched that paper I put there tonight I'd a killed you quick," Hayden said.

"What is it?"

"Somethin' maybe you wouldn't understand, I reckon; not from a gent like me. It's from the calendar that was in Mrs. Long's café in Marlinville this mornin'. Link was makin' fun of it. I brought it along to put here, damn him." He continued roughly, "Sit down on that old stone. Comin' here saved your life, Jonathan. If you hadn't, I'd a shot you dead without warnin' when you turned to go."

Carr seated himself on a red sandstone block of an ancient grave—some forgotten sodbuster killed by Commanches, he remembered. Hayden stood with legs apart, looming high in the night.

"Why," Carr said in surprise, "I've always come to this grave for a few moments, Dale, on every visit I made here."

"Well, I never did! Not even when we buried Luke last spring. I find it all cleaned off, same as the judge's. Miss Melissa, huh?"

"She's that kind of person."

Hayden sighed heavily and grounded the butt of the rifle. Somewhere out on the plain a coyote cut loose and another one answered and the sounds were lost as the two animals moved toward each other. Hayden spoke and his voice and words were clear to the ears of Pedro Viejo lying just outside the south fence of the cemetery.

"Poke don't know it, Jonathan, but the old man double-crossed him tonight. Said you an' Delaney could leave town. He knew Poke would come tell you. Soon as him an' them lawyers left, he had Jules have all his men strung out on the east side of town to kill you when you left. My job was to trail the hack or Miss Melissa's buggy, kill Lee, an' then hit for my shack down in Double Mountain breaks. I come here to kill you instead."

"I'm glad Ples didn't think of my visits here."

"I did. I knew you'd be here before leavin' town. Then I find Tom's grave all fixed up, an' it got me. You come on over an' that sorta got me too. I used to figure how I'd kill you an' show old Ples I wasn't no low dog among his outfit. I thought all those years it was him ordered your father killed. I found out a couple hours ago it was Alma."

"She's already told me, Dale. Said she intended for Tom only to hurt my father, not kill him."

"She lied to you!" Dale Hayden cried. "Tom was crazy for her. If she'd a said hurt, he'd a hurt. But your Pa was shot right through the back with a rifle!"

Carr knew this bitterly agitated man was speaking the truth. Alma had offered herself to him, wept a woman's tears of regret and remorse, tried to make up for everything by offering to drive Delaney and his wife to safety. She had been taunted by her father for years and unable to fight back. Today at the crossing, and this evening at the barn, she had tried every trick she knew to save him and her brothers. She was *still* all Kendall. And she'd come a damned sight closer than she realized!

Carr pushed back the brim of his hat. He wanted a cigarette but didn't dare light one. He had to think. If he could keep Hayden out of town until morning. . . .

"I'm not much of a hand at this hating business, Dale," he told the angular man in whose belt Carr's pistol reposed. "And Alma will suffer enough unhappiness the rest of her life without me adding anything. But when Ples Kendall finds out you disobeyed his orders to kill Lee you'll be finished here."

"She won't live long enough to suffer anything," Hayden cut in caustically, "because tonight I'm goin' to kill that damn woman! Then I'm leavin' the country. If you try to stop me, Jonathan, I'll leave you here dead!" The rifle came up, and Hayden backed off a step. "You'll find your six-shooter on your saddle. But don't try to follow me till you hear my horse go. Good luck."

Carr didn't move. He sat there as Hayden's figure gradually faded. A sick dread came up inside him. He'd been on his way to freedom and no more gun trouble. Now he had to go back. He couldn't let this man walk into the Kendall home and shoot down a woman.

He heard Hayden's horse leave, and he strode through the grass to the big double gate. The roan had pricked up its ears and Carr thought he heard another horse not far away. One of the K Cross punchers, probably. He untied the trigger guard of his Colt from one of the reins on the ground, blew dust from it, sheathed the weapon and mounted again.

Carr knew what the chinless roan had already been through that day, but he struck with the four-pronged rowels at its sides, calling upon it for the one final burst of power the animal always had had in the past. He rode hard down to the dam and across it, pounded along a wide cattle trail and then onto the slope of the flats, toward the jail and saloon and the rear of the hotel.

Something had broken loose up there and he thought he knew what. Ed and Link had been down in the brush with the K Cross men. Poke and Bert Burton wouldn't throw their guns except in last ditch defense. That left one man. Ples Kendall—against MacNab. Ples had made a promise and kept his word.

He and MacNab had shot it out in the hotel dining room!

A galloping horse, haunches pumping, loomed up ahead to the right. Carr swung the roan over and began to close in, pistol in hand. The frightened rider flung a look over his shoulder and bent to lay on the quirt. At Carr's strident command to halt the man straightened in the saddle and pulled up.

At a walk Carr edged the panting roan in close and saw that it was not Hayden. This man was shorter and older and his words when he spoke carried a Spanish accent.

"Don't shoot, mister! Please don't shoot!" he begged. "I do nothing. I hurt nobody."

"I thought you were Hayden," Carr said and sheathed his gun. "You're Pete Viejo of K Cross."

"Yes, mister. Dale is up there ahead."

"Where have you been?"

"I don't hurt nobody," protested the Mexican.

"Talk!" Jonathan Carr ordered him.

Old Pete removed his big hat and wiped at his forehead with a sleeve. Even in the night it gleamed white. He put the hat back on his gray-streaked hair and night shadows swallowed his face.

"It's like this, mister. Ples tell me to go up to Lennox saloon an' wait there. He think you come there to ask questions, maybe. He afraid maybe you don't go from town. If you go an' his men don't catch you, then he want to know where so they can follow. Me, I trail nights. Comanches teach me a long time ago when I live with them. One time Ples an' Poke kill some Comanches an' I come home with them here. Thirty years ago. Long time I work for Ples."

"I see. And you were on the floor in a corner, playing drunk, when I was in the saloon."

"Yes, mister."

"And you trailed me to the cemetery when I left town?"

"Yes, mister. I hear you an' Dale talkin'. Everything."

Carr felt suddenly relieved. He didn't know if Hayden had swerved from his purpose and gone to the scene of the firing uptown, or headed on straight for the Kendall home with anger and bitterness still washing at his brain. Dale must have guessed from the firing that one or all of the Kendalls were involved.

He might be shrewd enough to take advantage of their presence up there and kill a woman first and *then* come back uptown.

"Pete, put the leather to your horse and cut off across

the town section to Ples Kendall's home as fast as you can. Tell Alma what you overhead—that Dale has found out the truth about her and has sworn to kill her. Have you got a gun on you?"

"No, mister." Old Pete shook his head vigorously.

"You'll find one in the back of Ad Slocum's hack, that Alma drove home from Miss Melissa's. Get it, get inside and pull the blinds. If Hayden comes, you know what to do."

"Yes, mister."

"Hurry it up, Pete! I'll try to get down there after I find out what's taking place up there at the hotel."

"Old Ples and the Ranger, mister. He was going to arrest Ed."

With the courtesy inherent among his former people, Old Pete doffed his hat, and then the quirt slashed into his horse's flanks. He rocketed away across thes north slope of the town section. Carr sat there for a few moments, jerking back and forth in the creaking saddle as the roan panted. He moved it out and eased it into a gallop, heading for the stables back of the hotel.

The feeling of dread was still in him. If MacNab had come out winner in a gun duel with old Ples, then the men led by Link and Ed would tear the little Ranger captain to pieces.

Chapter Fifteen

CARR RODE boldly past the hotel's corral and the outlines of the six tired coach horses munching roughage in long plank troughs. At least a dozen or more men were swarming around the front of the hotel and inside, and yet there was a strange quiet, an air of awe and dread in their subdued voices. He bent from the saddle and peered through the open front door of the frontier saloon, but not a person was inside. Lennox had broken from the place and run to the hotel when guns began to crash.

Carr swung from the roan, leaving it to regain its wind, and stumbled over trash as he crept to the rear door. He opened it and a gust of murmured sound swept at him. Through the length of the darkened hallway he saw the huge figure of Jules MacCandless standing with a big paw on the newel post of the stairway. Jules's scarred face was glum.

Carr turned left and eased open the door to the kitchen. Two pairs of frightened eyes saw his marked face and a low cry escaped one of the women. Carr glanced at the swinging door leading into the dining room and then drew a long breath. In the light of the kitchen lamps he looked pale and drawn. He'd been held and beaten savagely, and he was tired. But a Ranger was in trouble, and that man had been his superior.

He shook the Colt free in its sheath, pushed aside the swinging door, and went in. A man cried out, "Hell's fire! There he is!" and then the place went silent.

Tables had been knocked aside and in a cleared area in the center of the big room Captain MacNab lay stretched out on his back. His black knee-high boots, heels in and toes out, shone like polished ebony. Wadded beneath his head was the long coat Judge Tullock had worn. The judge, a bloody white napkin in one hand, knelt beside MacNab.

As Carr stood coldly poised, the judge sighed heavily and rose to his feet. He let the napkin fall helplessly and looked at Carr.

"This is a terrible thing to have happened, Mr. Carr," he said quietly, though his voice sounded loud to Ples Kendall's uneasy men. Working under Ples Kendall's orders was one thing. Getting involved in the killing of a Ranger—a famous man like MacNab—was quite another. Grim manhunters like Jonathan Carr himself would spare neither time nor horses until somebody paid in blood for this night's work.

Carr looked down at the inert little man who lay with black eyes closed, his face the color of dirty putty. Blood stains covered the brown coat and white shirt that was beneath it.

"Is he dead, Judge Tullock?" Carr asked softly.

"Not yet. The doctor attending young Evans upstairs had just come for a visit and gone home again. Somebody rode hard to his house to bring him back here."

"Who did it? Ples?"

"No," Tullock shook his head. "It was the boy MacNab had intended to arrest. Ples was eating supper over there at another table when young Ed came in. He got to his feet and leveled his gun at us and dared MacNab to arrest the boy. Before either of us were aware of what happened Ed Kendall snatched out his pistol and shot Captain MacNab twice. MacNab toppled out of his chair but Ples Kendall wouldn't let me touch him. He was like a man gone crazy, Carr. He said to leave him there and let him die. In courtrooms I've seen men under stress become irrational, but never anything like this. When Link came in, Mr. Kendall ordered them to go with him. He stated that as long as they were at it, they might as well do the job up right."

"Where did they go?" Carr asked, but he knew the answer. A lash of apprehension coiled through him. Delaney, of course! They knew where he was because Carr himself had told them there in the saloon!

He had asked MacNab to protect his client in the cellar of Miss Melissa's house, and Miss Melissa had left the place with Alma.

A commotion broke out among the men packed around the door. They split apart and Poke Kendall pushed into the dining room, his face haggard but determined. He'd been at home, helping what little he could while Miss Melissa and Mrs. Beecroft and Mrs. Deen had prepared his stepmother for burial.

"I just heard," he said grimly. "Met one of the boys who was comin' after me. What are you doin' here, Jonathan?"

"I was paying a visit in the cemetery before leaving town, and met Hayden. He found out the truth today about who instigated the murder of my father and caused him to lose his brother. He's on the loose with a rifle somewhere around here, and I sent old Pete to warn Alma. Hayden swore to get her and then pull out for Mexico."

"What are you goin' to do now?" the sheriff asked as though he hadn't heard.

"You ought to know. Your father and two brothers have just left to drag Delaney out of the cellar. Get your men out of my way, Poke."

"No, by hell!" the sheriff said. "The old man is wrong an' I admit it. I warned him, but he wouldn't listen to me. But he taught us Kendalls that come hell or high water we stick together. I been sidin' him a long time, Jonathan. I'm still doin' it! Jules, come in here!" he called.

Big Jules MacCandless's figure shoved through men packed shoulder to shoulder around the dining-room entrance, towering above them. He moved lightly for such a big man and his crudely cobblered shoes, always without spurs, made scarcely a sound. He looked like a huge mastiff, he walked like one.

"Jules, take him!" Poke Kendall snapped and pointed a finger at Jonathan.

"Not this time, Jules," Carr spoke up softly. "Once today has been enough. No hard feelings, friend. Just don't try it again."

"Take him, Jules," Poke repeated harshly.

MacCandless tugged at his burned ear and looked at Poke. Unbelievably, he shook his head. "Not tonight, Poke. All my life since I been out here I never question what Ples do. Now, because of the men, I refuse."

He looked down at MacNab, still lying with eyes closed, and then his eyes met those of Judge Tullock. He turned and faced the men of the outfit.

"You got one chance to escape being run down by Rangers and sent to Huntsville for what we were going to do tonight. Get on your horses. Go to the chuckwagon and stay there. I follow you later."

Carr said softly, "Jules, I won't forget this." His eyes met Poke's and held them. He spoke tonelessly, without emotion. "Ples and your two brothers have gone down to Miss Melissa's house to drag out a wounded man and kill him, Poke. The way your father has gone blood-crazy tonight, anything could happen to Delaney's wife, too. You can come after me and try to save your father's life, and perhaps lose your own. Or you can make a run for your own home and try to save Alma's. The choice is yours, Poke."

He backed toward the kitchen door, whirled through it, and plunged for the one leading into the darkened hallway. In him now flashed the frantic desire to get going without the loss of another second. They already had three or four minutes' head start. Carr's only hope to get there in time was based upon Link's cruelty, the desire to hurt the man who'd killed Luke Kendall before finishing him off.

Carr jerked open the door and almost collided with Bert Burton, who, gun in hand had sneaked from the lobby and was coming in through the kitchen to shoot him in the back. He swung his left fist at Burton's face and drew his pistol at the same time. Burton's frightened yell was cut short as Jonathan Carr smashed him alongside the head with the gun barrel.

He jumped over the pudgy sheriff's body, jerked open the back door of the hotel, ran to the roan and mounted it. Its hoofs began a tattoo on the hard-packed earth, made that way by untold numbers of ox wagons and buggies and hacks, the plunge of Kendall horses carrying Kendall plains riders. The roan shot along the north side of the square, turned the west corner past a dead man's bank and vault, and went down across the flats.

The night wind pressed against Carr's face and his hat went flying. He felt the roan falter in its stride and knew that it was foundering. Two hundred yards from the front of Miss Melissa's white picket fence he felt the roan falter again and then a warning quiver.

He tried hard to hold its head up as he pulled it in, but

the chinless roan was finished. It went down as Jonathan
Carr kicked his booted feet free of the stirrups.

He saw the outlines of three horses there by the front
gate. And as he reached them he heard the muffled
scream of a woman in the huge cellar beneath Miss Melissa's kitchen.

Jonathan Carr stopped at the porch and slipped off his
knee-length black boots. Six-shooter in hand, he opened
the front door and eased into the darkened living room. A
lamp gleamed from the table inside the kitchen.

Ples and his two murderous sons had lit one boldly
in order to do their job of cold-blooded murder.

The woman screamed again, and mingled with it Carr
heard the louder sound of Link Kendall's laughter. In the
cellar Link stood holding the struggling woman in his
arms. In the light of the lamp behind covered ground-level
windows his boyish black mustache was skinned back in a
cold grin over white teeth. Ed had Delaney by his good
arm, stretched out behind his head, gripping and twisting
it. One of his booted feet was placed firmly as a brace
in the hollow of the helpless man's neck and shoulder.

Old Ples, gone momentarily mad now that he had his
son's killer in his hands, was beating at Delaney's face. He
straightened, panting, and grabbed the wounded arm. "All
right, boy," he wheezed at young Ed. "Let's drag him up
the steps into the kitchen."

Link laughed again and flung Ruby aside. She struck the
mortar wall and sank down at the foot of the bunk, burying
her face in her arms, without the strength or will to fight
back any more. Link bent and got Delaney by his ankles
and lifted him as his father and brother backed up the
steps.

They came out into the kitchen and dropped the man
to the floor with a crash. Link slammed down the cellar
door and straightened. "That'll keep her down there, I
guess," he grinned at his father. "You goin' to finish him
off here, Pa, or outside?"

The old man wiped a hand across his mouth and
brushed at a lock of hair in front of his face. He flung
back his head as Jonathan Carr's voice cut in from the
doorway.

"Neither, Link. I never wanted it this way, but you're
all finished."

Ed's right hand stabbed down to his hip, his eyes cat-like. Carr had never dreamed that old Ples's youngest son could pull a gun so fast. Ed, the quiet one, as fast and deadly as Duval had been.

Chapter Sixteen

As Ed Kendall's gun flashed out before Link's hand came up from leather, there was an instinct in Jonathan Carr's reflexes that none of them knew and would have only vaguely understood. It came from working a horse, feet muffled in gunnysacks, along a trail in the brush country where outlaw firelight pinpointed the night. You felt it when you quietly surrounded a darkened house and then crept in under lightless windows where a desperate man sat waiting with a cocked gun in his hands.

It razored your senses, and it was Carr's one bet against three tough men; the old Comanche-killing prairie wolf and his two merciless cubs. Plès had ordered most of his killing done in later years. Link had had the K Cross to back him up and had missed developing the extrasensory perception of a man who had to go it alone. But Carr had badly misjudged Ed, despite having known that he was a very dangerous man.

That was why Jonathan Carr turned his spouting pistol first at young Ed, the instinct of his manhunting years paying the dividend that could mean the difference between life and death. Ed had shot a Ranger, before the lawman could fire his gun. Carr felt the hard impact of the walnut-handled weapon as he drove a bullet into Ed and then another, the room beginning to rocket in ear-splitting concussions. He was aware of pain in his bruised hand that shocked and sharpened his reflexes. He saw Ed reeling backwards with one hand palmed over his shirt front, heard some kind of animal scream come out of the old man who had sent Duval and Evans that afternoon to save his sons. The harsh, booming roar of a Walker cap-and-ball began adding its voice to the din.

Carr placed his shots with cool deadliness. Link, too, went down. He stumbled over Ed's body and fell backward into the china cabinet. He rolled off it and crashed to the floor.

Ples Kendall dropped his gun and began to cough, the two horny hands that had pummeled Delaney now clawing at his buttoned shirt as though he were suffocating from lack of air.

"Ed!" he called out brokenly. "Ed, where are you? Ed—"

He received no reply. His right hand jerked convulsively and a string of buttons went flying as Carr, sheathing his emptied Colt, leaped forward and caught Ples in his arms and lowered the cattleman to the floor.

"Ples, it will do no good to say it again, but I never wanted it this way," was all that Carr could say. Men like Ples Kendall had fought the Comanche, pitting their lives against the Indian, drenching their minds in mercilessness against equal ruthlessness, because it was the only language the Comanche knew and respected. The only tragedy now was that a very few of them, Ples Kendall for one, had been unable to accept the changes brought about as the plains country was finally occupied and ranched.

The old man hadn't been able to change. It had cost him his life, and the lives of two of his sons.

Carr saw the piercing blue eyes, devoid of the insane rage of moments ago, looking up at him. "Ed," Ples Kendall whispered. "Where is he, Jonathan?"

"He shot a Texas Ranger tonight, Ples," Carr tried to explain. "He would have spent the rest of his life in Huntsville. If MacNab dies, he would have hung."

Ples Kendall's eyes brightened. The wrinkles around them intensified. "They would've never . . . hung that . . . boy," the old man said.

Carr rose to his feet and a tremor shook his body. He began to tremble and had to put a hand on the cold kitchen stove. He looked down at Lee Delaney and saw that the man was unconscious. For the first time in years he needed a drink badly, and the only one in the house was down in the cellar.

He went over and got hold of Ed Kendall's right hand, the one that had thrown a gun so fast. It looked chubby and boyish. Twenty-two years old, and dead. Such were the things a man could think about in the aftermath of violent death.

He edged Ed away from the trap door and opened it. He had to steady himself as he went down the stairs and

saw Ruby Delaney's frightened face peering at him with
the largest pair of eyes he'd ever seen. She pushed herself up heavily and stared at him with a hundred questions.

"It's all right, Ruby," Jonathan Carr assured her. "If you
can nerve yourself to go to your husband, he'll be a free
man after tonight. He'll never be brought to trial now.
But first hand me that opened bottle of whisky. I'm going
to need it."

He sat down on the bunk from which Lee had been
dragged and shoved the palms of both hands hard up
across his battered face. It hurt, but the pain was welcome.

Poke Kendall would be coming hard very shortly, and
both he and Carr knew what Poke had to do. Carr took
the opened bottle and drank and the unaccustomed fire
of it in his throat began to take the shakes out of his
legs. He heard the swish of Ruby Delaney's skirt as she
mounted the steps to the kitchen.

Without thinking, his hand went to his hip and withdrew
his gun, and his right thumb flicked open the loading gate.
He thought, No, there's no more killing left in me, and rose
to his feet as he returned the gun to its sheath. He padded
up the steps and went through the kitchen and out to the
front porch. He sat down there and pulled on his boots
again.

Three hip-shot horses stood in front of the white picket
gate, and he saw the outlines of another, standing dim in
the night. The chinless roan had regained its feet, broken-
winded and through. He looked out through the night
and heard the sounds of still another horse coming at a
hard run from Ples Kendall's house.

Poke was keeping his word, too. Still siding the old man.
Carr got up and went into the living room and struck a
match. He lit the two lamps and waited.

He heard the crash of the sheriff's boots as they struck
the front porch and rose to his feet from the chair where
Miss Melissa had sat and knitted. The front door flung
inward on its hinges and Poke Kendall stood there, his
eyes wild with anxiety. He gripped a pistol in his right
hand.

"Where are they?" he cried harshly, and headed for the
kitchen.

He found Carr blocking his way, a man drawn and haggard and sick inside. Carr said, "Don't go in there, Poke. They had torn off Lee's bandages and dragged him up into the kitchen. I had to stop it."

"Any of them left?" Poke Kendall asked.

"None of them." Carr shook his head.

The six-shooter in the sheriff's hand lifted and its metallic click seemed to ring through the room, the black muzzle lined at Carr's midriff. It held, wavered, and then something convulsive took hold of Ples Kendall's last son. He wagged his head from side to side and slowly sheathed the weapon.

"This leaves you and Alma as owners of K Cross," Carr said. "Did you get home in time?"

"She was waiting for him with a rifle—a Sharps with a busted glass sight. It ruined her aim. She couldn't see. She missed, and Dale hit his horse running. I don't think he'll ever come back here now."

Carr walked over and blew out one lamp and then the other. Darkness blinded them both for a few moments. He could hear Ruby's voice in the kitchen and that of her husband coming reassuringly. Carr said, "Poke, this thing will haunt me as long as I live. It started five years ago and ended tonight. It will brand me in Texas as a killer. I always lived with the hope that some day I could come back here and take over where my father left off. But as long as men pack guns in Texas I'll never be able to walk down a street without fear that at the end of it will be another kid like Evans. Men won't remember me for the cow thieves I ran down, the five murderers whose horses I brought back. They'll remember me only as the man who killed Ples Kendall and one of his sons who shot down a Texas Ranger."

He felt his way through the darkness to the hazy rectangle of the opened door and Poke Kendall followed. He took the first horse of the three there and found that the saddle carried an apple-knob horn.

The stirrups fitted his legs. He and Ples Kendall had been about the same height.

MacNab was conscious when the two of them entered his upstairs room in the hotel. Stripped of clothing by the doctor, he lay beneath a white sheet, his chest swathed in bandages. His bright black eyes flicked from Carr to the sheriff as he listened to the brief account of what had happened. When he spoke his words were labored, but clear and precise.

"Jonathan, because of your legal training, the adjutant's office in Austin has had its eye on you for a long time. They were pretty unhappy when one of the best sergeants in the service resigned his commission. They sent me here on a special mission to keep an eye on you during this court trial, which now presumably will be dismissed, Captain."

"Captain?" Carr asked.

"I told you in the saloon that I'd talk with you. You didn't give me the opportunity. I tried to put you under arrest to save your life, but from the looks of things you came through. You're wanted and needed in the office in Austin. As far as the records go, you were never out of Ranger service. If at the end of another year—"

He broke off and twisted his head to look at Poke Kendall. "Sheriff, I'm the only person to whom Jonathan ever confided his hopes of some day returning to Salt Fork and taking up law practice and ranching. Your father built that courthouse and ended an era on the plains frontier. Would this time next year be about right for Carr to come back here and start another one?"

"Just about," Poke Kendall nodded. "The old man just couldn't change. I warned him but he wouldn't listen to me—" He turned and went out.

Jonathan Carr followed him out a few minutes later. He heard the hubbub of voices down in the lobby, Porter Beecroft's loud and expostulating. He heard them only in the background of his mind because his tired, unhappy eyes were upon Laura, standing at the head of the stairs. In her own was an understanding as she came toward him.

"I suppose you know everything," Carr said.

She nodded, and then slid her arms around his waist and put her head against his shirt front in almost the same way Alma Kendall had done earlier that evening.

"I'm going down the back way and get my saddle on a fresh horse and ride out tonight, Laura," Jonathan Carr went on. "I have a year of legal work in the adjutant's office in Austin, and then I'm coming back home. Are you leaving on the stage to Fort Worth in the morning?"

He heard her words in soft reply, muffled because her face was pressed against him. "No, Jonathan. I'm going to wait and go home with Judge Tullock to Brownwood. I'll take another stage out of there—to Austin."

The Exciting and Beloved Characters of

ZANE GREY

Brought to life again by his son

ROMER ZANE GREY!

Classic Western Action

_____2530-2 ZANE GREY'S BUCK DUANE:
KING OF THE RANGE $2.75 US/$3.50 CAN

_____2553-1 ZANE GREY'S ARIZONA AMES: KING
OF THE OUTLAW HORDE $2.75US/$3.50CAN

_____2488-8 ZANE GREY'S LARAMIE NELSON:
LAWLESS LAND $2.75 US/$3.75 CAN

_____2621-7 ZANE GREY'S YAQUI: SEIGE AT
FORLORN RIVER $2.75 US/$3.75 CAN

PONY SOLDIERS

They were a dirty, undisciplined rabble, but they were the only chance a thousand settlers had to see another sunrise. Killing was their profession and they took pride in their work—they were too fierce to live, too damn mean to die.

_____2620-1   #5: SIOUX SHOWDOWN
$2.75 US/$3.75 CAN

_____2598-1   #4: CHEYENNE BLOOD STORM
$2.75US/$3.75CAN

_____2565-5   #3: COMANCHE MOON
$2.75US/$3.75CAN

_____2541-8   #2: COMANCHE MASSACRE
$2.75US/$3.75CAN

_____2518-3   #1: SLAUGHTER AT BUFFALO
CREEK $2.75US/$3.75CAN

SPUR

The wildest, sexiest and most daring
Adult Western series around.
Join Spur McCoy as he fights for
truth, justice and every woman he can
lay his hands on!

_____2608-2   DOUBLE: GOLD TRAIN TRAMP/RED ROCK
REDHEAD $3.95 US/$4.95 CAN

_____2597-3   SPUR #25: LARAMIE LOVERS
$2.95 US/$3.95 CAN

_____2575-2   SPUR #24: DODGE CITY DOLL
$2.95 US/$3.95 CAN

_____2519-1   SPUR #23: SAN DIEGO SIRENS
$2.95 US/$3.95 CAN

_____2496-9   SPUR #22: DAKOTA DOXY
$2.50 US/$3.25 CAN

_____2475-6   SPUR #21: TEXAS TART
$2.50 US/$3.25 CAN

_____2453-5   SPUR #20: COLORADO CUTIE
$2.50 US/$3.25 CAN

_____2409-8   SPUR #18: MISSOURI MADAM
$2.50 US/$3.25 CAN

PREACHER'S LAW

In the aftermath of the Civil War, Jeremy Preacher, late of Mosby's Rangers, rode home to find his plantation burned to the ground, his parents slaughtered and his sister brutally raped and murdered. Blood would flow, men would die and Preacher would be avenged—no matter how long it took. Join Preacher's bloody crusade for justice—from 1865 to 1908.